Look Where
You Are Going
Not Where
You Have Been

Steven J Dines

First published by Luna Press Publishing, Edinburgh, 2021

Men Playing Ghosts, Playing God. First Published in *Black Static* #35, Jul 2013.
So Many Heartbeats, So Many Words. First Published in *Black Static* #46, May 2015.
The Space That Runs Away With You. First Published in *Crimewave 12: Hurts*, Nov 2013.
The Broken and the Unmade. First Published in *Black Static* #39, Mar 2014.
The Things That Get You Through. First Published in *Black Static* #31, Nov 2012.
Pendulum. First Published in *Black Static* #70, Jul 2019.
The Sound of Constant Thunder. First Published in *Black Static* #37, Nov 2013.
The Harder It Gets the Softer We Sing. First Published in *Black Static* #63, May 2018.
Looking for Landau. First Published in *Interzone* #275, May 2018.
This House is Not Haunted. Original to this collection.
dragonland. Original to this collection.

www.lunapresspublishing.com
ISBN-13: 978-1-913387-67-9

*This book is dedicated to all those
with absent fathers.
Look where you are going
not where you have been...*

Contents

Introduction

Later This Evening

Ralph Robert Moore

From the quiet street, looking at a house, no matter how neatly-mowed its lawn, how rainbowed the flowers in its beds, you can never really know what goes on behind that varnished front door.

Every Steven J. Dines story I've ever read—and I've been fortunate enough to read quite a few—invites you in its opening paragraphs past a white picket fence and into a home, and as you're walking into the front hallway, looking up at the paintings, the architectural details, decorating decisions, certain you saw something running past the rails upstairs, you fall through the floorboards into the real rooms of the story. Again and again, Steve creates a world we know—the world we all believe in—breakfast, office jobs, children—then shows us how much of that world is nothing more than cardboard props.

At the center of each Dines tale is a man or woman caught in their own obsessions, unable to escape. Often the stories are first person, so that we the reader are scarily trapped in the protagonist's head, only able to see the world through their eyes, and much of what we see through those eyes we strongly suspect is unreliable. This sense of claustrophobia is so pervasive that often it doesn't even require a supernatural agency. The world itself, with its playgrounds, attics, and sounding beaches is enough to impose a closeness as suffocating as anything found in Poe.

There's a quality certain writers have. Reading their stories, you sense they're not writing just because they enjoy writing, or are good at it, but because they are compelled to write. What is inside their head has to be pushed out through their hands. Onto a sheet of paper, a blank monitor. Into our head.

William S. Burroughs had that quality. So did Philip K. Dick, Charles Bukowski, a few select others.

I would include Steven J. Dines in that group.

Start a Dines story, and after wading a few sentences in, you've left the solid, sunlit world we want to believe is real, sinking in a blue and black sea, and what's swimming around you—what has just now noticed you, circling back—is rarely friendly. There are very few dolphins in a Dines story.

Horror exposes the unfairness in life, everything from the death of a child to the sand within the spinach salad, and Steve excels in exploring that wrongness. An old man falls in love with an old woman at a nursing home, and pretends to be the ghost of her husband. A young couple live in a mold-infested flat, their young son getting sicker and sicker. A father tries to find his kidnapped son. A survivor of the concentration camps in World War Two lives into our modern age, but with a terrible burden on his shoulders. A husband has difficulties adjusting to the death of his wife. A young boy raised by a troubled mother and absent father. A lonely man gets by on the banks of a river after the apocalypse, his life stunted but bearable, until one day a young woman shows up with her baby. A writer deals with the tragedies in his family. In the American southwest, a man hunts for answers. A wife loves a child who doesn't exist. Two brothers try to survive in a forest on the back of a dragon.

One of Steve's greatest strengths, to me, is that he writes about the world as it is now. What I admire so much about the authors that rose to fame during the time I was growing up—Richard Matheson, Charles Beaumont, Fritz Lang—is that they were writing contemporary stories about their own time in history, about suburban life, the threat of atomic annihilation, the great social changes that were occurring. I love old-fashioned tales about crumbling castles, horse-drawn coaches traveling through night-time forests, foggy graveyards, but to be honest, I prefer stories set in our own age of technology, diminished expectations, social media. Capturing that feel of how we now live is where Steve excels. In a Dines story, you're not experiencing something that happened to a character generations ago. You're experiencing something that could happen to you, later this evening.

Another great strength in Steve's writings is that they are not vignettes. We get the full story, moving from one well-written scene to the other, to the next, to a devastating conclusion. What makes life meaningful is not one moment, but how one moment leads to another, completely unexpected moment. What would *Night of the Living Dead* be like if it were only about Johnny and Barbara trying to escape the zombie at the cemetery? *Texas Chainsaw Massacre* if it were limited to how they deal with a strange hitchhiker they pick up? When I start a

Dines story, I know I'm going to become completely immersed in that world, and changed by it.

The seed was planted early. Steve started writing, as the best of us do, when he was a child. Around the age of ten, he was asked by his teacher to write about a dream. He didn't complete the story in class that day, so took it home, sat down by himself with a pen and paper that evening, and wrote nineteen pages. Over the days that followed, the story grew longer and longer, his classmates eventually getting included in the narrative as characters, to where they'd come up to him in the playground and ask what was happening next to their fictional selves in the stories. Over the course of the next three months, he ended up writing 120 pages. And the seed sprouted, twinned green hands reaching up, rotating, emerging from the brown nubble, palms raised, finding the moonlight.

I've known Steve for years and years. He's a good man. An inspired writer who knows how to get inside your head, and take you for a midnight joyride, which is what we should demand of all writers. Reading him, you're not going to read about different people. You're going to become different people. And that's exhilarating. He has an excellent writing style, brimming with insights, perfectly-turned phrases, and a deadpan humor. As unsettling as his stories can be, every one of them is an immensely satisfying read. I slowed down towards the end of this collection, because I didn't want to leave this amazing world Steve has created for us. I wanted it to go on forever.

Look Where You Are Going Not Where You Have Been is a perfect introduction to the world of Steven J. Dines. Steve is one of the most important writers working today, and this first collection of his is a book I highly recommend.

Go past the white picket fence. Open the front door of his house. But be very careful. You're about to fall. And it's a long, long drop to what is waiting for you.

The End Is A Monster

Johnny Mains

A long time ago, in a dank corner of the internet, there used to be a website, now defunct. It's full address was www.eastoftheweb.com/uncut. *Short Stories Uncut* was a forum dedicated to those who wanted to hone their craft. The boss of the forum was called Icasa. There were authors who didn't use their real name or only used partial names such as Lance, Lila, The Harlequin, Capulet, Amphritrite but there were other authors who used their full names; Martin Abraham, Diete Nickens, John Ravenscroft and Steven J. Dines. I landed on that forum in 2005 with the pseudonym 'Johnnyelvis' and I didn't bring much to the table writing-wise; there were early kernels, such as 'Jesus Wept' and 'Small Town Life'—the latter being the birth of Effingham-on-the-Stour, the town where a large part of my fiction is now set—but it was mostly bad.

The forum itself was a pretty intimidating place. You would post a story and it would be critiqued and scored by your peers, then you would do the same when one of their short stories was posted. It was certainly a proving ground, a necessary bear pit for writers who were serious about the art of the short story. It was where Steve and I met and we would leave comments on each others stories and also chat away on the general discussion page. This means that Steve and myself were both around when the other was starting out, and 16 years later, in 2021, I've waited longer than most (apart from Steve) for him to get this collection out.

Steve's early website, *Crayons in the Dark* (use the wayback machine: www.sdines1975.demon.co.uk) states that in 2004 he was putting together a short story collection. It would have contained, I'm sure, 'The Beautiful Game', 'Night Monsters', 'What Trevor McDonald Doesn't Tell Us' and maybe other stories such as 'Leaving the Picnic' from the Australian e-zine Skive or 'Unzipped' from *Underground Voices* would have made it in. These early stories see the steady, assured steps of someone who was writing their socks off, making mistakes along the way, as we all do—but look at some early examples and tell me that Steven J. Dines wasn't put on this earth to be a slave to language:

He imagined walking back into the room downstairs only to be confronted by a dozen or more ghostly pale faces lined up outside his window, every one of them staring in at him through the glass; ghostly pale faces with rivulets of rainwater running over their unblinking eyes [...] Light flared and, lying on the floor next to the double bed, his wife flinched and shut her eyes. He turned her over with his foot. Her wrists and ankles were bound with lengths of electrical flex; the lower half of her face mummified with brown parcel tape. When she opened her eyes again, they pleaded with his.

-from 'What Trevor Macdonald Doesn't Tell Us'

From the way you were lying broken and covered in dust, at first I thought you were a child's doll. Then I saw you were really a little girl. Then I saw you were my little girl lying dead beside me. And you're not, are you? You're at home, safe, with mom. She never insisted I take you with me. Right?

-from 'John Doe's Oklahoma City Turnaround'

From these early, tantalising kernels, we come to this debut collection, containing none of these stories from aeons ago. While I hope that one day you see these stories, I am happy to report that Mr Dines, at the controls of the good ship Never Stop, has never stopped writing; that he has put in his 10,000 hours of practice that it takes to become brilliant at something. What he is offering you, is something I've never seen before in a debut work. This remarkable collection isn't just a totem to the hours put in and the leaps he has made—it's about how an author has managed to balance the constraints of their chosen genre with the overwhelming, exhausting demands of crafting emotional literature and created a landscape of love, loss, pain, regret and hope, if I may be so bold to say. With tales such as 'The Broken and the Unmade' and 'Pendulum' you know that you are in the hands of someone who isn't afraid to go to those places in their soul where others would drive a thousand miles at 100mph to steer clear of. Of course this is going to embarrass the hell out of him, but I will say that the trilogy of interlinking tales that hold this book together—'So Many Heartbeats, So Many Words', 'The Harder It Gets, the Softer We Sing' and 'This House is Not Haunted' contain some of the best writing I think I've ever read in my life. The latter and most recently written sees Steve tap into the pain of a happening in his personal life and that writing is raw, angry and heartbreaking to read.

Take the following paragraph from it:

Got pregnant. Lost a baby. Invited the monster in while never letting our ghosts leave. And we are reading every chapter of this horror story except the last because we don't want the story to end, because The End leaves us in an even more vulnerable position—with a choice to make: what now? The End is a monster. All endings are. It is the silence that drops after the final full stop on the final sentence, when we think the nightmare is over, the story's been told. But it hasn't. The monster won't be done with us until there is nothing of us left. And I am doing that thing again, burying the problem under an avalanche of the figurative: simile and metaphor held firmly over my face like some sweet, chloroform-soaked rag. And there's another. Any more? No? Good. Because enough is enough.

"The end is a monster. All endings are." I mean...*fuck.* I don't know how he can dip in and out of such strange waters without remaining unscathed. Maybe these stories have taken their toll on him or maybe he sees them as therapy; with each story he dives deeper into the easier he sleeps at night. I've not asked him, and a small part of me is afraid to discover the answer.

The end tale of this book contains a fallen monster in the shape of 'dragonland' and sees Dines in unfamiliar territory, sword and sorcery, fully-blown *Game of Thrones* fantasy, but he manages to create something fresh and full of wonder. He made me, for the very first time in my life, want to read more fantasy, a genre I do not get on well with at all. I hope he continues with the rich saga and mythology he has created.

So here we are, I've run out of words. You know how highly I rate this collection; you know how highly I think of Steve as an author and a friend. Look Where You Are Going; the path ahead is dark and explored by very few. You may hesitate before you take the next step, but have faith, Steve will make sure you get out in one piece.

Mostly.

Men Playing Ghosts, Playing God

Age will not be defied
-Francis Bacon

Let me tell you about the time four old ghosts held death captive in a basement. Let me tell you what that power can do to a man and the sacrifice he will make for the gift of time. But first, let me tell you how we became ghosts in the first place.

At the age of seventy-seven, I, Henry Eddowes, died. Nobody seemed to notice, nobody seemed to care, which only made it harder for me coming to terms with my demise. Not my literal demise, you should understand, otherwise how would I be writing this account? But there are other ways to die, just as there are other ways to live.

The name of the one who took my life away was Russell Hobbs. That's right, it was one of his toasters that caused the fire, his defective workmanship; not me, not mine. All I wanted on that September evening of last year was to put my tired feet up, eat spaghetti and sausages on toast, and listen to a little Piano Sonata No.14 until I fell asleep. Contrary to what the fire inspector concluded I never turned the dial all the way to the darkest setting, and even if I *had*, which I cannot completely disclaim since I don't have what you might call 'one hundred percent recall', the fool contraption still should not have flame-grilled the toast, the toast the kitchen window-blind, and so on.

Being old is worse than being a child. When a child sets fire to something, they get a ticking off or a slap on the wrist, but do the same thing at my age and the powers that be—and I am referring to *my* children here—are prepared to throw you in a padded cell.

Or worse.

They call Wintercroft a residential home. I call it the waiting room to Hell. The brochure boasts it is situated in four acres of landscaped gardens on the outskirts of the city. It does not, anywhere, use the phrase, 'out of the way.' But it is and we are.

And that is an altogether different kind of death.

*

When we first heard of Constance' husband's passing, it was one minute to midnight and we were playing cards. It was quiet, the lights were low, and everyone else had been fed and bedded, except the four of us with our special pass, paid for with sixty cigarettes and the assurance that we would keep it down. We were in Wintercroft's communal room. Kensington chairs lined two of the walls, hand upholstered, red floral pattern on a backdrop of somnolent green. In time, our bones turn to straw; in time, our brains too. None of the residents were really capable of lying on the grass to look at the sky anymore, so that was as good as it got: a chair and a window. We were scarecrows, propped up and left to watch the black birds circling.

But the four of us—we had poker.

Forget Bridge and Canasta, we left those to the nonagenarians. We young ones in our seventies, Walshy, Bullamore, Sheldon, and myself, we enjoyed nothing more than a game of five card stud. All right, so we used onion rings instead of actual poker chips, and our table, a walnut coffee commandeered from the women's corner, was a little on the low side, something our backs incessantly complained about afterward, but we could lose ourselves, *really* lose ourselves: in the cards, in our hand, in the game.

The scream changed that. One soul-torn scream from just along the corridor.

Her scream.

It changed everything.

Walshy looked at Bullamore then Sheldon; Bullamore at Sheldon then Walshy; Sheldon at Walshy then Bullamore. Then all three turned to look at me.

None of us needed to say anything: we all knew what it meant. We were all putting in our twilight time in Wintercroft, and darkness was never too far away.

"So he's gone," I said in a low voice, raising my coffee mug in the air. "To George."

"To George," the others echoed.

We touched the rims to our lips and drank to him, or rather we breathed deeply of the aroma lingering at the bottom of our near-empty cups.

And then we played another hand.

I forget who won it. Not me. My heart was no longer in the game. It was, with my mind, just along the corridor...with Constance.

*

It was no secret among the other residents that I was madly in love with her. There is no time for secrets when time is short. Even George had known my feelings, but he'd also understood that I was nothing if not honourable. I respected the sanctity of their marriage as much as I respected the sanctity of my own. A growing shortness of time on this earth does not make licentious wolves of us all.

But I do love her.

Before we ever met, on my first day in Wintercroft, I heard someone mention her name, and the jolt I felt as a result rattled my heart. I fell in love with her name before I met and fell for the woman herself. Constance. Constance. And when I learned of the others they fell one behind the next, like a trail of warm autumn petals across a slab of frozen ground: Constance Harriet Willington-Wright.

Petals, yes—or four elegant train carriages lighting up the walls of a darkened tunnel: me.

But I digress.

Back to what happened.

*

I could not visit Constance in her room that night. The staff would not allow it. So I spent the hours until morning pacing my room like some poor love-starved teenager. When I grew tired of pacing, I stretched myself out on the bed and traced the cracks in the ceiling, imagining that I was somehow clinging to a comet up in space, looking down upon the rivers of the Earth. It was a game I used to play as a boy while my parents argued in the next room, after someone told me there was no sound in space.

It isn't true.

The words become lost in the great vacuum of time and distance but somehow the screams never seem to lose their power. If anything, they become comets themselves, orbiting the world right alongside you.

The next morning I was a Jack-out-of-his-box, hurrying along the corridor to Constance' room. I found her curled up on a large chair, a little girl in posture but an ancient woman in appearance. Who knew one night could last so long? Enough to add years to a woman's face when years were the thing none of us really had.

I stood before her, trying not to block her view out of the window. She needed distance—if not the ability to distance herself then at least the ability to see something distant. A lone-standing tree. A car coming over a hill. The sun climbing the sky.

"Four years ago, when my Mary died," I said, "the window became my best friend too."

Constance' eyes changed focus, narrowing in on the movement of my lips, a matter of feet and inches from her own. A pained expression flitted across her face before she turned her head slightly, back to the distance on the other side of the glass. It was like she had not recognised me.

"I'm sorry about George," I said.

"He was a good man," I said.

"A loss to us all," I said.

And I meant it, every word.

Constance said nothing, only nodding in places. Whether it was in response to me or to some other conversation playing inside her head, I did not know. I only knew that I was completely alone in the room with her.

And that somehow I had to bring her back.

*

"Eddowes—no. No! It's madness."

I opened the door to my room and hurried Sheldon inside, out of earshot of the other residents. The service wasn't over by thirty minutes and we were both still dressed in our funeral attire, but it had been two days and Constance was slipping further and further away.

Sheldon had been the one to share my idea with first. He was a cautious soul; he only ever went in on a winning hand and never, never went for the bluff. He had the scars to prove it too: every one of his three wives had been unfaithful, leaving him for other, *less* cautious men. But, bless his heart, some people never change and some people never win at poker; it didn't stop them anteing up.

"I need to do this," I told him. "Something to stop the rot setting in."

Sheldon loosened his black tie but left it on. "It's an awful risk, Henry," he said. "If she finds out, if she *catches* you, she'll never forgive you. And you'd be giving them grounds to throw you out of here. There are worse places than Wintercroft, you know."

I could think of only one.

"I can't do this alone," I said. "Are you in or not?"

"Christ, Henry, his ashes have hardly had a chance to cool and you're talking about...well, let's just say it, you're talking about sneaking into his widow's room and planting clues—"

"They're not clues," I corrected, trying to placate him. "This isn't some treasure hunt. Try not to get over-excited. They're messages. Simple but clear messages—from George to his wife."

"And what do you hope to achieve by doing this?" he asked.

I had given the question a lot of thought, and it boiled down to a single grain of truth.

"Time," I said.

"With Constance?" he asked, suspicious.

I nodded.

Sheldon shook his head. It was a cautious shake.

"There are other, better ways to steal a man's wife—widow or not."

Before I could stop myself, I reached for the loose tie around his neck and yanked it up and around like a noose. A tiny puff of air escaped from his mouth and passed into my nostrils the sweet-sharp smell of peppermint on his breath. Reality struck me then, and I snapped out of my rage in an instant, letting go of his tie and backing off to stand next to the window. Sheldon fixed his tie, trying to maintain his composure as he struggled to catch his breath. Suddenly the room felt smaller, the walls pressing in like hands around a bug.

"I'm not trying to steal anyone," I said. "I simply want a little more time with her, that's all. More time. Do you understand?"

Sheldon nodded.

With three ex-wives, he understood better than anyone.

*

To sweeten the mood, later that evening I folded on a Three of a Kind and two Flushes. The other two saw through it right away. Sheldon was *too* quiet and I rarely, if ever, lost at cards. Walshy, ever the clown, got a kick out of just playing the game, good hand or not. Bullamore always went in too heavy and came out light.

"You're one sick old dog," Walshy said, once he'd heard my plan. "But I'm in. Just try and keep me *out*."

Bullamore took a little more convincing. He huffed and puffed but in the end blew nothing down. "As long as no one finds out and no one gets hurt then I'm in too."

And so four ghosts we became.

I should have been pleased, and I was, briefly—my plan to rescue Constance was in early motion. But my tired old skin went cold as I watched myself gather up all of the cards and shuffle them in readiness of the hand about to be played. The sun was sinking outside, pouring in through the windows of the communal room a kind of thin, jaundiced light. It clung to the backs of my hands, to all of our skins in fact, and made of us strange yellow men. Men who had no right to think of themselves as ghosts, who had no right to meddle furtively in the lives of another. Men, strange and yellow.

And before a card was dealt, my hands began to shake.

*

The plan was a simple one. Simple enough for four septuagenarians with—at least it seemed sometimes—one brain left between them. Walshy and Bullamore were to sit at the card table on opposite sides, watching opposite ends of the corridor. If they spotted anyone, resident or member of staff, they were to either give a warning or create a distraction, depending on the risk involved. Sheldon was to stand outside Constance' room and cough once, loudly, just in case I missed the other two's signal. Meanwhile, I'd be inside the room doing my ghostly business.

At eight o'clock some of the residents began shuffling out of the communal room, slippers whispering on carpet. You can tell which ones have lost their husbands or wives; they are the first to head back to the privacy of their rooms. Some like to pray or meditate; some—and I say this with confidence because the walls are thin—want to talk to their loved ones on the other side. I don't judge; I've done the same thing myself once or twice, and sometimes Mary even gave me the gift of a few words in reply. We four were not the first ghosts in Wintercroft, by any means. They came and went with the living, part of their luggage, you might say. However, we *were* the first to break into someone's room and move their things around.

When everyone was out of the way and we had bribed the night staff into allowing us an extra hour for our card game, Sheldon and I made our way to Constance' room. We loitered outside the door for a few minutes, shaking with nerves and trying not to breathe too loudly. Sometimes the harder you try to do something the harder it becomes. It might have been astute to heed that thought *before* I opened the door and slipped inside, but I didn't. Love is deaf as well as blind.

The ceiling light was off, but the curtains had been left open slightly. The moon sat low in the sky, a crooked smile. I remained in the shadows on the other side of the room. For a while, I could only look at her, watching her sleep while feeling a surreal connection to her deceased husband. After all, we were but two of a small number who had enjoyed the privilege. Constance looked tired though, weary of the waking world and wading through the other. Her eyes rolled under the lids, no doubt tortured by dreams of George. I stood and watched and listened long enough to hear a low moan escape her lips and, a few moments later, a single soft tap on the door. Sheldon. Get on with it. Two taps in succession meant somebody was coming, stay put. Yes, I thought. *Get on with it.* And it was at that precise moment Constance spoke, plaintively, from the depths of her sleep.

"*George?*"

Any residual doubt I had vanished. Even asleep, Constance could sense him in the room beside her, and he *was* there, in me. I was the ghost of George.

I crept across to his chest of drawers and opened the drawers until I found something I could use. While I pushed aside the socks and peered under the pressed shirts, I wilfully opened my mind to prior conversations I'd had with Constance about him. A happy, loving wife will share the minutia of her husband with anyone who will listen. But most of us do not listen; we smile, we nod, we make sieves of our mind to let the words fall through—unless, that is, we are in love with the woman ourselves. Then we listen; then we store; then we remember...

Everything.

The ruby cufflinks she gave him on their fortieth anniversary. How he wore them every time they went dancing after that. The cufflink he lost, perhaps to the dance floor during an over-enthusiastic spin, like the ones I would watch him inflict upon her in the communal room in front of everyone. Constance never seemed to mind it though, often slipping into fits of giggles as if she had somehow shed ten or fifteen years with the completion of each turn. The painful truth was George had inflicted them upon *me*—as I stood in the crowd and watched them, close and together.

The stuff of life collects in the corners. It is where the good—and the bad—invariably end up. It is where I found the remaining cufflink. A silver oval with a ruby 'star' set in the centre and an engraved starburst around the jewel. I picked it up and transported it carefully on my palm over to Constance' bed, where I placed it on the empty pillow next to hers. My hands shook. If it were caused only by my age then I was two hundred years old. I was frightened, terrified. Constance' face was turned toward me, the tip of her nose within touching distance, her lips...only a short lean away.

I am a ghost, I reminded myself. And I have outstayed my welcome.

Wait—what welcome?

I backed away. My eyes lifted from Constance' face to the moonlight caught in her silver hair to the gap in the curtains through which the moon and...something *else* watched.

My heart paused, and threatened to stop. When it started again, it raced fast and hard in my throat and ears. My hands shook, out of control. I felt them at my sides, gripping the air spasmodically; seeking purchase, finding none. If the trembling of a man's hands is the measure of his age, I was Methuselah.

Something watched me from the garden.

It—he—stood beside the trunk of the willow tree, whose shadow-branches seemed like cracks across the pale, moonlit ground. I remember thinking that he had climbed out from one of those cracks to enter this world, which seemed a stupid and skittish thought at the time, but not so much later on; not so much at all. The figure wore an ankle-length overcoat and a hat with a wide brim. In his left hand he held a cane of sorts. But it was when he turned his head to one side and revealed the silhouette of the mask he wore that my fear bubbled over and carried me out of that room in great haste.

His mask had the long curved beak of a crow.

What frightens a ghost, you might ask. Let me answer.

Not much. But that? Yes.

I almost pushed Sheldon onto his backside in the corridor, but I managed to grab onto his shoulders before he fell and stood him back upright. His face was entirely *un*-ghostlike, unless ghosts can sweat profusely and look terrified. Then I thought of how I looked to him. *I* was the cause of his fear. For the moment I decided to keep the cause of mine to myself. We hurried back along the corridor to the communal room and the game, where we retook our seats as the cards were swiftly dealt.

"Are you happy now?" Bullamore asked. "You know—with what you've done."

I looked at my cards for a very long time. "I am," I said. "I think it was the right thing to do. For Constance," I added.

"Good," Sheldon said. "Let this be an end to it."

He folded. It was Walshy's turn.

"I'll raise you two onions," he said, meaning rings. "I've got two pair and the worst are tens. Do the right thing, Eddowes, and throw in your hand."

I looked at Walshy. Although the moment called for a knowing smile, the muscles of my face refused to cooperate.

"I can't do that," I said. "Not with what I'm holding."

It was a bluff, and I lost.

*

The next morning she found me on a bench in the gardens, gazing at the spot on the lawn from which the figure had watched me the night before. The willow tree's branches shivered in the breeze. Constance sat beside me, drawing a shawl about her shoulders. She said good morning. Her voice was different. In my distraction, I forgot to say good morning back.

"You can feel it, can't you?" I said, not turning. "Snow on the way. The air's got teeth. Bite." I turned then and prayed the guilt of last night's intrusion would not show upon my face. "You should be inside, dear. Somewhere warm."

She shifted closer, leaned against my side, gave a long sigh. I wanted to curl my arm around her and draw her in close, but something choked me. The feeling of eyes watching us—even though the gardens were empty, entirely ours.

"Henry?" she said. I noticed that she was looking where I was looking: toward the spot under the willow tree. She saw nothing, no one, but we were looking at the same thing from different sides of the night. "Do you think there is something after...this?"

If she felt me tense beside her, she did not show it.

"What do you mean?" I said, knowing precisely what she meant: a ruby cufflink on a pillow; love undying, love undiminished, love... underhand.

"Promise me you won't laugh," she said. "I have to tell someone and I'd like it to be you, but promise me first."

"I promise not to laugh." It was the easiest promise I ever made.

She took a moment. While I waited, I watched the first snowflake fall from the sky, land on the back of her hand, and melt into a tear. A speck of dirt floated in it. I peered at it, leaning closer as it grew in size, until the speck outgrew the tear and became a single rheumy eye, crow-black.

Malignant.

"I think George visited me last night," she announced. When I looked from her face to her hand again, I saw the eye had reverted back into snow-melt, and I—I was losing my mind. Turning the toaster to the darkest setting.

"What makes you say that?" I said.

I listened to her tell the story I already knew; the story I had written last night, myself, not George. And long before she was done telling it, I was no longer focussed on her words but on the modulation of her voice. Gone was the flat-line of the grieving widow, replaced by the rise and fall of a woman revived.

"Do you think it was a one-off?" she asked later, toward the end of our conversation. "Or might he return to me again soon?"

I checked the back of her hand for eyes. When I found none, I shrugged and said, "Who can say, my dear. But if I were you I'd check the pillow each morning, just in case."

*

We waited nearly a week before becoming ghosts again. Following her discovery of the ruby cufflink, Constance' mood stayed elevated for a day or two but soon began to wane when there were no further messages from George. She suspected that he would never return and even began to entertain the notion that she had somehow put the cufflink on the pillow herself and forgotten about it. And so, I felt compelled to act, but I did so with growing reluctance.

It was the same setup: Walshy and Bullamore were on lookout from the communal room card table; Sheldon waited for me outside her room. I considered leaving a handwritten note on the pillow but realised she could easily tell that the script did not belong to George, and a typewritten note was too impersonal to convince. So, I circled three lines in one of her favourite poems—Robinson Jeffers' "For Una":

These are the falling years,
They will go deep,
Never weep, never weep.

Early the next morning she knocked on my door, pulling me from a night of fragmented sleep. I had been dreaming of the figure I'd seen on my first visit to her room (and indeed on my second visit also, on the exact same spot): a standing shadow beneath the willow tree, eyes hidden behind the black glass eye-covers of a mask with a long beak; a mask that seemed maddeningly familiar to me, but which I could not place. Constance kissed my cheek even as I tried to rub the tiredness—and the unsettling memory—from my eyes.

"He came," she said, holding the book of poetry in her hands like one might hold a delicate bird or a book of prayer. "George. He left me this beautiful message. I'll read it to you." She did, and it took huge restraint on my part not to move my lips along with hers.

"That *is* beautiful," I said, savouring the look of desperate joy on her face despite knowing that this had to stop; *I* had to stop. I decided to test the water. "But maybe it is a parting message," I said.

The joy drained from her face, leaving only the pale look of desperation. "Whatever do you mean?"

"Nothing," I said. "Forget it. I spoke out of turn."

"Henry, please..."

I shrugged. "It sounds like a farewell message to me. Who knows—maybe you were right and it isn't possible for him—George—to continue making these trips."

"Why not?"

"I don't know. Look, forget I said anything. I've just woken up, I'm—" *being watched* "—still half asleep."

"No, tell me why you think he can't continue," she insisted.

Suddenly she was seven-years-old, a slightly petulant child looking for answers.

I told myself to keep silent, but it wasn't me talking anymore: it was the dark, bird-faced figure from the previous nights. He'd somehow displaced himself from the lawn outside Constance' window to the darkened corridors of my sleep to the waking thoughts wriggling through my mind.

"Constance, I don't know. I don't know anything. Maybe George *will* come back. All I'm saying is you should try to get accustomed to the idea that at some point he won't. I'm sorry."

She looked at me for a moment, studied me, then closed the book, gently, hiding the words her dead husband had circled for her. Or so she believed. Foolishness, what we use to fill the hollows of our grief. Then—

"You're right," she announced suddenly. At that, I snapped fully awake. "My George might not be able to make too many more visits. Thank you, Henry, for your honesty. You've been most helpful."

She said no more, but slipped the book of poetry into her cardigan pocket, turned, and walked away, back along the corridor to her room, I assumed. I stood in the empty doorway for a short time after she left, bemused by what had transpired between us. Indeed, feeling like an insignificant minnow caught and left to wriggle on a hook.

When I finally went inside, I glanced at the window and saw the heavy snowfall. Winter had come to Wintercroft. The ground was completely white.

*

I spent the day reading in my room, or rather staring at the words on the pages as if they were peculiar footprints in the snow. At some point, Walshy knocked on my door, invited me along to play cards; I declined, said I had a headache, and that wasn't a lie. When someone compliments you on your helpfulness and you cannot understand the way in which you have helped, it kneads your mind like dough.

I did not want to go back. I did not want to face her. Twice, I'd seen that strange bird-like figure standing out there on the lawn, watching me. I knew not what to make of him but he knew what to make of me, the hopeless meddler.

I no longer wanted to be a ghost; I wanted a life, *my* life. But what I had once, house, home, wife, family were lost, either stolen from me or dropped by my own tired and slackening grasp. The nearest of my two boys lived four hours away in a big house with a wife and my grandchild and at least one spare room for visitors. He refused to give me those four hours or that room because I refused to release my Mary's ashes and kept them still in the bottom of my wardrobe. My other offspring lived farther away and hated me more. I was sorry for the way things were, but I was also stubborn. Mary was not meant for wind or worms or columbarium niches. She was meant for me.

Constance... Constance was warm petals on snowy ground...an elegant train passing through the dark, lonely tunnel of me, there for a moment and then gone, never truly there, never truly mine. But the tunnel does not forget the train; it embraces its fading echoes and in infinitesimal ways quietly shapes itself around them.

I gave her two days and then went to find her. I wanted to know how she was coping. And I missed her. She hadn't been seen much outside of her room, but when I knocked and entered she wasn't there, and I eventually found her in one the conservatories. She was standing with her nose almost touching the glass, breath fogging up the pane, looking for signs of George in the snow, like he was lost out there and due to return anytime soon. I approached and stood beside her. Constance looked up at me, teary-eyed. I reached for her hand and gave it a gentle squeeze. I wasn't being tender, particularly; my hand felt unclean.

"There's been nothing, Henry. No communication from George at all. Something is wrong."

I opened my mouth to say something, but my throat was dry.

"I wrote to him," she said.

My heart nearly stopped.

"Three whole pages," she went on. "I left it on his pillow two nights ago and then last night too, and since then—nothing. It's still there now."

I moved my tongue around the walls of my mouth, spreading moisture.

We ghosts, we crave the life we leave behind. But sooner or later the truth gets through: that life is no longer ours, and we can never reclaim it.

The ghost of George would return, of that I had a sudden, nauseating certainty.

"Give it time," I managed to say. "Give it a little more time."

*

Something felt wrong from the moment I informed the others that we were "going in one more time." I had a heavy feeling in my stomach, which I attributed to having been pushed into a third visit. I disliked and distrusted that number. Bad things tended to happen either in threes or on the third time you did something. Like enter Constance' room. But you couldn't skip it or o'erleap it and move straight on to four; no, you could only go through or in this instance, go *in*.

I decided that I would risk everything and write a response to

Constance' letter in my own hand. I am left-handed, so I used my right to produce a scrawl that I thought could be attributed to that of a dead man communicating with his wife from the other side. I thought it was transparent nonsense, and of course it and I depended upon poor Constance' willingness to believe my fakery was in fact a heartfelt message from George. I wondered when it was I had stepped willingly off the path of right into the gutters of wrong. Worryingly, I had no recollection.

We all felt it. The weight of that number on our shoulders. Three. Like an eight half-hidden by shadow. But I was bound to this thing; the others not so much, but they gave me their grudging allegiance nonetheless. Bullamore and Walshy went to their stations and Sheldon to his, while I, letter in hand, turned the handle of Constance' room door and slithered inside.

It was black as pitch in there. Unlike on the previous two occasions, Constance had drawn the curtains, denying the moonlight. I hesitated, unsure of what to do next: my old eyes asked for too long to adjust themselves to the dark, and would have been beaten in the race by the approaching dawn. So, I could either turn and leave or walk and pray I didn't bump into any corner-posts on my way over to the empty pillow, assuming Constance slept on the same pillow every night, of course. Two options. But as I was deliberating between them, a third presented itself—not as an option but as an obstacle—when a tall shadow, darker and deeper than any around it, rose from leaning over the far side of the bed. Someone turned toward me in the dark, the sound of his brushing against the blankets overhanging the bed a soft hiss in my ear.

I tried to speak but I was as voiceless as...as any ghost. That, and I did not want to risk waking Constance. And I was, undeniably, quite petrified by this point, too.

One of the curtains decided to speak for me, however. Caught by a blast of icy wind through the open window, it flew up and, twisting as it fell, allowed the moon to illumine for a moment the figure standing beside the bed.

It was, of course, the same figure I had observed on the lawn during my two previous visits. Now, he was inside Constance' room. When he had uncoiled in the dark, he must have been hunched over her sleeping body, the tip of that crow-beak mask almost touching her soft, oblivious cheek. He leaned over her still, one gloved hand on the corner of the headboard while the mask threw a black accusation my way.

In a matter of seconds I knew that *he* was not a man—not one of us. What I did not know was everything else. But I understood one other

14

important thing when I saw the empty pill bottle lying on the bedside table a second before the curtain fell and the room plunged back into darkness: he was not there for me.

He was there for Constance.

*

What Happened Next.

It's getting late and my fingers are stiff from holding this pen, so allow me please to skip to the next part, or at least to summarise briefly what happened...

I went for the son of a bitch. Like a rabid old dog.

And he went down easy.

Too easy.

Bizarrely, there was no strength in him at all. But then, they say the most dangerous creatures in this world are often the smallest and most vulnerable. Perhaps the same rule applied to those not of this world, to the things that inhabited the corners, out of sight from the rest of us. For now, take my word for it: taking him down was no problem whatsoever, not even for this old man. I should have known something was wrong—something *else*—but all I could think about was putting a distance between him and Constance. When I had him pinned to the carpet, I whispered to Sheldon on the other side of the door. He came in on my third attempt; the third stab at anything is never a whisper but a shout: the rule of three. I told him to get the others and fast. I cut him off dead when he started firing questions into the dark. "Go, *now*," I said. "And one of you call an ambulance."

God bless him, he did.

The ambulance station was three minutes from Wintercroft. I knew that because we were regular customers. In *two* minutes, and with a promise to explain everything later, I convinced Sheldon and Bullamore to help carry the intruder to the end of the corridor, into the south stairwell, down, down, down, to the basement and the boiler room—a room with four walls and a door and a lock and a key that nobody ever bothered to remove *from* the lock. We left our prisoner on the hard stone floor, locked the door, pocketed the key, and raced the swelling sirens up the stairs and back to Constance' room in the one minute we had remaining.

We made it. Several hours later, the district hospital confirmed via telephone that Constance had made it too.

But I'd forgotten the rule.

The rule of three.

And later that night, Sheldon died in his sleep.

*

Before we all went into the basement and discovered otherwise, I'd hoped to learn that it was a heart attack brought on by the stress and demands of that night. After all, Sheldon had helped to carry our captive down two flights of stairs and across a cluttered, murky basement. Then there had been the sprint back to Constance' room. It had taken a lot out of all of us, and I could see how it might have taken that little bit more out of him, a man who had gone through life in first gear, who had worked in the same garage office all of his life with only one promotion, who, when his last wife suggested they retire to Malta, said he liked the idea but could never bring himself to commit, and so she went anyway, without him.

But it wasn't a heart attack.

The results of the post-mortem stated: cause of death unknown.

We'd arranged to meet in my room after breakfast and after I had checked on Constance, who had been delivered back to us by the hospital but given strict instruction to get bed rest following the pumping of her stomach and her miraculous recovery. She would miss Sheldon's funeral. And I wasn't comfortable with the knowledge that while she was lying weakened and vulnerable in her bed, our prisoner would be right under her nose, pacing the floor of his makeshift cell, possibly planning an escape.

"Where the hell is he?" I said, meaning Bullamore. "We need to talk...we need to figure this out and come up with a plan." I glanced out the window at the wall bordering the snow-covered gardens and thought it seemed a little bit taller today. "The snow isn't melting," I said just to be saying something. "If anything, there's more of it."

Walshy, sitting in my armchair, gave a quiet snort.

"What?"

"I was just thinking," he said. "Sheldon. That poor bugger never caused anyone any problem until now."

"What do you mean?"

"Well, think of the other poor bugger who's trying to dig his grave through all of *that* shit."

I laughed. I couldn't help it. It tore right out of me. But all it left was a hole, and a smile melting down my face.

Why is it always the good ones? I thought. Mary. George. Sheldon.

"The meek will never inherit the earth," I said. "But they make it a far, far better place to live."

Walshy was about to say something when the door opened and Bullamore's face appeared in the gap. He looked troubled. "You two," he said, "come with me—now. It's been nagging me ever since we carried our intruder friend downstairs. I thought there was something familiar about that mask with the beak, but what with my brain being a little slower than it used to be it's taken me a while... Anyway, I've figured it out—some of it at least. It's time to pay the doctor a visit."

Walshy got there first.

"Doctor? What are you talking about?"

*

Bullamore led us down to the basement. Never a man of many words, despite forty years teaching History to disinterested secondary-schoolers, he seemed unusually taciturn that night. There were no windows in the basement, but two low-wattage bulbs emitted light enough to push the shadows back and allow us to navigate our way through the bowels of Wintercroft. Some of the detritus ended up in local charity shops, the rest ended up down there with the dust and the spiders.

He halted us halfway to the boiler room on the far side of the basement level, in a small pocket of darkness between the reach of either bulb, and pointed at something hooked over one foot of an upturned walking frame.

A glove.

We stood there and stared at it for a moment.

"I found it this morning," he explained. "Came down here with some food and water for our friend, and to get a proper look at him, and came across it. It's off his right hand."

I gave him a quizzical look. I wasn't sure if he saw it through the gloom. Anyone could tell looking at the glove that it was meant for someone's right hand. Bullamore was holding back, taking his time instead of going all-in. I'd never known him to play it cautious.

But then I realised: he was scared.

I laid a reassuring hand on his shoulder. "What is it?"

"When we carried that thing down here," he said. "I had him by the left arm and shoulder. You, Henry, had both his legs... Sheldon took the right side, do you remember?"

"I remember," I said. "But what are you—"

Wait. The *right* side.

"I think the glove came off when we were carrying him through here. I think Sheldon touched him—touched his hand. And now Sheldon's dead. What is it we're dealing with here, Henry? If you know something, you'd better share it with us."

"I don't know anything," I replied. "At least, not for sure. Not yet."

I saw Bullamore shake his head in the dark. "The mask with the beak and the hat with the brim, the cane...they're things I'd seen before, back in my teaching days. But I couldn't make the connection until this morning when somebody mentioned something about a doctor's appointment they had coming up. The word stuck in my head for some reason, but it wasn't until an hour later that it came to me. Whoever... *whatever* it is, the uniform he's wearing—it's consistent with what a seventeenth or eighteenth-century plague doctor would have worn. The mask protected them from infection borne by a miasma, or what they called 'bad air'."

"A plague doctor," Walshy repeated, dubious. "As in, someone whose job it is to *treat* the plague? I don't think so, Bull. For starters, there are no plagues anymore. Secondly, how did he get here—by travelling through time? No, this is somebody's idea of a joke. Sneaking in, frightening people while they're asleep, that kind of thing. We should've rung the police by now and let them handle this."

"That doesn't explain what happened to Sheldon," Bullamore said. "I'm going in there. And he's going to answer some questions."

I thought of our captive in Constance' room, leaning over what I had assumed was her sleeping form. But she hadn't been asleep; she'd been unconscious, in a pill-induced coma, skipping along the path to some imagined reunion with George.

Depending on one's perspective, I had either prevented death from taking her or kept her out of the loving arms of her husband.

So it wore no hooded cloak and carried no scythe, and it clearly did not match the archetype of Death, but my encounter with it inside Constance' room convinced me that our captive had the ability to end a life with the ease of snuffing out a candle. Sheldon, were he able, would testify to that; and Constance too, had I entered her room but a moment too late, I'm sure. It *was* death, make no mistake; perhaps not with a capital 'D', perhaps just a servant or an underling—one of the elves—but evidently more than capable of carrying out the same work.

Treating a plague.

I reached out and seized Bullamore's arm. "We can't go in there," I said, pulling him back toward the stairwell. "It's dangerous. Not human. Not like us at all."

"So what is it?" he asked.

I tried to explain my theory. I described how I'd tackled it with ease in Constance' room, and how under that long coat there couldn't be much to it. Hollow bones, I thought. We took turns looking at it through the porthole window of the cell door. It sat on the floor and faced the wall in front, though I doubted that was what it saw: the glass eye-covers revealed no eyes, only the impenetrable darkness of a mine, and the assurance of a long drop should one lean in too close. Its gloveless hand was thin, long-fingered, black as coal. No fingernails. There was no smell coming from it either, at least none that reached us under the door. It ignored all offers of food and water and conversation. It sat, and it waited.

"What are we supposed to do?" Bullamore asked, later. "We can't hold it here indefinitely."

I glanced around at the discarded furniture and personal effects that once belonged to some of that creature's family-less victims, and gave Bullamore a long and serious look.

"Who says we can't?"

*

Two days later, Constance invited me to a private lunch in her room. Since returning from hospital she had been confined to her bed, by precaution rather than necessity. She appeared to be in good if not magnificent health, suffering no ill effects from her attempted reunion with George. Her only affliction, it seemed, was boredom. When I pulled a chair over to her bedside and sat down to sip my tomato soup, I detected an energy in her that I had not seen since prior to her husband's death. Indeed, she seemed relatively youthful, although I credited that to a fine application of make-up powder, which in itself was rather startling since the grieving widow tends to stay free of the stuff for a while after the loss of her husband. In the early days after Mary, I refused to shave and took to roaming the house wearing her bathrobe, until the scent of her faded and the stench of me took over. You find a way back, or perhaps it finds you; but life—or at least some approximation of it—goes on. But Constance seemed different since her return: rejuvenated; positively vibrating with energy instead of tremulous from her eighty-year-old bones. Perhaps I describe it from a skewed perspective; our captive in the basement had a far-reaching influence that we remaining ghosts were only beginning to understand. And feel. The three of us were barely managing an hour or two of sleep each night, and I was tired if not exhausted if not on the verge of collapse. Indeed, as I tried to eat, most of the soup on my spoon invariably splashed back into the bowl from the unsteadiness of my hand. I ate less than a quarter and finally gave up.

"You seem much better," I said. "How long before you can get up and move around?"

"They said another day but I feel better *now*," she replied. "I hate this bed. It feels like a coffin, and every day in it feels like a week. At my age, that's not even an exaggeration."

I laughed, while behind it I recalled our prisoner brushing the tip of that beaked mask against that fair, powdered cheek of hers. *If only you knew, Constance; if only you knew just how close you came.*

"On the other hand, you're looking tired, Henry."

I nodded in agreement, too weary to pretend otherwise.

"Where there is Yin there is Yang," I said. "But I'll be fine."

"Is it just me, or has everybody been acting a little odd these last couple of days?"

I sat up straight in my chair. "Odd, how?"

"Perhaps odd is the wrong word. *Different* might be better. I don't get to see much being stuck in here, but I can hear it in people's voices when they walk past my door. Of course, *I* feel it too."

"I should hope so," I said seriously. "It was a close thing. You almost didn't make it."

"I know, I know," she said, burying her face in her hands. "It was a stupid thing to do, and I've been lectured by everybody and his dog about doing it. Please don't tell me off too, I beg you. I already know what you must think of me, but try to understand something: I never expected to be here, having to face you, or anyone. I took the whole bottle, Henry. It should have killed me. I didn't want this second chance—"

"Don't talk like that," I said, shifting uncomfortably. "You belong here. There's still plenty of life left in you yet."

Constance nodded. "Yes. Yes, I think you're right. I also think me being back here might've been my final gift from George."

I did not have to feign my surprise. "Really? You believe he did this?"

"He was never much of a letter writer, was my George," she said.

"More one for the big, overblown gesture. Never a single flower but a whole bunch. I'm not disappointed anymore that he did not reply to my letter, because he did much more than that. He gave me a second chance."

In my mind, a voice roared out in protest. *Tell her! Get up and tell her it was you. You gave her the second chance, not George. You're the Yin to her Yang. Not George. YOU!*

"If you love someone," I said, "you should let them go. I've never understood it, personally. The cold, hard truth is if you love someone you want to hold on to them, keep them, *never* let them go."

When Mary was at her worst, I stood at her bedside and swore to that effect. After she succumbed, after the rise and fall of her chest stopped, after the tears and the eulogies and the world going up in smoke, and after they handed her back to me in an urn, I remained a man of my word.

I stood and moved the chair back to its original position, then went over and stood in front of the window with my back to Constance. For a moment, I thought I felt her confused gaze on the back of my neck, and I held my breath, waiting for her to say something, to toss me a rope so that I might pull myself out of the cold, cold waters I suddenly found myself in, drowning; but in the end she said nothing, threw nothing, and I breathed again, not an ocean from my lungs but mist on the windowpane.

The disappointment I understood...but why did I also feel relief?

Some esoteric balance perhaps; Yin and Yang.

Or perhaps the ghost of Mary haunting my heart.

Not letting go.

I let myself be distracted by a sudden small commotion outside. Eleven Wintercroft residents were lining themselves up in the snow, having abandoned the comfortable Kensingtons and safe views of the communal room for winter coats and wellington boots.

"Constance, you must come see this," I said.

I helped her get out of bed, and walked her over to the window. We watched the activity outside for a full minute before one of us found the words. She was smiling when she looked at me; a beautiful smile below two beautiful eyes imbued once more with a *joie de vivre*.

"Something's different around here, all right," she said.

I had no argument.

Outside, in freezing temperatures, six old women and five old men laughed as they made angels in the snow.

*

Two weeks later, as the snow began to thaw and the angels to melt back into the ground, the cancer showed up. No more than a wisp of smoke on the X-ray, but inoperable nonetheless. Chemo and radiotherapy were two options put on the table. Any hair that survived the chemical warfare would fall in battle against the radiation. There would be fatigue and swallowing difficulties and sickness and increased shortness of breath and coughing *at least*, for the possibility of weeks, months, maybe a year (because miracles do happen, they say). Constance Harriet Willington-Wright was told by doctors in no uncertain terms: she was going to die.

But I knew different.

Constance wasn't going to die.

She was going to suffer.

*

I held her, she cried; she clung to me, she cried. A woman drowning in a sea of confusion, questions like sharks tearing hunks from her haemorrhaging faith. "Maybe George changed his mind," she said. "Maybe he decided he wants me with him after all. What do you think, Henry? Could it be that?" I shrugged and shook my head, knowing that it was nothing to do with George, something to do with our doctor friend, and *everything* to do with me.

*

The basement felt like the right place for us to meet. Although it remained unspoken between us, it was clear we all felt the same: like ghosts, wandering through the place in which we once lived but lived no more. Indeed, several weeks on and every day spent up *there* with the laughter and frivolity was made more difficult by our secret in the basement and our exhaustion; every night made more demanding with the incessant groaning and knocking—an indication of the return of libido to Wintercroft—while the staff stood around looking bemused and we three lay in our beds too afraid to close our eyes for what new death our prisoner would show us next.

Our prisoner.

Right.

Imagine every time you closed your eyes, you saw only death. The victim of a heart attack. The smoking, silent aftermath of a car accident. A man's head kicked like a football. Or picture the bloated victims of a tsunami; the broken victims of an earthquake; the melted victims of a fire; or the bloated, broken, *and* melted victims of a plane crash or terrorist's bomb. A little girl run over by a bus while crossing the street. A boy turned inside out by a paedophile. Every night, different images on the same theme. Every night, waking sweat-drenched and furious because you know that as sure as night falls there was someone who could have prevented those things from happening, but they didn't. And that maybe the ones you love don't come back because they hate you for letting them go.

Walshy and Bullamore arrived armed with a small battery torch. Bullamore carried it. We arranged ourselves outside the boiler room door as Bullamore played the torch across our haggard, unshaven faces. Walshy blew into his cupped hands and tried to shake the cold from his feet. Finally, Bullamore shone the torch on himself, and my mind leapt to Piggy, holding the conch in *Lord of the Flies*.

"We need to talk about what we're going to do with him," he said. "I vote we let him go, tonight. And that's all I have to say on it." Typical Bullamore, I thought. All in. He moved out of the light, toward the door.

I stood in front of him and placed a conciliatory hand on his chest. But if it was conciliatory, why did I put so much weight into it?

The torch illumined my face.

"Think very hard about what you're doing here," I said. "You've seen the difference in Wintercroft already. If we let him out, everything changes back. People will die."

He pulled the torch under his drawn and shadowed face. "I'm so tired, Henry. It doesn't ever let up. I can't sleep. Besides, think of Constance and what's *she's* going through."

"I am," I said from the darkness. "I'm trying to convince her to stop treatment. It's not making any difference to her anyway, not with him locked up down here. All it is, is self-inflicted pain. If I can convince her to stop, then we can have more time. But if you let him go, it's the end of her—of all of us."

Walshy reached for the torch and angled it in his direction. He looked the worst of any of us: shadows had made permanent homes in the hollows of his cheeks and there was no humour whatsoever left in his deep-sunken eyes. "What about the next poor bastard that falls sick?" he said. "I mean, really sick—something life threatening. How many are we going to let suffer before we do something about it? No, Bull's right, Henry: we have to stop this thing and put everything back the way it was."

"The way it's supposed to be, right, Walshy?" I said, bitterly.

Bullamore took the torch. "Death must go on, Henry," he said.

"Don't open that door," I warned.

Bullamore turned on me then. "Constance doesn't love you," he snarled. "She loves George. Just like you love Mary. Let him have her back, Henry."

"Don't open the door. Please. All I want is a little more time with her. Then I'll let her go. I promise."

I watched the anger leave Bullamore's face. He placed a hand on my shoulder. "There's never enough time. For any of us."

I nodded in the darkness. He shone the torch in my face, and I batted it away; I did not want them to see my tears.

"Who's got the key?" Walshy asked.

"Here," I said, pulling it out of my pocket. "Be careful when you open the door. Make sure that thing hasn't moved. And watch for its right hand."

There was a moment when Bullamore's fingers touched the key and we both held onto it, both reluctant to let go. The moment passed, and he was the one left holding the key.

Walshy glanced through the porthole. "He's standing," he said. "But he's backed away from the door. I think it's okay. It's as if he knows we're letting him go."

Bullamore handed Walshy the torch and told him to keep it trained on the prisoner, especially its exposed right hand. Walshy shone the light through the window. The thing's hand was thin, practically skeletal, like black spun glass. Long fingers, no fingernails. Beneath the long coat, the brim hat, the mask, the gloves, the boots, there was something ancient and perhaps as frail as the rest of us. Bullamore put the key in the lock and turned it. The door swung open unassisted, the key still in the cylinder. The prisoner did not move; not yet. He stood. He waited. Bullamore went in first—all in, as usual—while Walshy kept the torch trained on the creature inside as he followed Bullamore into the room. Which left me standing outside...with time in the palm of my hand.

You know what I did.

But believe me when I tell you: I did it for Constance.

So Many Heartbeats, So Many Words

10. Woe-cake

Don't let the sunshine fool you. That beautiful, yellow bitch may be out today, but she's been hiding for months. They say we had the wettest winter and spring on record. But here she is, back. Like nothing happened after she left.

Like all is forgiven.

Earlier, I stood at our bedroom window and watched through a frame of mould as my neighbours emerged from their homes looking uncertain, stooped, braced for the sudden impact of precipitation; looking, in fact, for the all-too-familiar English rainclouds. Seeing none, they straightened their backs, lifted their knuckles, and went inside, returning moments later dressed in shorts and T-shirts, some not even wearing the latter, going bare-chested for their blonde goddess, trying to impress her whilst conveniently forgetting that she hasn't so much as called never mind dropped in for a visit since September.

It isn't just the adults either. Children love her too.

Even Alfie.

As I sit cross-legged on the grass and nurse a cold beer, he kicks a football around the garden. There is a lot of shifting of feet before each kick, an odd little dance, but it doesn't keep him from losing his balance. He falls, he gets up. Failure is still new to him, a pebble on the path instead of a wall.

Like most children, Alfie has many curious habits and customs. His Dance Before Kicking a Ball is but one, like the lining up of his Fisher Price Little People along the length of the television unit, facing the TV if it is on, facing out if it is not. Or that thing he does sometimes with the bucket of plastic creepy-crawlies. Or the wonderful way he tackles the dense jungle of language, reshaping its landscape with a kind of verbal machete in order to make his way through. A magical place in which finger becomes *nin-ga*, look becomes *yook*, elephant becomes *entint*, and purple *pee-pail*. *Lego* is yellow. The sun is *lego*.

On paper, I am good with words too. Over one hundred short stories published. A dozen appearances in "Best Of" anthologies. Two British Fantasy Award nominations.

The jungle is ours, you might say; his and mine.

But if that's true, why is there so much talk of Alfie having delayed speech? Why appointments with a Speech and Language Therapist?

She'd summarised it in two words: precautionary measure. I had two words for her, too: they involved sex and movement.

"Alfie, it's time for lunch," I tell him. "What do you want?"

"Bit-it," he says cheerily.

"Not for lunch, Alf. Something else, more nutritious."

"*Choccit* bit-it."

"Nice try, but no."

He stops what he's doing to glower at me with those strong blue eyes of his, cartoon-expressive eyebrows furrowing into a scowl. I hate that so many of my bad habits and none of Sue's have stuck to him, but she is the one out there in the real world, at work, while I watch him and snatch moments to write when I can. He curls his top lip, affecting a silent snarl to accompany the frown.

"Nice," I tell him.

But there's no real malice on his face; he's merely mirroring something, or someone, he has seen before. Besides, he understands that there is only one way to achieve his goal of getting that chocolate biscuit, and that is to eat his proper lunch first.

"So, what'll it be?" I ask again.

"Woe-cake," he says with apposite gloom.

I find it a strange association. I mean, *weambow* sounds like rainbow, right? But *woe-cake* doesn't sound much like the real thing at all.

I stand up, set my beer aside to warm in the sun. I don't feel like drinking just one anyway. Let the *lego* bitch take it. She's taken so much from us already this year.

"Woe-cake it is, son."

I don't bother to correct him as I lead him inside. Sometimes the words he chooses have a logic of their own.

9. Coffee Sunset

It took me three years to ask Sue Leonard out, and then my hand—or rather my tongue—was forced.

"I'm leaving Salisbury," she said to me one day over lunch. This was fifteen years ago. She was eighteen and mature to my twenty-two and not. We were casual friends. She had long hair, dyed black, a square fringe. I liked that she'd chosen that colour over any other. Her eyes were beautiful, too. A coffee sunset you could gaze into forever.

"Where are you going?" I asked. My heart knocked on my ribs as I waited for her to answer.

"Mum and I are thinking of going back to Oz."

Sue had spent a lot of her childhood in Oz. I had spent most of mine in Middle-Earth. Only, Oz was Australia, and I'd never heard of any flights to Rivendell. I was stuck here.

"When was this decided?" I asked. "When is it happening?"

"About a month ago," she replied. "And not for a while yet."

"How long is a while?"

Forever? I wondered.

"A few weeks," she said.

"And this is—this is a permanent thing?"

Sue nodded.

The knocking in my chest became a hammering. Sweat popped out across my forehead, and my tongue tasted suddenly like a fat slug.

"We'll keep in touch though, right?" she said, genuinely hopeful. This was in the days of email but before the rise of social networking. Still, I couldn't help but love her slightly naive optimism. Then, as I took another bite out of my sandwich, something struck me, hard.

Without her coffee sunset, each day is going to seem like forever.

I quickly sank into a black mood after that. When I tried to eat what was left of my sandwich, all I tasted was salt and the withering of that dead thing inside my mouth.

8. The Monster in the Room

My eyes snap open to the darkness of our bedroom. I could use a drink of water, if only to wash my mouth of the bad taste—not the taste of my dream but the monster in the room.

I don't know the precise time, but I sense we are somewhere in the hours after midnight but before dawn when silence smothers the world and the world holds its breath for dear life. Two or three hours from now the first timid rays of sunlight will reach under the blinds to touch the skin, to check that we are still alive. Sometimes, in these lost hours it can be hard to tell. Sometimes, in these lost hours, you don't give a fuck either way.

I turn my head to check on Sue. Usually, she sleeps facing the edge of the bed, and on those nights, when I am still crawling out of the netherworld of my dreams, I find her back toward me and her face concealed. And it is at those times I think about secrets and about lies, and about how lies push secrets around like dung beetles rolling their giant balls of shit.

But tonight, thank you for small mercies, she is facing me.

Four years...and you still can't let it go.

It's unfair, and I know it; just like I know that we should talk about it, about everything. Marriage is a living thing. Its heart is communication—words: those we give, and those we receive. They say that every living creature has a limited number of heartbeats. How many heartbeats does a marriage have? How many words?

And what happens when they run out?

These are the things that I think about in bed at night. No wonder my GP keeps trying to push antidepressants on me.

In the next room, Alfie begins to cough. It's worryingly chesty, like something has got inside his lungs and taken a firm hold. Something has, of course.

Months of incessant rain has led to increased humidity. Add to this the zero ventilation upstairs: no trickle vents fitted to any of the windows; the windows themselves long overdue replacement, crying out for just that every morning when I find tears of condensation streaming down the glass. Add to this the winter temperatures in England making it too cold to leave the windows open through the night unless the central heating is burning alongside, and with Sue the only one bringing in any real money it is too expensive to maintain. Besides, there is no guarantee that it would make the difference needed to prevent the mould from forming. Add to all of this a landlord who couldn't give a fuck, leave in darkness for several hours, and what you have is...

...a serious mould problem.

...a fat slice of what I should like to call henceforth, "woe-cake." Alfie's words, but I'm sure he won't mind if I borrow them.

"Thank you, Alfie."

Again, coughing from the next room.

"He can't help it."

Sue's voice startles me. I turn to look at her again and find that her face is nestled in the other pillow just inches from mine, eyes wide and staring as if she had never been asleep, or was merely pretending.

"He has a chest infection," she continues. "You need to take him to the doctor. She'll probably prescribe a course of antibiotics. I also think we need to move, sooner rather than later."

"Move?" I say. "We can't. I have three deadlines this month. Besides, moving is a lot of added stress and hassle, not to mention expense."

"You did mention it. You always mention it. This house isn't good for him, Simon. For any of us. Alfie's sick: *listen* to him. Me, I'm getting sick. And you'll be next, I'm sure."

"Wait—you're ill too? I didn't know. Why didn't you tell me?"

"You've been too busy writing," she says, making it sound like an accusation, which of course it is, and there are no secrets about *that*.

I say nothing for a moment, only retune into our son's room instead, the muscles in my arms and legs tensed, ready to propel me through to scoop him up should his coughing become choking. Thankfully, it subsides.

"Fucking mould," is all I can say when I finally think of something. "I'm so tired of this."

Rolling over, her back to me, Sue quietly says, "Me too."

7. The Long Walk (in Short)

Fifteen years before, once I resuscitated my tongue and found the words, I asked Sue if she would like to join me for a walk. We left behind the busy city centre and followed Odstock Road past fields dotted with grazing horses, past Salisbury District Hospital, and on to yet more fields. Somehow we ended up in one of them, wading through grass knee deep toward a copse of trees. The sun was hot, bringing out the greenness of the grass and the redness in my cheeks. A light breeze created beautiful, emerald waves around us and caused the trees to whisper at our approach.

I tried to relax, but the simple fact was I knew too much, even if I could not seem to find a way to say it. For instance, I knew that the grass was green because of chlorophyll and that my cheeks were red because of adrenaline and increased blood flow to my face. I also knew—and with only slightly less scientific basis—that Sue's move to Australia was a mistake, and that given half a chance I could fall soul deep in love with this girl.

"Why did you take me all the way out here?" she asked, leaning against one of the trees, the bark coarse next to her soft skin.

She watched me with those coffee-coloured eyes. Calming as a sunset, usually. But now it felt like staring into the sun as it was dying, as it sank below the horizon for perhaps the last time.

And, again, my tongue refused to co-operate. My lips went dry, my mind blank. Eventually, my thoughts flashed upon the stories lying on my desk at home; the thousands upon thousands of words I'd written, every one of them useless to me here and now. Maybe, given a week, three, and the ability to redraft and redraft again, I might have found the right words.

Might.

But since I definitely could not risk saying the *wrong* ones...

I stepped forward.

Leaned in.

Kissed her.

6. Fit It

In another millennium, Sue leaves me asleep in bed while she goes off to eat breakfast, shower, dress for work. But I am only half asleep and she is like some vengeful phantom stalking the periphery of my senses, banging cupboard doors, scrubbing me off her skin, undressing in reverse.

Whether she is pissed off with me or the mould problem or both I do not know. I could ask, but I'm worried she will answer.

And then comes the slamming of the front door. A full stop to end her sentence.

Fifteen minutes later, I drag myself out of bed. Squint through sleep-sealed eyes at the dressing mirror. Adjust my balls inside my boxer shorts. Sniff one armpit (because one's enough). And decide that if I skip the shower this morning I can squeeze in fifteen or twenty minutes of writing time before Alfie wakes and announces that he's *hun-gwee* and wants some *eatbix*.

Really, who's the child here? I spend most of my time making stuff up. I don't make a living at it, though: short stories sell for a pittance and the horror e-book I self-published last year, despite an award nomination and some glowing reviews, had a sales rank of 1,256,447 the last time I checked, and I check *every fucking day*.

My mania is wearing Sue down. She doesn't read books. She exists quite happily in a cultural vacuum, hating Bob Dylan and foreign cinema while adoring Richard Marx and the films of the Eighties, the oeuvre of John Hughes in particular. But I suppose emptiness has its own reward, because she is also responsible and kind and loving; a good mother.

What do I know about being a good father?

I take a long, deep breath. Look up at the ever-growing patch of black mould in the corner of the room. Feel anxiety spread across my chest. It is because of my shortcomings that we cannot afford to move into another house. We are trapped here, just us, and the mould.

Right on cue, Alfie coughs in the next room.

Get your black fingers out of my son.

"Daddy?" he says in a searching voice.

The dressing mirror looks at me. *Is 'Daddy' there?* it asks.

Sometimes, I stand in front of the mirror when I'm alone, holding up another, a shaving mirror, in order to create a kind of tunnel of duplicated images. I'd like to find out what lies at the end of that tunnel someday. They say it goes on and on, into infinity. I like an impossible challenge. It's just the possible ones I struggle with.

"Daddy?" he asks again. "*Sow nin-ga.*"

I don't know what Alfie means, so I turn from the mirror and walk through to his bedroom, where I find him sitting up in bed, holding his index finger aloft in the air. On closer inspection, I can see the problem.

"It's a hang nail, Alfie. Nothing to worry about."

"'ang nail," he says. "*Sow-a.*"

"Downstairs," I tell him. "We'll fix it."

"Fit it."

"No, *fix*, Alfie. We'll fix it."

I can do that much, I tell myself. I haven't wandered that far down the tunnel quite yet.

I wait as Alfie bumps-and-slides his backside down the stairs while he holds his *sow nin-ga* in the air. Sue has left something for me in the kitchen, right where the bar of nine a.m. sunlight strikes the countertop. She used to leave me love notes under my pillow. Now I hold this thing up, turn it over so I can read the single word written inside the digital display in what seems like ten-foot-tall capital letters.

PREGNANT.

"Fit it," a voice says somewhere behind me.

I wait until I catch my breath.

"Alfie," I say. "I think it's probably too late for that."

5. Q*bert Has Hopped His Pyramid

That afternoon, while Alfie is in nursery, I drive to the city outskirts and Wintercroft, the residential home where I left my father two years ago after mum died and his episodes started taking over.

Some days he's lucid. He'll talk incessantly for hours on different subjects, hopping from one to the next like Q*bert across his pyramid of blocks. Those are the days when I don't recognise my father at all, when I wonder if perhaps this garrulous septuagenarian bent on the chair in front of me is the real man, hidden from me all these years.

On other days he is quiet: introspective or distracted—I can never tell which. He refuses to leave his room, choosing to look out of the window instead, at green fields and distant tree lines and years lost and buried like bodies in the woods. It's like I'm not even in the room with him. That's Mr Fenwick. *That's* my father.

And then there are days like today when he shifts effortlessly between the two: from loquaciousness to being completely off the grid.

"That Eddowes fellow's got someone locked up in the basement," he says.

I am feeding him tomato soup. Although he can still feed himself, it's sometimes too agonising to watch the slow, unsteady movement of the spoon toward his wavering mouth, or the drips spattering across the white tray, like a path of blood toward a dying man.

"Who's Eddowes?" I ask.

"George. He lives right here in Wintercroft. Hangs around with those three cronies of his, playing poker after lights out. I heard them talking about it, this thing they've got trapped in the basement."

"That's nice, dad," I tell him. "Maybe you should ask them to let you in on a game."

"You're not listening. They're up to something."

I bring the spoon to his mouth.

"Sue's pregnant, dad."

Spoon goes in. He slurps the soup from it, licks his silver whiskers. I can almost feel him leaving the room then, in much the same way as I can feel the presence of the black mould in the bedroom when I turn the lights off. Sue thinks I'm paranoid, but there's a subtle yet palpable change to the molecules in the air: in the case of the mould it's a thickening; in the case of my father, it's a thinning or a spacing out.

Q*bert has hopped his pyramid.

Someone else is at the controls now.

Or maybe no one is.

"I don't know how I feel about it," I confess to my vacant father as his eyes start to turn toward the fields. A man is out there walking his dog. Enjoying the air. The dog running off all of its excess energy. My father smiles, remembering. But if there is some recollection there, I will never know it. "The timing couldn't be any worse," I tell him. "Alfie is having problems communicating." I cannot contain a snort at the irony. "There's mould in every one of the rooms upstairs. We're all starting to fall ill because of it. I clean it, it comes right back. And I really don't think I *should* be cleaning it because it's a rental property, but the landlord won't do a thing about it. Meanwhile, Sue expects me to be happy that we're bringing another child into this mess—at least, I expect she does: we haven't talked about it. What do I do? Dad?"

This.

This is rock bottom. Seeking advice from a stranger, albeit a *blood* stranger. A carpenter who craved sixteen hour days his entire working life. Fifty years of pulling stuff apart and putting it together again, and always, always for somebody else. He never quite got around to those jobs waiting for him at home. Waiting and hoping.

My father tilts his head toward the window. I can see the dog squatting on the edge of the field.

"Follow that there example," he says. "Deal with your shit then walk on. Live, son. Because there's nothing in this world more horrifying than a life *not* lived."

This is possibly the worst—or best—piece of advice my old man has ever given me.

I just don't know which it is.

4. I, uh...

The sun rises on another day. Our respective doctors have confirmed we each have a chest infection. Alfie's breakfast is a slice of toast followed by five mils of banana-flavoured antibiotic. Sue poaches some eggs for me and her, serves them on toast. Afterward, I pass out the amoxicillin tablets and the water with which to wash them down.

"It's like medication time in Cuckoo's Nest," I joke after swallowing mine.

If Sue gets either the joke or the film reference she doesn't show it. She has only one thing on her mind, the same thing I have been fidgeting around for days.

"I was sick this morning, around five," she says.

I realise Sue is opening a door, saying—without saying, of course—*Let's walk* this *way*.

But I am not ready to follow.

"I wrote something," I tell her. *Here's another door, sweetheart. Come this way, instead.* I know she doesn't want to open it never mind enter Simon's Writing Room, but maybe it's enough to lure her away from hers long enough to drop the subject.

"I couldn't sleep because of the mould," I go on. "So I went downstairs and just started tapping keys. I managed to get a whole story down in first draft by the time I heard you in the bathroom. Four thousand words."

"Why didn't you come up?" she asks, sounding hurt.

Why did I say that? Why did I say that and turn the conversation back to that *door?*

Because I am an arsehole. Four thousand words last night and not one to her about our unborn child now.

"I, uh, assumed it was morning sickness and, you know, par for the course. You're okay now though, right?"

Sue nods, then storms out of the kitchen, slamming all doors real and metaphorical on her way.

3. Dying More Than Living

The tunnel stretches far in front of me, curving into the shadowy distance. I start to run, feet splashing through dirty water. Each breath sounds like a furious gale railing against my ears.

The train platform is littered with paper and broken glass. I run up one stalled escalator and before I head down the next spot the colourful graffiti messages scrawled across the walls. I do not understand the words. Written in a foreign language.

English?

No, French. This is the Paris Metro.

But now isn't the time for words.

It is the time for killing.

I dash across a stretch of open platform, heading toward the conflict. In the distance, the staccato report of gunfire. From the bottom of another unmoving escalator, I hear the blast of a rocket propelled grenade as it slams into a wall somewhere on the floor above me, spraying bricks and debris everywhere. The response is swift and decisive. As I breach the top of the escalator, automatic gunfire rises in a colossal wave and breaks upon the enemy ranks. There are no more RPGs; no further explosions. The push is on: toward the exit, outside, into the open air. I finally catch up with the others, a dozen or so soldiers grouped in chaotic fashion, bearing various kinds of gear, sporting various types of camo. I join them as we carry the fight outside onto the Parisian streets, where I notice the sunlight dancing on the bodies of our fallen comrades a split second before a bullet to the head adds me to their number.

"That is such bullshit," I yell, tearing off the headset and rattling it in my hands at both the TV and the games console. "I didn't even see the son of a bitch!"

Sue's head appears round the door jamb. "Are you forgetting someone? Watch your language."

I nod grudgingly and glance at Alfie in his pyjamas, Alfie playing with his plastic wetland creatures on the rug. I ask him to tell me what they are to distract him from absorbing any of my cursing a moment ago.

"*Yook*," he says. Look. "A *nake*...a *spy-door*...a *corfee-in*...a *graf-foffer*, a *lee-zad!*"

I notice that they are all lying on their backs, legs in the air.

"And where's mummy? What is she doing?"

"Mummy kitchen. Woe-cakes."

"Yes, she is," I tell him.

It is eleven o'clock, long past Alfie's bedtime, but within fifteen minutes of putting him down earlier he began coughing and couldn't stop; not a tickly cough either—nothing about the air in the house tonight is tickly—but a bronchial hacking instead. A short while downstairs, out of the affected areas of the house, and his cough subsides, mostly. It should come as a relief, but it also underlines how at night in particular the house no longer belongs to us but to the monster in our lives.

"Sue?" Her head appears in the doorway again. "I called Coombes today. No joy. He says he'll get the windows looked at in the next two or three weeks, to see if something can be done to improve the ventilation upstairs. Until then, he says to leave the windows open and the heating on."

"And who is paying for that?"

"He didn't answer that one."

"The windows need replacing," she states. "He might not like to hear that little piece of news but it's something he needs to deal with."

I know she isn't talking about Coombes or the mould problem anymore. She's talking about me and the word on the stick. And now I regret taking off the headset and breaking the barrier I put up between us. I need more time to think about what another baby means. At the moment, it feels like a car crash from which I feel compelled to drag myself away not toward. I cannot find a job, I cannot provide for my family, and this house is slowly eating us all from the inside.

It's easy for my old man to say "deal with it and move on," but he never showed me how. Whenever mum and he had a fight he just took on another project or worked an extra shift until the dust settled. Me, I escape into creating stories about other people and their problems, and when I can't face that, into videogames.

Sue walks into the living room carrying a plate piled high with homemade pancakes. Alfie instantly leaps onto his feet and, with the warm smell exerting a kind of gravitational pull, orbits his mother like a small, hungry moon.

Onscreen, the round comes to an end. The scoreboard appears: kills 10; deaths 11. I calculate that it gives me a Kill/Death or K/D ratio of point zero nine. Less than one. Translation: I am dying more than living.

And the creatures on the rug lie on their backs, motionless and forgotten.

In war, arsehole, nobody wins.

"Woe-cake woe-cake woe-cake," Alfie exclaims, tears welling in his eyes.

Calmly, I set the headset and control pad down on the floor, get up, and walk out of the house.

2. A Late Night Launch Pad

One hour later, I'm in the same place: crouched under the climbing frame at the play park less than sixty seconds from my front door. Sometimes we take Alfie here. Typically, he plays alone. It never starts out that way, but it's where he finds himself more often than not. Children his own age try to talk to him but when he cannot find the words they lose interest and walk away. He looks four, but he's only three, and speaking like he's two leaves him at one: on his own.

Countdown to a life of loneliness.

God, I hate that he's so much like me.

I glance at the time on my phone. Hopefully, Sue has managed to put Alfie back to bed. She'll be waiting up for me, probably in the kitchen, concerned, angry, most likely both. She's already assumed this little demonstration of mine is because of the pregnancy, and she's right—to a point. It's about me failing my existing child, too. The Wonderful Fenwick Family Heirloom: my father rarely talked to me, which led to me being withdrawn and awkward around other people; and here I am, the great writer and communicator, perpetuating it into another generation.

Wood or words: change one letter, add an 's', what's the difference, really? We both failed our kids for our craft. So, why add another one to the mix?

"Jesus, he's three years old. He's not lost. It's not too late." I sound like Sue.

Isn't it? Me again.

Then a moment of penetrating self-awareness: it is midnight and I am hiding from the world under a children's climbing frame tower. This is not the strongest place from which to start a recovery. Problems have rarely been solved from such a dubious—

I have a sudden frightening feeling that someone is watching me.

I peer into the darkness. No one. The play area is nestled in the far corner of a small park unlit by street lamps, which is why I came here in the first place: the perfect hiding place. I crawl out of the shadows, standing to greet or confront the person or persons out there. Indeed, I have an inexplicable sense of number—of there being several pairs of eyes watching me from the dark, pulling me toward them. I suddenly wish that I'd had the forethought to bring a torch. One broad stroke of its beam would put me at ease.

"Is anyone there?" I ask.

No answer. Instead of allaying my anxiety, however, the lack of response heightens it. Why would someone not talk to me if they mean me no harm?

Shit. There's nothing like opening old wounds to make you feel wretched.

"Look, I'm leaving," I say, taking several steps toward the gate. "I just wanted some fresh air."

Now I *want* to go home and find my wife waiting in the kitchen with a hot cup of tea and a forgiving smile. But from the far corner of the play park something grabs my attention: a shadow hunched on the back of the elephant springer. From this distance, the shadow looks like it might be a rabbit. I cannot see its ears, but maybe they're flattened against its skull in fear of the strange man peering back at him. Maybe the playground is a particular haunt for the local population, and here I am, intruding.

I begin to relax, turning once more toward the gate and home, when the unmistakeable cry of a baby jolts me to a stop.

I turn around, peer through the dark at the hump-shaped shadow on the back of the springer. A baby—really? Out here, at this time? Judging by its size it must be a virtual newborn. Naked as the day, too. Where is its mother? Father?

Nowhere to be seen.

Thirty seconds pass before I'm forced to conclude that this child has been abandoned and I have a duty to protect it and to contact social services. The night air has real bite to it when the wind blows, and an unclothed baby will not last long. I have no choice.

The playground mulch mutters under my feet as I make my way around the other playground apparatus toward the springer in question. A blast of cold air reminds me of the urgency, so I pick up the pace until I am within an arm's length.

But something keeps me from reaching out to lift the child.

At the same time, it occurs to me to use the screen of my phone as a light source. The touch of a button provides a few seconds of low radiance...

When the display light fades, a cold prickling sensation runs up my neck and across my scalp. I start to rub at the crown of my head even as I stumble backward from the baby on the springer. I regain my balance, but keep rubbing. The last time I did this was when Alfie came home from nursery with lice.

I glance around for help, but despite the persistent feeling of being watched there is no one there, not even a dog walker or a junkie looking for a quiet late night launch pad.

My thumb wavers over the buttons on my phone. I'm not sure I want to see any more, but what I *did* see in those few seconds was its back and legs mottled by some kind of black fungicidal...

Mould.

No, infection. Mould can't grow on skin. Can it?

I hold my phone out at arm's length and press a button for the answer.

The baby is lying on its stomach in a tight bundle, knees folded underneath itself, almost touching its elbows, oversized head turned to one side, thumb pushed into its toothless mouth, and...

The light on my phone dies. I press another button.

Two arms reach from its empty eye sockets, fingers opening and closing on the cold air. I scream and drop the phone. Stumble backward across the mulch. Fall. Get up. When the light on the display goes out this time, I am already running.

1. An Unexpected Smile in the Dark

The kitchen is dark, the house unquiet, disturbed by sporadic coughing from upstairs. Sue has gone to bed, leaving the countertop bare. No tea, no smile. Running the tap, splashing cold water on my face, I realise she didn't wait up at all. This shouldn't bother me, especially after what I've just seen, but I feel like I need someone to talk to, to tell me I'm not losing my mind.

When I go to bed, I find Sue in a restless sleep, coughing against the wall. Leaving the lights off, I tiptoe across the floor and slide into the empty side of the bed. I sit up and count off the seconds it takes my breathing to return to normal. I get as far as eighteen and give up. Under the quilt, my hands won't stop shaking.

Through a gap at the top of the curtains the glow from the street lights outside illuminates the mould on the wall. It looks like mottled skin.

Infected.

Skin.

My eyes focus on the clear line where the light ends and gives the room back to the dark. If I didn't know any better I would think the entire wall might be covered with the stuff. *Every* wall. Perhaps it crawls out of the pores of the house at night while we dream. Perhaps it isn't even night here at all and we are so utterly surrounded by this black infection that no light can ever make it through. I can feel not only the walls closing in but the air getting thicker and harder to breathe.

A sudden burning sensation in my throat threatens to make me cough. I try to contain it by placing a hand over my mouth, but in doing so it only makes the damn thing seem more determined to find a way out. Finally, I relent, cringing inwardly at the loudness of the cough inside the room. Beside me, Sue joins in but doesn't wake. Then from the other bedroom the hack of what sounds like a three-year-old chain-smoker. And then it is back to me, Sue, Alfie again, and so on, passing our misery around like a parcel at a children's party. Except the happy music died a long time ago and we can't stop going through the motions.

It starts to rain outside. I lie in the dark, listening to the rain fall and watching the mould for movement while staring *through* it at the baby in the park. Telling myself: it wasn't real. Babies don't reach for you with their eyes. Not like *that*.

The rain grows heavier, overflowing from the gutters on the roof, hitting the surfaced driveway with a sound like meat splashing from a tall building. It's raining suicides out there. You can close your eyes to everything, but you cannot close your ears, or your mind.

If I can't make someone give me a job then I can write a new novel and sell it to a publisher. It might cover the deposit for a new place. A house that can breathe instead of rotting in front of our eyes.

May as well rob a fucking bank, comes the reply. A novel will take me too long. The first took five years and didn't sell. We don't have five years. We don't have five months, and I worry if we even have the weeks. Jesus, everything seems to be counting down.

To what?

"Zero."

I kick the sheets off of me. Stand up. Walk through the dark to the top of the stairs. Curl my toes around the lip. Teetering, I tilt my head and tune in to the suicide rain outside.

Where is the sun when you need her? Where is she? Where is that lego *cunt?*

One of Alfie's words paired with one of mine.

An unexpected smile finds me in the dark. And then laughter, right there at the top of the stairs; the kind of untethered, hysterical laughter that can only tickle you late at night when things make no sense at all.

I uncurl my toes from the step and walk downstairs into the living room, where the rug is still a battlefield littered with insects and creatures lying on their backs.

One by one, I pick up their rigid bodies and place them back inside the tub.

0. A Terrible Kiss

Even though Sue is still angry with me, even though we haven't really spoken in days, I ask her to join me for a walk. Just as those plastic corpses had to be put back inside their container, I realise that we need to remove ourselves from ours.

"Toss some things in a cooler bag," I say. "We'll have ourselves a picnic."

"Where'll we go?" she asks.

"Leave that to me," I answer.

Sue packs the cooler bag quickly and what we do not have in the cupboards or the refrigerator we pick up from a petrol station shop on the way. We—Sue, Alfie, and I—hike towards the edge of the city and Odstock Road. If Sue remembers this route at all, she doesn't say. Instead, she points out some grazing horses to Alfie, who grins and calls them *houses*.

Not quite, but close.

But maybe close is enough.

The air feels clean against our skin and sweet inside our chests. Each step, each breath away from that house with its cancerous walls somehow helps to cleanse our lungs of its impurities. I can almost bring myself to forgive the sun for abandoning us over the wet winter months, for shining on lands other than ours. Indeed, now that she has returned, her radiance is second only to the glow of my own pregnant wife.

That's right.

I can love her again.

Eventually, we arrive at the field. The hike takes a little longer than it did fifteen years ago but back then we did not have a three-year-old with us to stop and point and mispronounce everything he saw. Now, he is a valuable distraction whose voice spills into all of the silence and space between us.

When we reach a break in the fence, we leave Odstock Road and step into the long grass that reaches above Alfie's waist and our knees.

"It *tickoes*," he says, wriggling on the end of my arm like a hooked fish.

I release his hand and watch him run, laughing, through a sea of sighing green.

"To be that age again," I say to Sue. "When every wrong thing you do is considered cute, and every mistake is fine. Do you remember this place?"

"Of course," she says, sounding either slightly irritated or disappointed that I felt the need to ask.

I point to the copse on the far side of the field. "Let's do this over there."

"Do what?" she asks, suspiciously.

Bounce, I think. *Because that's what you do when you hit rock bottom.*

In the shade of the broadest, tallest tree, surrounded by an audience of dandelions, we place the blanket on the grass and start unpacking the cooler bag.

I open a Coke can and that little carbonated genie suddenly appears in front of me before the hiss is even half done, eyes wide, jumping up and down on the spot.

"You can have a sip, Alfie," I say. "But one. Otherwise it will rot your teeth."

Alfie takes two, of course, because sips are like wishes are like children: one is never enough.

I watch him run back through the tall grass, chasing a honey bee until it starts chasing him back.

"You're pregnant," I say to Sue, without looking at her.

"I'm pregnant," she says.

I leave it at that for at least a full minute, watching Alfie run from a sting.

"This is the spot where we kissed."

"For the first time," she says.

"For the first time."

"You didn't know what to say to me then either."

A faint smile flits across my lips. "I couldn't find the words. Too busy thinking about all of the things that could go wrong. You rejecting me, for one. Telling me you were leaving for Oz regardless of how I felt. Or worse, staying because I wanted you to stay and then resenting me for the rest of your life."

"And now?"

"Now? I'm fifteen years older and thinking of all the things that *did* go wrong. You having an affair. Me wasting the majority of my life chasing some foolish dream. I have no job, and no prospect of finding one either in the current climate. We have a son with his own set of problems and a house that is trying to kill us. No, not even trying. And words fail me, Sue. They fail us all. And now...now, you are pregnant. Is there really anything else to say?"

"It was a terrible kiss," she tells me in a watery voice. "The worst."

Then Alfie runs out of the tall grass and stands in front of us, holding up a dandelion and smiling broadly.

"Oh, to be that contented in a world where words don't work for you," I say.

"In fact, it was possibly the worst kiss in the entire history of first kisses," she says. "But...I'll never forget it."

"Why?" I ask, eyes fixed on our son.

"Because the worst things stay with you the longest. Nothing overshadows them. They don't fade. But what happens is you look back on them later and realise that what seemed bad for you at the time was actually, in the grand scheme, pretty good."

Pollen keeps irritating my eyes. I rub it away.

"Even my terrible kiss?" I ask her.

Behind me, Sue is crying.

"Even your terrible kiss," she says.

And then there is no pollen. Only tears.

"I'm sorry," I tell her. "About everything."

"Me too."

"I'll try harder."

"Me too."

And so, in the quiet shade of the copse we eat our sandwiches and drink our drinks and open ourselves to the sun.

When the picnic is over, we pack what's left inside the cooler and start to walk back across the field toward Odstock Road. On a small hill on the other side of Odstock stands Wintercroft, the residential home in which my father waits to be reunited with my mother. Dragging our tired legs and full stomachs through the long grass toward the road and the place I hesitate to call home, I wonder if he is sitting at one of the windows I am looking at, looking at *us* crossing the field below him. And with that comes a sense of *déjà vu*; an awareness of my father being present during another of my life's big moments and somehow remaining, as always, utterly detached from it.

Live, son. Because there's nothing in this world more horrifying than a life not *lived.*

If only for that, I will pay him another visit tomorrow.

Walking back to the house, Sue and I each take hold of one of Alfie's hands and swing him between us. Although there are still a lot of things unsaid I cannot help but feel better. Sue is pregnant, our heart is still beating, and I have bounced. So, we swing Alfie higher and we listen to his laughter and we smile and put on a show for my father, who may or may not be watching from his window on the hill. Strangely, it doesn't feel dysfunctional at all. Indeed, this might be the closest we ever come to being one of *those* families, the kind that exist only in television adverts and magazines.

Even the house does little to dampen our spirits as we cross its threshold and breathe of its mould-infected air. I carry the cooler into the kitchen and start to unpack the leftovers while Sue dashes upstairs to pee and Alfie sprints into the living room and cannonballs into the beanbag, giggling for no reason, which, as I was reminded the other night, is perhaps the best reason of all.

"If we're going to do this again," I call up to Sue from the bottom of the stairs. "Then we need to look for another place. As for the cost... we'll figure something out."

I'll quit writing. I'll focus everything on finding a job. If my marriage has only so many words then I'll stop using them in other ways. And I'll try not to be bitter about it.

Sue doesn't answer, so I start patting my pockets for my phone, wanting to somehow maintain this momentum I have accumulated by contacting the rental agent and getting the ball (*bouncing*) rolling.

But I can't find my phone.

I can't find it because I dropped it in the park that night after I saw that...thing—with the mould on its skin and the arms reaching from its eyes. Although, picturing it now, the arms are retreating into its sockets like snakes down a couple of holes.

A chill swims down my back.

I hear crying.

At first I think it is Alfie, but then I hear the word, "*Gwibber*," from the living room, which means he is likely standing at the glass patio door, watching a squirrel cavort through our garden.

"What is it?" I ask the top of the empty stairs.

Her sobs meet me on the first riser, putting pressure on my chest and gluing my feet to the floor.

"Sue, what's wrong? Tell me."

Sometimes we crave the words we need to hear.

And fear the ones we don't.

"Sue?" I urge. "What's happened?"

She walks into view at the top of the stairs, her cheeks streaked with—

mould

—mascara and tears.

"I'm bleeding," she says.

The Space That Runs Away With You

A motorway runs through my brain tonight. Loud traffic—thought traffic—crams every lane, bumper to bumper, refusing me any hope of sleep. I get up and walk the darkness. I should switch on a light, I know; four nights isn't long enough to get accustomed to all of the tics and tricks of a new place. But Heather is still asleep somewhere behind me, and the room at the end of the landing, softly breathing, means Max is alive too—

Asleep.

I mean asleep.

And this was supposed to be a fresh start.

Beige walls, neutral colours; *safe*.

In the kitchen I open the fridge and most of what's inside I do not like. Mature cheese. Breaded ham. Eggs. I haven't eaten an egg in fifteen years, but Heather insists on keeping us stocked, and whenever I ask why she does this she inevitably answers with a question, because everything with that woman has to be a question and what fridge, she will ask, doesn't have eggs in it? But no one eats eggs in our house. *No one*. I don't, Heather doesn't, and Max is four-years-old; he would rather paint monster faces on the shells and throw them at the walls. Why is it always the same monster? I never ask because I know he'll tell: *it's the monster who stole my brother*. And sometimes I wonder if Heather is seeing someone else, a man who likes to down eggs raw after completing one of their exhaustive and exhausting sessions. But Heather can stomach *that* sort of thing even less than I can stomach eggs.

She isn't cheating. She'd need to open up more than just her legs for that. Besides, a dozen eggs tell me she isn't. Like twelve bald-headed jurors mired in deliberation, they'll sit untouched on the shelf-racks until the fridge begins to smell like halitosis, and that is how I know everything is fine; that is how I gauge the status of my marriage; how I know with any degree of certainty that things have not gotten any worse.

The jury is out.

Forever out.

And in the darkness I find a seat in which to dig in and wait for morning.

*

It takes another four days for Max to feel hungry at breakfast time. It is a relief to see his appetite return, however, and he makes short work of the bacon rashers on his plate. I cannot touch mine. It sounds like he is crunching on bone. So I eat just my toast then push the plate to the middle of the table and point out to Heather that she cremated the bacon again. Death by a thousand cuts, divorce by a thousand digs, I realise that, but I cannot help myself. If we can't control the little things, like timings, then what hope is there of finding him on this, the sixty-seventh day?

And it is raining out.

He doesn't have his jacket on. I put it on the hanger myself the morning I unpacked his things. Heather didn't see the point; Max either. Pretending only underlines it isn't real, she said, and left me to it—the boxes, the clothes, the toys, the anguish: everything.

"Put his stuff in the loft until they find him."

It is her way of dealing with this thing, a defence mechanism, like a shopkeeper nailing boards over glass in an attempt to keep the looters out. What she doesn't get is this: nothing will keep them out; not if they want to get in.

Besides, the loft is a no go zone. We can use it, according to the rental agent when asked if we might utilise it for storage, but no one knows what is up there. Apparently, the owners bought the property as an investment and put it straight onto the rental market. They didn't inspect the loft space. Nor did the agency. Is it floored, do you know? I asked. She said she didn't. Which sounded a little incompetent to me at the time, but now I've thought about it, now that we've had that space, empty or not, floored or not, sitting above our heads for over a week now, I'm beginning to think it is actually pretty cool. Like a lottery ticket no one has bothered to check or an unopened box on Deal or No Deal. I doubt there is any money up there, certainly no treasure—the house is a recent build, not much older than the twins themselves—but then again there *could* be. Besides, what *is* up there remains untouched.

Untouched.

I like that.

"They're going to find him," I announce. Him, or the one who took him. Which goes in the face of everything that we, the police and ourselves, have accomplished so far. The search of our house, our street, our neighbourhood, our city, and all of the surrounding countryside has turned up nothing. It feels like we may be chasing a phantom. Or God. "I know they will find him," I tell my wife. "We just need to have some faith."

Heather stops pushing her watermelon chunks around the bowl as Max snaps a rasher of bacon between his fingers, and both of them look at me across the table.

"Do you think so?" Max asks. He looks down at his plate, a frown worrying his face. "Do you think he...remembers us?"

I reach across and ruffle his hair. "Only every time he looks in the mirror, son."

"What if he doesn't have a mirror?" he asks. "What if there aren't any where he is?"

"And where is that?"

Heather grimaces at me. *Don't.*

Another ruffle. This one feels mechanic. Like I am touching his mother. "Where is he, Max?"

"I don't know...*heaven*?"

"Your brother isn't in heaven."

"*Rob.*"

"He is missing, Max, not...not lost. He could be anywhere. Five minutes away or, or..."

"Five hundred," he suggests.

"Yes, or that," I say. "No one knows but him and the man who took him. The police will bring him back though. We need to believe that. All of us."

I look at Heather; she looks away. The watermelon pieces in the bowl look like chunks of flesh to me. I've lost my appetite. "I'll give them a call today."

"Dad?"

"Yes," I say, slowly turning from his mother to look at him again. "What is it?"

"When do you think they will find him?"

"I'd only be guessing, Max. I'm sorry."

Do you think he remembers us?

An innocent question but a terrible black bean I must not let become a terrible black bean*stalk*. Children forget far easier than parents—

Stop.

Think about something else.

His jacket. Hanging in the wardrobe like some butterfly chrysalis.

But it's raining out. It is raining hard out.

When I drew it out of the suitcase, I found a single blonde-brown hair stuck to its collar. Over two months old.

I take a deep breath.

"Don't worry," I say to Max—and to Heather through him. "He will remember us."

I take a deep, deep breath.

The jacket lining had remembered him, too.

"So, Max, what do you think of the house?" I ask, hastily changing the subject.

He shrugs. "It's okay, I s'ppose."

"And you?" Heather. She looks at me with a start, as if she has just wandered back into the room. Where does she go, I wonder. And why does she never invite me along?

"It's fine," she says, nodding. "Different and...smaller, obviously."

Our four bedroom detached sold quickly once we dropped the asking price to fifty grand below the market value.

"The money will help with the costs," I assure her. Max doesn't know about the two private investigators we've hired to help with the search. Moving to this rented three bedroom on the other side of the city was supposed to be a distraction for him too.

"I'd move into a caravan if I believed it would make a difference," Heather says.

"I know that," I reply, arranging my facial muscles into a smile. "We're going to find him." Untouched.

"You keep saying that," she says. "You keep saying that but..."

"What?"

"I can't, Max is here."

"It's okay, Mum," he says. And then, turning to me, he fills in the gaps. "Dad, what she wants to say is she thinks Michael isn't coming home. She thinks Michael is killed."

Hearing his name acid-burns the back of my throat, even though I am not the one who said it out loud. I cannot speak. Likewise, Heather cannot seem to find her voice either. Instead, she nods her head and looks at me, her eyes like glass, wet with the tears of the rain.

*

After breakfast, I decide I don't feel like working with zombies today. I have a commission for an undead design from an American skateboard company and a similarly-themed cover proposal to complete for an indie book publisher. But following the conversation at breakfast, I don't really care to see Michael's face appear on any of my zombie fodder.

Jesus, no.

So, I get up from the dinner table. It is also my workstation—I don't have a proper drawing table because it isn't my proper job, as Heather is keen to remind me; my proper job is working part-time at The Last Bookshop.

Why does everything feel so *apocalyptic* today?

Maybe they're going to find him, I think. Maybe today is the day. In which case, this won't do. Zombies or the last *anything*—it won't do at all.

"Max?"

He is in the next room watching a film, but there is a moment when I feel the veins in my throat tighten as I think he is not going to answer. I have a lot of moments like this, usually until he is standing right in front of me, an inquiring look floating up from his innocent face as I arm the dust out of my eyes.

"Max, let's do something. What do you say?"

"But I'm watching *Toy Story*."

"You can stop it and watch it later. Daddy doesn't feel like drawing today. We should do something."

Max turns to listen longingly to the room in which Woody and Buzz are having a heated argument. Finally, he turns back to me. "We could look in the loft?"

"We could," I say. "We *could* do that, but wouldn't it spoil things?"

"How?" he asks.

I cannot tell him I don't want to know what's up there. That I would rather live with possibility and with hope than knowing.

"Well," I say, thinking fast. "Remember how I told you nobody's been up there since they built this house?" He nods, attentive while the toys in the room next door come to blows underneath a truck. "We've joked about what might be up there too, haven't we?"

Another nod. "That was fun."

"Exactly. And we don't want to spoil that." Suddenly, I am inspired. "It's like the toys in the film, Max. They run and hide when anyone is around. They only come out when you don't look."

"It spoils the magic," he says.

"Yes," I say. "It spoils the magic. Good, son."

"Can we play Duplo instead?" he asks.

"Of course we can play Duplo."

"And build a tower?"

"We can build the *biggest* tower."

"And watch *Toy Story?*"

"Absolutely."

"And can we talk about what's in the loft?"

I hesitate. It isn't uncertainty. What I feel is *excitement.*

"Yes, Max, we can certainly do that."

And we do.

*

Part one of our conversation:

Aliens...left behind on our planet like E.T. Or spacemen, like Armstrong and his crew, who some say never even landed on the moon. Maybe they didn't and ended up in our loft instead. What do you think? What, cowboys? Yeah, why not? Gunfight at the O.K. Corral. Doc Holliday and the Earp brothers. What else might be up there? Yes, well, obviously there are dinosaurs in our loft, Max. How do I know? Because it's like Jurassic Park up there at night when you're asleep...

It isn't a lie but a gift, much like the gift of Santa Claus or the Tooth Fairy. Except it is long after midnight and Max is asleep and I cannot hear gunshots or booster rockets or the scrape of a single claw across the ceiling. The house is quiet, and the space over our heads seems to stretch and contract, stretch and contract—breathing, almost, with a life of its own.

"Heather?" I ask the gloom. "Heather? Are you awake?"

Nose to the wall, she doesn't stir beside me. Even if she is awake, she won't stir. She avoids this insomniac's middle-of-the-night conversations whenever she can. The witching hour is when our missing son haunts me the most; when the membrane between the present and the past and Here and There is at its thinnest; when memories flow with ease into words and hope crams the spaces between.

Heather cannot cope with memories.

Heather cannot cope with hope.

Suddenly I am out of bed and walking through the darkness toward the landing at the top of the stairs. Old before its time, the house ticks and creaks all around me. Max's door is open. The glow from his night light projects diluted green stars onto the walls outside. Most of them appear elongated and distorted, like a bunch of odd accidental spills. But the star on the loft hatch looks perfectly formed to me.

What about monsters, dad?

Part two of our conversation earlier.

I don't believe there are any monsters in the loft, son.

Why not?

Because I don't think there should be. It's not that kind of space.

Sitting on the landing floor, the hard balustrades at my back feel like the massive, knuckled fingers of some giant's hand. And I am in his palm. Between the balustrades—or his giant fingers—cool night air reaches up from downstairs to gooseflesh my back. I have left a window open in the kitchen. Heather would be mad. I always leave a window open. She sees burglars and thieves; I see Michael, having found his way home after three long months. Heather sleeps in the same room as me, but lives in a whole other world. She sleeps in a room. Tonight, I sleep under the stars.

*

The morning drive into work is a long spiral of one-way streets and intensifying traffic under a bloodshot winter sky. Faces—long, slack, empty—peer back at me from rear-view mirrors, Munchian characters riding the Helter Skelter, at the bottom end of which is an eight or nine hour long shift. Fortunately for me, mine is four hours and I found an email in my inbox this morning that changes everything.

Behind the counter in The Last Bookshop, Emily's is the first kind face I see. The upper half, anyway; she is shielded behind a novel called Dark Matter. She's a fan of ghost stories. She understands that people are energy: they don't die; they just take on different forms.

"I got it," I announce to the shop, drawing a curious glance from a browser over in the Health & Well-Being section. "Emily, I *got* it." I'm going to be the lead illustrator for a major US-based role-playing games company. "Covers, interiors, everything. Oh, and if this new R.P.G.

system takes off, I'll be working on the scenario modules too."

"That's wonderful news, Rob," she says. "Congratulations." She puts down her book without even marking the page and runs out from behind the counter to hug me. I let her. She's warm—inside and out. If she wasn't nineteen and I wasn't approaching twice that age, I would reconsider my life. But my love for Heather hasn't died yet; it's just taken on a different form. And my arms never leave my side.

"Thank you," I say, smiling, and blushing like a fool. "But don't think you'll be getting rid of me just yet. The initial contract is only for six months."

"But it's doing something you love, Rob." She steps out of the hug, and the space between us is immediately filled by the warmth of her smile. "You don't get the opportunity to chase after your dreams very often in life. Congratulations, man. And hey, lunch is on me today, all right?"

It is more than all right. It is twenty-eight minutes of the first real cheerfulness I have felt since Michael went missing. He doesn't enter the conversation or my thoughts during this time: Emily and I talk about me getting the job and where I'd like to take this thing if I could take it anywhere; we talk about books and stories, particularly ghost stories since it is Emily's specialist subject, which doesn't make me think of him because from where I am sitting the world is good and boys do not die, boys go missing then return safe and well and whole.

Twenty-eight minutes.

And then my phone rings.

*

Michael isn't dead.

My mind clings to those three words as I speed home, having made some poor excuse to Emily about Max being ill. But Max isn't ill, he is...

What *is* he doing? I think, trying to decipher Heather's message on the phone. Not a message, an actual live conversation, but she'd delivered it *like* a message—a cold, distracted reading. I can imagine her calling me under different circumstances. *The house is on fire, Rob. The house is on fire and maybe you should come home.* This, as she stands in the living room and lets tongues of fire wrap themselves around her.

"Get hysterical," I say, demonstrating my point by thumping the steering wheel again and again with the side of my fist. "Give me *something*, woman."

But the house isn't on fire, I remind myself. It is just Max acting up. Getting the wrong idea.

It's me, she'd said on the phone. *You need to get back here and let your son see what's in the loft.*

Forget the part about *your* son. She disowns the poor kid every time she loses control. The crucial and most-worrying part of the message is *see what's in the loft.*

At the house, I leave the car running and rush inside. Heather is on the two-seater settee, curled up so that she will fit, nursing a headache with one hand and pointing toward the stairs with the other. The television is off and there is a half-empty bottle of white wine on the floor nearby. No glass.

"I don't know what kind of ideas you've been putting in your son's head, but he thinks Michael is up there." As I move to the bottom of the stairs, she spreads her fingers—stop. "I don't know how much more of this I can take, Rob."

"I'll talk to him."

"Where'd he get the idea?"

"The other day when we spoke about..."

"What?" she snaps.

"What we'd like there to be in the loft. Michael's name wasn't mentioned, though."

She turns her head to look at me, daggers blunted by alcohol.

"Why not?" she asks.

Which ambushes me.

"What?"

"Why wasn't his name mentioned? Why didn't you want to find him up there?"

"What *is* this? What are you saying?"

"... Nothing."

"You don't honestly think I don't want him to be found..."

"I *said* 'nothing,' Rob. Stop being paranoid and go fix your son."

"He isn't broken," I tell her. "And when did you start drinking from the bottle?"

"It saves time," she says. "When did *you* start paying such close attention?"

I will not go there. I will not go there. I will not go there.

Two boys were in the garden, and then there was one.

"Did you go up?" I ask, looking at the dark reflection of her in the television screen. "Into the loft."

She makes me wait, as if somehow she knows the importance of her answer. Or maybe she begrudges me the gift of more words today.

"No," she says finally. "I didn't go up. Michael is dead, and there is nothing up *there* that will change that."

I want to say, How can you be so sure that's true? Anything is possible. *Anything*. Because when you have a space to fill, you can fill it with whatever you want.

And Max wants his twin brother.

"I'll talk to him," I say again, and head upstairs.

I find Max on the landing, sitting below the loft hatch with his legs tucked underneath him. He has a small mountain of loose Duplo Lego bricks on the carpet beside him and he appears to be building some kind of stepped tower.

"What are you doing?" I ask, taking a knee. I know the answer, but I want to hear him say it. Maybe I also want it to be true.

"I'm going up there," he says, "to get Michael."

There aren't nearly enough bricks for what he has in mind, but he's four and doesn't plan ahead. He has Ideas, capital I, and acts right away to realise them: Michael is up there; he will go get him; everything will be okay. A-B-C. I should have seen this coming. He wanted to look up in the loft, and I told him it would spoil the magic. But there is no magic that can keep him from trying to reach his brother, not when that particular Idea has taken hold.

"Max, listen to me," I say, trying to sound firm, but wondering, wondering—"You can't go up there. You're going to hurt yourself if you try to climb. I need you to stop...please." Need you to, not want you to, I think.

He creases his brow and gives a dramatic shake of his head.

"You said."

"I said what?"

"You said there wasn't any monsters. You said that."

"Yes, I did, Max, and it's true." I take his small hands in mine. "Up there is a good place. I meant that. But we don't know that's where Michael is."

Now, he puts all of his theatricality into one seemingly never-ending nod. "That's why we need to look, daddy. Before it's too late. We need to look."

"No, Max, I don't think I was clear enough. We won't find him up there. *Michael isn't in the loft.* Do you understand?"

Right before my eyes, something inside him crumbles, and he pushes the Lego tower before he runs, crying, into his bedroom. The tower sways, topples, hits the wall, and breaks into a dozen smaller pieces that crash to the floor.

I feel like a terrorist. Like I have destroyed something sacred and holy—not just a tower of plastic but the Idea that built it. Max's Idea. And if I am truthful, my Idea, too.

That Michael is still alive.

*

It is the day of Michael's disappearance. I am drawing at the dinner table. The front door stands open and each blade of grass on the lawn stands out in high definition. The boys are playing outside, and one of them flits across the doorway every so often as they run around in their bare feet. I can't always tell if it is Max or Michael, but most of the time it is easy: Michael's hair has a cowlick and is a lighter shade of brown. I leave them for just a moment, to fetch a box of fresh drawing supplies from the loft, and when I return, they both stroll out of the kitchen carrying a tall glass of Robinsons orange and pineapple. Like his hair, Michael's juice is a lighter shade; Max likes his strong. I keep telling him his teeth will pay the price one day. He keeps telling me the Tooth Fairy will make him rich.

"How's the war going out there?" I ask. "Who's winning?"

Michael sips his juice. He is panting, thirsty. "Max lost half his army."

"Oh, why?"

"He can't find them."

Of course—green soldiers, green grass: they keep going AWOL out there.

"Well, you better look for them," I say. "Otherwise, the next time I mow the lawn it's going to get pretty messy."

"Ew," they say together, thrilled. "Daaaad."

Fade to black.

"DAD!"

Max is standing in front of me. His lips continue to move but I cannot hear a word. It is like someone somewhere pressed a mute button. It isn't just Max; the whole world has stopped talking. Outside, all of the light has gone out of the day. Did I fall asleep? I don't think so. I walk down the hall to the front door and look up—

This is a dream.

The sky is hanging beams, roof joists, boards.

Stars.

No, not stars: knotholes. Through these knotholes, the sun burns holes in the lawn. Tendrils of grey smoke rise from the grass and the smell of burning plastic fills the air. And...are those tiny *screams?*

Something taps me on the lower back. The screams are growing louder on the lawn. I turn around and it is Michael standing there in the hall, not Max; Max is gone. Max is not in the garden. Then I awake on damp sheets and realise the screams are mine and my mouth is full of them, toy soldiers, melting plastic.

But this is a dream too. And when I finally wake up, it is to a house holding its breath. I stumble through the dark, along the landing into Max's room, where I find him in bed, Max not Michael, stirring in his sleep. His hair sticks to his skin and his head twitches on the pillow. I want to reach down and save him from his nightmare, but I cannot do it. The best I can do is run my fingers through his sticky hair and raise my eyes to the ceiling. To the loft. He needs to ride this thing out. He needs to believe he can.

We all do.

*

People are energy. They don't die; they take on different forms. The energy flooding out of the loft is good. I sense it, and Max senses it too. It is a space of infinite possibility and inspiration; a space that runs away with you; a blank page longing to be filled with lines and scratches of pencil and ink. However they land, they land in the right places, in the right shapes. This is my best work so far and the loft is my muse. The R.P.G. box cover illustration is finished, scanned, emailed, and now I am working on an unplanned side project. Something special: a coffee-table book about everyday life after the end of the world. *Living with the Apocalypse*. Four sketches done and I have found him on every page. Michael. Sometimes he is in the foreground, sometimes his is a face at the edge of a ragged crowd, but he is always there; a survivor. Even on day seventy-five.

I almost forget about Max. When he interrupts me at the dinner-cum-drawing table, I can hear his stomach complain. He doesn't look too happy either, bored, and with a lost look in his eyes. His hair needs to be introduced to a comb and there's a blackcurrant juice stain drying on his collar. Michael, at the end of the world, looks in much better shape. I am a bad father.

"Christ, Max, I'm sorry. I got caught up in this thing and completely forgot—" *about you*, I almost finish. Max isn't stupid though, and stomps through to the kitchen. "I'll make you something to eat and then we can go out, if you want."

What are you doing? my muse protests. Never mind going anywhere, there is work to do. Great work.

Before I can retract the offer, Max asks me from the kitchen, "Can we go to the park?"

I *am* a bad father, but the apocalypse will have to wait.

*

Give me four walls and a ceiling.

Max feeds the ducks and swans as I keep watch in case he slips on the muddy bank and falls in the water or one of the swans decides he is having a bad day and wants to pay it forward. Anything can happen. The world is a dangerous place. Children drown all the time and swans can kill a man never mind a four-year-old child. And all of this open space only steers my mind back to the loft.

Maybe this is the start of me becoming an agoraphobic, I think.

Since Michael's disappearance I don't go out unless I have to. Part of me believes, foolishly, that if I can make the world smaller there will be a better chance of finding him. Ergo, with space to run and an infinite sky over our heads, there seems to be little hope. Madness has its own unique logic, I suppose.

"Stand back from the water, Max."

There are already two dozen ducks waiting for his next offering of stale bread. The swans hang back at a cool distance, knowing they can muscle in at any time, while a lone seagull skulks right at the back, wings raised in readiness for the swoop and steal.

"Son of a bitch."

"Rob?" A woman's voice at my back.

I turn around and there's Emily, standing on the grass with a white Pomeranian on a leash. Max hears the thing yip and turns to see what it is, forgetting the ducks and their hangers-on for a moment.

"Hello," Emily says. "You must be Max. This is M.R. James. Would you like to play with him?"

Max gives her a slow, shy nod. He can't look her in the eye. I'm not the only one withdrawing from the world in small, hard-to-see stages.

Emily unclips the leash, and M.R. James drifts away like a small white cloud in a gusty breeze. Max hands me the leftover breadcrumbs and follows, crouching in imitation of the dog's size.

Emily offers me a smile. "He's cute. How is he?"

"Fine," I say. It's easier than telling her I don't know because I've been too busy looking for Michael in my mind and on the page. "You called your dog M.R. James?" She laughs, a shy, slightly embarrassed sound. "No, that's great," I continue. "Naming your white Pomeranian after a writer of ghost stories. I should get a Saint Bernard and call him Stephen King."

I manage a smile of my own when she laughs, but behind it I'm aching with the effort of trying to be funny while Michael waits for me in the unfinished drawing back at the house. And did I remember to lock the front door?

She asks me about my work and without hesitation I tell her that I've never been so productive in my life, like the stuff won't pour out of me quick enough.

"You sound inspired," she says.

"You know what," I say, trying to play it cool as a swan. "I think I am."

Emily's cheeks turn scarlet and I realise she thinks I meant her when I meant the loft. She looks into my eyes then glances at my lips and—this can't be happening. Is someone in the house? She cannot want me to kiss her.

What are they doing in there?

Emily is waiting. For something that will never happen.

Michael is waiting, too. Somewhere. For something that...

We kiss.

Emily's lips are young, soft, so full of hope.

Someone is inside the house...looking my drawings.

An intruder. Heather, maybe.

Looking in the loft...spoiling the magic. Fucking with my muse.

"I'm sorry, Emily...I think—I think I have to go."

"Wait, was it the kiss? I'm sorry."

"No, it wasn't that. Something is wrong. Back at the house."

"What is it?"

"That's just it, I don't know."

"Can we talk about this sometime? Over Starbucks, maybe?"

I nod. "Where's Max?"

Twice in one day; what is wrong with me? Why can't I stay focused on him instead of—of *this*? And why can't he stay in my sight?

We find him standing on the bank a short distance downriver, eyes overflowing with tears as he hurls one stone after another at something in the water. I don't want to look but—

It isn't Michael.

"Max, what are you doing?" I ask, suddenly furious.

"That seagull over there," he says, broken-hearted. It's the son of a bitch I called a son of a bitch a moment ago. "It stole the last piece of bread out of my hand."

One of his fingers is trickling blood. The world is a dangerous place. We need to get back.

Emily passes me a handkerchief, which I wrap around Max's hand. What he can't see won't hurt him. Which is crap, because what you can't see hurts you the most.

"It was just a kiss," I tell him, trying to make him—or myself—feel better. "That's all it was. Just a little kiss from a seagull. Come on, let's get you home."

*

There is no intruder and the front door is still locked. Inside, I clean out Max's cut with antiseptic wash and put an extra-large plaster over it to make him feel like a battle-wounded soldier. Still it doesn't stop him crying.

"You're going to be all right, Max. It just nicked the skin. It'll heal, son."

I will be drawing the seagull later on, I realise. Shoved into a pot of boiling water and suspended over a roaring fire. Supper for my apocalyptic family. And maybe—maybe Michael will find his way into camp for a bite to eat himself. After all, he must be hungry wherever he is.

"I want to look in the loft, dad," Max says.

"You're not going up there," I tell him. "Nobody is."

"Please, daddy. I want to see if he's up there. If Michael is up there."

It is the kiss in the park; it is the seagull stealing Max's last piece of bread; it is Max, crying because he has a bleeding finger when his brother has been taken from us. I grab hold of Max, clutching the tops of his arms in a grip strong enough to cause him some discomfort.

"He is up there if you close your eyes and wish it, Max. He is up there with all the other things you want to imagine are there with him. But if you look, the magic will spoil. You'll ruin everything. Do you understand that?"

It is the kiss in the park. Full of hope in the moment but dying slowly on my lips.

"I want to look, daddy."

"Be quiet, Max. Let me think."

"Let me go up. I want to see my brother."

"You think I don't want to see him too?" This is not a good idea, I think. "Come on, upstairs."

Then I am walking up the stairs two at a time, pulling Max behind me by the hand not bitten, until we are standing underneath the loft hatch, both of us looking up as though expecting something to happen on its own. After a moment like this, I drag a chair through from the bedroom and position it below the hatch. Standing on the chair, I reach up and slide the lock bolt and push the hatch up and to the side.

A black rectangle looks back at us.

But I realise I cannot do it. I cannot climb inside. Every instinct tells me that if I look there is only the disappointment of answers waiting for me up there. It is Oz, the great and powerful, behind his curtain. If I do not look, maybe I can keep the kiss with Emily and leave it at that, maybe I can keep drawing and continue to find him through it, but my gut feeling tells me that preserving these things somehow depends upon me *not* looking. Or it might. Either way, I cannot risk it.

But maybe Max can; he has less to lose.

"Do you still want to know what's up there?" I ask.

He nods solemnly. I reach down, place my hands under his arms, and lift him toward the space, averting my eyes downward in case I catch even a glimpse of what it contains. It is at this moment I realise that superstition has completely taken over my life. But I do not care. I am hoping this is a doorway to another world and that Michael is awaiting our rescue there. Then Max's head enters the open hatch and, swallowed by the dark, vanishes from the neck up. Glimpsing this from the corner of my eye, I am tempted to pull him back and lower him to the floor.

"Dad, I can't see," he says. "I need some light."

"All right. Climb up and I'll get you something."

"Don't let me fall."

"Max, don't worry, I won't drop you."

I wait until he has climbed all the way into the loft before I step down from the chair. His face peers down at me from the shadows enshrouding the hatchway, eyes wide with fear.

"How long will you be, Daddy?"

"One minute," I tell him. "I'll get the torch from the car boot. Just hold on."

"It's cold up here. And stuffy."

"I imagine so. No one's been up there since the house was built, remember?"

"There's a funny smell too."

"Dust, probably. Stay next to the opening until I get back, okay?"

"Okay."

It takes me less than the minute I promised to locate the torch and return to my place under the hatch.

But Max is gone.

Then, "Daddy?" His voice, tremulous and faint—almost far away.

"Have you found anything, Max?" I don't want to know but at the same time I feel compelled to ask. I find myself hoping that he won't tell me.

"Daddy, I think there's somebody up here."

A shiver takes it's time to slide all the way down my back.

Is it Michael?

"Can you see him?" I ask. "Who is it?"

No answer.

"Max? What do you see?"

"He isn't up here." A disappointed reply. "I want to come down now. I don't like it. I want to come down."

A four-year-old scared of the dark. Nothing more.

Meanwhile, my heart aches in my chest, caged in the moment when I walked into the front garden and found Max standing next to the space where Michael should have been. It is like losing him all over again.

"I'll shine the torch in the hatch," I say. "Walk toward it." When he is standing on the landing again and the hatch is locked, I ask him, "What did you see, Max? Anything? Anything at all?"

He looks pale, like a ghost himself. But he is also frightened, upset, trying to be strong and not cry again, rubbing at his eyes so hard they are swollen and bloodshot. Heather will slaughter me tonight. I've let my four-year-old son peek behind the curtain because I was too afraid to do it myself. And Oz isn't just a disappointment, he doesn't exist. I am a bad father and this was a terrible idea.

"Okay, Max, tell me what you think you saw?" I ask, trying again to get through to him.

"Michael," he says, matter-of-factly. "But it wasn't him. It was nothing. Nothing at all."

A sad figure, he retreats into his room, silently closing the door in my face. In an example of perfect acoustic coincidence, the front door slams closed.

Heather is home.

*

When Max comes out of his bedroom later, he is still in bad shape. Heather pretends not to notice, busying herself in the kitchen by throwing out a dozen old eggs and replacing them with a dozen fresh ones. And suddenly I know why she does it. I feel more attuned to her tonight than I have in months, and I realise it is because of the kiss with Emily. Guilt focuses the mind while ripping at the heart. And Michael liked eggs. Soft boiled usually, with toast soldiers to dunk in the yolk. I mention it to Heather and she gives me the kind of contempt-filled look she cannot produce in a moment but must have constructed over a period of months.

After dinner, we sit on the couch and point our eyes toward the television. But it is abundantly clear we have all retreated into other rooms of the house: Max to the solitude of his bedroom, Heather to the kitchen with a bottle of wine, and me, to the landing under the loft, where I stare through the open hatch at the black rectangular abyss, wishing it would swallow me up.

*

I wake up and moonlight is crawling across the bedcovers. Underneath, the bed is hot as a furnace. She has forgotten to turn off the electric blanket again. I want to wake her and say, *Look, you forget things too.* But blankets do not compare to boys, and besides, her cold, cold bones could use the warmth.

You took your eyes off them, she said. *It's all on you.*

The ghost of our argument.

I forgot about Michael liking eggs...

Everything happens for a reason, Rob. That reason is you.

...I forgot about him liking eggs and suddenly I am to blame for everything.

I walk downstairs to the kitchen and look in the cupboards. I don't know what I am looking for but I'll know it when I see it. I have been telling myself this for seventy-five days.

"It isn't my fault," I say. "Don't you ever buy any soup?"

So, that is what I want. Soup. There is a tin of Heinz Tomato and Basil on the shelf. That is what I want. And that is what I'll have. If not control then Heinz Tomato and Basil Soup.

Sometimes things just happen, Heather. There is no reason. They just are.

I can feel the ghost of Heather's cold fury in the kitchen beside me. It leans in close to whisper in my ear—

Bullshit.

*

I wake up this time to the wail of a carbon monoxide detector in the kitchen and the smell of gas throughout the house. Heather switches on her bedside night light, pulls on her dressing gown, and throws open the window. I am much slower to rise, still drowsy from having had less than two hours sleep. I am wondering if this is in fact the tail end of another nightmare when Max wanders into the room, rubbing the sleep crusts from his eyes and wrinkling his nose.

"What's that smell, mummy?" he asks. "And what's the alarm for?"

"Gas," Heather replies. "Carbon monoxide."

Carbon monoxide is odourless, actually; it is the coward hiding in the skirts of butanethiol. I read that somewhere; I don't forget everything. But I don't have the will to point it out to Heather; she hates me enough already. Call me a coward; call me carbon monoxide.

Wait. This isn't a dream; this is real. In my dreams, I can say anything to Heather and we usually end up fighting or fucking. What I never do is bite my tongue.

"We need to get out of the house," she says, panic rising through her voice. "Max, don't put on any lights, okay?"

Max is nodding. Crying, too.

"What's wrong?" Heather asks.

"I was dreaming," he says, "about Michael. Then the noise woke me up."

"That's nice, honey, but we need to leave the house, okay? Give me your hand."

Max shakes his head. "Don't you see? It's him. He did it. He made the gas come out."

"Michael?" I ask, incredulous. "Max—no, it wasn't him. And now isn't the time. It wasn't him, it was..." *Me*, I realise. The soup earlier. I forgot to turn off the burner or I did not turn it off enough or— "Christ, it was me. I forgot..."

"You left the gas on?" Heather yells. "What were you thinking?"

"I don't know," I tell her. "I thought maybe I'd try and kill us all. Look, just give me a second. I'll run down and turn it off. Meanwhile, open all of the windows up here. I'll do the same downstairs."

But Max won't move from the doorway. He makes himself into a spider web across the lower half of the door.

"Get out of the way, Max."

"No, daddy," he says. "It wasn't your fault. It was Michael."

"He didn't do this. We've been through this already, this afternoon, remember? I let you look in the loft and he wasn't there. Now let it go and let me past."

"Why did you let him look in the loft?" Heather interrupts.

"He thinks Michael is up there, doesn't he? I was trying to fix things like you asked." I turn back to Max. "Are you going to move or do I have to move you?"

He shakes his head.

"I left the gas on, Max, *me*. It was a very stupid thing to do, but I did it, not Michael." I ruffle his hair to soften his will. But we aren't on a football field and he hasn't just scored the winning goal; I am angry—with him as much as myself—and he is determined to get in the way of me fixing this. During our fight earlier, Heather mentioned the word divorce for the first time, and I am going to find a way to make everything all right.

Somehow.

"I forgot too," he says.

"The gas isn't *your* fault either," I tell him.

Max nods but remains an X across the doorway. "Michael put it on," he says.

"It wasn't Michael," I yell at him.

"He's mad at me too."

Tears. The house is filling with gas and the boy gives me tears. I've tried the assertive approach and I've tried softly-softly, but if I go hard on him now Heather will do more than talk about divorce. There's nothing else for it. "Okay, Max, why is he mad at you?"

"I told you," he says. "I forgot."

"And what did you forget?"

"I don't want him to hurt me."

"Max, it's all right. You can tell me. What did you forget?"

"I forgot to let him down," he says.

Not this again, I think. "He's not in the loft. We've been through this. He's not there."

"Yes, he is."

"*No*, Max; he isn't."

"He is," Max screams, running for the sanctuary of his room. "THIS ISN'T OUR HOUSE!"

*

The journey to our old place is ten minutes by car. I spend nine of them looking at the empty car seat in the back. I know that space. I do not know the child sitting in the other seat, staring out of the window at the night closing in fast around him.

Michael wouldn't let me find my soldiers. He said he won the game and laughed at me.

I park in the old spot.

It is 3 a.m., a thin layer of frost covers everything, preserving it until the morning when the temperature will rise and the world will thaw but a little. Brittle flowers line my old flowerbeds. Each blade of grass is almost ready to snap. And I forgot—not the window or the eggs: the ladder to the loft.

But we looked inside the loft, I think. Me and the police. We looked and found nothing.

This is where I found Max on the day his brother disappeared. He was picking soldiers up out of the grass and humming a tune to himself. *You've Got a Friend in Me.*

I knock on the door. No answer.

There was wire in the loft. I put it round his hands and feet. There was tape. The silver kind. I put that on his mouth. Then I hid him in the corner behind the big tank, under the smelly old rug.

And while we all looked with our eyes, we searched with our minds—out. Outside. Me, Heather, the police, we fixed ourselves upon the man-sized space that took away our boy.

I press my face to the glass panel and peer inside. I see a decorator's ladder in the hallway and old sheets covering the wooden floor. A glance through the kitchen window offers empty countertops, no appliances. The new owners have not moved in yet.

The rock feels cold in my hand.

"Stay in the car, Max." I wouldn't want him to get in the way.

Inside, I turn on the lights in every room on my way to the landing under the loft. The lights reveal the walls; the walls have changed colour. Repainted beige, every one. For one head-spinning moment this is déjà vu and I am back in the rental property, looking up at the loft hatch, swimming in idle dreams, the stuff of hope, washing my skin with it, while here, here in this other space, I feel sick to the pit of my stomach.

The Broken and the Unmade

One

The German SS arrived in December, 1943, and announced that our deportation would commence the following morning. In our schools that evening, the teachers gave us no homework.

Mothers stayed with young children, washed them from head to toe, hung their wet clothes on barbed wire. I was fourteen and big for my age. My mother busied herself cooking the last of our food and packing a suitcase. My father, unable to look at either of us for very long, sought without success that level of drunkenness that might allow him to forget the coming morning. I went for a walk.

Everywhere, the dark, bare soil was set with Yahrzeit candles; the camp like a mirror held up to the late night sky. I wandered among those stars for hours before I finally returned to my parents.

We prayed and wept all through the night.

*

When will it end.

I'm so tired it is not even a question anymore.

I sit up in bed. Stretch the ache from these ancient bones. Somewhere in the gloom of the basement the boy from the train is standing, watching me. I don't have to see him to know it. Eyes open, eyes closed, he is always there, timeless as a photograph. The cap turned sideways. The yellow Star of David stitched to the left side of his coat. Pupils swollen so large by the dark it is like staring into two pits rimmed with blue fire.

I get up, slowly. Put on my dressing gown. Stamp slippered feet to announce that I am climbing the stairs and entering their world. Saul

Aaronson, persona non grata.

My family are already sitting around the breakfast table. They don't bother to get me up anymore. They don't wait. They conduct breakfast as though they prefer the company of an empty chair over me.

My son, Nathaniel, is wearing the T-shirt again, the one I cannot bear to look at, but I say nothing and take my seat. The cereal bowl in front of him is almost empty and he has some splashes of milk clinging to his beard as if he hasn't quite been able to find his mouth this morning. Anger will do that, make you miss the mark when you ought to be stepping up to it.

Sitting opposite him is Aliya, my daughter-in-law: her face is spotless, beautiful, troubled. The bowl in front of her is full, but it saddens me to watch her stir the milk as if she has lost something in there that she can no longer find. At least my grandson doesn't notice any of this stuff. Joshua is too busy playing with one of the Star Wars figures his father gave to him, in-between oblivious sips of his orange juice. Darth Vader. Right. Surely there must be better things a father can pass on to his child.

But who am I to say? I no longer have a voice in this family. I am too old and I see some fucked-up shit; Nate's words, not mine. So, no one talks to each other, and maybe that's all because of me. It is these moments that are the worst, when we become ghosts ourselves, silently haunting each other during meals I can no longer bring myself to eat. And the boy from the train, he stands behind me, close enough to feel his breath on my neck; that is, if he had any breath to give. He watches us. Watch is all he ever does: the ghost of a memory that refuses to go away.

When will it end.

*

On the way to the funfair, I ask for all of the windows to be down. This invites cool air into the car at something like fifty miles per hour, which in turn invites Nate to curse under his breath. But even with the windows open the entire way they feel like no more than a slit, particularly inside a vehicle containing three adults and two children. Yes, the boy from the train is here too, sitting between Joshua and I on the back seat. Not that my grandson knows this. When I tried to tell him the story of the boy a few months ago, or at least a watered down version of it, he looked at me like he didn't believe a word about either the death camps or my ghostly parasite. To a boy of twelve, even one who likes to live in his imagination, it must all seem so far-fetched and far off.

He sees what he wants to see. Like the rest of us, I suppose.

At the funfair, I trail behind Nate and Aliya as Joshua races ahead through the huge gate.

DREAMLAND. *Where Dreams Are Free.*

This is, of course, an outright lie, because everything comes with a price. Everything.

Nate walks ten feet apart from Aliya while he reheats some previous argument. There is anger in my son's bones, and I find myself staring at the ground, too ashamed to see—or hear—it seep into the rest of him.

Two large inflatable skeletons greet me at the gate. Keeping my eyes down, I walk swiftly past them and inside. I glance back to see the boy from the train loitering near the entrance before vanishing into the crowd. I wonder if I am to have a few seconds of respite, but then the boy's face appears on a teenager over by the hotdog stand, and then on another, queuing for a ride, and then on every teenager's face I see, flitting from one to the next like some mask passed around.

"Three shots for a dollar!" someone yells.

I turn to see the barker at a shooting stall holding up what looks like a Luger that shoots corks. I beat a shuddering retreat.

It's happening again, I think.

The screaming children. Beeping arcades. Flashing coloured lights. It's too much.

Inflatable skeletons...because it's October and Halloween squats right around the corner...inflatable skeletons everywhere. Hollow-eyed grins of bone. And Nate...the T-shirt. Pink Floyd's *The Wall*: a screaming face of red on a background of blue, mouth opened impossibly wide and nothing, nothing inside it but yawning, unending darkness. And more children, screaming behind the face of the boy they wear like a mask. And that gaping, agonised mouth on the chest of my good-for-nothing son. And the boy from the train suddenly standing next to me, mouthing words I cannot hear, cannot lip-read. *Why can't I hear you? What is your name?* I don't remember. Did he ever tell me? On the train maybe...or beneath the mottoed gate.

Arbeit Macht Frei.

Screams.

Bodies.

Bodies.

Bones.

The boy—

"Take me home," I say, heart pounding inside my chest. I find my son and pull the sleeve of his T-shirt, half expecting the elongated mouth to turn and swallow my hand up to the wrist. "I have to get out of this place. *Now.*"

*

On the car journey home everything is Aliya's fault, according to Nate.

"It was your idea to invite him along," he says.

I listen to them talk about me like I am not there in the car with them, like I am the ghost. My daughter-in-law starts to cry. She hardly makes a sound, and it occurs to me that with walls between us I probably would not hear her sob. Which makes me wonder about the silences in that big house we share...are they all filled with her tears?

And what else? What else does he do to her?

I shut my eyes and imagine a car crash in which everyone dies. It is beautiful, both in its simplicity and its symmetry. The line ends as it was meant to end back in 1943, either on the train or as the outcome of one of the thousands of coin-toss moments inside Birkenau. But it didn't end, of course, and when I open my eyes my *farshtinkener* son still lives and breathes and drives safely under everyone's radar.

Someday, though...someday my crash will come.

Tuning them out, I glance sidelong at my grandson on the back seat next to the boy from the train. The boy stares at the side of my face like I have a dirty stain on my cheek. I rub at it, even though it isn't there, even though it will never come off. Meanwhile, my grandson is clutching something in his hand.

The Reichsfuhrer-SS...

Darth—

Himmler.

—Vader.

"Lift the mask, son. You'll find him wearing round spectacles over a toothbrush moustache."

My grandson can only give me a vacant look.

*

Back at the house, I stand in the hallway and watch my son and his wife carry their fight upstairs and left, into their room. Joshua follows close behind, sliding Vader up the banister, although on the landing he turns right. He stops and flinches at the sound of a slap behind him, then quickly resumes walking toward his bedroom door with Vader—*Himmler*—flying alongside him like some angel of darkness.

I listen for another slap.

The boy from the train brushes past me to stand on the bottommost step. He turns to face me, the weight of his stare chilling me marrow deep.

I hear no further blows.

But the silence is choking.

And the boy's stare...feels like sympathy, compassion. But by the time my brain is done with it, it seems to only feed my ravenous guilt, which I carry with me, down and down into the basement.

*

The sun betrayed us. By rising, it condemned us all. The SS carried out roll-call, at the end of which five hundred and fifty "pieces" were crammed inside ten wagons. What are we pieces of, I wondered as I listened to the doors being locked from outside.

The train did not move until evening, and then it moved slowly, with long stops on the way. Through a slit in the wall I watched our homeland disappear behind us.

The wagon was cold. Dark. Some light and air entered through a slit, but not enough; not nearly enough. We were pressed together, painfully so in most cases, and I could hear my parents' cries of discomfort from the far end. Pinned in a corner as I was, I had ho hope of reaching them.

The boy was roughly my size, perhaps a year or two older. I understood it wasn't his fault; fate had forced us together. In fact, fate had shown us a small mercy for the boy might have been heavier and crushed the life out of me before we ever arrived.

In a way, he saved my life.

Still, it was difficult to breathe. And terribly cold.

And loud.

Folk do not go quietly to their deaths, nor with dignity; blows were dealt indiscriminately in the dark.

Thirst became a real problem too.

When it snowed I collected what I could from the slit and drank the melt. I shared some with the boy. He said nothing but drank gratefully from the cup of my hand.

The journey took three days.
Three days to reach bottom.
The train stopped.
The boy and I exchanged our first word.
Farewell.

*

The boy is waiting for me by the foot of the bed. The shadows in the basement rally to hide him. I lie back on the covers. The springs squeal, reminding me of the brakes of the train. I don't even try to push the memories aside anymore. They're immovable as boulders anyway.

I see the officer strike the woman for taking too long to answer his question. I see the angry mark it leaves on her cheek: a Nazi flower. The woman does not allow herself to cry because she knows the officer will only plant more, entire beds of the plum-coloured blooms, all across her body.

I see the officer's jacket fall open to reveal a T-shirt underneath. A howling, bloodied face on a background of blue.

I see my grandson, lining up storm troopers outside a hijacked spaceship, Darth Himmler hovering over the captured prisoners, an angel black, capable of flight and things beyond belief.

Open my eyes.

The boy from the train is gone.

I rise cautiously from the bed, peering through the gloom. On the far side of the basement, I see a hole in the wall and light spearing through it. I cross the floor and raise my hand. A tiny sun appears on the centre of my palm. It is cold. The sun is cold.

I move my hand closer to the hole, pushing the cold light back until my hand is over the opening and the light stifled. I can hear feet shuffling behind me; many feet. Then bed springs squeal as someone's weight settles on them, squeal again as the first weight is joined by a second, then a third, a fourth, and so on until it sounds like punching brakes. I am too afraid to turn around, to discover how many others have joined me inside the wagon. And it *is* the wagon. The walls may move, the walls may vanish, but they've been here inside me for seventy years and they're not going anywhere.

The air is being used up, thinned out; it is getting harder to breathe.

A part of me knows that it must be all in my mind, because *real* ghosts do not use up air molecules but inhabit the spaces between them.

I pull my hand away from the wall. The hole and the spear of light are gone.

Panic rises in my throat.

I lift my hand, look at the place where the cold light kissed my palm, and see only darkness clinging to my skin. I turn from the wall and hurry across to the bed. The other passengers are no longer there, but I can feel the weight of their stares from all four walls.

I lift the pillow, snatch the gun from underneath.

On the other side of the bed, on the other side, the boy from the train waves his arms at me while shaking his head, just as he did when those Nazi sons-of-bitches sent his mother to huddle and weep with the old and the young, the broken and the unmade.

The boy mouths something but no sound can escape his lips. You need air in your lungs to deliver words. Otherwise, they simply slide back down your throat.

"And I don't have the imagination to give you any," I tell him. "Not kind ones. Not for me." My mind flashes to Joshua role-playing with his Star Wars figures. "Go see my grandson. They're all about that at his age. Making stuff up. I'm done talking. It's nothing but a waste of good air anyway."

I point the gun at the wall, pull the trigger.

Inside the tiny basement room it is a thunderous sound. But the hole I hoped to see materialise does not; it is little more than a pock-mark on the face of the wall. And that wall's many eyes, starved of oxygen, bloodshot from the tears of strain, continue to watch me from behind their shadow-veils. I fire another shot, another. But the brickwork is too tough and there is no light to be found.

No light to be found anywhere.

Then the door to the basement opens. Nate and Aliya appear in the doorway with the same look on their face.

At last, I think, *they've found some common ground.*

A look that communicates a simple message, loud, clear: *What have you done, Saul?*

I start to say the words, *It's what I* haven't *done*, but then I see the flower peeking at me across the shoulder of my son, the deep purple blossom on her smooth cheek. I see the necklace of Nazi flowers about her throat and realise—finally—that it has to end. The hurt.

Everything.

Now.

Two

The Germans ordered us to disembark. The platform was vast. Bright lamps struggled to hold back the night. A line of idling trucks awaited us a short walk away. As soon as our feet touched the soil, twelve men swooped upon us, an odious jury with hate in their bones and long shadows that darkened our startled faces.

They made us leave our bundles and luggage beside the train. I heard my mother call out to me in a whisper, but I was too afraid to reply.

An officer asked for her age and if she had any illnesses.

"Can I see my son?" she pleaded.

"Yes, yes, later," he replied curtly.

When she persisted, he planted a bruise on her face with the butt of his Luger. Then he pushed the barrel hard into the same cheek and asked his questions again.

She answered, and he motioned toward a fast-growing group of women, children, and old men.

Someone spun me around. A blonde tower of a man held me by my collar and asked my age. His voice was polite. Was I to be murdered by courtesy? As I opened my mouth to reply, the boy from the train suddenly appeared behind the German, holding up two hands, four and three fingers respectively.

"Seven," I answered, quickly. "Su-su-seventeen."

In his courteous brain the officer flipped a coin. "Over there," he said.

Away from my mother.

Away from my father, too, whom I saw embracing her, until a sharp kick buckled his knee and put him writhing on the ground.

The boy from the train joined our group and stood beside me.

I realised that he had possibly saved my life for a second time.

"Tell me your name," I said, at once mortified that my voice seemed to echo the Germans'.

We stood and watched as the group containing my parents was led away at gunpoint.

The night swallowed them up and never gave them back.

"Saul," he whispered. "My name is Saul."

"On the trucks," a voice ordered us. "Schnell! Schnell!"

*

Six hours out of the hospital and my new foster parents mention the new bike they have waiting for me in the garage. It's not the smartest move ever, but I understand that Mr and Mrs Weissmann know about Grandpa Saul and what he did. Clearly, they want to be seen as good, kind people—good, kind *parents*—by giving me this two-wheeled symbol of freedom and hope.

"Once the rest of your bandages come off, Joshua, you can take it for a spin," Mr Weissmann says. "Wearing your helmet, of course."

He is not only good and kind, my new dad, but he seems pretty funny as well.

Somewhere, though, they're missing the point. I've died twice, so far—once in the ambulance and then on the surgeon's table as they attempted to prise the bullet from my brain—and while I don't know if the third time will really be the charm or not, I know I've been too long in a hospital bed with an itch I couldn't scratch to wait around for trifling things such as bandages or permission or anything else for that matter.

"Let me ride it now and I promise I won't go farther than two hundred feet from the driveway," I offer.

While Mr Weissmann relents, Mrs Weissmann stands up from the table and walks out of the kitchen. At least there is no sobbing or, later on, bruises poorly disguised by facial product. She just seems worried, no more, no less. It's sweet and it's refreshing.

And it's one of those mid-sized mountain bikes. Silver and green. Somewhere between a BMX and an adult model. I like it because it doesn't know *what* the hell it is.

Mr Weissmann adjusts the seat height, checks the brakes four times, and ensures the helmet chinstrap is secure before he presses the button to raise the garage door.

Mrs Weismann reappears, bruise-free and dry-eyed. I feel bad that I expected anything else. She even smiles as Mr Weissmann puts an arm around her shoulders and they walk out onto the driveway to watch me under a Spring sun as my tyres purr against the blacktop.

Two hundred feet come...

...and go.

*

I feel bad, wracked with guilt in fact, deceiving my new family like this. They are barely out of the wrapper and I am already breaking their rules. The world seems to grow a little bit darker for a moment until I glance up and see a lonely cloud stealing across the face of the sun.

"I need to know, Grandpa," I manage to say between gasping breaths. "Why—why you did it."

"Did what?" a voice startles me from behind. "Oh wait. Never mind."

I peer over my shoulder at a boy pedalling hard to keep up.

"Thomas Weissmann," he says. "Jim and Debora's kid. We missed each other back at the house. Mum said you took off on the bike, so she sent me after you. I'm supposed to bring you back in one piece."

"Tell your folks I'm sorry. Tell them...I had to go somewhere." To avoid any confusion, I add, "*Alone.*"

"It's cool, bro. But I got to tag along. Sorry. I promised I would."

"I'm not your bro."

"True," he says. "But for the purposes of this little trip of ours it looks like you are."

"All right, but swear on your life you won't tell them—anyone—where we're going."

"I swear. Now, care to fill me in?"

I consider trying to make a break for it but I am already snatching breaths and cramping in one leg.

"I'm going home," I tell him. "I need to know why I made it and no one else did. Why I survived..."

"How are you going to do that?" he asks.

For a moment I can only hear the sound of bike tyres ripping along the road. Then I realise that Thomas is waiting for my answer.

"I don't know," I tell him. "I guess I'm hoping something will come back to me."

*

When we reach the house I find a For Sale sign leaning on the uncut yard. I push it facedown on the grass. I find a rock, pick it up. Break a window. Climb inside while my new brother loiters on the yard, kicking rocks, pretending not to look at the house of horrors.

Realisation dawns: this is precisely how all of my fellow students and teachers will react to me once I return to school—with hesitation and avoidance. I am condemned to carry this house on my back, forever. A snail with its shell on fire.

"Maybe you should call your folks," I say to him. "Tell them we're all right."

It took us ninety minutes to get here, the old house on the hill. Blood is spreading across the sunset sky, congealing toward night.

Thomas shakes his head. "I left my phone. Besides, they'll only ask me a bunch of dumb questions. Are you ready?"

"I think so."

I sigh along with the house's old timbers then climb the stairs to check my old room.

Somebody has hoovered the place, stripped off the bed sheets. Probably the clean-up crew. Only they've missed a spot on the wall next to my bed. There is a spatter of blood on my *Ironman 2* poster. Blood...red exoskeleton: easy to miss, I suppose. But the tears sting my eyes as I start to see what it all means.

Superheroes bleed.

Superheroes die.

"Everybody knows that," I say.

What they might not know is that they can also point a gun at your head and blow a piece out of your skull.

I drag a forearm across my leaking eyes.

Fuck you, Grandpa.

*

Thirty minutes later, I am sitting on the topmost stair of the hall staircase, looking down at Thomas standing on the bottom and looking up. In my hand, my favourite of all the Star Wars figures dad gave to me. Darth Vader. I found him under the edge of my bed. Now I turn him in my restless fingers, cold plastic refusing to warm.

"The house is empty," I declare.

"What did you expect?" Thomas's voice rises up the stairs.

"A clue, maybe. Something."

"A clue, to what?"

"I dunno. Why Grandpa Saul killed us."

"But you're not dead. You made it."

"It doesn't feel like it. It feels like a big piece of me's gone and there's a hole in its place."

"You're only what—twelve?" Thomas says. "You can come back from this. It wasn't your fault he got all twisted up."

"Maybe," I say, squeezing Vader in my hand. "Or maybe I should have known something was wrong. He freaked out when we took him to the Halloween fair. One of his flashbacks or something. He seemed much better on the ride home. But then dad was yelling at mom about all kinds of stuff, so I probably wasn't paying much attention. He saw ghosts, you know. Grandpa did."

Thomas's eyebrows climb his forehead halfway. "Ghosts? Really?"

"Well, one ghost apparently. The same one, every day. He told me about him. Some boy he met on a train during the war. Y'know, the one where they put all the Jews in the gas chamber. I'm not sure I believe it."

"Which part?" Thomas asks.

"Either. I mean, how can ghosts exist? And how can anyone kill sixty million people? Without a nuclear bomb, that is. It's impossible."

"I think it was six million," Thomas says. "And all the history books say it happened. As for ghosts, well, I can't explain that, but there are books about them too."

"Maybe," I say, standing up, brushing dust from my knees. "I think Grandpa Saul saw what he wanted to see. But here I am, and I can't see anything." I glance at Vader in my hand. "Who knows, maybe it's all some kind of Jedi mind trick or something."

We laugh; but behind the laughter I can feel a sadness creeping up on me. A wave rising. Ready to fall. Break. I want to run from it, hide, but at the same time I want to stay and search for answers. My scalp itches underneath the bandage.

I close my eyes. Breathe. Let my mind replay what I remember.

I see the front door crash open. My father and mother walk inside the house. They are arguing. Dad is winning, if volume and profanity are a means to measure such. Dad has on the Pink Floyd T-shirt he only wears because he knows Grandpa hates it. He doesn't even like their music. But he likes to poke the bear (although if Grandpa *is* a bear he's an old and sick one) because Grandpa drove Grandma away many years ago, when dad was still a boy, by playing genie and hiding in a bottle, not wanting to come out. And Mom is wearing the same long dress she wore to the fair...

I open my eyes. See my parents walk through Thomas. Not ghosts but living memories from that day. They walk upstairs toward me, Dad's voice growing louder with each step. I stand aside and let them pass—stupid, I know. They walk through their bedroom door, but I can hear it slam and feel the shudder run through the timber frame into the floor, into the balls of my feet.

Whoa.

"What is it?" Thomas asks from the hall downstairs. "What's wrong?"

I turn to answer, but the front door closes and standing there on the rug is Grandpa, before he took a gun and put it to work.

*

I'm standing behind my bedroom door, ear pressed to the whispering timber. Dad wants Grandpa out of the house and into a facility. Mom says, *Your father, Nate? Your own father?* Dad throws some curse words at her, and maybe a couple of punches to the stomach, too. Except it isn't Mom he's hitting, not in his mind; it's Grandma, for leaving him all on his own with Grandpa Saul.

I turn to Thomas sitting quietly on the bed.

"Hide underneath. It might not be safe in here."

"Why?" he asks.

I don't want to believe a bad thing can happen twice but what I'm hearing is telling me different.

"I think it's happening again," I tell him.

"You're remembering things," he says. "Replaying them in your mind. You mustn't do that. You need to move on. Come on, we should get out of here."

My head seems to shake itself. "I don't think I *can* move on."

"You have to."

I turn on him then. "You don't get it. I've lost everything."

"I know."

"I should have died—with my family."

"But you didn't."

"They might have answers. Some answers, at least. This could be my one and only chance—"

"They don't, Joshua."

"You don't know. You don't know anything."

"They're not real. I know you want them to be, but they're not. This is all you, brother."

"I don't think so. They're showing me what happened...things I didn't—*don't*—know."

"Who is?" Thomas asks, spreading his arms wide. "I don't see anyone. Why *is* that?"

"They're not your ghosts," I tell him in a calm voice. "They're mine."

It is a poor choice of words and I don't have time to correct myself. On the other side of their bedroom door, my mother's cheekbone meets my father's knuckles—hard. Then I hear her gasping for air. He is choking her. I remember running across to my bed, thrusting my head under the pillow. Vader dropping to the floor. Me pressing the pillow to my ears to block out that terrible, gasping sound. Now, I listen as he throttles her to within seconds of her life.

Then from the guts of the house: a gunshot.

Suddenly their door opens and the landing groans under their weight. Mom is crying. Dad tells her to quit.

Quit.

Like it is *her* bad habit.

I listen to their footsteps descend the staircase, punctuated by tears, whispered threats, confused questions, and finally, towering silence.

"Come on," I say to Thomas. "The basement... That's where they die."

Then I am racing downstairs, careful to avoid the ghosts of my parents, soon to be made ghosts again when the bullets shred them like tissue. I wonder how many times this can happen; if I come back tomorrow will the whole thing reset like some computer game I have the inability to save?

I'll find out tomorrow, I think. *And tomorrow and tomorrow and—*

"—Stop beating yourself up," Thomas yells after me, leaning over the balustrade. "There's nothing you can do about it now. It happened. You're only punishing yourself, and for what? Nothing!"

I am no longer listening.

*

The basement is dark as a cave or a hole or a longing. I can feel the presence of Grandpa Saul and, oddly, others; many others. It is as if the darkness is packed with people—not quite people and not quite touching, but packed nevertheless. A draught like someone's breath prickles the back of my neck, spinning me like a top, and I see first one face then a whole crowd of faces, men, women, young, old, leaning in, leaning out of the gloom.

"I don't want to see this. Grandpa, take it back. Someone...please."

The room is moving.

Unseen wheels spin along an unseen track.

The air, too: shifting. Sucked into gasping mouths.

In this breathing, shifting dark, I squeeze Darth Vader in my hand, finding comfort and strength in his familiar shape.

I know Grandpa wasn't fond of the toy, but sometimes he saw things that weren't really there. Like ghosts. Or the bad in everything.

The bedsprings squeal and the room comes to a shivering halt. My eyes follow Grandpa through the gloom as he shuffles over to the bed to retrieve something from beneath his pillow. Moments later, the deafening sound of a gunshot ricochets off the walls and fills the entire basement. I duck instinctively, anticipating the bullet that shattered part of my skull. Underneath my bandage, bone starts to itch.

I rise to my feet again, ready to flee the basement. But the door opens and into the light spilling down the stairs enter my father and mother. Before I can reconcile Then with Now and warn them of what is about to happen, two further shots are fired.

The first enters the screaming mouth on my father's T-shirt, puncturing his chest and one of his lungs.

The second carries the short delay of indecision, but finds my mother's neck regardless, severing the carotid artery. A doctor provided this detail to me the day after I regained consciousness. Now, I watch the wound spray crimson as the strength rapidly leaves her legs. She falls, beating most of her own blood to the floor.

Seconds later, my father collapses on top of her.

I turn slowly to my grandfather, who looks at the gun with an expression of shock and horror and disbelief; similar to mine, I expect. A moment passes. During it, he and the gun appear to confer psychically on what they should do next. Finally, he mutters, *It should have ended with me*. Repeating it to himself, he steps over the two bodies slumped in the doorway and staggers upstairs.

It should have ended with me... It should have ended...

Thomas steps into the doorway, seemingly oblivious to whom he just passed on the stairs to get here and to the ghostly bodies piled at his feet. He spreads his arms wide in appeal. *What are you doing?*

I hurry to him, mindful to not look down.

"Come on," I tell him. "Grandpa's heading upstairs to kill me."

*

Posters cover the walls of my old room. Marvel heroes, The Lord of the Rings, Star Wars. Tableaus of Good versus Evil. Standing in the middle of this is an old man, stooped as if by some invisible weight on his shoulders, holding in his loose grip a smoking gun.

I can't tell which side he belongs to anymore.

But I realise something: I am responsible for this not him, because this would not be happening if the shot he is about to fire had done its job. If I had not survived.

My bed lies empty. It is empty because I am here, alive, standing in the doorway, with Thomas behind me and peering in. The ghost—or memory—of the bullet, of the weeks I spent in hospital and the darkness that found me there in a brightly-lit ward is enough to make me hesitate before moving any farther into the room.

When I am alongside him, Grandpa Saul suddenly looks away from the bed to where I am standing. For a moment I feel his eyes connect with mine. A chill shudders through me.

The bullet...the bullet comes next.

He lowers his eyes to look at what I am holding in my hand. The Darth Vader figure. I watch as Grandpa's pupils swell to twice their usual size. In response? I have no time to decide, because the hand holding the gun rises suddenly through the air and brings the weapon around to point at the bed, empty now but not empty then.

He weeps as he mumbles the words, *Forgive me, Joshua, but...the line—*

He fires the gun.

Pain flares inside my skull. My fingers spasm and drop Vader to the floor. He bounces and comes to rest under the bed. I can smell the burnt powder in the air.

Weeping uncontrollably, Grandpa Saul staggers from the bedroom onto the landing outside.

There is another gunshot, and his body tumbles loudly down the stairs.

The echoes fade and silence falls over the house.

It is a heavy silence.

Full of tears.

*

I survived four days in Birkenau. Longer than most.

I never spoke again to that boy from the train, Saul, who had by my reckoning saved my life on two separate occasions, but I saw him, glimpses of him anyway, crossing the camp on the way to his new job.

He was chosen to join the Special Works Unit, or Sonderkommandos; perhaps because of his size.

I was forced to dig trenches. Back-breaking labour. Many men with weakened hearts simply gave up, falling right where they stood. Some were taken away; some—if the trench was being dug with the intention of refilling it the next day (before digging it again)—were left in the hard, winter soil to draw flies while the rest of us dug around their bodies.

Some prisoners were made lieutenants or kapos. They supervised fellow prisoners in exchange for small privileges from the Germans. I will call this one dirt. No capital 'd'.

Late afternoon, dirt stood on the lip of the trench and regarded me from a height for several long, uncomfortable minutes.

Finally, he said, "You there. Yes, you. What is your age?"

Being a Jew and a prisoner like me, I did not think it necessary to lie to him.

"Fourteen," I answered.

He walked away. I thought that was the end of it.

Seconds later, dirt returned with a German officer, trailing him like a dog. The officer grabbed me roughly around the bicep and dragged me out of the trench.

"Come with me, Mister Su-su-seventeen."

I was frogmarched away, to a group of prisoners corralled outside a nearby barracks. I was sent sprawling amongst them. The guards laughed.

I turned onto my back to watch the officer walk away, and finally recognised him as the one from the platform who had asked my age. He said a few words to dirt, motioned for something to be brought over, then handed him a hunk of bread. I realised two things: the first was that I'd been made part of some trade-off; the second was that I was going to die. Today. Now. I did not even know the date.

They pulled me onto my feet, cuffed me around the head for sport, then led all of us to our end.

Sore and stumbling, I glanced back for one last scathing look at the mongrel who had betrayed me. I saw him, pushing another prisoner toward my shovel, which stood, still upright in the earth.

I never again spoke to the boy, Saul, or got the chance to tell him my name, but I saw him, once, crossing the wastes of the camp like some beaten angel, and then again, often, after the end.

As we lay—or stood, some of us, propped against the cold stone walls— inside the gas chambers, the Germans sent in the Sonderkommandos to remove and dispose of our bodies.

Saul came to me and carried mine out into the open air. The sky looked beautiful and frightening, as things that are out of reach so often are.

Saul looked at me, tears filling his eyes.

I wanted to thank him but I had neither the air nor the working lungs with which to begin the process. So, I made a silent vow instead, to my saviour and friend, to never leave his side until I was able, somehow, to say those words.

*

Breakfast with the Weissmann's is different.

Different bad and different good.

Bad because mom and dad and grandpa aren't here. Good because things don't seem so awkward anymore. Not since I went back to the old house yesterday.

I feel like a book has been closed. Closed on a story that wasn't really mine in the first place. It was Grandpa Saul's story, and I know now that he didn't want to do what he did. But it wasn't exactly an accident either.

More important, I think, *it was something inside him and not me that caused it. Something that got twisted.*

"It's okay that I'm okay," I say to the table. "Isn't it?"

I notice that Mr Weissmann has some cereal milk on his chin. I wonder if he's mad about something; maybe about me going back to the old place. He didn't seem angry last night when I got back, but then you never know with parents—especially foster ones, who aren't even the real kind.

He reaches across the table and pats my hand.

"Yes," he says. "Yes. It's okay."

I blink. Sip my orange juice. Which, it turns out, is possibly the best that I have ever tasted. I make a mental note to ask Mr Weissmann— Alan—later what kind of oranges go into making it. I want to know. I want to know because he said it's okay to be okay.

"What do you want to do today?" he asks after we're finished eating our breakfast. "It's the weekend and you've been cooped up inside that hospital for so long I figure we need to do something fun. What do you say?"

From the other side of the table, Thomas nods his head rapidly in agreement.

Maybe the book isn't quite closed yet. "Can we go to the funfair, maybe?" I ask, nervously.

Mr Weissmann—Alan—claps his hands together.

"There's no maybe to it, Joshua. We're going!"

"And Thomas is coming too, right?"

"Thomas?" he says. "Sure. If Thomas wants to come, he can come."

*

A clear day. The sun is out. The spring weather isn't all that hot but it's comfortable if not welcoming. The year seems slow to get out of bed, stretch, put on its clothes before summer arrives. In the car, my stomach does flips long before I step on any of the rides. I feel as if I am standing on top of a tall tower with a beautiful view spread out in front of me, but when I look down I see a thin glass floor under my feet. And there's a crack in the glass. Close one eye, look at it a certain way, certain angle, yes, I think I can see it.

DREAMLAND. Where Dreams Are Free.

Words above the funfair gate. I can't help but think there ought to be a question mark at the end. In fact, my life feels like a giant question mark at the moment. A crack in the shape of a question mark.

After a few minutes inside I am struck by how quiet the place is; how bare it all seems. Everywhere, row upon row of light bulbs that are not only unlit but seem empty, incapable of light. Everywhere, litter blown in gusts across the ground so that it seems to creep when you are not looking. Everywhere, rides going through the motions with mostly empty seats.

It occurs to me that this is the kind of day that Grandpa would have appreciated here. He'd wanted to keep his distance from everything and everyone. He would have been able to see the fair without actually seeing it come alive. Even the calliope music sounds more subdued than usual, as though pacing itself for long, empty days and nights ahead. Which causes me to wonder, *Will the summer ever return to this place?*

Thomas gives me no time to answer as he appears at my side, takes my hand, and drags me at a run over to the rollercoaster.

Over to the helter skelter.

To the hurricane.

And it begins to dawn on me that even with no crowds, even with the lights out and the bulbs empty, this can still be a fun place to be. It's about what you give to the funfair not the other way around.

A couple of hours later, we find ourselves with no rides left but the last: the ghost train.

Excited, I climb into the front wagon and wave for Thomas to join me.

He shakes his head.

I wave again, harder. *Come on.*

Another shake of his head. *I can't.*

"What's wrong?" I ask. "We're going home after this. Get on."

His eyes fix themselves on mine, shining with blue fire. "You're going to make it," he says. "You're younger than he was and not quite broken. You still have the ability to dream. You gave me my voice back."

"What are you talking about?" I ask, but his words feel like a cold hand caressing the back of my neck. As soothing as they sound, I want to scream.

"You're not broken, Joshua."

The motor sputters into life.

"Wait," I tell him. "Wait! You're going to be here, right? When the ride ends and I come out the other side, you're..."

The wagon begins to move, a slow, jerking motion along the track.

The mouth of the tunnel, black curtain obscuring what lies beyond, looms closer and closer.

Thomas keeps pace with the train until the curtain blocks him from my sight. Even so, his voice manages to find me edging through the dark on my own.

Thank you, it says.

The Things That Get You Through

I. Lilac is the colour of denial

The news of Eedee's death isn't forty minutes old before James Graves is in the bedroom pulling on white coveralls and cracking the seal on the can of purple paint. Correction: lilac paint. Edith hadn't known her own mind on many things—the important stuff mainly, like what career she wanted or how many kids, if she even wanted kids at all—but she'd known she wanted lilac for the bedroom; she'd known that much. And lilac, he thinks, is what she's going to get, even if she is never coming back.

But then, she just might.

James dips the brush into the paint, doesn't bother to wipe the excess back into the can, doesn't think of spreading an old bedsheet across the floor to catch the drips, but *does* go to the trouble of zipping his coveralls all the way up to his throat and checking the rubber bands that hold the clear plastic sacks on his feet are both tight and secure. Along with the latex gloves, Edith's old shower cap, and the pair of sunglasses that are, praise the Lord for some luck on this morning of none, keeping the sunlight out of his red-rimmed eyes, the coveralls make him feel protected, or at least like someone else. Someone far removed from who he was this morning: the Claremont High English teacher with twenty-seven essays to red-pen by the end of the holidays. The thirty-five-year-old who started breakfast by saying to Edith, "If Banquo had only slit Big Mac's throat in Act One he would've saved me a whole lot of hard work today," and ended it in the upstairs bathroom blubbing like a baby. Somewhere in-between Edith had dropped the *it's over* bomb. Shrapnel flew: *there's someone else, James... I don't know, a few months... Yes, it's serious... Yes, I'm moving out... No, we can't talk about it... I'm pregnant... No, it isn't.*

It's his. That word—*his*—had stuck between James' ribs like a hunk of ruined metal, and led him to push the button that launched his full counter-strike, a napalm tirade bursting with abuse and curses, as if he had been saving it all up somewhere for weeks, perhaps even months. Like a fucking squirrel storing fucking nuts for the fucking winter, he thinks, and slaps the paintbrush against the wall, producing an ugly lilac splatter.

She'll come back, he thinks, watching the paint runs race each other toward the floor long enough to realise he isn't watching but staring. She'll come back. And then they'll fix this whole rotten mess somehow.

But it finally occurs to him with one wall finished and a second underway: what if she doesn't? What if the hysterical phone-call from Edith's mother wasn't a sick joke and Eedee, in her hurry to reach lover-boy's address, really had run a red light into the path of another vehicle? At first, James snorts and shakes his head like a horse irked by a cloud of buzzing flies, but the idea just isn't that easy to dismiss. Bus, truck, or car, the outcome would have been much the same; she had taken off from here on her 1995 Vespa, aka Kermit because of its colour, without wearing her crash helmet.

He lays the paintbrush across the mouth of the can. Takes a step back. "What'll I do?" he asks the room, specifically the one-and-a-half lilac walls still wet with the hope of Eedee's return. "If she's...what'll I do?" The answer comes to him not in words or sound but as the powerful smell of emulsion paint. It is the only thing keeping him on his feet right now; the only thing preventing those idea-flies from peeling off from their cloud one by one and making kamikaze runs at his nerves. Eedee has been pushing him for six years to spruce up the place, but he's always been busy doing something else. Even when he wasn't. And so he decides he will finish what he has started: he will paint the walls; he will give the ceiling a fresh coat of white. He will make Eedee proud.

With all four walls done, the first coat anyway, James descends into the gloom of the basement garage in search of white paint for the ceiling, taking the stairs two and three at a time in his bagged feet and sunglasses. He trips, almost falls, barely notices. He wants this momentum he has built up over the past few hours to carry him through to the end of the day, but it's barely noon and there's no white paint to be found anywhere in the bowels of the house. Among the clichéd basement fare on the shelves, between old electrical goods and cardboard boxes crammed with everything from paperbacks and CDs to his aborted attempts at The Great American Novel, there are ancient rusting cans with rubbery paint-skins inside, but nothing he can actually use.

Most of this stuff, he realises, belongs to him. While Eedee held on to nothing—except that goddamn green scooter of hers—he on the other hand never could let anything go. With the exception of the empty floor space where Kermit usually spent the night, the entire basement belongs to him. *Is* him. And there is something comforting about that, something deeply, vitally reassuring, like a lighthouse light to the captain of a vessel crashing through one colossal wave after another. But he cannot allow himself to stop and think on it. The paint won't find itself and the bedroom ceiling won't become white on its own. He is, today at least, a man of some importance and responsibility. The rest of it is junk in basement boxes, stuff lying around waiting out the ten years it takes the average suburban home to digest it and then crap it back out for either the trash or a yard sale.

Rather than return upstairs empty-handed, he grabs a box of old CDs and a Sanyo ghetto blaster. He needs to hear something other than silence or ringing phone up there.

You knew this was coming.

Something other than the voice of his conscience.

It might as well have been you behind the wheel, Gravesy.

Nobody called him Gravesy but Edith—just as nobody calls her Eedee except him—and he doesn't like it; no, not one bit.

What's the matter, Gravesy? Don't want to face up to the fact that I'm gone?

It's as if she is inside him. As if she has moved in. And she can't be allowed in there.

The phone is ringing somewhere.

James knows he should answer it, if only to hear someone's else's voice, but there is the getting of the paint and the painting of the paint to be taken care of before Eedee's return.

Return? Who says I went away?

"Who said that?"

God yes he must evict her, he thinks, looking around the basement. Send in the removal guys and get her the hell out of his mind before she opens the box in there marked PRIVATE and takes a look inside.

"Who said that?" he asks again.

Then he sees her. Under the stair alcove. The mannequin from his bachelor party.

She is leaning against the Fifties-style refrigerator Eedee loved so much that she cried when it stopped working. In build, she is ten, maybe fifteen pounds on the lighter side of Edith (although Eedee's shed some weight recently, he thinks—*And you know why I lost it, Gravesy, don't you?*), but she's got the same auburn hair and folded arms and—what else? Aura? Yeah, he thinks, it could be that. The same aura.

James walks over to her, and before he can think to check his hands he touches her face, leaving a smear of lilac across her cheek.

He nearly apologises but checks himself in time to mutter "damn it" instead.

However, less than a minute passes before it gets the better of him.

"Go on," he says in a hushed voice. "Say something."

But if Eedee's mannequin lookalike was talking before she isn't talking now.

I don't have time for this, he thinks. So he carries the mannequin upstairs and returns for the ghetto blaster and the box of CDs. The white paint can wait, for now. In what will be (when it is finished) the bedroom Edith always wanted, James plugs in the ghetto blaster and plays one of her all-time favourite songs, *Nothing's Gonna Stop Us Now* by Starship. He plays it loud and on repeat as the mannequin looks on. It is an irony that is not quite lost on him as he goes to work applying the second coat of lilac.

II. Anger is the smell of turpentine

One afternoon, sometime after he painted a room and found a mannequin, James Graves puts on a black tie. This is the last surreal moment of the day for him. By the time he is standing in a room full of people watching Eeedee's casket disappear into a hole in the wall, he is, combed hair to polished shoes, numb.

Everything has been arranged by Edith's mother. He is no more than a guest at the funeral, and perhaps less than that—a *ghost*. Condolences, so freely shared between Eedee's closest friends and family, are given to him with palpable effort and restraint, when they are given at all. He feels nothing. The only flicker of emotion occurs when he realises one of the men in this place could be the one she was riding so quickly toward on the morning of their huge fight. But it passes and he becomes frozen again, scarcely mindful of the tightening of folks' eyes at the sight of his hands, which are when they are drawn from his pockets, a noticeably different colour. "You're all purple," someone whispers or hisses. Perhaps Eedee's mother. "I'm not, I'm lilac," he answers coolly. "You really didn't know her at all, did you? None of you." And then he leaves, moments before a door closes and she becomes so much smoke and ash and nothing.

Outside, he keeps walking, he doesn't look back, and by the time he does look there is a parking lot and a line of very tall trees between him and the chimney stack. The sky is blue and clear. It is not the kind of sky he expects to be standing under and looking up at when—when his wife is dead and her family and friends are gathered to send her off. And she *is* dead, he knows that, but it doesn't mean she will be leaving *him* anytime soon. Not with this unfinished business they have between them.

He hears the phone ringing inside the house the moment he steps from his car onto the driveway. Walking toward the front door, he feels the weight of someone watching him, and stops. Turning around, he sees there are in fact *three* someones: a trio of teenage girls on the other side of the street.

They are standing around the open mouth of a garbage can on the grass verge, ceremoniously passing a lit cigarette around. Pull, exhale, pass. Pull, exhale pass. And so on, until the ash tip lengthens to breaking point and drops inside the can. All three wear black mini dresses and black skyscraper heels. The ridiculous shoes force them to keep their feet moving to prevent the spikes from sticking in the soft ground. It seems a curious and strange sort of dance.

Dressed as they are, he wonders if the girls were at the cremation service. By now the news must not only be out but circulating vigorously throughout the neighbourhood. He cannot remember seeing them in the small crowd though. And they appear a tad overdressed for a funeral. Still, they keep staring at him from across the street. Three Little Witches.

"Can I help you?" he asks.

"No, sir," one of them says.

In Macbeth, the witches were brought on when there was no other explanation for a major change in the behaviour or actions of an individual.

Here they are, he thinks. So what is it they think they know about me? And what are they telling people?

He stops himself. A little irrational. And possibly paranoid too.

Inside the house, the phone is still ringing. But the witches command his full attention.

"Do I know you girls? Maybe one of you is in my class..."

"Have you found a new girlfriend yet, Mister Graves?" one of them asks. He isn't sure which one; he didn't see anyone's lips move.

He doesn't answer. He watches as they pass the cigarette around and wonders if there's possibly more than tobacco in that thing. Because they are not witches, he thinks. Some teenage girls getting stoned in broad daylight, maybe—probably—but not witches. They are no more witches than the mannequin in his bedroom is Edith Graves, his deceased wife. It is all just some stupid game of role play.

Theirs? he thinks. Or mine?

As he turns to go inside the house (even though the phone has stopped ringing), a second voice speaks up: "I bet Mister Graves has found someone new already. Boys don't tend to hang around."

"If he hasn't found her already," a third added, "I'm sure he will before long."

"There's no future in wasting time," says the first. "The sun will go down soon and life's too short."

"True," says the third. "Life is *very* short. And maybe one of these days the sun won't come up again. Think about *that*, willya?"

"I will," says the first.

"Me too," says the second. Then: "Aw, look, Mister Graves is leaving. Goodbye Mister Graves!"

"Oh yes, goodbye!" says the third.

Then all together: "GOODBYE, MISTER GRAVES!"

Suddenly the key in his hand is the size of his fist and the lock is a pinhole. It just won't fit. And these girls (*witches*), they give him the creeps. And the phone is ringing again. He decides it is crucial he answer it, even if he has to toss the key and kick down the fucking door. Then it's in, he's in, and the handset is in the palm of his hand like a screaming newborn.

He doesn't answer it until the front door is closed and locked and he is ensconced upstairs in a bedroom of calming lilac. Eedee's mannequin lookalike stands in the corner with her arms folded. James almost doesn't answer the phone. But those witches outside...he needs to talk to someone. *Hear* someone.

"Hello?" he says.

"It's your brother." There is a pause, like this is a test or something.

"Paul. Hi. It's—good to hear from you."

Paul lives on the east coast now, having left Claremont soon after the death of their father in '99. Coronary. Ovarian cancer took their mother four years before that. He is doing all right for himself over there, running his own plumbing supplies company out of Boston— when he isn't laying pipe in the Biblical sense, that is. A line that gets no funnier each time he tells it.

"Listen, I heard what happened. Why didn't you call me? I would have caught a flight."

"Thanks, but it's okay. I'm fine. I'm handling it."

"That's good, that's good." There is a silence, interrupted by a woman's voice asking him a question, something about orange juice. Whatever time it is in Boston, it sounds like breakfast over there. "Not for me, babe," Paul answers.

"Is that Denise?"

"Naw, just somebody."

"What happened to Denise?"

"We're fine. Listen, Jim, I'm here for you if you need me, okay? I know this is some real messed up shit you've got to deal with, but you gotta keep in mind it's all just a process. What you need to do is work *through* that process, y'know? All the different stages 'n' shit. Right now, you're standing on the start line, and there's a long road ahead."

"But I've only got four weeks," James says, hearing the panic rise in his own voice. "Then the new semester starts."

"Take some time off."

"I, I can't, I... All I've got is this teaching job. I've lost everything else. Jesus, if I go back there and I'm not over this, those kids are going to chew me up and spit me out. I've got to be over this."

So what happened to Denise?

"Take one stage at a time," his brother says. "You can't rush these things."

I have to, he thinks. What happened to Denise, Paul?

"I think I've done the denial part," he says. "I think this is stage two. That's anger, right? Yeah, I'm all about stage two." If it isn't Denise then who is it? Who is he screwing now? Screwing and getting away with it.

"Then get angry, brother. Rage against the world for a couple of weeks. It might do you some good to let that shit out."

James thinks, he's right, it would. But I don't have that time to spend on one stage. I've got to be over this thing fast.

"Do I have any other choice?" he asks.

"I don't think so. But listen, you'll be fine. I promise."

"Yeah, sure, I'll be fine. Look, I gotta go, okay?"

"Okay."

"Paul?"

"Yeah, what?"

"Say hi to Denise for me." And he breaks the button ending the call.

There is a tack sticking out of the wall. He sees it, over there in the corner, two feet above Eedee's old wicker chair. There is a tack he either didn't see before or forgot to pull, and he's painted over it lilac. Eedee used to hang something from that, he thinks. What was it?

He looks at the mannequin standing in the other corner, half expecting her to provide him with the answer. Before she does, he remembers.

"It was one of those little dreamcatcher things," he says.

Eedee must have taken it down.

When she quit dreaming, he thinks.

Then he starts searching the bedroom for something to prise the tack out with. Now that he has noticed it, it won't go away, it won't blend back into the wall; it will jut out instead, like some unsightly skin tag.

He finds a pair of nail clippers lying under the bed. Eedee would sit on the edge of the bed and fire toe bullets across the floor for the hoover to crackle over later. Stuck in its jaws is a toenail clipping. James teases it out, holds it up to the light. Chipped pink nail gloss, a cracked pink smile. One of Eedee's. Nails are one of the last things to go, he thinks, then walks over to the tack in the wall. Hooking the mouth of the nail clippers around the rim of the tack, he tries to worry it free. But his grip is poor and the lilac paint acts as a kind of glue holding everything in place—and boy doesn't he know that?

When the tack finally gives up the fight, it pops right out of the wall. With no resistance, the clippers recoil like a fired pistol, taking a small bite out of James' cheek, under the left eye. The cut isn't deep, but it starts to bleed. James wipes the blood with his thumb, and looks at it. He turns it this way, that, and looks at it some more. Then he presses his thumb to the wall and drags it diagonally downward, leaving a short crimson slash in the midst of all the lilac. Then he waits for another bead to swell from the cut, and presses it to his forehead. The next two drops he applies to either cheek, like war paint.

I need a soundtrack, he thinks, searching through the box of CDs. Something I can play loud. Guns 'n' Roses. *Appetite for Destruction*.

But it isn't there.

Wait a second: Edith held onto Starship but she tossed out *Axl Rose*? *What a cunt.*

He turns to look at the mannequin. She still has the lilac smudge on her cheek from when he first touched her in the basement. She is looking at the ceiling as if rebuffing his presence in the room. Irrational or not, James feels humiliated. What's that? he thinks.

He can hear something. A sound coming from the direction of Eedee. Correction: the mannequin.

It doesn't sound like words. It is more like a tapping or a ticking or a—no, something else, he thinks.

Scratching.

He listens to it for a while. And the longer he listens to it, the more it begins to fit a sound buried deep in his memory. It reminds him of the four years he spent writing his novel. Four years of sitting in front of the computer, producing word after word, page after page of flaccid prose. And it reminds him of those pages, stacked beside him on the desk, and the sound his uncut fingernail made as it scratched the top sheet, sometimes for seconds, sometimes for hours.

Scratch, scratch...scratch, scratch.

The sound of failure.

And then he is running downstairs into the basement for a bottle of turpentine. The space where Kermit once stood is empty but for an old oil stain on the concrete that needs a double-take to identify as anything but blood. Back upstairs, he picks up the mannequin and carries her across the hall into the bathroom, where the steam of the running water mixed with the turpentine burns his face and sticks to the insides of his eyelids.

And she will not fit.

Either the tub is too small or she is too rigid, but she will not fit. As intractable, he thinks, as Edith on the day of their huge fight.

James yells up at the ceiling through the billowing clouds of steam, and starts yanking the shower curtain down from its rail, hooks snapping and firing across the room like projectiles. Or cut toenails.

Plick. Plick. Plick.

Later, when he is done and cool and composed, and the shower curtain lies over the toilet bowl like a sheet draped over a body, he heads back down to the basement again.

This time it's for the handsaw.

III. Bargaining is the sound of one man talking to his mannequin

Over two weeks have gone by without Eedee and James is sitting cross-legged on their old bed, staring at the telephone handset while The Jackson 5 sing *I Want You Back*.

Outside, the temperature is reaching into the high eighties. James closes the windows and draws the curtains in Eedee's lilac bedroom to keep out the sun and the heat and the prying eyes. The Three Little Witches walked by the house a half hour ago, and he does not want them seeing or hearing what it is he is about to do.

Standing in the corner, the mannequin stares at the space above James's head as if he is a character from a comic book and she can read his thoughts. She is wearing Eedee's pink Alpaca fur slippers. Eedee loved them. She never took them off when she was in the house. Since they have the same-sized feet, he figures why not let her wear them, that is, let the mannequin wear them. Besides, he thinks, what's the point of leaving that sort of thing lying around the house like exhibits in a museum? So they belong to her now, together with the half-roll of duct tape he used to put her back together again.

The phone has finally stopped ringing this week. It got so bad that three days after the funeral he went out and bought a digital answering machine to handle the incoming calls—her relatives and friends mostly, as well as one or two of his teaching colleagues. It couldn't have been any simpler: every morning he got up and erased the previous day's messages without listening to any of them. But today is different. Today, he wants to use the phone.

He wants to call Eedee.

I'm not crazy, he thinks. I'm just running out of time.

He knows she isn't going to pick up and he isn't going to hear her voice on the other end of the line, like in that Twilight Zone episode with the kid and the toy phone with a connection to his dead grandma. Actually that would be great. But, no. He is going to use an old classroom trick and do some simple role-playing—for peace of mind, closure, whatever clichéd label you cared to lick-and-stick on it, just as long as it gets him through stage three. The phone is nothing more than a prop, although come to think of it, what *did* happen to Eedee's cell?

Curious, he scoops up the handset and speed-dials her number.

It rings. Surprising.

And rings. Not surprising.

When he's sure she won't be picking up anytime soon, a judgment call that takes him longer to make than he might have predicted *before* ringing her number, he thumbs the big oval button—now fixed with superglue—to cut off the call. Then he lifts the handset to his ear.

"Hello? Edith? This is...uh, it's me."

There is a strange, suggestive silence. It is the silence of a large cave or a deep pit, neither of which feel entirely empty.

"Edith? It's James. Can you talk?"

Nothing.

"This is stupid," he says, dropping the handset on the bed like a hot coal. "I can't do this. This bullshit only works with kids. I'm thirty-five-years-old talking to a lump of plastic."

Talk to me then.

"I don't know why I'm doing this. I don't know if I can. It's all happening too fast, I..."

What is it you want to say, Gravesy? Spit it out.

"I want to tell her that I forgive her," he says. "I forgive you, Eedee. Okay? And I hope you can forgive me too. Whatever happens, I want us to work this out. No, that's not what I mean, I—I want us to lay down our swords and stop with the jabbing and the poking and... What I am trying to say is... Jesus, you're not even here and I can feel your eyes drilling into me... What I'm trying to *say* is—"

He stops with the realisation that he is not only looking at the mannequin while he is talking but he is in fact talking *to* the mannequin while he is talking. What frightens him the most isn't that he's talking to an inanimate object. He was, after all, about to have this conversation with the telephone handset. No, it is how natural and ordinary and comfortable it feels to do so, to talk to her like this. Eedee the mannequin. Like pulling on a pair of shoes or sliding into a coat.

"What I'm trying to say is that you weren't the only one. There, I said it."

There is a long silence.

"Say something."

But Eedee the mannequin has nothing to say. She just stares at that space over his head, arms crossed in pending judgement.

"You can't even look at me, can you?"

Or is it that you won't? he thinks.

"Look, you know how these things happen," he says, figuring that if he is already standing on hot coals he might as well walk to the cool safety of the other side. Assuming there *was* another side and not just endless insufferable heat. "A little flirtation on Facebook goes too far and suddenly you're into sex talk or cyber sex or whatever you want to call it. I realise there is a fine line of distinction between what's okay and what is not, but I did not sleep with her. We came close, we talked about it enough, but it *never actually happened*. It's important you understand that, Eedee. I know, I know, it's still cheating. It can happen in the *mind*room as much as the bedroom. God knows, you said that to me often enough. I guess if you really want to put it that way then yeah, I cheated on you before you cheated on me. But you slept with yours, you fell pregnant by yours, you were running off with yours. You met him on the internet too. Online gaming. Y'know something? I hate all that shit; I can't stand it. These things that get us through the day—the texting, the picture messaging, the video messaging, Facebook, Twitter, the whole fucking lot—they have too much power over us. Do we control them or do they control us? I know, I'm veering a little off track here. As usual, right? But I do have one more thing I need to say to you, Eedee, and then I'm done.

"You never let me fix us. That's what bites me the most. You never let me fix us."

He feels better for having it out in the open. The atmosphere in the room feels almost electric, the molecules in the air thrumming all around him as he looks across the room to the mannequin and for a fraction of a second believes he sees Edith Graves' eyes glaring back at him, out at him.

Is she inside that thing? he thinks.

Scratch, scratch, scratch.

"Don't do that, Eedee," he says. "You know that sound drives me nuts. Don't."

Scratch.

"Goddammit!"

It stops.

An awkward silence wafts into the room.

Where do we go from here? he thinks, looking around at the lilac walls. He remembers asking himself the same question after the words dried up and his novel slipped into a long coma. Where do we go from here?

The cold, serene face of Eedee the mannequin only has one thing to say.

Nowhere.

There's my answer, he thinks. I can repaint the room, I can confess my secrets, try to make things right between us again, but what does it all achieve, really? I have to get past this, and faster than I am. Time's running out.

"You still won't talk to me, will you?" he says, looking at the mannequin in Eedee's pink Alpaca fur slippers, head and limbs fixed to her torso with long, winding strips of duct tape. It's so like you, Eedee, he thinks.

"So like you to keep it all inside and under wraps," he says. "I grew to hate that about you, you know. Because it was never me, was it? I never had control of anything."

Scratch, scratch.

"Fuck you," he says, rising quickly from the bed. "I'll show you I can do this. I'll show you. Have your precious lilac bedroom. Take it. I only did it for you anyway. And newsflash—I never even *liked* lilac. And you can have the rest of the house while you're at it, too. Me, I'll be in the basement if you need me, going stage four."

He makes it as far as the bedroom door.

"So are you coming or what?"

IV. Depression is the touch of a dust angel at your back

The new semester at Claremont High is right around the corner, eight days from now to be exact, and James is holed up inside the basement garage with Eedee the mannequin and a Whole Bunch of Other Crap, which at another time he might have described as the summation of their life together. He's been down here for three whole days, listening to Leonard Cohen, drinking bottled water and urinating into the floor drain. So far, he has only needed to use the bucket once.

Today, James is lying on the dusty concrete floor, staring up at the rafters and the tube lighting and the crisscrossing wires, all too aware that were he to want to walk outside—which he doesn't—he would be faced with a short but steep climb just to reach street level. It is too much for him right now. So, he's decided to lie in the dust and make snow angels, like the ones Eedee and he made a century ago, or at the very least he will make something with wings. Dust insects, maybe.

Besides, isn't he better off in the dirt? Smoke rises, that is, while there is room for it *to* rise, and the portable barbecue in the middle of the garage is filling the space with the smell of grilled hickory chicken wings and yes, smoke—a lot of it. There is supposed to be a window down here somewhere, if it can be called a window, and the smoke is queuing up, trying to get out and really getting nowhere. Who knew it didn't like fire?

And I thought there couldn't be one without the other, he thinks. But the reality is smoke can't wait to get away.

"Then let me be smoke," he says. "Please."

The rest of it pushes its way upstairs into the house, under the door. A new kind of fumigation. If he is to claim back his life, or indeed have any life at all, he figures he needs to reclaim the house for himself. Smoke her out.

But I'm right here.

I'm dealing with the house first, he thinks. Then you.

Eedee the mannequin stands in the corner by the roll-top door, facing the wall. Her head is tilted to one side as though she is listening to something. A tell-tale heart perhaps, he wonders. No. She'll find nothing like that inside these walls. Or in her own chest, for that matter. The source of that incessant scratching, maybe, but no living, beating heart.

So, he has food, although after this latest batch is cooked, the chicken breasts in the cooler bag will be a trip to the ER waiting to happen. But there are plenty of canned goods left: soups, beans, vegetables, and so on. He has the drain and the bucket for any toilet requirements and a sleeping bag for some comfort during the colder nights.

When the chicken is ready, he fumbles on the floor for the smoke alarm batteries from upstairs, and feeds six of them into his heavy-duty Man Torch. Capital M. Capital T. No penlights or overhead lighting for him, no sir; he wants to disconnect from the entire grid. A total reboot. He eats with his fingers, doesn't brush his teeth, and later on, he thinks, he might go ahead and draw on the walls with the charcoaled hickory sticks. Because the way to start over is to start over. To go back to the beginning.

It has to be this way. Quick and drastic. No one else can help him over this hump in time. His parents are in the ground. As for colleagues: eighty percent of the other teachers at Claremont High are women. The only male teacher he knows—or rather, knew—in a speak-to-on-a-daily-basis-in-the-hall kind of way was Mr Morrish of the Chemistry Department, and he is sodium in water now, gone, two weeks past, after an incident in which he got caught browsing porn on his iPhone and fondling himself during class—a class he was supposed to be teaching. A siege mentality has developed among the staff since then, meaning now was most definitely not the time to be a lonely screwed-up male educator appealing for any kind of understanding or support from his mostly female colleagues. As for James' friends, that is, *his* friends and not Eedee's, they *are* those teachers and colleagues. For a moment he considers getting in touch with Paul again, but something tells him being around another lying, cheating husband is not exactly the fast track to a successful recovery either.

It has to be this way.

But the chicken wings are burnt—again. This should infuriate him, but it doesn't, because lately he can't bring himself to eat them anyway, not with that bucket in the corner, which instead of collecting his bodily waste seems to break it down and concentrate it into something more foul-smelling than anything he could have ever produced had he chosen to shit all over the floor instead. And Edith isn't talking to him. And the nights are chilly. The nights are *cold*. The concrete floor is a glacier under his hip. The sleeping bag zipper sticks halfway. Every time, he swears, it sticks halfway. Which is somehow worse than it not moving at all, because what it says to him is *I can, but I won't*. And for James his time in the basement is supposed to be a matter of *I can, and I must*. So he burns scrunched-up pages of his great unfinished novel for heat, and is surprised when they do not burn with a purple flame. He makes dust insects on the floor. And he superglues Eedee's old toenail clippings, having found a stash under the bed, to Eedee the mannequin's feet, telling himself it is just something to do, something to pass the time.

Which it does.

Until on the seventh day James Graves presses the button on the garage remote and from the basement staggers, blinking, into the sunlight, a new man, and if not new then undoubtedly changed.

V. Acceptance is the taste of a mocha latte with a beautiful blond

On the Saturday before the Monday on which James must face a roomful of fourteen and fifteen-year-olds for the first time since Edith's death, he leaves the last few Macbeth essays unmarked, gives Eedee the mannequin a goodbye kiss on the cheek and leaves for a relaxing stroll through the neighbourhood. The late evening air is cool, sweet to the taste, and a gentle following wind provides some soft cadenced encouragement to keep moving forward, to not turn back.

I think I'm going to make it, he thinks. I really do.

Then, turning left onto Bradburn Street, the acrid smell of cigarette smoke carried by the breeze reaches his nose.

If you are going to bring me this then we are no longer friends, he thinks jovially, and walks on, assuming the smoke will disperse and he will be allowed to continue his walk without any further interruption. However, the smell grows stronger, and the air surrounding him is filled suddenly with long grey wisps.

"HI, MISTER GRAVES! REMEMBER US?"

James glances over his shoulder, trying not to look affected by the chorus of voices he has just heard. They are walking a few feet behind him, following him, he presumes. The Three Little Witches. The girl in the middle has a cigarette and she is blowing smoke rings into the air. What leaves the O of her mouth as a perfect white circle reaches him a shredded grey ghost of its former self.

Edith liked to smoke. She *loved* to smoke, in fact. Thirty a day, but that could reach as high as fifty if she was out drinking with friends. She smoked in the house, too. With no kids around, she didn't see it as a problem. She never once tried to quit either, even though he begged her to stop on many occasions, telling her it would likely kill her before the age of fifty. She was right though, it didn't.

James starts to cough; great, chest-wracking coughs. Turning around gave him a face full of the stuff. He can feel it, clinging to the insides of his lungs, making it hard for him to breathe. Since his daily barbecues in the basement he has found it a struggle to catch his breath sometimes, but this is something different. He has gone four long weeks without cigarette smoke invading his lungs, and now, this evening, one deep breath of the stuff and it feels like he's choking. Why?

Easy, he thinks. Your body has woken to the fact that it's poison. When you breathed that shit in all the time when Eedee was around, you must've forgot that one important little nugget. *It wasn't good for you.*

"Are you ready, Mister Graves?" one of the witches asks.

Ready for what? he thinks.

Part of him wants to stop walking, to turn around and confront these girls for harassing him. But he's not sure that this even qualifies as harassment. And there's the other part to consider; the part that believes if he did confront them, if he reached out to lay his hand on one of them, on her shoulder, say, it would simply pass on through—

Like she's made of smoke, he thinks.

The door to the local branch of Movies-4-U stands open on the corner up ahead. James waits until the very last moment, then turns and hurries inside, glancing back to see if the Three Little Witches keep walking or follow him in. They do neither. Staring at the empty doorframe for several seconds leads him to consider two other possibilities: either they have stopped outside to wait for him or they are indeed smoke in the wind. In his shaken state, one seems as likely as the other.

Compose yourself, he thinks. If they want to hang around and wait for you, let them *wait* for you. Look around.

The long girl behind the counter looks up from a magazine, smiles her tongue bar at him, and goes back to reading. She has red hair, mostly, shocking red, a home-dye job by the look. The roots are black. Edith used to wind her finger through her hair when she concentrated, but this one plays with her mouth ornament. It looks like she's chewing a bag of screws, he thinks.

He knows what he is doing. It is a game he plays sometimes. He calls it Distraction or Look Away Now. You focus on one thing to keep yourself from looking at or thinking about another. By unfairly judging the girl behind the sales counter, James knows he is successfully *not* thinking about the Three Little Witches outside or the slight, blond woman inside, the one wavering irresistibly between the Drama and Romance sections.

Game Over, he thinks.

Late thirties, early forties. Short blond hair. Natural tan. Iris print blue silk chiffon dress that doesn't quite reach the floor.

Edith had been thirty-two. She never wore a dress after her wedding day and she hated the sun. That auburn hair of hers was never anything but shoulder length and always, always had some curl to it.

"Can I help you, miss?" he asks, the words out of his mouth before he can check himself.

"Oh. Do you work here?"

She smiles. She doesn't know it, but what it says to him is: *I am not Edith Graves. I am not a Little Witch. I am someone you have never met. I am new.* It is a good smile.

"Do I work here?" he asks, glancing over at the counter girl. She is too busy moving her tongue bar around the inside of her mouth to notice anything. "Yes. Yes, I do."

"Good. For a second there I thought you were just some creep trying to hit on me."

"Me? No," he says, reaching out a hand. "Jim. Jim...Barr."

"Maureen Hodder," she says.

"Nice to meet you, Maureen. I have a tiny confession to make. This is actually my night off."

"Really?"

Still smiling. Good.

Good.

"Sure," he says. "I mean, I'm here most nights, *obviously*. Most days too, in fact. And weekends. *All* week really. Although, when I'm not here, I work as a teacher over at Claremont High School. English Department. That's just a part-time thing though. You know, something on the side."

The wait is torturous. He feels as if his shoulders are touching his ears. Then, she smiles and in an instant all the tension evaporates.

"Well, I'm sorry to bother you on your night off, Jim Barr of Movies-4-U, but I was wondering if you could possibly help me out. See here, you seem to have put *Before Sunrise* under Romance, and its sequel *Before Sunset* under Drama. I would argue that they are both either Romances or Dramas and shouldn't be put on different shelves as they are now. And I'm sure that in your capacity as a *dedicated* employee and expert you would be inclined to agree with me."

James can't help but smile. "I *would* like to," he says. "But you'd have to let me buy you coffee first."

"I'd prefer a Mocha Latte."

"Fine, a Mocha Latte it is."

He thinks, this is wonderful, like a kind of jazz. Or an open-top car ride with the wind in your hair.

"So which one of these do you think I should rent?" she asks.

"Of the two?" James looks at the covers of both titles.

Wait, he thinks. That day after the funeral, the Three Little Witches outside my house. They said something about this...

But he doesn't want to remember, because he's been trying to forget them ever since he walked in here and laid eyes on this woman. However, Distraction is a game that by its nature can only last until the thing you are trying to forget makes its inevitable and unwelcome return.

There's no future in wasting time.

True, he thinks. But it wasn't that.

The sun will go down soon and life's too short.

Again, true.

The sun will go down soon...and maybe one of these days the sun won't come up again.

I'm doing it again, he thinks. Seeing what I want to see. One second they're three girls who like to smoke a little weed and play silly games on people, the next they're three Shakespearean witches. Back and forth, as it suits. I did it with Edith. I knew she was messing around and I turned a blind eye to it. Hell, I practically *encouraged* it. I stood back and saved that poison inside me for the day she finally confessed, thinking it would get me off the hook and we'd somehow clear the air—fool that I am.

"*Before Sunset*," he says, handing Maureen Hodder the box. "The timing seems right and I guess maybe I have a soft spot for inferior sequels."

"That is assuming we will be watching the movie together," she says.

James hopes she cannot see the falter in his smile.

"Of course, that's entirely up to you."

A few minutes later, they step outside onto a deserted sidewalk. The Three Little Witches have gone—as have the three weed-loving girls. However, the smell of cigarette smoke remains pungent in the air.

VI. The Things That Get You Through

She takes it from behind. Always from behind.

James Graves—who even after four months remains James Barr to Maureen—never puts up a fight or suggests they try switching to other positions for two reasons. One, because she has an undeniably great ass. Two, because with him working behind the scenes it means she will never see the guilt-swell of his face while they fuck. He can't help it. Sometimes this still feels like betrayal.

Every time, really.

Maureen is a good woman though; a divorcee with no time to waste. She has four children, all grown, all flown the nest. She works for an advertising agency, which means she's on the road or in the air four days out of seven. On those mornings, she leaves little notes and paper hearts lying on her pillow for James to find. He is suitably sad to see her go and suitably glad to see her back. She is moving her things into his drawers and cupboards one piece at a time. A slow home invasion. She wants to introduce him to her children and then take a trip to the east coast to meet her parents. She says the Florida sun will do him a world of good. Rid him of his pasty-coloured butt and help him get over Edith's death. He says Florida is for tourists, sunbathing is not his thing, and he got over Eedee Graves some time ago.

They are taking things slow at his request.

It is not that the days aren't good. He gets up, he takes a piss, eats breakfast, showers, drives to a place where the people that he is around, mostly high school kids, do not ask too many questions. On the first day or two, sure, there were plenty. But it wasn't quite the open forum—or autopsy—he had feared it might be. Typical, this complex and difficult thing he had built in his mind was as straightforward as popping a balloon. Eedee was right to have called him The Worry King of The Western States. Eedee, it turns out, was right about many things. Then, everyone has their plus points, he thinks. Even Hitler.

So, questions were asked, questions were answered, some with more difficulty than others, but eventually everyone in his class turned their attention back to Macbeth and the grades from their pre-holiday assignment. By day's end, one thing is clear to James Graves; his love of teaching has not waned in the slightest since Edith's death.

It is not the days.

It is not Maureen either.

It is the nights.

The nights are bad.

On this particular night, James cannot sleep. Since Eedee left him, insomnia has been no stranger, but tonight it is a visitor who simply refuses to leave. The clock on the nightstand reads 03:48 when he is awakened for the umpteenth time. Maureen lies facing him in the dark, asleep, snoring, a constant reminder of the very thing of which he is being deprived. James turns onto his side, faces the other way, faces the door. Maureen's snores cannot drown out the boom of silence emanating from the basement.

She is still down there. In the basement. His basement. Eedee the mannequin. Standing in that corner with her back to the room, listening to sounds in the walls that only she can hear. On some nights, he wonders if she listens to him, to what happens with Maureen in this bedroom he painted lilac just for her. It is another reason why he insists they keep the lights off. In darkness, he can pretend the room has no colour at all. But he is only lying to himself. He knows the lilac is always there, beyond the veil of the dark, much like his memories of Edith, stored behind the colourless appeal of Maureen. Tantalisingly out of reach. And so his mind wanders downstairs into the basement to be with Eedee. They do not talk at such times, but instead let the silence of understanding heal old wounds. An understanding that began with his confession, he believes. In this case, two wrongs do make a right, or so it feels to him in the darkest hours of the day.

But this isn't moving on, he tells himself. This isn't moving forward. It is moving *sideways* and taking someone else along for the ride.

I have to do something. I have to make this right.

It is time for another game of Distraction.

No, not tonight. Tonight, he feels he cannot commit to a game. The game is a lie, which is what it should be called. How about turning the board over and playing a different game? he thinks. Let's call this one Truth, or *Don't* Look Away Now.

Here goes.

As long as you continue to keep Eedee in that basement, you will never move forward.

A good start. Eedee is the reason he hasn't agreed to meet any of Maureen's four kids, and the real reason why he won't make that trip to Florida. And if we're playing by the rules of the game and being completely honest, he thinks, Eedee is always with me. Wherever I go, she's thereabouts, beyond the veil of the dark.

I have to take Eedee away from here. Which James knows in his guilty heart is a softer way of saying, *she has to be gotten rid of.*

The whole grieving process, rushed though it was, he realises, will count for nothing unless he removes the mannequin from this house and never looks upon her again. The things that got you through weren't necessarily the things you wanted to carry with you on the other side.

Eedee has to go, he thinks. Tonight.

He dresses in the dark, careful not to wake Maureen. Downstairs, he picks up his car keys and a roll of black plastic sacks before heading down into the basement. On the garage floor, where he made dust insects in a kind of tribute to Eedee, he uses the handsaw to remove her head. The arms and legs follow. By the time he is finished, she fills three plastic sacks. But he figures it is better this way than taking the risk of carrying her outside in the early hours of the morning and being spotted by one of the neighbours. But what if the police pull him over? Does throwing a mannequin in the city dump break any laws? He doesn't believe so. It might be a little embarrassing to explain at four o'clock in the morning, but what else can he do? He knows that if he waits for another night, he may never have the willpower to see this thing through. The situation isn't fair on anyone. The situation needs to be resolved. Now.

He opens the front door and checks the coast is clear, wishing he had left the car in the garage. But life throws a curveball sometimes and you either take a swing or strike out. You can't recapture what you had and lost, you can't simply patch it up with duct tape and expect it not to fall apart again. *It falls apart.* In the end, everything does. No game of Distraction can last forever. The street is empty. He carries the bags to the car.

One hour later, as the sun threatens to rise, James drives back into the street and parks the car in the same spot. An instant before he kills the low-beams, he thinks he sees them up ahead, the Three Little Witches. Maybe it is how the last of the moonlight falls through the trees or how the shadows move themselves around to get away, but it isn't them. Just to be sure, he waits inside his car for another five minutes, until it occurs to him that at any given moment one of the windows on the street could offer up an inquisitive face. Then he is out of the car and hurrying up the path to the front door. Then up the stairs and into the bedroom, where he undresses in a deeper darkness than the one he dressed in earlier, because in the past hour his eyes have grown accustomed to streetlamps and wild, irrational tears. The world is a blur, more so now than ever. Which isn't how this is supposed to be, he thinks. I'm supposed to be over her.

Lifting the covers, he slides into a warm bed, careful not to touch any part of Maureen's body with his street-cooled skin. If she wakes now, she could mistake him for that guy, the kind that sneaks back into the marital bed with the smell of other women on his breath. But he is not that guy, and he is glad to be home. Yet over time her sleeping stare presses at the back of his neck.

"Maureen?" he whispers. "Maureen?" And then a little louder: "Are you awake?"

The sun rises to unveil the walls in all their lilac magnificence, and he is still waiting for his answer. Reaching back, meaning to give her the gentlest of nudges, James brushes something else instead. Something his mind tells him it cannot be.

Duct tape.

Pendulum

Swing, says the pendulum.

This was supposed to be my life story. Instead, it's a tale unfinished, like a son stuck forever in a tilted uterus or some shy performer cowering in the wings with eternal stage fright. But my son arrived—to die, aged nine—following an arduous thirty-hour labour that came to nothing. In the end: ventouse. They sucked him right out of my aforementioned tilt with a bruised shoulder and a head like a football or an alien or an alien football, misshapen as the thoughts that would come to form inside it, that never did get the chance to become *shapen*, like your thoughts or...like your thoughts.

First we need to go back. I am writing this in stream of consciousness. Connected moments recorded in a continuous flow, one word, one sentence leading naturally to the next. Reducing my life to this.

This sentence.

My obstetrician looked like Steve Buscemi.

But we need to go further back than that. The pendulum swings over the same old ground every time to reach the beginning, to reach the end.

Back.

I went into labour while watching the HBO series, *Boardwalk Empire*. March 2011 that was. My waters broke, soaked the couch cushions, and to this day the season remains unwatched. Just one odd association in a story littered with them, you'll find.

Back. Let the pendulum swing all the way to the left.

Waiting. Sickness. Waiting. Cravings. Waiting. Sickness.

Peeing on sticks. A factory of sticks. Until you find the one, the golden ticket after you have already been to the factory so many fucking times.

Sex with Ellis, lots of sex. A factory of sex.

"Let's try for a baby," I said.

That was 2010. We were in a children's play park just off Venice Beach. I was twenty-three, Obama was in the White House, Katy Perry in the charts, telling us about *California Gurls* even though she was not singing about me. Ellis and I sat on the swings, two adults trying to recapture something, listening to the chains creak under the weight of our years.

"I've been thinking about killing myself," he said. "I'm so depressed. I hate my job. I hate this place. Let's go someplace else, Milly. Let's get out of here... I need to talk to you about something."

It's funny how, thinking back, Ellis starts with the line about wanting to die, just comes right out with it. Which is different to how it actually played out; the opposite, in fact. He took his time to tell me. Really built up to that shit. But as the pendulum swings back it all looks and sounds and feels so different: you pull the bandage from the wound before the wound is made. It makes it easier somehow. The scabs shrink, disappear, leave the smile of a fresh cut before the blade moves up and across your forearm to close the skin and leave behind the soft, perfect paleness of a blank page. Which is why I never liked tattoos much, because you're writing a story that can never be unwritten. Who wants that?

The sleeve unrolls down my arm.

And I get to *un*hate myself for wanting a child. It's like the tide slipping away from the shore and leaving me with the tiny, broken shells of my life gathered in the crook of my arm. Walking backwards, I get to place them back into their depressions in the sand. Lay them out across a stretch of empty beach.

"I want a baby."

Then I sit on the sand and wiggle my painted-blued toes as I stare down the retreating waves.

Let's stop here awhile. Let the pendulum hang for a moment. Let the forces exchange, one become another. Besides, there is no point going any further back than this. There is only the empty air of my life leading up to that day, aged twenty three on the sand. The pendulum can only go so far back before it stops to protect itself. Force it any farther (strange how farther sounds like father, right?) and something breaks. So let's stop awhile and let the waves stop with us. A perfect pause.

Calm.

Silence.

No friction, no drag.

Silence.

Calm.

Unpause, and the surf rolls toward me, waves rushing in like a bunch of fists at first but losing their power, their hatred, until they are fingers crawling ever-so-timidly across the sand toward the wriggling paintedness of my toes. All froth and foam and not a chance of undertow to drag me down.

"I want a baby."

I jump up and start combing the beach for shells or anything precious. At first, I pick up the prettiest shells, the smoothest ones, the most-perfect, but soon I am gladly picking up whatever I can find, seeking reassurance from the thing taking shape in the crook of my arm: my shell baby. But then I get spooked and lift my arm and with this foolish notion of having a child with Ellis I let it all fall to the ground like a bunch of collapsing bones. I hate myself for even thinking it, but then those are the ideas that tend to stick sometimes: the ones with barbs.

The sleeve rolls up my arm.

I have locked myself in the bathroom of our Venice Beach apartment. Ellis is in the bedroom playing Xbox, streaming to his building fanbase as he yells his frustration at his teammates and the television screen. The sound of the surf reaches me through the open window, a lulling effect, drowning Ellis. You step outside yourself to remember how daddy used to say it was all your fault. Mommy leaving? Your fault. Losing his job? Your fault. His being stuck in the house, looking after some kid? His kid, *your* fault. Meanwhile, Ellis rages and curses at the TV screen as you make a fist and take the cuts.

"I need to talk to you about something... Let's get out of here. Let's go someplace else, Milly. I hate this place. I hate my job. I'm so depressed. I've been thinking about killing myself."

I had sensed he was building up to something; maybe not that but something. Walking through Venice with Ellis, he took my hand and led me into some children's play park and sat me on a swing. And I was five-years-old again with my father, begging him to stop pushing the swing so hard and him laughing at my fear. He never hit me but maybe he liked to see me cry. Daddy. Ellis. Daddy with his pushing, Ellis with that way of his, how he built himself up to telling me something big, little pushes of words at first, then harder and harder until the chains went slack and it became less of a swing and more of a series of falls.

"Let's have a baby," I say.

Sex with Ellis, lots of sex. A factory of sex. Peeing on sticks. A factory of sticks. Until you find the one, the golden ticket after you've already been to the factory so many fucking times.

Sickness. Waiting. Cravings. Waiting. Sickness. Waiting.

My waters break during the seventh episode of season one of *Boardwalk Empire*. Right there on the couch in our Venice Beach apartment.

You're in labour but you decide there is time to take a shower and shave your legs while Ellis goes insane with panic. But you've got this.

Don't panic, he says, panicked.

So cute, his male ignorance.

There *are* some things you love about him.

Hospital labour ward. Pushing for hours. A Buscemi-lookalike obstetrician, a theater with a line of doctors and students observing your distended vagina, and Buscemi peering over the stubborn roundness of your belly, those piercing blue eyes of his tightening with concern. Between the doctors, the nurses, the student doctors, you have never seen so many furrowed brows. Suction, suction, suction, before finally the head, the trapped shoulder come loose, pop loose, and a child is born.

Your child.

Your fault.

Equilibrium.

Staring at his misshapen head, Ellis says, "I think there's something wrong with it."

He actually says those words.

I get as far as thinking *maybe something* isn't *right*, before I consign it to exhaustion and the fear of becoming a new mother. But maybe Ellis senses something that I cannot. That happiness is merely dancing in the cemetery. Flossing on someone else's grave.

"Maybe there's something wrong with *you*," I tell him.

Swing, says the pendulum.

Swing, says the axe.

Ellis does not argue but begins to let his absences speak on his behalf. Plugs himself into his fanbase and unplugs himself from us. And when he leaves, when he finally builds himself up to telling me he is leaving, the silence that remains feels like the sum total of all the arguments we've never had.

So infuriating, his male ignorance.

Jack is a good boy. Too good. Maybe that should be the loudest alarm bell but he is my firstborn and so my only point of reference.

As a baby there are tears but not a lot.

At two, three, four years old, there are words but, again, not a lot.

In kindergarten, he plays on his own in the sandpit or finds a quiet spot and builds towers with wooden blocks. Not towers, not really: they are Jenga blocks stacked end to end on top of each other, thin, frail structures with weak foundations, destined to fall when they reach a certain height.

I see nothing wrong with it. He builds those towers higher than anyone else in his class, and that makes mommy proud. But I mistake ambition and drive for what is really Jack's simple need for order, structure, repetition.

I start to become more...erratic, which is a soft way of saying I am a fucking mess. I miss Ellis, I hate Ellis, I miss Ellis. Back and forth.

Son of a bitch.

We see him on the beach sometimes, taking time out from *Call of Duty*. Jack is oblivious to his sperm donor being out there (I call Ellis that because he is no father to Jack; where is *that* call of duty?). We will be walking along the boardwalk, watching the street performers, Jack alongside me with one of his Jenga blocks clutched in his hand, and then I'll spot Ellis sitting not so far out on the sand that he could not see us if he just lay down his guitar and turned his head. But he never does. He is usually with a different gamer girl every time: thin girls with big chests, bright hair, tattoos, piercings.

That used to be me, I think, except for the tattoos. Now my tits are deflated, the dye long washed out of my hair, the holes closed and healed over but for the scars. Still, it's hard to see different versions of yourself out there having fun.

Living.

We usually stop at Zelda's Delicatessen for mini-donuts, although on the days I see Ellis I cannot eat, so we get them to go and head back to our apartment where I sit on the couch and smoke a joint as Jack eats a cinnamon sugar and adds to his latest tower. Both of us chasing our high.

"Mom? What was the man playing?" he asks me one time. The *only* time.

"What man?"

"The guitar man on the sand," he says. "He had a pink girlfriend. She had drawings on her neck."

He means pink-*haired* and neck tattoos and holy shit he means Ellis. His—

"Why do you wanna know?" I ask, trying not to sound defensive but sounding precisely that.

"I liked it."

"So now what? You wanna meet him? You wanna meet the guitar man and, and—what?—become his friend?"

"No..."

"Then what do you want, Jack? Because I can tell you something: the guitar man doesn't want to meet *you*." I stop, put my head in my hands. "Sorry. I didn't mean... I'm, sorry. Okay?"

Jack nods but he looks hurt in the way he always looks hurt. Like he's just swallowed a hot chip and he's trying to hold it together.

One too many tokes for me, I'm afraid. Rolling the j, I had been thinking of Ms Neck Tattoo, about the naked branches reaching up from her collar, of the trunk down the centre of her back, of the roots perhaps spreading across the skinny white cheeks of her ass, of Ellis's hands foraging around in the dirt down there, foraging around in the moist, dark dirt... Really, I just want to forget what happened. To look forward to the undoing of it all; to the unsaying of every stupid, hurtful word.

"I'm sorry," I say.

Swing forward.

"What did they do to you?" I ask.

Jack, aged seven, with a bruise blooming under his right eye that told me they had done something if not the instrument by which they did it. He stood in the corner of our kitchen, a little boxer who has never thrown a punch. I drop to his eye level to try to make some kind of connection but his gaze traces the perimeter of my face as though it is too dangerous to venture any further in. He looks everywhere but *at* me, like I am off-limits or don't exist. He's just like his sperm donor, I think. But Jack can always look at the tower, at the top and the space he aches to fill with the next block, and it *is* an ache, a biological need for structure. And just for a moment I don't blame the bullies for wanting to hurt him. Maybe they only crave some kind of a reaction, like me.

I hate myself for writing those words. Good thing the pendulum keeps moving.

Let's leave it to talk about something else. Only, it's me talking while you don't say a word in reply. You're just like him. Jack.

I can't catch a break it seems.

Have you ever watched a pendulum? You tend to take sides. To focus on one, either the left or the right, to get a feel for the swing—to see if it will go farther out or start losing its momentum. For me it tends to be the right, the end of the swing. But is it the end? We're taught to read words on a page from left to right, so maybe it's that early association. The right is the end. What if there is no end, though? What if the end is the right *and* the left and every point in-between?

Jack's favourite movie is *The Lion King*, but Sir Elton John had it all fucking wrong. Life is not a circle but an arc. A great, invisible blade, scything nearer and nearer to the centre of us. Our memories are its swing. Jack is not even his real name, you know.

Jack turns nine. I throw a party and nobody shows up, just Jack and his newest bruise. Venice, for all its oddballs and freaks, is no different from the rest of the world. When you have a child like Jack you get used to people's excuses. Hell, you make enough of them yourself. I hug him and say the other kids must have forgotten the date. He nods and retreats to his room. I can hear him in there, watching a gaming stream on his Xbox. I spent over two hundred on that thing for him to watch other people play.

Jack falls asleep watching these streams. He goes to bed early but stays awake late most nights. He keeps the volume low, so it doesn't really bother me what he's doing. As long as he eats (he does) and finishes his homework (he does; he's good at math but reads like a robot—no expression in his voice) then I don't mind. A mother just wants her child to be happy, and Jack is, in sips: I can hear him giggling in his room sometimes. I can hear it now. Such a beautiful sound. An elixir of youth pressed from the petals of the world's rarest wallflower.

Three weeks after his ninth birthday, I hear the soft snores from his bedroom and creep inside to turn everything off. The gamer Jack has been watching, sillEboy, has paused the game (some cartoonish affair called *Fortnite*) and left his chair, possibly to take a toilet break. I don't think anything of it at the time but read that gamertag backwards or in a mirror and you'll see it, if you haven't already.

Go on.

And even when I did see it, I didn't stop it. You don't, do you? You let a thing like that continue to see where it might lead. Besides, I had my hands full trying to make Jack's school take the bullying seriously. They denied it was happening. Said he was misinterpreting things. They all but said his diagnosis made him unreliable. And yet every week my boy had a new bruise somewhere on his body. *Someone* was beating on him but he would not give up the name.

There was no name.

There was no boy planting bruises on him to see what might grow. There was only ever Jack, just Jack, invisible Jack, alone with his tiny, angry fists.

Swing, says the pendulum.

Swing, says the axe.

Swing, says the little boy who can't take his father to task.

Here is the fight that led to Jack running away that night. Here is the exchange of words that led to him walking out the door.

There is no fight.

There are no words.

No name, no boy, no fight, no words.

Sometimes the momentum is already there, built up inside a situation, and you do not see it and you cannot stop it because you do not see it. You are looking the other way.

Swing.

Swing.

Swing.

Says the axe.

After we eat a late supper, leftovers from the restaurant I waitress at, Jack heads for his bedroom and settles in for another night of watching live stream video games. That night, he closes his door. He never closes his door. He closes it that night. I have seen that door open, seen that door closed a thousand times in my mind since, as the pendulum swings. It's like the bruises on his body that fade in and out of his skin, that crawl up, down, and all across his upper body and arms like some kind of weird insect train in a stop-motion movie. It's a little different every time without anything important ever really changing at all.

At eleven o'clock, Jack is in his room.

At eleven-thirty, he's gone.

At eleven thirty, *Ellis* is in Jack's bedroom, occupying the lower left-hand corner of his television screen. Ellis, sitting in a high-back racing chair, wearing a headset and mic, talking shit about the game he's playing on the rest of the screen to his two-thousand-plus audience. I turn up the volume, currently low because Jack doesn't like anything loud and maybe because he's trying to keep this thing a secret.

Ellis looks at someone off-camera. I hear a female's voice but cannot make out her words.

"Is the little creep gone yet?" Ellis responds, laughing and shaking his head in disbelief.

"Yeah," the female says. "I think so."

"That was some crazy *shee-eet* right there," Ellis say, pausing the game. "Some creepy little bastard just showed up at my door! I know, right? How'd the son of a bitch find me so fast?" Ellis scans through some of the comments scrolling up the right side of the screen. "I know! I only gave out my general vicinity, man, and boom, some kid's knocking on my door, asking me to hang out! I mean, what the actual fuck?"

The comment stream is scrolling swiftly now, a few LOLs and a *Go fuck him up, sillEboy!* among other, more graphic encouragements. At the top right-hand corner of the screen, I see a comment from Jack's gamertag, Simba0326, one second before it is pushed out of sight. *Where do you live, sillE?*

Then Ellis looks off-camera and I watch his eyes widen at the same time as his mouth falls open. The blood drains from his face. I recognise that look from when I told him I was pregnant. The urge to run. The comments stream goes crazy, scrolling upscreen almost as fast as I can read it.

What is it, sillE?

Has the creep come back?

Tell him Halloween is five months away, bruh.

Everything okay, bro?

Talk to us.

What is it?

What's wrong?

By the time I fumble with the remote and + the volume to max, Ellis has ripped off the headset, sprung out of the chair, and dropped the controller onto the floor. The game unpauses and the last thing I hear as I sprint from Jack's bedroom is Ellis somewhere behind me saying *no, no, no* in a small voice that is all but drowned out by the loud report of an automatic rifle filling Jack's bedroom.

I glance back to see the killcam tracking through Ellis's final, defenceless moments right up to the headshot that sprayed his brains.

I run from the apartment in my bare feet, leaving the door unlocked. Run down Canal Street, left onto North Venice Boulevard, right onto Dell Avenue—all the way to the Venice Canals. There is a lot of light down here and a lot of it is reflected in the still watercourse, but darkness being a deluge and not a trickle, the night cannot be held back everywhere. There are pockets all along the lit canal paths where a boy can hide.

Where a boy can become lost.

I find Jack.

I lose Jack.

His real name isn't Jack.

I lied because his real name is all I have left. Because you pray that by using a different name it will lessen the pain somehow.

It doesn't.

Jack, Peter, Paul, George, Ringo, or John—it hurts just the same.

I find him hanging from a rope tied to a tree branch outside one of the small bungalows, hidden from the canal path by a row of tall hedges. He is still swinging. Swinging. Still. His feet tapping the tree bark. Tap. Tap. Tap.

I want to scream but I can't. We scream when they come into this world, we scream when they go out. But I am not ready to unbirth my son. Not yet. So, I look at the tree, the rope, his feet. And the tapping tells me there had been purchase there had he wanted it: a way back. Which makes it worse and then better and then worse and then nothing at all.

I turn to the front door of the house. Ms Neck Tattoo has her pretty little pink head buried in the chest and arms of a man crying as many tears as drops of sperm it took to make our boy. To be fair, he doesn't know Jack is his. But who wants to be fair? Nothing about this is fair. And that axe will swing at him later, soon, moments from now, and when it does, it won't *stop* swinging, just like the boy at the end of his rope.

Let's stop here awhile. Let the pendulum hang for a moment. Let the forces exchange, one becoming another. Besides, there is no point in going any further forward than here. There is only the empty air of my life from that day. The pendulum can go only so far before it stops to protect itself. Force it any farther (funny how farther sounds like father, right?) and something breaks. Let's stop awhile and let the world stop with us. A perfect pause.

You forgot that he died, didn't you? Our son. I realise I may have made it easy for you to forget by placing it in the middle of a sentence in the middle of the second paragraph—our parenthetical boy—but still: shame on you, Ellis. You put him there.

You made him parenthetical.

I can't forget.

I won't. And neither will you.

As gravity takes over, the pendulum starts to fall, to swing back to the left, and I am running backwards along the canal path, away, away, away from that house, that tree, towards Dell Avenue, North Venice Boulevard, Canal Street, my heartbeat slowing as the fear in my veins starts to subside.

I like this part. It reminds me of the Sea Dragon ride over at Pacific Park on Santa Monica Pier—because when that back swing starts, as much as you know where it is going, you cannot see anything until it is there in front of you, rushing away from you. Untouchable.

That is how I want this thing to be. How I want to be.

Untouchable.

I am looking forward to all of this being undone, to the rope untied from Jack's neck, to the bruises fading to the colour of a punch never thrown, to taking back the Xbox, to Jack's towers of blocks unbuilding themselves one Jenga brick at a time, like a city slipping back into the marshland, to Jack pushed back inside of me by the doctor that looks like Steve Buscemi, to my cervix closing, closing, like an iris that does not want to see, to taking back the sex with Ellis, all of the sex, the words that led up to it, the words I write here, now, all of it, every brick, sperm, and word gone.

I am looking forward to the undoing of everything for it all to be done again.

I don't want to learn a thing. Fuck lessons. Besides, you don't get a chance to change what has already happened. The swing is the swing is the swing. Just ask the pendulum, or the axe, or our son. I want to *un*live and live these same moments, these same blessings, these same mistakes, over and over and over again.

Until this pendulum stops.

The Sound of Constant Thunder

Before the end I was a city council employee: a street custodian. I removed the litter they dropped on the pavement, the shit they let their dogs drop when they thought nobody was around, and the wild animals their big, fancy cars dropped on the way to their big, fancy jobs in the city. The city of No More. That was my nickname for it back then; as in, make it stop. And it was what I continued to call it after the war: No More, as in no longer there, as in vacant.

Every weekday, after eight long, back-bending hours spent removing all of the stuff they dropped, I rode my bicycle south of the city, to a small lopsided caravan stood halfway along a humpbacked dirt road between two fields. It was a beautiful spot: the headaches eased, and that din, like constant thunder in my ears, reduced to a less intrusive volume. It took me four years to find the place. Another twenty feet farther up or down the lane wasn't any good; it had to be right there. My GP called the spot an "aberration", that is, when he took my symptoms seriously for the first time following an incident outside the Old George Mall. I'd been litter-picking for thirty minutes when the Wi-Fi signal surged or something, because I fell to my knees, screaming and pressing my hands to my ears. Nobody picked *me* up. They all kept moving, like a river around some ugly-looking rock.

I wasn't making it up. At least, I didn't believe so. *Electromagnetic radiation is non-ionizing*, the doctor said. *It's harmless.* Really? I said. Tell that to my brain. Where did the crushing headaches come from? Or the noise like thunder? He was the sort of person who denied there was a war coming—until the first nukes pancaked the capital to the north, of course. Well, he was wrong about that, and he was wrong about me. We are *not* all wired the same. We are not created equal. We are snowflakes, and with just the right—or wrong—amount of heat, we melt and become nothing.

It is only when we are nothing that we become the same.

*

If that buckled front wheel on the pushchair had not given her away she would have crossed the bridge and been far away without us ever meeting. But that didn't happen. And so I lowered the dead child I'd fished out of the River Avon with my litter-picker just moments before into the wheelbarrow and covered him with a coat. Then I looked at the underside of the bridge and tried to figure out whether that clicking sound posed a threat or not. The stories my mother used to read to me had got it all wrong: the trolls tended to be the ones crossing the bridge rather than lurking under it. But I had not seen anyone in a month—no rabbits in three—and I wanted to hear someone else's voice, someone other than my father, gone sixteen years and yet still dishing out his judgement.

You're the cancer, son. I can't even look at you without thinking of everything that went wrong with her. You're the cancer.

I emerged from underneath the bridge into what should have been the midday sun but was, since the war, something closer to dusk. The sky was full of cloud, black on top, red underneath; ash on sunlight; dirt on anger. According to the last person to cross the bridge, a man in his fifties from Amesbury way, strong winds had blown most of the nuclear winter north from London, which explained why he had been heading south and why the sun with some effort could still make it through to us down here. He told me he was heading for the coast, which seemed true of most of the wanderers who approached the bridge from the north. I asked him why the coast, and he mumbled something about how in a time of crisis you should point yourself away from the source and head for the edges, where it's safer. I didn't know anything about that, it sounded like something he had made up just to keep his feet moving, but he said it with such conviction that for a whole hour after he'd gone it seemed to make all the sense in the world. I don't know, maybe the man from Amesbury was onto something; or maybe he walked himself straight into a gang of eaters. Either way, I was staying put. Before all of this happened, I'd made a promise to the rabbits that I would look out for them, and a promise was a promise was a promise.

The woman did not see me until she almost ran me over with

the pushchair. Startled, she jerked it to a sudden halt in front of me. Fortunately, the baby did not wake up. The woman looked at me. She was in her thirties, although surviving the war had aged us all by at least a decade, with dirty skin and medium-length hair, black, knotted at the ends, at the middle, at the roots. She looked at me as if I wasn't there. I noted her long, delicate fingers, the knuckles white from gripping the pushchair handles too long. She might have been pretty, once and long ago, but now she only looked at me and through me as though she were counting the dead flowers on the grass behind my back.

You'd have to be *really* distracted to bump into anyone in a world with so much space, I thought.

That morbid notion amused me, and maybe it was the smile on my lips that kept her from running off or pulling a weapon. She just went on looking. Finally, she seemed to snap out of it and positioned herself in front of the pushchair to shield the sleeping child.

"What's the little one's name?" I asked to break the ice or rather, the iceberg. I'd said 'little one' because it was impossible to tell whether it was a boy or a girl from the wisp of dark brown hair I saw poking out from its blanket wrap. And then there was the woman herself, blocking my...my what—attack? Her eyes shuttled between my face and the litter-picker I still held in my hand.

"This?" I said. "Oh, this is nothing. Not a weapon anyway." Attempting to demonstrate my point I picked up a wilted daffodil from the ground, but it fell apart and a breath of wind scattered its faded petals. "I use it to pick up litter," I said. And the occasional dead baby from the river, I thought but did not add. "That was my job, before. Please, don't be afraid of me. I'm Alan."

A tremor crossed her lips, and I realised that she might be smiling on the inside. "Alan, my name is Charlotte," she said. "And I'm not afraid of you."

There was something pretty about her, after all. Somehow it found its way through the dirt on her skin and the smell of her clothes.

"Hey," I said. "Would you like something to eat? For you and the baby, I mean. I have food."

Charlotte glanced over her shoulder at the pushchair. "Ella's still on the breast, but I would love something if you've got enough to spare— if this isn't an inconvenience..."

"No, no inconvenience at all," I said. "I live here, in a tent there under the bridge. I've got some tinned food round here somewhere— soup and vegetables mostly—and there's some cream crackers in one of the rabbit holes on the bank. They let me hide a few things down there in case somebody tries to steal from me again."

"They let you," Charlotte said with a smile; this one she wore on the outside. "The rabbits?"

I shrugged, and nodded. "They're my friends."

*

A glorious morning before the end. The kind of morning that made me glad I had an outdoors job; the kind that could make me almost forget the thrumming in my skull as I neared the city. Almost.

As I often did on New Bridge Road, I stopped halfway across the bridge and climbed off my bicycle to gaze down at the river. Traffic whooshed to-and-fro behind me as the waters flowed underneath us all, slow and steady. A short distance downstream, an old oak leaned halfway across the river with its branches lowered just far enough to trace the surface. Cool water ran between its wizened fingers.

I tensed as someone blasted a horn behind me three times to make their point: a point that was lost on the river and lost on the tree. But not so much on the rabbits, who popped out of several holes near the riverbank, five rabbits in all, ears pricked, eyes widened with alarm. I had time to wonder, in the moments after they vanished again with flashes of white, how deep their burrows would need to reach before they completely escaped the sound of the traffic on the bridge. Or did the racket vibrate down through the bridge's foundations, into the earth, into their home, and chase them through tunnel after tunnel into the deadest but noisiest ends?

I decided to be late for work that morning.

I walked my bicycle back across the bridge, around, and down onto the riverbank. The traffic noise continued to spill over the barrier and fall into that peaceful pocket like a waterfall into a soup bowl; the voice of the river silenced by the rip of tyres across tarmac and the clearing of so many throats by the blasting of horns. Never had so many with so little to say been quite so desperate, it seemed, to carve out the opportunity to say it.

I lay my bike on the grass, found a space between the rabbit holes, sat down, and massaged my head as I listened to the river struggle to find its own voice in the din.

Do they scream down there? I thought. Where no-one can hear. Do they think about bashing their heads against the buried rocks until either the rocks or their skulls split apart?

I massaged my head and knew that they did.

I was two hours late for work that morning.

I was late three times that week. My supervisor gave me a verbal warning in an email and then again in a letter, which I held in my hand and looked at, confused. People didn't talk to each other anymore. They'd forgotten what the word meant.

And so I stopped picking up the litter on the city streets—I said no more to No More—and focussed instead on tidying up that stretch of river. If I could not do anything about the traffic noise then I could at least do *something*. I picked up the litter that collected at the water's edge so that the rabbits would have a clear spot on which to stand when they wanted to drink. I picked up the plastic bottles and the sweet-wrappers and the cigarette ends that drivers threw out of their car windows onto the grass. I did that, and more, every day, until my supervisor discovered that my assigned streets were not getting their due attention. He handed me my second verbal warning without saying a word. I took it and went right back to the river, where I talked to the rabbits while they took turns lying out in the sun and listening to everything I had to say.

We became friends. More than that, we became brothers—brothers in arms united against the sounds of constant thunder: Wi-Fi and tyres; tyranny and horns.

But every storm reached its climax, usually that moment when it landed on your doorstep. For the rabbits, it was the deafening convoy of armoured vehicles crossing the bridge and heading north. For the rest of them, the storm landed a few days later, when the first nuclear strike on their capital killed millions.

After that, the world seemed to draw a long, ragged breath, and fall blissfully silent.

*

Charlotte agreed to stay for something to eat but maintained what I suspect *she* thought was a safe distance. I wanted to tell her that she was kidding herself, that she could be reached no matter where she put herself in the world, but I thought better of it just in time. When it doesn't hurt, the truth can frighten, and I did not want her running off. So I built a fire while she continued to relax and build her walls of illusion. Behind these walls she tended to her baby's needs, washed it in the river, changed its nappy, whispered private things into its ear. I gave them their time together.

Fire gave us light and warmth and something at which to stare and distract our thoughts. Like when I glimpsed Charlotte unbuttoning her shirt and scooping out a breast in order to feed the child: the heat from the flames disguised the warmth that rose into my cheeks, and the snap-crackle of the burning firewood hid any suckling sounds. Thank God. Finally, she covered herself and put the baby down for the night inside the tent. She wrapped it well. Days were cold enough, but nights—nights were deadly.

"You've got a good one there," I said from the other side of the fire. "Quiet, well-behaved. Even so, it must be difficult for you, you know, on your own with a baby—with the world the way it is now."

The flames doused Charlotte's face with a pleasant orange glow. She'd washed herself in the river too, after bathing the child. The dirt was gone from her skin but her clothes still carried an awful smell.

"Why do people say that?" she asked.

"Say what?"

"That you're on your own with a baby. It's contradictory. You're never alone with a baby. You *have* the baby."

I laughed nervously. "It's one of those stupid things people say, I suppose. Sorry." We stared into different sides of the fire for a moment. "According to my father," I continued, "I say—and do—a lot of stupid things."

Charlotte looked at me across the tops of the flames. "We're all guilty of that, Alan. Don't be too hard on yourself."

"He used to tell me I entered the human race from a standing start. That I'd never amount to anything. He disappeared when I was thirteen, two years after my mother died. He never got to see me grow up and become nothing. He would have been really proud of himself. Being right was what he lived for. What's the little one's name?"

"Ella," she said.

"That's a pretty name. Does she have a father? I mean, is he still alive?"

Charlotte gave a slow shrug. "I don't know, and truthfully, I don't care. He never gave one shit about us before the end so why would he give one now it's every man and prick for himself?" She laughed to take some of the bitter indignation out of her words, but the wound was unmistakable; deep, raw. "Love is listening to someone else's madness and not listening to your own. To hell with him. Life goes on. Nothing dies, it just changes, right?"

"... Right," I said, looking beyond the fire and across the darkened river—at the man stood on the far bank, half-in half-out of the shadows, watching us.

*

My eyes snapped open on a starless sky and the kind of darkness you might find at the bottom of a well. I heard the river flowing somewhere beyond the ends of my feet, but it seemed far off, like an echo from my dream. I listened for other sounds, and heard nothing. Charlotte and her daughter, Ella, were fast asleep in my tent underneath the bridge, while I lay on the riverbank twenty feet away. The fire was out. The air smelled and tasted of ash.

Why won't you teach me how to swim?

Something I've learned: memories can be thrown away, but they end up in the landfill of your dreams.

We were in my father's Toyota, me in the back, the two of us having one of our conversations via the rear-view mirror; the only time I was ever able to hold his gaze for more than a few seconds. Objects—and fathers—may appear closer than they really are.

Why won't you teach me how to swim? I heard myself ask again.

Because you have that look about you, he said.

What look? I asked.

The look of someone built to drown.

At which point the memory warped itself into my dream, or my nightmare rather, as my old man's eyes went from looking at me perched in the gap between the two front seats, me hanging on his every word like some starving bird praying for a crumb, to them stretching wide an instant before the rear-view mirror glass blew out to let countless gallons of water flood inside the car and wash us both away.

At which point I woke up. On my back. Poised under a night sky or above a deep well: soaring, familiar space, dark, clutching water; not sure which.

I sat up, tried to shake the dream from my head, then got up to pace the stretch of riverbank. The darkness was pitch. Only the whisper of the tall grass against my legs convinced me that up was up and down was down and that the dream was finally over. I turned myself to face the river, my one true friend, constantly carving out his own bed but never actually sleeping in it, choosing to talk—*and* listen—to me instead, and

I peered at the far side for the man who'd watched us earlier.

If he was still there, the darkness refused to give him up.

For now.

But he would be back tomorrow, that monster of a man with his particular taste. I knew that much. Perhaps on the other side of the river.

Perhaps not.

*

In the morning, the sun rose somewhere behind the cloud-veil and reverted night to dusk. Charlotte emerged from the tent underneath the bridge with a blanket around her shoulders, looking almost refreshed. She spotted the soft billows of steam rising from the pot over the fire, and smiled.

"Please tell me that is for coffee," she said.

I lifted a cup and shook it gently in the air. "Since you're my guest, you can use it first."

"There isn't another one?"

"Cup? No. I didn't expect the company."

"Why, thank you, Alan. I really appreciate it. I haven't so much as sipped a coffee in a fortnight."

Last night, she'd told me how she'd spent the first weeks of the conflict barricaded in a country hotel in Wales. She'd been there for a business conference and had brought her daughter along only because the child minder had cancelled at the last minute. Conditions had been good, she'd said, until the pantries were picked clean. Then things quickly went sour: guests became survivors. She fled, taking Ella.

"I wish I had some eggs to give you," I said. "Or some bread for toast. Or some butter *for* the toast. But all I've got are Jacob's crackers and some cheese and pickle, if you want it."

"That's fine, Alan. Thank you."

"I had a live chicken for almost five days. But an eater stole it," I said. "I'll make a trip into town later if you want—if you're going to be staying for more than a day or two..." The words hung in the air as I poured the hot water into the cup and let the scent of instant coffee drift into the silence between us.

"I hope you like it black," I said. "They've made off with all the cows from around here too. All the cartoned milk has turned sour as well. There's no cows, no hens, no sheep, dogs, cats, mice, squirrels—

everything's gone except the rabbits. And that's down to me being here to guard them. Otherwise, they'd have been dug up a long time ago, too." I offered Charlotte the cup. She took it, smiling, and sat down beside me. She smelled bad, worse than last night, like she needed a whole day in the river rather than a five-minute dip, but then she had on a Stones World Tour T-shirt, the one with the lips and the tongue, and the tongue kind of rolled itself out and over the swells of her breasts and—and I suppose I convinced myself that the smell wasn't too bad after all. She took a mouthful of coffee, just plain old Nescafe out of a one kilo tub, swallowed, and gave the kind of sigh a man tried hard not to forget. And I found myself wondering how she might react to the good stuff, to a Starbucks or a Costa, to an Espresso or a Cafe Mocha. Oh Lord, the possibilities...

"What are you smiling at?" she asked finally.

I blushed and looked away, toward the river, at the cold empty space on the opposite bank. Within seconds the heat left my face again, and my cheeks returned to their usual colourless colour.

"How's Ella?" I asked.

"Asleep," she said. "I'll see to her soon. Thank you for letting us use the tent last night."

"No problem. I often sleep out here anyway. It's good, and it helps."

To see him coming, I thought but did not say.

Another quiet divided us for a while. We sat and listened to the fire and watched the river and thought our thoughts. Charlotte threw back the last of her coffee and then after gazing at the grim-looking clouds not so far over our heads, she said, "Do you think they'll ever clear? I'm starting to forget a lot about the old things: the taste of coffee...what the stars look like on a clear night...*clear nights*. Other things too."

The warmth returned to my face, and I stood and moved away from the fire and Charlotte and the tongue on her T. I spotted the litter-picker lying in the grass, scooped it up on the go, and walked down to the water's edge. Lowering the picker's claw into the flow, I felt the river try to pull it free of my grasp. Part of me wanted to let go, perhaps so I could turn my back on my responsibilities, but another part told me to tighten my grip.

"This river used to be full of bodies," I said, recalling the early days after the end, when the world and its Wi-Fi had come to a sudden stop and I emerged from my caravan into this new place, this new world, headache-free and thinking clearly for the first time in my life. "Children, mostly," I said. "Babies. Don't ask me why or how they ended up in here—I don't know. But something I've learned from my job is: people throw away the things they think they don't need or the things they can no longer afford to keep. Anyway, I stood right up there on the bridge and watched them go floating downriver. Some of them spun like stars. And I started to play a game. Whenever I saw one pass under the bridge I had to hold my breath for five seconds. There was this one day when they just kept coming and coming and coming, and I—I nearly passed out."

"Why don't you leave?" Charlotte's voice behind me: dry, cracked, drained of the oil of its earlier suggestion. Confusingly, that came to me as a relief.

"And go where exactly?" I answered. "I'm needed here. I'm wanted here. I still have a job to do. I'm guarding these rabbits. Eaters have slaughtered everything else. There's nothing left—only what passes through the city, and they'll have that too if they can."

"Is what we're talking around here cannibalism?" Charlotte asked.

"I just call them eaters," I said. "There was one hanging around here last night."

"WHAT? Why didn't you say something?"

I turned around. The appalling smell in the camp struck me anew and almost sent me stumbling backward into the water. I glanced at the rabbit holes farther up the bank and wondered if the bad breath was coming from one of those small mouths...if down there in the dark there might be some rotten, decomposing things...

No. I refused to believe it...because of what lay inside the wheelbarrow underneath the willow tree on the edge of the camp, hidden behind the veil of branches and a waterproof jacket.

"He was on the other side of the river," I said, attempting to calm her down but seeing by the reaction of her face that I was failing miserably. I decided to try a different tack. "Look, I've seen him before. He's one of a half-dozen or so who have stayed in these parts. The rest moved on a long time ago. This one comes around from time to time and watches—from over there." I pointed at the far side of the river. "Usually it's for a couple of days. Once he realises that he won't find what he's looking for around here, he steals something and goes off on his merry way. Usually."

Charlotte stood and folded her arms. The lips on her T-shirt became more of a pout as her breasts squeezed together underneath. "*Usually?*" she said.

"I've never been a good liar."

No, you're the cancer, son.

"As I said," I went on, "I've seen this one around here before. He seems to have a particular...preference. It's why he keeps coming back to the river."

There was a pause, and then we both turned at the same time to look at the tent underneath the bridge.

Charlotte shook her head vigorously. *No.*

I said nothing. I'd never been a good liar. My father, on the other hand, was not only a good one but the best.

"I have to get her out of here," Charlotte said, panic rising in her voice. "If Ella's in any danger then I have to go, leave, right now."

"Go where?" I asked, exasperated. I had it on the good authority of others who had come this way and gone that and were never seen again—by me at least—that: "There is nowhere to go and everywhere's the same. Please. Stay here. With me. I'll protect you both."

"Bournemouth," she said. "That's where I was heading before you stopped me. I'll go there. There's supposed to be a treatment centre, right out on the pier. I'll be able to get Ella checked over."

"You'll never make it," I said. "It's too dangerous. The eaters have set up ambushes along all of the major roads. Taking the A338 won't be an option. You'd have to use back roads the entire way or else go cross country. No, you're safer here, Charlotte."

"We made it this far on our own," she said. "I think we can make it to sodding *Bournemouth*." Her tone softened. "Why don't you come with us? It's not as though there's anything here for you. Throw that stupid thing away and come along."

I glanced down at the litter-picker in my hand. How could she possibly understand? I looked back at her, and gave a slow shake of my head.

"I can't," I said. "I still have a job to do here. A promise is a promise is a—"

She spread her arms as wide as the world.

"*What* job, Alan?" she said. "What bloody job?"

I waited until the echoes of her voice died down before I walked over to the willow tree and pushed the wheelbarrow out from behind its screen of branches. Charlotte watched me in silence. I wanted to talk about coffee some more; I wanted to feel that heat rise in my cheeks again; I wanted to...never mind.

The tall grass at the top of the riverbank tried its best to tangle itself in the wheel, but I fought and pushed my way through it until I stood on the pavement at the beginnings of the bridge. Finally, I turned to Charlotte.

"I'm going into the city for some supplies." I hoped she did not hear the nerves in my voice. "You're going to need some things for the road. Please—don't leave until I get back, okay? Stay here and look after your daughter."

She gave me a hard look. "What if this—this *eater* sees you gone and decides to make his move?"

A good question. I glanced down at the blue waterproof jacket spread across the top of the wheelbarrow. There was a waft of algae and early decomposition from underneath it. I realised that the smell was similar to that which had invaded the camp and clung so doggedly to Charlotte's clothes and skin. Maybe it clung to mine too, only I hadn't noticed.

"He won't," I said. "You'll be safe."

Charlotte looked unsure. "How do you know that?"

I started up the gentle rise of the bridge.

"Because he'll be coming after me."

*

Walking into the city felt different from all of the times I'd done it before the war. The streets were deserted—of the living anyway; the dead, mainly adults, lay everywhere, too rotten even for the eaters. The quiet seemed bottomless. But it was hard to miss people and their prattling when your skull was filled with helium and silence. No Wi-Fi, no headaches. It was as if the storm-clouds in my head had leaked out through my ears and packed the sky instead, taking all of the pressure and thunderous noise with them.

Everything was covered in broken glass. With fat clouds smothering the sun, the glass had no sparkle. It was strange, because you could see that it *wanted* to. Maybe it was time for the world to be grey and the people to shine rather than the other way around. A switching of places.

I felt a little guilty that things had had to end for me to feel better, but I couldn't do anything about it or take it back. And would I if I could when the world and the people in it had only ever held me down?

The broken glass crunched under the wheelbarrow's tyre as I walked on. I listened for a sign of someone following. Not Charlotte: I hoped that she had listened to me and stayed put with Ella in the camp. No, the eater. Gollum to my Frodo. Which I supposed made the child's corpse lying in the wheelbarrow the precious.

As good a name as any, I thought.

I remembered my father telling me in another one of our car journeys to or maybe from the hospital that if my mother beat the cancer he would like her to give him a second child. Another boy, he hoped. I asked him what they would call him, my little brother, and dad looked at me in the rear-view mirror and said, "Alan. I always liked the name but it never really stuck with you."

My mother never did give him that second child, and the trips in the car stopped a couple of weeks later. Then, every time my father said my name it was obvious to anyone that he wanted to take it back. That he wanted to take it all back.

Halfway along Exeter Street I stopped and lifted the waterproof jacket from the wheelbarrow. Using the litter-picker, I lifted out the five-litre jerry can and stood it on the road. I flipped the hinged lid and pulled out a length of siphoning hose. I left the wheelbarrow where it stood to inspect the nearby cars for my mark. In this case, an 'X' below the left wing mirror did not mark the spot but instead a vehicle with an empty fuel tank. When I found one without the mark, I siphoned enough fuel for a fifteen pound baby. And a little extra to be sure. Then I returned to the wheelbarrow and stood the can on top of the waterproof jacket. I looked around. No one was watching me. The fine hairs on the back of my neck weren't standing to attention but perfectly relaxed.

No one was watching.

I continued along Exeter Street until I reached 92, a number with no particular significance other than it allowed me access to a rear garden from which the cathedral spire was hidden from me—and me from it. There was a four-foot pit, already dug. An empty washing line hung limply between two metal poles, the only reminder that anyone had ever used the place as a garden. All of the grass was gone; half of the space taken up by the pit, the other by huge mounds of dark earth.

I threw the jacket onto the floor of the hole. There was no way I could ever wear that thing again anyway. I took the litter picker from its belt clip and used the grabber to first lift the child out of the wheelbarrow and then slowly lower it into the hole. I lay him on the jacket's padded inner lining and arranged his limbs in such a way that he looked less like a casualty, more like a boy at peace. Then I poured on the petrol. I saw the jacket lining darken as it absorbed the beginnings of the fuel, and then I looked away.

You remind me of everything that went wrong.

My father. Right on cue.

And if I stick around any longer I'm going to drink myself to death or hate you forever. Probably both.

The jerry can grew light in my hands as that all-too-familiar smell filled the air. Some people liked the smell. Not me.

I drew the matchbox from my pocket and stared at it in my hand.

"Cook's Matches."

I wanted to laugh, but nothing was funny. So I muttered a few words under my breath and lit one of them, watching it burn itself down until half of it was no more than a black and twisted thing. Then I spread my fingers and let it fall.

That familiar sound, like a soft explosion, and then all of the air in the tiny space that used to be a garden, all of the air inside my lungs was sucked into the pit's dark and hungry mouth.

I stood back, out of its searing breath, and let the precious burn.

*

Exeter Street was empty.

As I pushed the wheelbarrow across the broken glass and wove around the abandoned vehicles, I began to wonder where he might have hidden himself. Maybe he was lurking behind one of the doors, a shadow hunched behind frosted glass, or maybe he watched me through an eyehole or from behind the curtain of an upstairs window; any window, for that matter. But I saw nothing, and worse: I sensed nothing. Meanwhile, the smell of the pit-fire clung to every part of my body. I could feel its smoky fingers lingering too long in my hair. I felt unclean, and I considered drinking the dregs of the jerry can to rid my mouth of its taste.

Sometimes I hated my job.

I picked up the things other people didn't want and threw away, and I got rid of them, whatever *they* were; I put them out of the way. The end took away my headaches and I owed it something in return: a chance of a clean start. No dead child dumped in that river was ever going to be someone's next meal. Not on my watch.

All the burnings in the world won't get rid of the cancer, son. Not unless you go ahead and throw yourself on there, too.

"Where are you?" My raised voice echoed up and down the empty street. "Come out and face me." I waited. Nothing stirred; the breeze too weak to move so much as dust. I lifted the jerry can from the wheelbarrow and flung it high and far. It spun slowly through the air and took an age to land. I braced for—I don't know—an explosion or perhaps just a loud clang, but it landed squarely on its side in the middle of the street with the disappointing sound of a hollow drum struck once and weakly. "Son of a bitch," I said under my breath. "Why aren't you here?"

Why won't you teach me how to swim?

I had the answer to my first question a moment later when a woman screamed. Once, then abrupt silence.

The silence lengthened and grew terrifying. It crawled all over my dirtied skin.

You have that look about you.

What look?

The look of someone built to drown.

I snapped into a run, splinters of broken glass spraying from my heels.

*

I stopped on the bridge to catch my breath. Below, the river flowed past an empty bank. The fire was out, the firewood scattered as if there had been a struggle. I spotted footprints in the ashes. The only sounds were the river and the breeze whispering through the tops of the tall grass. Fifty feet back from the river, the willow tree stood on the edge of a field that cattle had once grazed in. Now there were only some graves I had dug in the early days. Under the willow, behind its umbrella of branches, I saw him standing behind Charlotte with a hunting knife pressed to her throat. I looked away again, quickly. I had not seen them. I was looking around for clues of her whereabouts and I had not seen them. I crossed the bridge and walked into the long grass. From the corner of my eye, I watched for sudden movement or a spray of crimson. Either would force me into action. The litter picker was fastened to my belt loop, but I had no weapon.

Staying close to the bridge, I walked down the riverbank to the walkway underneath. The camp smelled of death. I wondered if any of those graves had been dug up during one of the nights, its contents exposed to the air. I stopped at the tent and thrust my head inside, looking for Charlotte's daughter. She wasn't there. The whole campsite reeked of death and decomposition. I went to the river. I cleaned the stench of the fire-pit from my face and hands. I stood, turned, and risked a glance at the tree. No one had moved: the eater, Charlotte, and the new thing I saw—the bundle lying on the ground at their feet. Ella. I looked around for something I could use. The firewood would crumble on impact. A rock. But there was nothing small enough to pick up unnoticed and nothing large enough to inflict enough damage. He would get a bruise; Charlotte would get her throat opened up.

Then I thought of something.

I moved into position, turned and faced the tree.

"Come out," I said. "I know you're there."

They edged forward together. Both of Charlotte's hands gripped the forearm he had pressed into the underside of her jaw to expose her neck. She looked petrified. Tears slipped slowly from the corners of her eyes.

He was the antithesis of the word "eater": malnourished and weak-looking, his face gaunt. There was hair missing from his head too, clumps of the stuff. Burns on the side of his neck. I felt anger rise through me. Whether he escaped today with any food or not, he was a dead man. One week, two, a month at a push. Radiation sickness was eating *him*.

"What do you want?" I asked.

His eyes were lifeless as the nuclear sky. "You know what I want," he said. "You've been keeping them all to yourself. Keeping them and, and *spoiling* them. It's my turn now. A man's got to eat. Do you understand? A man's got to eat." Saying the words brought tears to the eater's eyes. He blinked and shook them off like annoying flies.

"That can't happen," I said. "But I can give you food. Take it. It's yours. Take it all. Just leave the—"

He pointed the knife right at me. He was thirty feet away, moving slowly toward me, and in his imagination cutting my face into ribbons.

"No," he said. "*No*. I want the meat, man. *Protein*. I'm not interested in anything else you've got. I'm taking the kid. You can have the bitch—I'll come back for her later—but the baby's mine and it's coming with me."

Charlotte screamed; a shrill, desperate cry. The eater tilted her head farther back and warned her to keep quiet. "You don't want to wake the baby," he said. "Believe me. You don't want her to be awake."

Charlotte twisted in his grip, but despite her best efforts and his lack of weight he had the strength of desperation on his side. He adjusted his hold and pressed the tip of the knife into her neck, drawing a trickle of blood. Charlotte closed her eyes and stopped struggling.

I stole a glance at the area in front of them. They moved to within a few feet of one of the rabbit holes. I willed my friends to stream out of there and climb his body, to go to work on his face and eyes with their large incisors, but nothing happened. They were gone. I was guarding an empty warren and they were never coming back. If they had survived the clamour and stress of the war then they were probably far, far away by now, in a new warren, breathing air that wasn't killing them softly. The rabbits were gone and all that was left was a hole in the ground. A hole in the ground was my only hope.

And the eater stepped over it.

My heart sank all the way down to my feet.

I raised empty hands. "Take her. She's yours. I can't stop you."

Charlotte let out another scream. The eater pushed her toward me, and sent her sprawling in the grass. She was on her feet again in a second though, rushing back toward him with no thought other than to retrieve her baby. As he backed toward the tree and his prize, the eater lifted the knife to his face and held it across his mouth. Its curved blade resembled a cruel smile.

Charlotte stopped, dropped to her knees in front of him, and begged for her daughter's life. Both of them were crying, albeit from different kinds of hunger. Charlotte walked toward him on her knees. He took another step backward.

Into the rabbit hole.

We all heard the sound of the bone crack, but only one of us felt the pain. He stumbled backward, dropping the knife on the ground, and reached down to try and free his foot from the hole. When he realised what he had done, he reached back with one hand and searched frantically for the weapon.

Charlotte fell upon him then, raining blows like bombs. He tried to protect his face with his hands and arms, but too many made it through. Blood ran from his eyebrow, from his nose, from his ears as Charlotte pummelled him to within a minute of his life. She did so in eerie silence, other than the huffs and puffs of her exertion, and then a thought occurred to me: She doesn't want to wake the baby.

I found the knife and pulled Charlotte from on top of him. She fell onto her side on the ground beside him, gasping but kicking at his injured foot. He had meant to eat her child just as he had eaten others, and I felt reluctant to stand between them, but finally I did. Holding the knife in one hand, I helped him to his feet with the other. When he was upright, swaying but just about able to support himself, I pressed the knife to his back and said, "Walk."

He walked. Or rather, with a broken ankle, he limped.

He limped down to the riverside.

He limped into the shallows.

And then, when I told him to keep going, he shook his head and put up one final struggle, which I cut short with a slash of the knife across his back.

"Either you walk into this river," I said, "or I give her this and I walk away."

He chose the river, and made it halfway across before the strong current swept him off his injured foot and carried him away. I stood in the shallows and watched his struggle to keep his head above water. He went under once, twice, a third time, and that was the last I saw of him before the river carried him under the next bridge and out of sight.

Maybe he made it up for air a fourth time.

Maybe he made it.

Charlotte stood behind me. I turned and saw her cradling a tightly-wrapped bundle in her arms. I smiled, but Charlotte was outraged.

"Why did you let him go? He was going to kill—*eat*—my daughter."

"I didn't let him go," I said. "I gave him a chance."

The same chance my father gave me, I thought.

Charlotte walked away. She would come back to me later, by the fire, when the night had leeched all of the light and colour out of the day and time and distance and firelight had given her the opportunity to reflect; she would come back and she would be grateful for what I had done.

Meanwhile, I remained in the shallows after she left to tend to her daughter, watching the long, reaching tendrils of river algae, striving to understand what it reached for, what—if anything—it hoped to catch.

*

Later, I huddled close to the fire. But no matter how close I sat, I felt cold. I put on an extra coat; it made no difference. I sat there, shivering, in two coats right next to the flames. There was a frost in my bones.

The eater was gone but Charlotte paced the camp for hours, cradling Ella in her arms, the baby wrapped as always in blankets, a lone wisp of dark brown hair visible from the top of her cocoon. Charlotte sang to her in a low voice; a lullaby. Between the sound of her voice and the song of the river, I wanted to let everything go and fall and fall and fall.

At some point Charlotte put Ella down inside the tent. Their tent. I would offer it to Charlotte tomorrow before she left. She approached the fire and stood on the other side, staring down at me. I waited for her to share whatever it was she was thinking. The tension between us had not faded since that afternoon. I knew that I had killed that man, even if Charlotte doubted it, and now words seemed far beyond my reach. Charlotte, meanwhile, roved the camp like a confined animal. I looked up and across the tops of the flames into the shadows of her face. Her pupils looked huge in the low light, hungry as pits. I ached to burn inside them.

Then suddenly I had some words to share with her.

"A man came through here," I began, "not long after the bombs fell. He told me about this—I dunno—this *thing* that was going to go down on Salisbury Plain. Some kind of orgy or something, right out in the open air. In plain sight of God, he said. One big fuck you to Him and the world. Hundreds of people were going to take part. Thousands, maybe."

"Did you go?" she asked.

"I didn't see the point. I wasn't sick or dying or desperate. I wasn't even angry with the world. I told him I wasn't interested."

"What did he say?"

"Nothing. He went on his way, recruiting or whatever he called it. But I—I couldn't seem to let the thing go. I kept thinking about all those people out there and what they were getting up to...I just had to take a look. So on the day he'd said it was going to happen, I waited until near enough dark then hiked out there." I stopped for a breath. Despite the smell of death lingering in and around the camp, it tasted all right, pretty good even. Maybe I was growing accustomed to the smell. Maybe I just really needed the air. "Anyway, by the time I arrived it was dark. I could barely see my own hands in front of my face. But I thought my eyes would adjust given time, so I kept on walking. Then, then I stumbled on something. I felt around in the dark. It was a body. I got up and walked two steps and tripped again. Another body. I got up, same thing happened again. And again. And again. And so on, until eventually I just stopped walking and stood right where I was, too frightened to move, too frightened to breathe, listening to their so-called fuck you to everything; this big statement they'd wanted to make. And do you know what it sounded like?"

"What?"

"Silence."

She circled the fire and sat next to me on the grass. She was looking at me in an odd way; intensely focussed. I drew the back of my hand across my mouth, assuming I had something stuck there that had caught her attention. "What?" I asked.

"I forgot to thank you," she said. "For coming back."

"I never should have left you alone here. I took a stupid risk and I was wrong."

"No, Alan, you saved us."

"In that case, I'm sorry I put you in a situation that left you needing to be saved."

Charlotte smiled. Her teeth were white. How long before they started to turn yellow? To rot? There was still plenty of toothpaste left in the world but toothpaste only bought us a little more time; sooner or later, we would need dentists. And dentists were the least of what we needed. We were falling, all of us, and clutching at air.

I shifted uncomfortably next to her. She moved closer.

"You have trouble accepting compliments, don't you?" she asked.

I looked at her. Her teeth were white and there were no dentists.

But her teeth were white *now*.

I shrugged.

She leaned in to kiss me. I leaned away.

"What are you doing?"

"Let's make a statement of our own," she said, and laid a lingering kiss high upon my cheek.

Before she could move away, I turned and found her lips with mine.

We kissed then, for an age. Until the odour lingering on her clothes dampened my passion—temporarily, anyway. It only put me in an even greater hurry to remove her from them, to peel the rotten skin from the sweet fruit inside. If she saw the clothes land on the fire, she did not speak up in protest. If anything, each blossom of flame mirrored our rising enthusiasm.

I did my best. But she was my first, and though I tried to make it last forever—and then to just make it last—it was over much too soon: for me and, I suspect, for her.

Later, at some unknown hour, as we lay side-by-side with the grass at our backs, the smell—the terrible smell—crawled back inside the camp. Or perhaps with my distraction spent, I detected it once again. Charlotte lay asleep beside me, snoring softly. I got up in deep darkness and moved carefully around the camp, avoiding the rabbit holes while

I attempted to trace the smell to its source. There was death all around us, every second, every day, but the smell had grown stronger, and in darkness with no other senses to rely on, it was almost overpowering.

As I walked toward the river's edge, it grew stronger. Mixed with the smell of river algae it became particularly unpleasant. I turned my head to the left, seeking a pocket of freshness, if there *was* one to be found anywhere in that camp, and found myself gazing underneath the bridge—at the dome-like shape of the tent.

I walked closer, and my heart sank. I unzipped the flap and pushed my head through the space, only to recoil from the stench. Holding my breath, I tried again. Then I squeezed my arms inside, and slowly, carefully unwrapped the bundle.

It was not Ella.

It had not *been* Ella for quite some time: days; possibly weeks.

It was bones and it was skin.

In shock, I carefully rewrapped the thing and placed it back where it had been. Then I returned to where its mother lay, asleep and snoring—and dreaming of what, I thought. Who could know?

I lay beside her, although not as close; not nearly as close. And then the ground seemed to spin suddenly, lifting me up, turning me around, so that I was fixed to a ceiling of grass with a long fall into darkness below me. My fingers tensed into claws and dug into the earth as I waited for gravity to realise that I was breaking its rules. And I lay there like that, suspended, disorientated, anticipating a fall that never came, for what was left of that longest of nights.

*

Charlotte rose late the next morning, ate a breakfast of beans, then went to see to her child. My skin crawled as I watched her cradle the corpse and rock the corpse and kiss the top of the corpse's skull. As always, she never came too close to me or turned the bundle so that I would see any more than that curling wisp of hair. I tried to convince myself that she was knowingly hiding the truth and that she knew what the truth was, but my gut assured me that all I was witnessing were private moments between a mother and her child. But when the shirt—one of mine since I'd fed all of her clothes to the fire the previous night—when the shirt got unbuttoned and a breast appeared, I turned away and rubbed my lips nearly raw.

And all I kept thinking was: Maybe the rabbits are fine after all. The smell wasn't them, so maybe they're alive down there. Maybe there's another hole I didn't know about and they've been coming and going all this time.

I didn't know if I truly believed it or not, but I wanted to—and wanting is as good as having.

Sometimes, it's better.

*

Charlotte put Ella down inside the tent for a nap after breastfeeding. She found me on the bridge, watching the river flow away, away, away. If I could swim, I could float; give myself over to it. But I never learned to swim because my father never taught me and he never taught me because he never learned to swim. Built to drown. Me. Him. Both.

Charlotte laid her hand on mine, but I wriggled free.

"Is something wrong?" she asked.

"He was a liar his whole life," I said.

"Who?"

"My father."

Charlotte reached to touch my shoulder, but I put myself out of range. Confusion slipped down her face like swell across a deep lake. I wanted to run, flee the camp and find somewhere to hide until they were gone. But I couldn't forget last night, and whether I wanted to take ownership of them or not, I could not deny the strong feelings I had developed for her either.

Love is listening to someone else's madness and not listening to your own. Her words to me on the day we met.

Part of Charlotte has to know she's dead, I thought. Part of her just has to know.

"So when are you leaving?" I asked. Charlotte stared at me; a crazy woman travelling with a dead child. I fixed my eyes on the riverbank below us, at the open mouths of the rabbit holes, and thought: I'll take my chances with them. "With the eater out of the way it should be safe enough to make another trip into the city," I said. "I'll get you those supplies. I'll get a car too, any colour you want, with a full tank of fuel. I can be back in thirty minutes; you can be on the road in forty."

"That fast?" she said.

"You'll be in Bournemouth long before it gets dark. Just don't pick up anyone on the way and don't stop driving until you get there." Then I thought of something else. I turned to look her in the face. "You can get Ella checked over. You know, at the treatment centre they've got set up down there." Something broke the surface of that deep lake for a fraction of a second and then vanished. Something, all right, but it wasn't enough. I was looking for the monster; or maybe some definitive proof that the monster didn't exist. But it was too fleeting to tell either way.

Tears slid from her eyes.

"Is that what you want, Alan?"

No, I thought.

"Yes," I said.

I left her standing there on the bridge and walked away. I broke into a half-run. Soon I forgot about the half and found myself barrelling toward the silence of the city's streets. The city I called No More. As in, make it stop.

As in, vacant.

*

They were gone by the time I got back. All she took with her was the broken pushchair and the clothes I'd given her to replace the ones I'd burned. From the riverbank I looked up at the car—a three-year-old Mazda 4X4—waiting on the bridge, engine idling, and considered going after her. Which was fine in theory, and quite possibly the right thing to do, but *what if* I found her—what then? I could not separate a daughter from its mother. Therefore, Charlotte was as dead as she. A zombie.

*

I put everything into trying to believe that.

But...

*

Three weeks later, I awoke to an unfamiliar noise. Over the crest of the hill behind me, a lone IFV, or Infantry Fighting Vehicle, appeared and rolled slowly down New Bridge Road toward the bridge and me. With no time to find a hiding place, I lay flat on my stomach amongst the tall grass and played dead. The tracks sounded like they were tearing up the road as the armoured vehicle passed within forty feet of where I lay before rolling over the bridge and into the city.

The sound faded and the vehicle never came back, even though I paced the walkway underneath the bridge for nearly four hours, anticipating its return. The light went quickly from the day then, and another premature evening pressed its freezing dark to my skin. I abandoned the space beneath the bridge for the open air to continue the wait. At which point I saw something lying on the grass close to one of the rabbit holes. My breath caught in my throat as I crept toward it, expecting the dark shape to suddenly prick up its ears and zip back inside. But it didn't move, not even when I bent and scooped it carefully from the ground and held it across the palms of my two hands. Then its side twitched. Alive? I thought. I peered closer only to realise it wasn't breathing at all. Instead, wriggling maggots had made a home of its lungs. I dropped the carcass and stood back.

But if it's been dead for so long, I wondered, how did it come to be out here?

*

I buried the rabbit and hung around the riverbank waiting for the others to show. Every so often I thought of Charlotte and the baby. I wondered if they'd made it to Bournemouth, if she'd even gone there at all. She was out there somewhere, lost in the nuclear wild, searching for who-knew-what, but it wasn't Bournemouth and it wasn't some treatment centre. The world suddenly filled with hope when it reached its most hopeless. It was pathetic, inspiring, confusing, maddening. And I missed her.

A week later, the IFV came back. Maybe it was the same one, maybe not; it didn't matter to me. Behind the armoured vehicle followed a long unbroken convoy of civilian vehicles: cars, vans, trucks, bikes. This time I did not try to hide. I stood and watched with a heavy heart. They moved slowly, like a funeral procession, but not so much in silence as a nauseating commotion of clattering engines and sputtering exhausts. They were moving back, in from the edges, cautiously working their way as far from the coast as radiation levels would allow.

The IFV stopped on the bridge in front of the abandoned 4X4. Three soldiers climbed out to inspect the vehicle both inside and underneath. Satisfied, they released the handbrake and two of them rolled it across the bridge and out of the way. The third soldier noticed me and made his way down to the campsite. He looked around but kept his automatic rifle trained on the space between my feet. He asked me some questions. I answered them. He asked me what I was doing there. I said, "I'm guarding these rabbit holes from the eaters and keeping the place clean until they return." I showed him the litter picker. The rifle barrel twitched. I told him that if they carried on along the same road they would pass a house, its number was ninety-two. I said it would be a good idea if they stopped anyone going near it. He gave me a strange look. Then I asked him if his people could keep an eye on it, because I couldn't be in two places at once. He didn't seem to understand, but nodded and said someone would come back for me later. I told him not to go to the trouble; I was happy right where I was. His laughter stopped when he realised I wasn't joining in. He went back to the others. People were pressing their horns like the starving rats I saw in a documentary once, pushing a button in their cage for the reward of food. But no reward was coming the way of that lot and they kept on pressing their horns anyway. The soldier returned to his vehicle and the convoy started to move again. The IFV's tracks sounded like they tore up the road. The vibration carried itself all the way into my knees. Then came the engines and the exhausts. Underground, the rabbits must have been going crazy. And over it all the horn blasts continued, talking to each other, saying nothing. Just like old times.

And then someone threw a chocolate bar wrapper out of their car window. The wind took it, lifted it over the edge of the bridge, and deposited it in the river. I raced it downstream to the bent old oak with his fingers in the water and clambered up his twisted trunk. I made my way along a branch that reached across the water, aligned myself with the fast approaching wrapper, and lowered the litter picker's grabber to within one or two inches of the water's surface. The outside of the wrapper was blue and red, the inside white. It floated toward me.

Hold on, I thought. What am I doing? I'm not going back to this. I'm not going back. Let the river have it.

It wasn't easy, but that's what I did.

*

The power came back on less than a week later. One minute I was asleep in the shadows underneath the bridge, the next I was shielding my eyes from a flare of tangerine light. I threw the nearest rock at the wall fixture, and the bulb smashed with a satisfying pop. Then I rolled over and went back to sleep. At dawn the following morning I walked out onto the bridge and watched the lights in the city switch on one by one; not all of them, but a lot. It was like watching some obsolete computer flicker miraculously back to life. I wanted to rip out all of its wires and short its electric heart. Because I knew what came next.

Not even two days.

I heard the first rumble in my dreams. Charlotte and I were standing in a graveyard; headstones everywhere, all directions, farther than the eye could see. There was a hole in the ground in front of us, freshly dug, large enough for a baby. Or possibly a man standing up, I thought, eyeing her for a sign, anything. Suddenly the sky went dark; dirty grey clouds rolled over us at time-lapse speed while Charlotte rocked her daughter in dreadful slow-motion, as though she might never stop, might never let go. I glanced back into the open grave and saw flame-tips licking the walls at the same time I felt heat spill out of its throat and heard that first low rumble. My initial thought was that the sound had come from the hole, but after the briefest pause it resumed, clearly overhead, no louder than before but longer and uninterrupted. Thunder. That terrible and frightening sound. And where there was thunder there was always lightning. Where there was lightning there was always the threat of a strike. Thunder was the threat of lightning. Thunder was the threat of the strike. And on and on it went. Then I said in a raised voice: *You have to choose, Charlotte. Now.* The graveyard was a vast, exposed space with no trees, and the tallest things for miles around were us.

I took her arm, she pulled away. I took it again, and not only did she pull away but she squeezed the bundle in her arms closer to her chest. And on went the thunder, on went the threat.

I woke with a start beneath the bridge. My head ached. I tried massaging my scalp to relieve some of the pain, but it did nothing; might as well huff and puff at the sky to clear it of the clouds. I prayed I was mistaken even as I peered out from beneath the arch at the sky. There were clouds up there but no rain and no flashes of light anywhere to be seen. But I could hear it...in the back of my skull, a sound like thunder.

Not even two days.

Two days and they had the Wi-Fi networks—some of them anyway—back online.

I got up and staggered onto the riverbank. The light was fading out of the day. It probably wasn't even five p.m. yet but shadows were drawing themselves up everywhere I turned. I'd slept for fourteen hours but I was exhausted. I hadn't eaten in days. With Charlotte gone I did little else except watch some holes in the ground or sleep. Perchance to dream? Yes, damn it. *Yes.*

I did not hear the IFV approach and come to a stop on the bridge. I did not hear the heavy boots beating on the pavement slabs. They simply appeared in front of me as if by some cruel magic, stood right there on the grass. Two soldiers. Their rifle barrels chose to ignore the space between my feet this time and settled on the middle of my chest instead. The tac lights mounted to their guns almost blinded me.

"Hands," said one. "On your head. Then turn the fuck around and drop to your knees."

I followed his instruction. My eyes went immediately to the river, running, running away.

"What's going on?" I asked. "What is this?"

One of them rushed forward to loom behind me. Something wet splashed onto my neck then oozed under my coat's collar and down the centre of my back. Spit.

"Ninety-two," he said.

For a moment, I did not understand and so did not respond.

"Number *ninety-two*," he repeated. "The house you told us to take a look at, you sick son of a bitch. What the fuck were you doing there? Cooking babies—what the fuck? I should put a bullet in your brain right now."

I opened my mouth to protest, explain, say something, but the words caught in my throat just as a small animal stepped tentatively from one of the rabbit holes in front of us and sniffed the air. I tried to get onto my feet for a better look, but a swift crack to my left shoulder from the rifle butt put me back on my knees.

"Wait," I said. "You don't—"

Right shoulder, that time. I went down, face in the grass. But I was back up, kneeling, an instant later.

The creature had turned around; its hindquarters jutted out of the rabbit hole. For a few seconds I tried to forget both the soldiers' misunderstanding of the situation at ninety-two and the constant dull ache edging forward from the back of my skull, and focus—*focus* on the activity around the hole less than ten feet in front of me. It looked like the animal was using its hind legs to brace itself as it tried to pull something up out of the ground.

"What *is* that?" asked one of the soldiers. The beam of his tac light strafed the grass and spot-lit the creature as whatever it had been struggling to pull out of there suddenly came unstuck.

The animal was a large rat, and held in its jaws was the carcass of a young, perhaps infant rabbit.

Suddenly one of the rifles spat a couple of rounds in the rat's direction. The rat dropped the thing it held in its mouth and made a run for the deeper undergrowth. A trained soldier would have had no problem hitting a rodent of that size from that distance: he had meant to miss. With the rat gone, the soldier fired another round and made the rabbit disappear.

I heard laughter.

Thunder.

I closed my eyes. There were no rabbits down any of these holes; not alive anyway. The ones that had left were gone; they were never coming back. The ones that had stayed were dead. Starvation, disease, fear, a combination of all three, it didn't really matter, because the rats—they were the ones moving in.

"This was a mistake," I murmured.

"You bet your bloody life it was," said the soldier directly behind me.

I rose to my feet on unsteady legs, expecting another blow from the rifle butt, but it never came. The soldiers' delight had bought me a few precious seconds.

I had to find her. I had to find her and tell her about her daughter. Love was listening to someone else's madness and not listening to your own. But even if she didn't love me, it was about something deeper; something far more important.

The inescapable truth.

"I'll come with you," I said. "I'll explain everything on the way. But please—just let me gather up a few things here first, okay?"

"Try anything and I'll put a bullet in your eye," the soldier whispered in my ear.

They would never believe me. They would never listen. I was an eater of children. My father's son.

Built to drown.

I kept one hand on my head at all times as I walked through the campsite, making much of collecting my belongings on the way. Soon enough I stood just a few feet from the water's edge. Another eight or ten feet and the darkness might swallow me. If it came down to choosing between their guns and the river then there really was no choice; no choice at all.

Time to find out how big a liar my father truly was.

The Harder It Gets the Softer We Sing

1. Never open a story with a dream

On our second night in our new home I have the dream again. I am sitting in a bar in Los Angeles, which in every sense is as far as you can get from Salisbury, England without leaving the planet. The place is empty except for me, Ray Bradbury sitting on the barstool to my left, and Charles Bukowski on the barstool to my right. Bradbury cradles a half-full glass of iced water between his hands as he raptly gazes at the abundance of tube lighting behind the bar. A myriad of neon hues reflect in his black-rimmed glasses. Bukowski drags on a cigarette in-between long pulls on his beer, the smoke cloud around him seeming to exude from his hulking, stooped frame. Both men have typewriters in front of them, old Royals, a sheet of blank paper rolled around the platen and carriages pushed to the right, ready. I have an empty stretch of bartop and a warm Coors, both of which are clustered with black mould where my hands have touched them.

"Got a problem there, baby," Bukowski says in his slow Californian drawl.

Bradbury glances to his right. "Not so much the Midas touch as..." He trails off, distracted by some unspoken thought or perhaps not wishing to hurt my feelings by stating the obvious. The science fiction writer, the laureate of low life, and me. This isn't a dream; it's a joke. I have no right to be here.

I would leave but it's raining outside. A hard rain that does not patter so much as slap the ground repeatedly. If a shower is a quiet conversation with a friend this can only be described as an argument you don't want to have with somebody you don't really like.

I turn to Bukowski who puffs smoke into the face of the empty page in front of him.

"What is it about this weather?" I ask. "Why does it always have to rain?"

Behind me, Bradbury pipes up: "A rain to drown all rains and the memory of rains."

Bukowski grimaces as though in actual physical pain then washes it down with another mouthful of beer.

"People run from rain but sit in bathtubs of water," he states with laconic finality before standing and hulking his way around the bar to fetch himself three more bottles.

"Anybody else buying?"

Bradbury shakes his head. I hold up my bottle of Coors, the one I am afraid to let go of, and raise it to my lips. Before as much as a drop can trickle out, the mouth of the bottle furs over with mould. I gag and try to spit out the taste of it, pushing the bottle away from me across the bar. More mould appears on the bottle and where my hand naturally fell on the bartop. A dirty handprint.

"I'm sorry," I say to my two companions. "I'm so sorry. I don't—" My face feels itchy. I *think* it is sweat (*it's mould*) but I am unconvinced and too afraid to touch it and see. "Jesus, that *rain*, it's—"

Louder now. It sounds as though the world is knocking, angry and itching for a fight.

"Ignore it," Bukowski says. "Have another drink."

"I can't," I tell him. "You saw what happened..."

"Then embrace it," Bradbury says. "Step outside and raise your face, your hands, your self to the rain. Greet it. With a smile."

"I can't do that either," I tell him, leaving my barstool to go stand by the window, peering out.

Outside, the clouds are dark and pregnant and desperate to give birth to something. But there is never any cloud-baby, never any birth, only an endless breaking of waters. I hate the rain. The cold, sticky feel of it on my skin, the tapping of it on my face, that way it flows from the rims of my glasses, the tip of my nose, like I am merely some conduit for where it really wants to go. Rain is bad news.

Somewhere on the other side of this, Sue and Alfie are asleep, snoring softly, breathing deeply, breathing well. The mould is a thing of the past, it's true, and yet it follows us wherever we go, as inescapable as the sound of the rain, or the silence of a heart not beating.

"Then you might just wanna stick around, kid," Bukowski says, as though reading my mind.

"He can't."

"Zip it, Bradbury. He needs to get what happened out of his system. He can't write for shit, so what's he supposed to do, huh? Kiss the *rain*? Kiss my *ass*. Listen to me, baby: find yourself a beautiful woman and fuck her. Fuck her good, fuck her bad, I don't care—just fuck her until the rain quits falling."

Bradbury has the words long before I do.

"And what then?"

"Send her ass home," Bukowski says with a shrug. "Sleep fourteen hours. Think about getting up at one but get up at two or even three o'clock. Have a drink, smoke, a little something to eat. Then, if you still feel the need, sit by a window somewhere—in glorious sunshine—and write about this beautiful woman you once fucked."

"He's married, Charles," says Bradbury.

"I know that, baby. I was only offering up one solution to his problem. *You* told him to walk outside and get his ass wet." He turns to me. "Why are you so afraid of the rain, kid?"

"It's not that I'm afraid, it's...more complicated than that. It's not even the rain, it's—"

"You," Bradbury says, turning away to face the typewriter sitting in front of him on the bar. He starts to type, slowly at first then picking up speed, typebars repeatedly striking the paper, leaving their mark.

Bukowski, seeing Bradbury at his typewriter, fingers moving, working those keys, swigs his beer, licks his lips, glances at me, shrugs, spins around on his barstool to the Royal in front of him, and starts to type.

Just like that, they are both gone. Bradbury on Mars, Bukowski on women. The sound of their typebars alternately kissing and punching the white page sends a long shiver climbing up my spine. It is a sound like mechanical rain. The longer I stand here and try not to listen to it, the more I can *only* hear its fall, the disparate sounds seeming to come together and merge to form words, sentences, a language all of its own. And when I think I am on the verge of understanding the language of the rain, it falls apart, reverting back to raindrops and letters.

And then the dream is over and I am awake, cheek-down on my laptop keyboard, a small puddle of drool around the R, T, D, and F keys and a stream of B's forty pages long running across the screen. You can depress several keys at the same time but one of them always rises to the top, negating all the others. Sometimes the B will make it, sometimes it won't. This is natural selection as applied to the QWERTY keyboard.

Onscreen, the cursor blinks at me and blinks at me and blinks...

Waiting.

Hungry.

Waiting.

I close the laptop.

Listen to the internal fan huff its last breath.

Look out the window.

It is raining outside.

2. Never end a dream and enter a flashback

The House of Mould. Me stood at the bottom of the stairs, Sue stood at the top.

"I'm bleeding," she said.

"What?"

The most impotent word in the English language. I said it again, with a different inflexion, because when something doesn't work, when something has no power or effect you try again, and again—and you keep trying until you realise it isn't the word that is powerless: it is you.

"But..."

The second most impotent word in the English language. An objection with zero weight behind it.

"How?" I ask.

Rhymes with 'ow'; something you might say after a paper cut.

"How do you think?" Sue screamed at me. "Come up here. Look in the toilet bowl. That's *how*."

"No, it's okay."

But it wasn't okay. It wasn't even close to okay. And every word out of my mouth was the wrong one.

And then Alfie, our three-year-old, appeared at my side, having wandered in from playing in the garden. He immediately noticed a spot of blood on the middle finger of Sue's left hand. I hadn't noticed it.

"You're bleeding, Mummy," he said. "Leave it alone."

"Go back outside, Alfie. Mum and I are trying to talk."

"But the *gwibber's* gone and Mummy's got blood," he said.

Gwibber was Alfie-speak for squirrel. Sometimes Alfie's words sounded like the correct word; sometimes they sounded like they came from another dimension, a kind of Twilight Zone of vocabulary and language. The speech therapist worked with him on eroding those glorious edges, on bringing him back to our planet—as if there was something so great about how *we* communicate.

"Maybe the gwibber is hiding," I said. "Maybe he's waiting for you in the garden with all his gwibber friends. Go take a look."

Alfie's face lit up for a second, and then darkened as he shook his head.

"No, he's gone," he said. "The gwibber's gone."

Children do not require proof or facts but have an innate sense of truth.

The gwibber *was* gone, and when I looked up the stairs for Sue I saw that she was gone too.

3. Never start the story proper in the third scene

The new house we've rented has a garage and by our first weekend I am inside it with the canopy door raised to allow the sun to illuminate the landscape of unpacked boxes within. I feel like Indiana Jones *sans* the Staff of Ra, searching out the location of the lost Ark. In my case, it is a cardboard box of irreplaceable first drafts, printed long ago but since lost from both laptop and memory stick. Until I lay my hands on the stuff inside, I cannot fully relax. Losing it would be like losing... something important.

One of my neighbours, British Indian, mid-forties, married, two young daughters, also rises early with the sun. We spot each other and both consider introducing ourselves but opt for the perfunctory nod and wave combo instead. I wonder briefly what he dreamed about last night, if anything. Something emasculating like my dream, perhaps? Who knows? He goes about his business, ridding the raised island on his lawn of its eyesore of dandelion rosettes; I go about mine, searching the garage for my cardboard Ark of dubious prose. We men, Lords of what little we survey.

Sue appears thirty minutes later, carrying a mug of hot coffee with two hands. She does not enter the garage but stands on the threshold as though wishing not to intrude; instead, waiting silently for me to come to her.

"Thanks," I say, accepting the drink and bringing it briskly to my lips to keep them otherwise engaged.

Sue's hands, warmed by the heat of the mug, move unconsciously to her stomach, rest there a moment, perhaps transfer some of their stored heat, then separate and fall to her sides.

"Where's Alfie?" I ask.

"Asleep still," she says. "Must be exhaustion from all the excitement of the move. Have you spoken to him—the neighbour, I mean."

"No, not yet."

"He keeps looking this way."

"I've noticed. He's just curious about the new arrivals, I suppose."

"Do you think he knows about—?"

"Why would he?"

"I don't know," she says. "I just...don't like the idea of people knowing and then coming up to me with questions."

"I doubt he'll do that, Sue. I doubt any of them will do that. No one here even knows you were pregnant."

Still looking at the new neighbour, Sue's hand slides across her tummy and absently rubs at it again. Eleven weeks may have passed since that day on the stairs but the memory, the pain, the loss is still evident. A new home, a new job (for me), new hope for the future did not necessarily ease any of it; perhaps it only created a fog into which we could lose ourselves—and possibly each other.

"I don't like how he's staring at us," she says.

Rub.

"A furtive glance isn't staring, Sue."

"Whatever it is, I don't like it."

"Look, we're new on this street. People can be wary of the new. Mistrusting, even. Give it some time. It *will* get better, I promise."

Maybe he heard us last night, I think. Windows were open to air the house as its lain empty for months and the three of us were coughing in our sleep from the chest infections we brought with us from The House of Mould. Or maybe he senses the hole left by what it took from us. Maybe it's written on your face, Sue, or tattooed on your belly by the constant rubbing—or is it searching? What is it you're looking for?

"We should try to unpack some more of these boxes over the weekend if we can," I say, changing subject. "I'm back to work Monday and we've not scratched the surface." I point to a couple of lonely-looking boxes off on their own in the far corner of the garage. "What do you want me to do with those?"

Sue looks. Looks away. She can read.

"What we don't need we can sell on eBay or give to charity," she says.

My mind goes to that Hemingway story of six words (*For sale: baby shoes, never worn*) and I want to say we don't need *any* of it, but it's a sign of how far Sue has come that she will entertain letting even some of it go. We are going to be okay, I think.

We are going to be okay.

I take her hand in mine—possibly intercepting it on its way to her abdomen again—and lean in for a kiss. Expecting Sue to turn her cheek and allow just a peck, she surprises me by offering her mouth, lips pouted and parted just enough to soften and prolong the kiss.

Eyes close.

Eyes open.

There is a moment in which we are alone but united, holding breath, seeing each other through half-lidded eyes across the length of our noses and the span of our years. Then the moment slipping as I feel a vague emptiness, a not-thereness, and follow its trail to my now unheld hand. Slipping as a pyjamaed and beslippered Alfie joins us outside, rubbing sleep from his eyes and yawning himself into a coughing fit. Slipping as I step back and look down, down at Sue's hand not in mine but on herself, cupping a palmful of soft abdomen over barren uterus. Slipping as our new neighbour drops the pretence of weeding and simply stares at us, at what we have become. The family of Mould. Then the moment gone, as I realise—no, *admit*—that my wife is still a haunted house, with the ghost of a child wandering her corridors, her tubes, her veins.

But we are going to be okay.

"Let's go inside," I tell them.

4. Limit your use of flashbacks

The House of Mould. Alfie and I stood at the foot of the stairs, while above us the landing remained empty and the ceiling over our heads seemed to sink to the sound of Sue's tears.

"This is *rifty*," Alfie said.

I had no idea what rifty meant but it seemed to sum things up rather well. Perfectly, in fact.

I started to climb the stairs slowly, to give myself time to think of something to say to Sue. When writing fiction I could usually find the right word with a little time and a lot of gazing at the Post-it note forest on my study wall. Or, if it was a first draft, I could simply type [insert word] and move on. First drafts meant that I did not have to think on my feet. When forced to do so, all I had were these slow, hesitant steps. Desperate to reach his mother, Alfie tried to duck and swerve around my legs and beat me to the top of the staircase, but misjudging his step he tripped and struck his kneecap on the nosing of the fourth stair.

Usually, this would have drawn tears, but he picked himself up and half-hopped the rest of the way to the landing, where he waited for me as I tried to fill in the square brackets in my mind.

We found Sue in the main bedroom, curled up in a tight ball in the centre of the double bed, hands clasped over her stomach, sobbing and coughing into a pillow. Sunlight invaded the room through the partly-open vertical blinds and seemed to cut her into slices of light and shadow, reminding me of the grim Damien Hirst sculpture of the dissected horse. My dissected wife. I berated myself: you'll have to come up with something better than that, you idiot.

The sound had brought Alfie running, but the *sight* and sound of Sue's grief overwhelmed his young senses and made him pause.

"Daddy? Why is Mummy crying?"

On the verge of tears himself, I patted his shoulder.

"Mummy's lost something special."

"I miss the special too," he said. "I wanted to cuddle it."

Then he limped round to the far side of the bed, rubbing exaggeratedly at his injured knee as he went. Reaching across the covers, he placed one small hand over Sue's two hands interlaced across her belly.

"We're both sore, Mummy," he said. "It's okay. You lost your special. But you'll find it."

5. You can't take the horror out of the horror writer

Two weeks in the new house (after The House of Mould I call it The House of Air) and we have unpacked and found a place for almost everything. We had to throw out a few pairs of Sue's shoes, a bunch of her dresses, and some of Alfie's soft toys after finding mould on them. It seems it wanted to make the move with us. I expected Sue to be upset at the loss of her property but she bagged up everything and dropped it in the wheelie bin with a gleeful grin on her face. Perhaps more than the move itself, letting go of those contaminated things confirmed to her that The House of Mould was behind us. I cannot recall ever seeing her smile this much.

Even my recurring dream has gone from visiting every second night to maybe once or twice a week. Sometimes Bradbury and Bukowski even let me sit between them at the bar while they write, although they never allow me to peek at the words on the page and it's never long before one of them (usually Bradbury), sometimes both, throw me out into the rain. Still, it feels like progress.

On weekdays we are up at six a.m. for breakfast (or as Alfie calls it, *breastfast*), either *eatbix* or *woe-cakes*, Weetabix or pancakes. On this Monday, we all float—not in a sewer but in the air, the *fresh* air, like kites or birds or beautiful insects. Alfie has finally made a friend at nursery (he is telling me), and I am working on a new short story (I am telling him), and Sue is full of the joys of Spring even in this rain-filled approach to winter. Her thin white nightgown floats behind her as she moves with purpose around the kitchen, making pancakes (without the woe) and singing, yes, singing under her breath.

Three Blind Mice.

A nursery rhyme I have not heard since my mother sang it to me as a child.

Thinking of my mother leads me to think of my father.

"I should visit dad today, after work," I say to Sue from the kitchen table. Sitting opposite me, Alfie does that thing with his eyebrows rather than nod his head—he bounces them up and down a couple of times like a cartoon character. It always makes me smile. "It's been over a month," I tell him. Which to a man in my father's condition is the equivalent to years. His is a dog's life. Time is accelerating him mercilessly towards The End, and we have little control over its nature, whether there will be time and opportunity for credits or just a simple (painful) fade to black.

Thoughts like this ambush me all the time. You can't take the horror out of the horror writer, I suppose.

"What's your new friend's name?" I ask Alfie.

"Kayden," he says. "He has a *Darf Vaver scoo'er*. Can I have a scoo'er too, Daddy?"

"A Darf—*Darth* Vader scooter, hm? Like your friend's?"

"No, that's Kayden's," he says. "I want a stormtooper one."

"Storm*trooper*," I correct him. "I don't see why not. What do you think, Sue?"

Sue is standing at the sink, cold tap running, water drumming on the silk steel. She fills a glass, tilts her head back and downs it in one. I watch her dance on the spot like she needs to go somewhere. Watch her long dark (bed) hair slip from her shoulder and reach down her white gown. Watch the swell of her backside. The nakedness of her ankles. What is it about ankles? We haven't made love since we conceived the baby she lost. How long has it been? Sue fills another glass, drinks half in one go this time, releases a little gasp, then finishes the rest. Water drums into the sink. A bass sound. Low. Deep. Like rain. She fills another glass, her third, drinking just a sip at a time now, but thirsty, persistent, until it's gone.

"Sue?"

She turns, distant look, glass in hand, but not before filling it for a fourth time and turning off the tap. More than the tap.

"Should we buy Alfie a scooter?" I ask.

"Isn't he a bit young?"

"*I* don't think so," I say. "All the other kids have them, so I don't see what harm it would do."

"That's because you won't be there when he comes off it and hurts himself," she says. "You'll be writing. Or working. If he sees one spot of blood on his knee he'll get hysterical."

Where is this coming from? I think. And so much to digest. The passive-aggressive accusation. The dismissal that writing isn't work. Condiments served alongside the main meal of *you don't know your son.*

Alfie has danced on the fringes of the autistic spectrum for a while now, displaying some of the standard traits but watered down *just* enough to not raise any alarms with his therapist or GP. Instead, he inhabits some murky, in-between world between 'normal' and 'diagnosed', a grey, lonely place where his peers are on one side or the other and Alfie is caught between the two like some ghost, rarely seen, never heard.

"Don't do that," I say to Sue.

"Do what?"

"Make him into an outsider."

"I'm not..."

"He should be like the other kids. Have what they have. That includes the scrapes and cuts that come with it."

"It's a *scooter*," Sue says, exasperated, eyebrows raised, but not in the way Alfie does; Sue's are high and fixed. Refusing to come down. "I don't see the big deal. All I'm saying is maybe not right now."

Leave him where he is, I think. Don't let him move on and be like everyone else.

And then I realise something: this is not about a scooter or Alfie; this is about something else. Although, I don't quite know what it is yet.

Sue knows; women always know. *Men* are the outsiders: slow, dim-witted animals rolling in the mud of denial that we are slow, dim-witted animals, which is precisely what makes us slow and dim-witted and animals.

157

"Alfie's not the outsider," I tell her. "He's the *inside*. It's their shitting problem—everyone else's—if they don't get him. Sorry, Alfie, bad word, don't repeat it, okay? Good boy. Sue? He's not the outsider. He's the inside."

Sue shrugs, calm (or maybe it's disinterested), and drains the glass she's still holding, still drinking.

"I know."

What is that, I think. Her fourth, fifth glass? I've lost count.

"I'm buying you a scooter, buddy," I tell him.

The first batch of pancakes end up a little burnt (ironically, it's because of all the water), so Sue cooks up a fresh batch. Somehow, I end up with the first, burnt side down, on my plate.

"Like I wouldn't notice..." I say to Sue, who is smiling at her own weak deception, our disagreement all but forgotten. And that is the fundamental difference between The House of Mould and this House of Air. In The House of Mould, words stuck and resentment spread. In the House of Air, they seem to float away—mostly.

Alfie lifts his fork and smiles at us both. Does that cartoonish thing with his brows.

"Woe-cake and maypole syrups for everyone," he says brightly.

Sue and I look at each other across the table and we cannot help but smile.

"Woe-cake and maypole syrups," we say in unison.

And as I reach across to touch Sue's hand, I am mindful of not toppling the tall glass beside her plate.

It's full again.

I make it her sixth.

6. You can't say you love someone then put a chasm between you

Stepping through the front doors of Wintercroft is like walking into one of my own stories. It's not as thrilling as I might have expected or even hoped. As the deep-carpeted hallways steal the sound of my footfalls, I often struggle to separate the reality from the fiction. Both Mum and Dad ended up in here, with Mum leaving three years ago the only way you can ever leave a place like this. And so I wrote a story about a group of care home residents who capture and imprison Death and in so doing take back the ability to choose between life and the other. See, everything is connected for writers. We see the world and try to make sense of it, which is probably why the suicide rate among us is so high. We are swimming against the tide of rationality: that this all means nothing and everything that happens to us is simply random.

Dad will be joining Mum soon, although it won't be the dementia that claims him. Something else has taken hold. Three months ago, I stood in the doctor's office at Salisbury District Hospital not far up the road from here and saw the two great black spots on my father's liver. The doctor zoomed in and the image looked not unlike the various ultrasound pictures Sue used to bring home of our unborn child. The tumours looked like eyes, and I may have even held my breath and waited for them to blink, but they weren't, of course, and they didn't—blink, or even move in any way.

I thought we were having a baby but instead Sue birthed a cancer.

Everything connected, see.

And then I went home, sat on my bed, and cried. When I eventually raised my head, my gaze went, as it always did in that house, to the mould in the top corner of our bedroom, the mould slowly taking over the walls, and I pictured its invisible spores getting inside our lungs, sticking to our clothes, our skin, and maybe...being passed to our loved ones.

Because... There has to be a reason.

Because... *liver* cancer?

Because... I never even knew the man liked to drink.

Here is my father's door. Plain, inscrutable, like the man himself. Before I knock, turn the handle, go in, there is a moment of disorientation and adjustment. As I cannot hear my footfalls on the thick hallway carpet, it is an odd sense of travelling while having no feeling of movement from my limbs.

"Dad?"

A question.

"Dad? You in there?"

Words carried on the shoulders of blind hope. Like Alfie on Christmas morning nervously saying "Santa?" one second before he walks into the living room to discover what the big man has left behind, except I *want* the room to be empty and my bed-ridden father to be gone, because then it might mean he is sitting in the TV room with the other residents, watching *Loose Women* and only *half*-hoping for a swifter, less painful death.

"I'm coming in."

No answer, just the silence of a breath drawn, held, hoping for release.

Here is my father's door opening.

He is inside, of course, in bed, of course, gazing out the window at the greying skies. Of course. I disregard the chair at his bedside, there's little point in me sitting there, choosing instead to stand in his line of sight with my back to the open window. The draught feels cold on the back of my neck, like a manufactured shiver, and a tsunami of guilt crashes into me (from behind, it seems), trying to force me closer to him. His white hair needs cutting and he has grown stubble (I have rarely seen stubble on my father's face) and I—I have not visited since the tail end of summer. A different season. And now winter is coming. There is no autumn; autumn is a lie. Winter is coming. Fuck you *Game of Thrones* and fuck you George R. R. Martin.

Hold it together, I think.

"They looking after you in here, Dad?" I ask in reply to the stubble and the smell I am getting wind of—not quite unpleasant yet but getting there. It might explain the open window; then again, it might not. The staff are usually excellent at Wintercroft and my father has always been a stubborn man. Alfie might say he's now a *stubble* man.

I decide my father probably declined the haircut and shave, or worse, fought them off.

"They're coming," he says.

"I thought as much."

Here is the starting point for today's visit.

"Hordes, son. Hordes of the undead."

"Riding on the backs of giant spiders. Yes, I know, Dad. We've talked about this before—at *great* length. How come you haven't shaved?"

"No point. I can't be myself. Not who I want to be anyway."

"And who is that?"

"Not one of *them*," he says.

"The undead?"

He nods his head, actual fear widening his eyes.

"There's no one out there, Dad. They don't come back."

I turn to the window and on the other side of Odstock Road there is the field and the copse where Sue, Alfie and I had our picnic that day, before Sue lost the—help me out here, Alfie—the *special*. There is no horde of undead, no giant spiders, just a young couple on the far side getting amorous in the long grass. As I am watching, the grey sky sends them a drizzle of rain and the couple leap to their feet, grabbing their socks and shoes and phones. It should be funny, watching them stumble and hop their way back across the field to their car but I cannot help thinking that if a little rain gets in the way of their love they won't last. But what do I know? Maybe they will go sit in the car and talk—just talk, no touching—exchanging words gentle and loving as any kisses. If my father can lie in his bed behind me and speak of the looming zombie apocalypse, I can at least admit something to myself: I envy this pantomime.

I want their words.

Breathe.

"Dad?" A question. All my life, a question. "You don't know this but... I always wanted you to tell me you loved me. Just once. I wanted you to say it and mean it and then do something that would make me believe the words were true. Actually that's wrong: you did say it once. New Year's Eve, eleven years ago. You were drunk—the only time I've ever seen you get in that state—but you said it, and I said it back, and then we didn't speak for eight months, which if I'm being honest just made me feel like you were taking the words back. You can't do that— say you love someone then put a chasm between you."

When he speaks, his voice startles me, because while I was talking I thought I was alone in the room.

"How's Sue?"

The sudden clarity in his voice, the words, tell me he is with me— for a while anyway. These days it's down to minutes.

I turn from the window to find him looking directly at me from his bed.

"She lost the baby. That's the reason I haven't been in to see you. She's hurting, Dad."

"That bloody house." It is the first time anyone has ever said it out loud: thrown the blame for Sue's miscarriage on the doormat of The House of Mould.

"I should have got them out of there sooner," I say.

"That bloody house," he says again, then sighs heavily. "I've got cancer." Changing subject like a child. "They break the treatment down into what they call fractions. Did you know that? I didn't know that. Fractions. I was never any good at those things."

Which I think is my father's way of telling me that he is losing the fight; that he too has failed. We have that much in common.

"They're coming," he says.

"... I know, Dad."

Here is the end point of today's visit. Ring a Ring o' Rosies. Around we go.

"Hordes, son. Hordes of the undead."

"Riding on the backs of giant spiders," I say, and turn to the window to hide my tears. "I'll bring Alfie next time. You really should let them give you a shave, Dad."

We all fall down.

7. Don't talk to me in metaphors

The server brings Sue's water as we wait for our starters to arrive. We got here late, the Thai restaurant's seats already emptying slowly and not being filled again. It is my least favourite time to eat (you can feel the staff hovering to take your plates, your card, to move you along so they can get home to their loved ones) but by the time we settled Alfie with the babysitter we were more than an hour late for our reservation. We were lucky we even got a table at all.

"You look stunning tonight."

"Thank you," she says.

"I can't remember the last time we did this."

Sue raises her eyebrows. "Talked?"

"Ate out. Just the two of us."

"I know. It feels a little strange, doesn't it?"

"It does, a little. But good, right?"

"Yes," she says. "Good. How is the new story coming along? I heard you mention it to Alfie the other morning..."

Sue rarely asks about my writing. Only when it serves a purpose. We rarely sleep together either. Same reason.

"It's getting there," I say. "Slowly, as usual."

"What is it about? No, wait; just tell me the title, maybe I can figure it out from that."

"It's called 'Perception', and it's probably the darkest story I'll ever write. After the year we've had I suppose that's where the mind goes."

She sips her table water. I sip my Corona beer. Our waitress emerges from the kitchen doors and makes her way across the floor to our table.

"Why does every word you write have to lead to some horrible conclusion?" Sue asks.

Her timing is impeccable. The waitress arrives and creates a natural dramatic pause for us as she displays the bowl of red curry and asks who it is for (Sue) and then the plate of vegetable spring rolls (also Sue's). I remind her that I only ordered the main, leaving out the part about how my visit to my father two days ago has left me with little appetite for anything but alcohol. And words. I wanted to cancel the meal tonight and retreat to the Post-It note forest of my study to write. But the sitter was already on her way and Sue was getting ready. I found Sue standing in our bedroom in front of the full-length mirror, pulling the thin, loose material of her dress taut across her belly and appraising it from every conceivable angle. I said nothing and put on my shoes. Our waitress smiles an oblivious smile and leaves.

"What do you mean every word leads to some horrible conclusion?" I ask.

"Your stories," Sue says, "they always end with some dark and terrible twist."

"You don't *read* my stories," I remind her. But we both know from my defensive tone that she is right.

"That's why I don't. I want a happy outcome, and if not that then at least a hopeful one."

Sue eats her two starters while I drink the rest of my beer and scribble notes on a few Post-Its I brought along for that very purpose. I eschew mobile phones and tablets for paper and pen, but I never seem to bring enough paper with me, and on those rare occasions when I do it never has a reason to leave my pocket. There is a life lesson in there somewhere, but Sue has finished eating and our conversation is far from over.

"You once said to me, 'You make me want to write stories that have a happy ending, where bad things don't happen to good people and the hero always wins.' What happened to *that* writer?"

I shrug and say, "He found horror. What do you want me to say, Sue? I think we learn more about ourselves from the bad things that happen to us than the good."

"You really believe that?"

"Maybe too much, but yes—yes, I do."

"You believe in monsters more than you believe in miracles? They do happen, you know."

"I know they do."

"I'm talking about the second thing."

"I know," I say, and then in reply to the look Sue gives me. "I *know*."

"Then why can't they happen to us?"

"Maybe the stories I write end the way they do because that's the right way for them to end, have you ever considered that? Things don't turn out well for us."

"The words every wife wants to hear spoken by her husband.

Thanks."

"I meant for *any* of us. Maybe that's why we—*people*—rarely speak to each other. We try to delay the end with silence in the hope that it will lull the monster to sleep. But the monster always wakes, Sue, and when it does that's the end. The end is the monster. It's coming for us all. I think that's why we only find the right words at the end—when time has all but run out."

"I think I'm still pregnant," she says.

The waitress arrives to collect Sue's plates and replace the bottle of water she has already drank. A cynical mind might think the waitress' purpose here was not to serve food but provide dramatic tension. She tells us our mains will be coming out in a few minutes and leaves us to talk.

I lean across the table, take Sue's hand in mine, the low-hanging paper lamps reflecting off her coffee-sunset eyes.

"You lost the baby, honey. It's gone. Now we have a chance at a fresh start. We can move on from what happened but...we need to point the ship away from the rocks."

She pulls her hand away dramatically. The few diners left in the restaurant glance our way.

"Don't talk to me in metaphors," she says. "You're all about the fucking metaphors. Nothing you say will change the fact that I am still pregnant."

Still? I think.

"But you told me you lost..."

The special.

"...the baby. Sue, what is going on? Did you lose it or not?"

"I'm still pregnant," she says.

"That's not what I—look, my father is dying. I won't...I can't... Let's not, alright?"

Sue says nothing. We look at each other across the table in the glow of the lamps and I try to focus on their reflection, my mind reaching for the paper light at the end of the tunnel of her eyes.

"Why are you mad at me?" I ask.

I know I will get there—I can feel the understanding coming like a freight train careening toward the back of my head—but for now we are Venus and Mars. I take a long sip of ice-cold beer. Look at the label. Corona. Mexican beer. I don't think I have written a story set in Mexico. I should rectify that, and perhaps I will, but after I stop stalling and deal with what is in front of me.

"They think I write about children a lot."

Or stall a little longer, perhaps.

"Who's 'they'?" she snaps.

"Readers. You know, the people who read my work."

Sue tries for confused but anger has moved into her face and kicked every other emotion out.

"And you know what your readers think, do you?"

"Well, *no*, but I'm guessing they think I write about children a lot because that's what's, you know, there on the surface."

"Right."

"But it's the fathers I'm really writing about, even in those stories where there is no father to speak of—particularly those."

"Okay."

"I think I write about the spaces, you know, in people's lives."

"Ah-huh."

"And I realised something recently: my father is in all the spaces. Every one. He *is* the space."

"This always happens when you visit him."

"What does?"

"This. This version of you comes out. The self-analysing, self-obsessing, self-loathing, self-pitying you. He brings it out. Squeezes it out of you like juice from a bitter lemon or, or poison from a wound. How's that for a fucking metaphor?"

"Those are similes not metaphors and what the hell are you talking about, Sue?"

"Every man does it," she says. "Tries to measure himself against his father. Except you never really had one, so you measure yourself against the idea of what a father is; in other words, a ghost. We chase the ones we cannot have, who are beyond our reach, but that doesn't keep us from trying to reach for them, does it? I'm sorry, Simon, but I can't think about him right now. Let me make our miracle, you deal with the monster. Sorry, I didn't mean—"

Right on cue: the waitress arrives with our mains. We both sit there, red in the face: Sue from anger; me from embarrassment. People are looking, judging; I imagine they will go home and we'll be the subject of tonight's pillow talk: the couple they saw arguing in the restaurant earlier. As the waitress lowers the plates, Sue sits back on her chair, hand on her stomach, rubbing. Feeling the warmth. I want to tell her it's just the red curry she ate but I don't, because the train has finally arrived in the station: Sue told me she is still carrying our baby and my response to that was to tell her my dad is dying, effectively countering life with death. I try not to be that arsehole but there's a saying (probably my mother's) that everyone has one, and every married woman has two. So for the rest of the meal and the walk home through the dark Sue says nothing while my head swarms with things I want to say but can't, won't, and I get the feeling that we are being followed by something small, something crawling.

Maybe I'm not a horror writer, I think. Maybe I'm just depressed. A depressed writer fooling people into believing that what I write is fiction. But when a depressed person opens up to you, you do not turn your back, Sue; you are handing him the rope and pointing out the nearest tree. And that tree is my father.

None of this is said. By the time we reach the play park a few minutes from where we live, we are walking a familiar path home, hand in hand. Hand on stomach. Until we find ourselves standing before the front door to The House of Mould. We laugh. We look at other.

We tell ourselves we don't live here anymore.

8. Never write about writing

Two o'clock in the morning and staring at the blank page.

This would be a suitable line to open a scene with if my protagonist was a writer. He isn't: he works in a bank and deals with numbers not words. His wife writes poetry but mostly in her mind.

I stare at the sentence and the white space around it. Sometimes you type something just to see the cursor moving, filling up the white space with letters, words, a sentence, hoping that one sentence will meet another sentence, take it out for dinner, fuck, and make baby sentences. Fragments. They treat cancer with fragments...or was it fractions? What did my old man say? Regardless, Sue and I treat ourselves with another baby.

Two o'clock in the morning and staring at the blank page.

The time suggests dedication, the 'blank page' hints at struggle, perhaps even writer's block. It's all in what isn't said. The words don't explain why, at two in the morning, you haven't just given up and gone back to bed. Or how Sue initiated sex earlier with a sigh, to which your inner Pavlovian dog responded, not so much with a pricking of the ears but a pricking of the prick. Or how two o'clock is the time for bad jokes. Like thinking you two could make love (or anything) without somehow messing it up. Teeth gritted, sweating, breathless, pounding from behind; one minute in and her head spun around like Linda Blair's in *The Exorcist* and she said, "Watch the baby."

Or that is how you saw it at the time it happened.

What actually transpired was: Sue said the words under her breath and you did not hear them, which made you lean forward over her and ask her to repeat them. You failed to catch them a second time, so you bent all the way over her, still inside and moving, pressing your chest against her back, your head behind hers, and she turned her face to the side and along with a strong pelvic squeeze she said, "Watch the baby."

You got up, rushed to the bathroom, closed the door. Splashed water on your face. Fogged up the mirror with your breath. Wrote the word 'LIAR' in the fog with your finger. Went downstairs. Switched on the TV, the PlayStation. Played a couple of rounds of Battlefield 1, which is the sequel to Battlefield 4. Set in World War I, with sharper graphics and improved sound capturing the cruder, simpler weapons of the time, things have moved forward but at the same time not moved forward at all. And it was the pelvic squeeze that killed it for you, the pelvic squeeze that felt like the clenching of some tiny fist.

Two o'clock in the morning and staring at the blank page.

You take a green Post-It note and draw between ten and twenty trees on it: a vertical line crossed through with carets, the proofreaders' mark for 'insert here'; then you add it to the hundreds of other Post-It notes already fixed to the wall. Sometimes you write a word in tiny script. It can be a thing, a feeling, a mood; whatever comes to mind. At two-thirty, you write the word 'baby' and surround it with tall trees. You fix the Post-It to the wall. Lose it in the forest.

It is only a temporary reprieve but it unblocks you long enough so that you can get some work done on *Perception*. By four a.m. you have two thousand words and realise what the story is about: a woman who cannot see, a man who needs to be seen, and a world that sees only what it wants.

9. O-O does not spell 'no'

I start what Sue calls my 'real job' on three hours' sleep. A week after Sue's miscarriage I landed this gig as a proofreader for a small publishing company on the outskirts of Salisbury. I work in a glass cubicle (fish bowl) with three women. There is a kind of reverse sexism that exists in the office. When I described it to Sue, she only rolled her eyes, pinched my backside, and said, "Welcome to our world, sweetheart. Suck it up."

"I'm serious," I said. "They don't like me."

"*You* don't like you. *They* are probably indifferent. But they don't know you like I do."

It starts the moment I arrive. Grace and Karen sitting there with their mugs of coffee greet my 'good morning' with silence or a subdued 'morning' without the 'good'. Then, usually a minute or two late, the youngest of our team, Holly, arrives to a 'good' *and* a 'morning' both delivered with feeling. Holly's cup sits next to the kettle, one spoon of coffee, one sweetener, the spoon leaning against the inside of the mug. My mug is left on a shelf in the cupboard.

I shrug it off and get to work proofing the words of others while mine sit at home, unnoticed. Which makes me think of Alfie and how other children his age treat him.

"Why am I wrong, Daddy?" he asked me one morning.

"You're not wrong, you're just different."

"Why?"

"Because sometimes you struggle with words." Even before I said it, I saw the connection and felt the self-loathing rise like bile in my throat. This curse we Fenwicks pass from one generation to the next, written (so poorly) into our genetic code...

When I left for work this morning, The House of Air felt more like a House of Silence. Neither Sue nor I mentioned the broken sex last night. But if anything, Sue seemed happy, chatting to Alfie about *Kissmas* and what toys he would like from Santa. When Alfie said, "I want the special", Sue glanced in my direction and it was as if she thought we shared some beautiful secret. What I felt was a sense of this thing careening out of control.

During lunch break, the conversation at work flows like a river around a rock, and as I sit at my desk and bite into my ham and cheese I get the impression that if the rock were removed the water would happily fill its place.

For most of the day, every day actually, there is an insidious and undeniable sense that I don't belong here, and so I allow myself to drift away and think about writing and Dad and Alfie and Sue and the miscarriage that never was.

When Grace sneezes at 14:33 there is a merry little chorus of bless yous from the other women. When I sneeze at 14:47 it is met with nothing—as though my sneeze is somehow less deserving—a tangible silence that gathers and shapes itself to form two simple words: *fuck you.*

"You keep note of the exact time someone sneezes?" Sue again.

"Not every time, no. Just when I'm having a bad day."

"And this makes you feel better how?"

"Well, for starters, it proves I'm not paranoid. Two identical situations—someone sneezing—with two different reactions. It's science."

Science is the word Alfie uses in place of silence. It's that too.

"It's silly is what it is," Sue said. "What is it you always tell Alfie? They'll warm to you if you just be yourself. Well?"

But Sue doesn't really believe that. We Fenwicks (men *and* boys) struggle to be ourselves. Alfie's speech and language therapist has mentioned ADD, ADHD, even Asperger's. Whatever it is, he is high functioning, as though that term is supposed to provide some comfort. Why are we so determined to diagnose difference?

Maybe at work it is nothing to do with gender, maybe it is too easy to go there. When you are different, those who share commonalities ignore you or treat you differently in ways they think are non-offensive but are often quite harmful.

The truth is we Fenwicks do not struggle with words, we struggle with silence. The silence of others. The words are ours. We *own* the words. If no one enjoys the stories I write or uses the words Alfie uses (words like *dusking* and *rifty* and *brinderful*, that gorgeous blending of brilliant and wonderful that only a child could create) then it is their loss. We are the inside.

I leave work at five o'clock, tired from reading all day, the dozens of little accumulated moments with Holly, Grace, and Karen like paper cuts to my brain, only now my brain holds the paper and is slicing itself again and again. *Look at this picture of my grandson. Six weeks old today...* Grace's mobile phone passed from one to the next like we were at a party, but with the music stopping before it ever reached me. Then, as we pulled on our coats and walked through the exit doors, Karen asked, *What are you doing tonight, girls?* I walked a few steps behind, not to my car (we cannot afford one) but toward Southampton Road and Churchill Gardens on the other side. Holly, key in her car door, said this over her shoulder: *Oh...bye, Steven.*

Oh.

An afterthought.

Bye.

Good. Progress.

Steven.

That is not my name.

With winter approaching, darkness falls early in the city, and there are few lights to be found anywhere in Churchill Gardens. At least in the near pitch dark I cannot see the trees or the branches or the spaces waiting underneath.

Following the winding path through the park, something bounds up to me from the dark and sniffs the air close to my groin. I cry out, but it is only a dog (albeit a Staffordshire Bull Terrier), and I am made to look a complete fool. The dog's owner drifts in and out of visibility, laughing like he knows some damning secret.

Shaken, I walk a little faster, hearing something behind me. Not feet or paws but something dragging itself through the brittle grass. I hope it is the terrier pulling its roundworm-infested backside across the park but I already know it isn't. Before the dog rushed me, before I even saw it, I heard its panting. I can hear no breathing now, only something hauling itself through the grass in breathless silence.

In *science*, as Alfie would say. Or maybe, *O-O spells no*.

Which of course it doesn't, but here, now, it does.

O-O spells no.

I arrive at the children's play park with its empty swings, its unmoving merry-go-round, its silent pirate ship, its climbing frame waiting for the attention of crows. It forces me to recall a different park on a different night and a baby with arms for its eyes. Here is the rope tower, a thick steel pole with rigging draped from it like a spider-web of intestines laid out to dry overnight, and the sound behind me closer now, shuffling, dragging, tiny legs, hands, hands.

"This is where the children play."

Not a cry this time, but an actual scream.

"I'm sorry, son. Didn't mean to frighten ye."

The voice belongs to a man sitting on a bench ten feet to my right, doused in shadow by the tall hedgerow at his back separating the park from the traffic on Churchill Way South. Homeless by the looks of him, wearing an ancient suit that doesn't fit him anymore, if it ever did, but still he's a hundred and eighty pounds; maybe one-seventy. A large green shopping bag stands next to him on the bench, mouth open.

"Dark for this time of the evening," he says.

He is right. It hasn't even gone six yet but I am feeling midnight.

I nod.

"Again, sorry if I frightened ye," he says.

"That's okay," I lie and pretend not to see his hand reaching for mine. "I'm just a little jumpy tonight. Long day."

He nods. "Same here. Name is Cutter, by the way. Nothing to worry about. I'm aw dull edges these days."

"Scottish, right?"

"Long time ago, aye."

"And now?"

"No fixed abode."

I glance at the shopping bag. It reads: *a bag for life*.

He's more like one-fifty, I think. The suit burying him like a clown's outfit without the laughs.

He reaches into the large green shopping bag and pulls out a McDonald's carton. Opens the carton and scoops out loose pieces of brown lettuce from around a half-eaten burger. Throws his head back, opens his jaw. Hand like a beak, he rams it halfway into his mouth, the way a bird might be fed by its mother. Only, she isn't around and he is a fifty-year-old struggling to feed himself.

He can't even be one-forty, I think.

"Can I give you anything?" I ask, reaching into my back pocket for my wallet.

"Naw, keep your money where it is, son. It's gone five and I'm off the clock."

"You're sure?"

Cutter nods. "I just like to sit here when there's no kids around," he says. "Otherwise the parents get a wee bit antsy: you know, a man minding his own business this close to children playing and having fun. I had a little brother once, you know. Maybe I just want to remember what that's like."

I wonder if I would be okay with Alfie playing on the play park apparatus while Cutter sat here on this bench nearby. The sad answer is probably not. Cutter weighed one hundred and thirty pounds at a push, but there was room inside that clown's suit of his for a child of Alfie's size...

"You know, they give to charity but they won't touch your hand," he says, causing me to blush with shame. "So I keep their kindness at a distance. Like chickenpox. But sometimes it gets so that you have to get ill to get better, you know?"

But I don't know. My father is up in Wintercroft getting ill, getting no better. Maybe it is a matter of perspective. Take this homeless man: not so frightening now.

What I say to him is: "I thought you were dull, Cutter, but you seem pretty sharp to me." It is supposed to end our brief conversation and allow me to be on my way but the old man wants to talk, probably hasn't talked—*really* talked—to anyone in months or even years, and I sense the stories lining up inside him, ready to pour out, the words floating around inside that empty suit of his like satellites through space.

"I have to go now," I tell him, but as I walk away I have a feeling we will meet again—and soon—on the white screen. Or at least some version of him.

He nods and gestures toward the empty play park—*his* white screen.

"This is where the children play," he says.

And I swear he cannot weigh more than one twenty.

Maybe even one ten.

10. Do not overuse italics

Nothing follows me the rest of the walk back to The House of Air. I leave it behind in Churchill Gardens with the crotch-sniffing dog and the homeless man. Or not quite. When I walk through the front door, all I see are hands. Sue and Alfie sitting on the bottom of the stairs, Sue with one hand on the back of Alfie's head, the other stroking her belly; Alfie with one of his hands in his mouth (sensory processing disorder is another diagnosis they want to throw at him) and his other hand under Sue's on her belly. They both look up at me when I walk inside the house. The House of Joy.

"Daddy! Mummy has the special!"

"That's nice, Alfie," I say then muster a little more enthusiasm. "That's so cool."

He rushes at me, hugs the tops of my legs.

"It's *brinderful*," he says. "All the sad can be happy now."

He means sad *memories*, but how could he be sad about something that never happened, memories that never were?

It's a simple answer: because Alfie created an imaginary life for himself with his little brother or sister, this giant vibrating picture puzzle in his mind, even while the final piece of it, the special, was growing and shaping inside his mother.

I never did that. Dared to dream of anything good.

I look past him at Sue. Tears in her eyes and a glow to her skin. The cynical deadvoice in my brain saying it's the cleansing effect of the four or five litres of water she pours into herself every day. Conversely, she has stopped going to the bathroom so often. There are times when we'll be sitting on the settee watching the latest episode of *Game of Thrones* (my preference) or *The Walking Dead* (Sue's) and her legs will be crossed, literally crossed, while she rocks backward and forward with her hand over her crotch and I pretend not to notice. Images of a dam springing a leak come to mind. Which isn't all that far from the truth. As Daenerys commands her dragons or Maggie takes down another walker, I have muted the television and heard Sue sat behind the locked bathroom door and sobbing while she urinates.

I detach Alfie from my legs, crouch to his height. Hold him at arm's length as I talk to him.

"Would you like to go visit Grandpa?"

Alfie nods. "Now?"

Something is different about his face but I cannot pin down what it is.

"Can I tell Grampa 'bout the special, Daddy? He's going to be my *bruvver* soon."

"Or sister," I tell him, caught off guard. "We don't know what...it is yet. Do we, Mummy?"

Sue looks at me; I look at Sue.

"I have a strong feeling it's a boy," she says from behind her smile.

"Surely it's too early to tell." I want to say it's too *not-happening* to tell but... "You were only what—thirteen weeks along?"

"Twelve. And no, it's not officially a boy but it's one or the other and you have to choose a side, so..."

"So, you've decided it's not a girl, then." I wanted a girl. One boy, one girl. The complete set. I even had a name picked out: Samantha. But wait—what am I doing? Sue lost the baby. Literally flushed it down the toilet.

I look at Alfie. Again, his face seems different. *Asymmetrical.*

"Are you okay, buddy?" I ask.

"Alfie, tell Daddy what happened today," Sue says.

"He can tell me on the way," I say, turning a half-circle on the threshold and reaching, fumbling for the front door.

"What happened?" I ask, not on the way to Wintercroft but when we are standing at the foot of my father's bed, faced with the sight of my frail old man lying in it, largely unresponsive. In the days since my last visit, he has lost weight. It isn't the cancer, they tell me, but the dementia. It seems like now it's a relay race to the finish. The fog of dementia has taken the baton and rolled into shore (and if I'm mixing similes or metaphors here I don't give a shit) because all he does is lie in the midst of all that cold greyness, reacting to shadows and refusing to eat.

And I cannot help but wonder: if you lose your mind first do you know you are dying—can you still feel the pain?

"So what happened, Alfie?"

"What about Grampa? Is she seeping?" Sleeping.

"No, Grandpa's awake. And it's he not she. Tell me what happened."

"Daddy, Henry's a bad boy," Alfie says. "Like Horrid Henry off the TV. He doesn't have *lisling* ears." Listening ears.

"Okay, what did Henry do?"

"He doesn't have *lisling* ears, Daddy. And he kicked me."

"Why did he kick you?"

"*I-cuz...*" —because— "*I-cuz* he wasn't *lisling*, Daddy. To Miss Brierly."

"He kicked *you* because he wasn't listening to Miss Brierly?"

"No, *i-cuz* I *told* him."

"Told him? Told him what? You're losing me, buddy. What did you tell him?"

"To *lislin*."

I can hear the frustration rising through my voice along with the heat rising through my cheeks. Ditto Alfie. Like father, like son. I don't think we've ever had a conversation that did not involve italics.

"Henry kicked Alfie in the eye," my father says, propped on two pillows but gazing at the ceiling.

I look from my father (they still have not given him a shave; I will have a word with somebody before I leave) to Alfie. The area above his left eye is a little red, a little swollen, but that wasn't what I failed to notice earlier at home; it was that half of his eyelashes are gone. Torn right out from the eyelids, a barren strip with just a few lashes left on either side, top and bottom, so that when he closes his eyes it looks like he is blinking on a spider.

I rub the back of Alfie's head. "What did Miss Brierly say to Henry?"

"Miss Brierly said Henry was naughty."

"Henry is a prick," my father states.

"Dad..." I begin, but whatever admonishment I was going to give him dissolves in my mouth. He is right: Henry *is* a prick. And Miss Brierly is something too. Where was the notifying phone call from the school? They sent Alfie home *damaged*, without a word. If he was any other child... "Dad, I'll deal with it, thank you. Alfie, say hello to

Grandpa."

"Hello, Grampa." Under his breath. To me, he says, "Why has he got old hair?"

"Because I'm old," my father says.

"But he's not even a granny yet," Alfie says.

He finds this hugely amusing and giggles into his hand. Age is funny to a child; it is foreign and non-threatening and out-of-reach, all the things it's truly not. It's slapstick or a magic trick. Wile E. Coyote falling off the cliff to become a cloud of dust.

"Can you go?" my father says. "I'm tired."

"We just got here. Alfie wanted to see you."

"No he didn't. Nobody wants to see me."

"That's not true and you know it."

"Do I? Just go, please. Leave."

"Not yet, I—"

"They're coming," he says. "The hordes. Hordes of the undead. They're coming."

"Christ, not now," I tell him.

But some of the colour has already drained from Alfie's face. He does not know what the words mean but the tone of my father's voice is enough to get him halfway to freaked out.

"Daddy, what is *whores*? What is undead?"

I feel like a contestant in some surreal episode of the American game show, *Jeopardy*. I'll take dementia for four hundred, Alex.

"Nice, Dad," I say. "You want to explain this one to him?"

"No."

"What is undead, Daddy?"

"Never mind, Alfie."

"Will undead kick me like Henry?"

My father laughs. "They'll do more than kick you. They will rip out your heart. Clean the fuck out. They'll squish it in their fingers like a piece of soft fruit."

"Daddy, Grampa's *scadey*."

"Jesus Christ, Dad, *enough*."

"Just...leave me alone," he says. "Come back another time."

"If you want us to go, Dad, then we'll go."

"I want you to go," he says.

But the waver in his voice makes him sound less sure. Nevertheless, I take Alfie's hand and lead him toward the door. He drags his heels, afraid to leave the room because *scadey* things lurk behind closed doors.

Of course, sometimes they're already inside the room with you. But when Alfie is scared, and Christ when Dad is too, neither will budge. It is the path of most resistance.

"How is Ruth?" he asks in a calm, if resigned-sounding, voice. "I haven't seen her around lately."

Not this. Not now. I just want to go home and write stories about shit that happens to *other* people.

Ruth, my mother, died in 2014. She became a resident of Wintercroft when her dementia took the reins. My father followed several months later after a series of falls at home due to his weak hip and shortly before his own encounter with the disease and, of course, his liver cancer. By then, he was already a stranger to my ailing mother. After thirty-seven years of marriage they came separately to Wintercroft, living in different rooms on different floors.

"You visited her room just last week, remember?" I tell him. It is a lie. It was three years ago. When this happens, I usually try to bring him back to me in stages. Dementia is a short-range time machine. We cannot visit medieval England or Italy during the Renaissance, but we can drop in on neighbouring years like a stone skipping across the surface of a lake. Forward movement is the key. "You brought her flowers, Dad. The kind she likes."

"Calla lilies," he says. "I went to her room. In a wheelchair. After I fractured my hip that time."

"Actually, I think that was the third time you'd fractured it," I say.

"Who got me there? ...Emily—*yes*, Emily. I had the flowers lying across my lap as she wheeled me around. She took me to your mother's room on the second floor and I knocked on her door. When I heard her coming over to answer it, I stood up and held out the flowers."

"Right, so you remember. Alfie, why don't you tell Grandpa—"

"No, no, no, wait a second," my father says. "Something happened. She didn't take the flowers. No, she *did* take the flowers. Something else..."

I sigh and resign myself to what comes next.

"She didn't know who you were," I tell him. "You held the flowers out to her, she took them and said, 'Thank you, *Evie*'. Then she closed the door in your face." I leave out the part about how my mother died in her sleep a month later.

I wait for him to agree and fall silent. We've been here before over the intervening years and I call it the death of silence. It is the moment he realises that the silence in his heart is gone. The absence of silence is want and expectation and disappointment slowly eating itself. It is the slowest of deaths, like a thousand cuts in which he forgets the knife until it revisits his flesh, and so every slice feels like both the first *and* the thousandth. She died.

She died.

Watch it sink in.

"Does that sound right to you, Dad?"

Skip, stone. Please, just *skip*.

Looking at the ceiling, he nods.

"All except one part," he says.

The stone stops. Freezes in mid-air.

"Oh? Which part is that?" I ask.

"The part where you said she didn't recognise me," he says.

11. This is not real. It's fiction.

I want a fucking time machine. I want to skip through time and space like a stone skimming across some beautiful blue lake.

Skip.

We are in a local Mothercare, looking at cots for the baby. I follow sheepishly, hands buried in my pockets, inches from my manhood. Alfie finds an emoji bouncy ball and throws it around the shop, chasing it headlong down the aisles. The staff look at him, but with no diagnoses of what is wrong with him I cannot offer an explanation, only shrug and say, "Kids, huh?" Sue chooses an expensive cot, which sees my hands ball into fists and drive deeper into my pockets. I'm thinking we really need to talk about this phantom pregnancy as the lining in one of my pockets tears and something round and yellow with a stuck-out tongue and a winking eye flashes past my face.

Skip.

Study. Door open. The sound of my fingers on the keyboard is a light shower. I'm working on *Perception*. The old man in the park may or may not be a bad person. Five hundred words. In bed by ten.

Skip.

As I leave the house one morning to walk the green mile to work (green because there are a lot of trees and grass on the way but by its end it only feels like dying) the neighbour I saw on the day we moved in stops me and congratulates me on the baby. He pumps my hand like we are old friends and offers me a lift to work in his rundown Nissan Almera while his two well turned-out children sit in the back seat. I say,"I'll walk, thanks," but really it's more like a run.

Skip.

Study. Door closed. The words rain in stops-and-starts as I work on *Perception*. Maybe the man who sits in the park and watches the children play isn't bad. Maybe he's trying to reconnect to something he lost. Should he take that hole that exists inside him and lock himself away from the world until he dies? Or maybe the old man is a pervert. Eight hundred words. Bed at midnight

Skip.

"The baby's coming," Sue says from the kitchen.

Alfie meets me on the landing upstairs, where Sue once stood and told me she was bleeding. "The special, Daddy. It's here!"

There is a white van outside. A knock on the door. The postman hands over a plain cardboard box; the kind of inconspicuous packaging reserved for pornography. Sue has a blanket at the ready and the Moses basket on the kitchen counter. She wanted a cot. It seems I only managed to talk her down from the roof to an upper floor window.

In the box there is polystyrene popcorn, dyed a hint of blue.

"I'm guessing it's a boy," I say.

Sue smiles and from the popcorn pulls out a bottle, a babygro, a bundle of outfits tied with a red-and-white ribbon, some paw-print mittens ("Cute," she says), a bunch (or is the correct collective term here a *neckful?*) of bibs, and an actual fucking nappy.

Next comes the baby, wrapped head-to-toe in a blue blanket with white spots. Sue lifts it out of the box, a few errant popcorn kernels sticking to the blanket, falling to the tile, and places it on the kitchen counter like you would if the thing was ticking. She teases out a foot and coos at the sight of its tiny toes, eliciting a similar response from Alfie, who is peering over the countertop, desperate to see.

My eyes are drawn to the bottom of the box. Under the baby, there is a keepsake picture of our new arrival. No one keeps print photographs these days, but then this is hardly a conventional childbirth. This is an unboxing, the kind of thing sad fucks post on YouTube and even sadder fucks watch. And I am starring in it. I think of our neighbour with his two bright, well-turned-out kids and my entire *being* cringes at the thought of introducing him—or anyone—to *this*.

As Sue carefully unfolds the blanket from around the doll I look away—into the bottom of the box. There, I make the rather grisly discovery of its belly plate, which at first glance looks like somebody has skinned a real baby from the clavicle to the pubus then fixed four white tiers around the edge. There is a back plate too. Spare legs. Spare arms.

Skip.

Skip.

It isn't working.

By now Sue has uncovered its face.

"Jesus Christ, Sue—what did you do?"

What I mean is how did they make this thing resemble one of us: not just a human baby but a Fenwick. The size, shape, and colour of its eyes, the creases underneath, the shape of its cheeks, the slight downturn to its mouth, the colour of its hair, the way the hair sits... everything.

"He's based on the two of us," Sue says.

"What do you mean?"

"I sent them photographs."

"You didn't."

She nods, mistaking my tone as light because she is not hearing me. Sue has not been hearing me for a long time.

They say no man is an island. No woman is either. But we often inhabit them, communicating with each other through smoke-signals and bottled messages we can only hope to see wash up on the other's empty shore.

Now Island Sue has gone swimming with the starfish.

"Is he my *bruvver*, Mummy?" Alfie asks.

"Yes," she says.

"No," I say.

Alfie's thick eyebrows furrow.

"But he looks like me."

It does. It looks like all of us. It's fucking spooky.

Without thinking, compelled even, I reach inside the box and take the spare arms and hold them in front of the doll's eyes. A shiver runs up my back.

"What are you doing?" Sue asks and slaps my hands away. "Don't do that to him."

What Sue doesn't understand—and I am only beginning to understand myself—is that this is how I have always seen him. Even when he was real, alive, growing inside her, growing inside both of us, he was never anything but a monster in my eyes.

A freak.

"What is wrong with you?" Sue asks, stroking the doll's cheek with the edge of her thumb.

"We can't do this," I tell her. "It's insane. You told me you were still pregnant, and—and I believed you."

The last part is a lie—or maybe an exaggeration because there was a moment there when... I am hoping something will snap her out of this—whatever *this is*. But Sue is crying, and Alfie is crying *because* Sue is crying, and the only ones not crying are me and our silicon son.

"What about *him*?" I ask, indicating Alfie with a not-so-subtle nod. "Have you thought about what this is going to do to him?"

"This isn't cancer," Sue says, picking up the doll, still wrapped in its blanket, and holding it against the warmth of her skin. "This isn't what's happening to your father—the zombies and the, the spiders. *This* is something good. For all of us. It's what we need."

"Grampa's *rifty*, Mummy. He says undead will hurt Alfie and Mummy and Daddy."

"You see?" she says.

I look between Sue and Alfie and the doll she is clutching to her chest and think, How do I tell my son that in the end the people he loves will hurt him the most?

"No, Sue. This is not real. It's fiction."

Sue leans closer to me, and I want to kiss her, to kiss away the pain and the madness spreading through her—our family—like mould, but instead she says to me in an angry whisper so that Alfie cannot hear, "You wrote a story about this once, remember? The teacher who lost his wife then replaced her with a mannequin. You believe in your stories, Simon. Let me believe in mine. Okay?"

"But Sue—*please*: that story did not end well. And neither will this."

But she isn't listening and we are islands.

Skip.

Study. Door closed. The time somewhere between late and early. The time for writers: when a door in the mind creaks open and the dark things pour out. Despite this, the words have been slow to hit the screen tonight, and there is a heavy rain outside. It talks to me, so I gaze out the window and listen to the words. In the woods behind our house, I watch, numb, as the baby crawls across the leafy floor, arms reaching from its eye sockets like insect antennae twitching, grabbing at the air. The sound of the leaves beneath its palms and knees like rustling paper. The wind through the rain like the howl of some incorporeal wolf.

In *Perception* I've reached a point where it is either the old man's fault or the husband's, depending on your point-of-view. But this thing with Sue and the reborn baby (I hate the word 'reborn'; it means 'brought back to life', but how can anything be brought back if it never was? It's a lie.) this thing with *the doll*, never mind what my father told me during my last visit, means all of the subtlety has gone out of the piece. I've lost any focus I thought I had and now *everything* seems to point at the husband. He was never supposed to be the bad guy.

I turn from the woods out back to the Post-It note forest surrounding my desk. My eyes skim across the trees and it takes a moment for me to realise that I am looking for something.

Something I buried.

I stand and lean across the desk. Start tearing Post-It notes down one at a time so I can peer closely between the trees. Soon it is handfuls and my desk and laptop keyboard are littered with crumpled green squares of paper. I run my fingers through this fallen forest and the sound is as crisp as dry leaves.

I don't need to find the word. It's like it has crawled out from the trees.

Like it's already inside the room with me.

Skip

Lying in bed, awake, the sun rising outside the window (or rather thinking about coming out of hiding, like Alfie when he used to wet himself), watching shadows try to find a place in which to hide for the day. Thinking, I feel like being a shadow.

Sue is asleep beside me, cradling the doll on her chest. It seems neither of us could sleep.

I sit up with a start and a shiver whispering against my neck.

"What is that?" I ask, shaking Sue awake. "What is it doing?"

Rhetorical question. The doll's chest is moving.

"Did you do that?" I ask.

"What?" she asks, muzzy. "No. No. He can do it himself."

"What is it, a mechanism or..."

"No, Simon, they're called *lungs*. Go back to sleep."

It takes me a full minute to remove the headboard from my back and slide back down into bed. This is how things are going to be from now on, I realise. Sue swearing pigs can fly, snow is blue, and that there's a guy down at the chip shop who swears he's Elvis—and, of course, he *is*.

My mobile phone starts to vibrate on the bedside table. Is that movement created by a mechanism or does my phone have lungs too, Sue?

Unknown number.

"Who is this?"

It's four-thirty in the morning, "Hello" does not apply.

Someone speaks. They have my number as an emergency contact but they've never had to ring me before.

"Who was it?" Sue asks after the phone hits the floor.

"Wintercroft," I say. "My father just died."

12. We are the inside

The problem with skipping like a stone across a beautiful blue lake is one of momentum: sooner or later the stone stops, sinks, and the lake is revealed as neither beautiful nor blue but cold, deep, and dark.

Over the next two days I deal with the business of my father's funeral. Deal is probably the wrong word: I carry out my duties as his son.

The staff at Wintercroft are compassionate and understanding. It turns out Emily shaved his face on the night of his passing. Apparently, he was wide-eyed and grinning throughout, like a baby taking its first bath. They all talk fondly of my father, recalling warm and humorous moments they shared with him. I do not recognise the man they are talking about. No one mentions the horde or the spiders. That was our thing, I suppose.

That, and our final conversation.

'All except one part... The part where you said she didn't recognise me.'

Collecting his things from his room, there is a sense of hope that I might find something: a letter, a clue, anything. A green Post-It note with trees hand-drawn on it and the word 'baby' hidden amongst them. But there is nothing other than the everyday, which is what he was all about. Nothing to connect the two of us, to make me smile a wistful smile and maybe bring a tear or two to my eyes (and perhaps to the reader's in the next story I write about him, because they are *all* about him). All I have are his last words to me, and I have dementia to thank (or blame) for those, so they might be true or they might not, and now—now I will never truly know.

And the saddest part is: dementia was probably the best thing that happened to us. Before, my father worked his long shifts and slept his long sleeps with little of anything else in-between. Words were his enemy (which might explain why they became my friends). He was a one-dimensional character in a story with no plot.

At least now I have a clue, a message in a bottle lying on the sand of my empty beach. I just don't know whether he wrote the words or not.

'*...the part where you said she didn't recognise me.*'

Enough.

While I make preparations for the funeral, Sue keeps herself busy with the reborn doll.

"He needs new clothes," she says to me one morning before my eyes are open and my nightmares have a chance to fade.

"Who does?" I mumble.

"The baby. They only sent enough to get us started. And we'll need more nappies and formula too."

My comment about how I am surprised she isn't breastfeeding goes unnoticed (or maybe it doesn't). We are entrenched on our islands, building shelters for the long game.

"You aren't taking that to the funeral," I say.

"Why not?"

"Do I need to explain?"

"Yes, Simon, you do."

"Alright: it isn't appropriate. This is going to be a short humanitarian service—he wasn't a religious man—and it's supposed to be about us saying goodbye to *him* not drawing attention to *that*. Clear enough?"

"If he isn't going then I'm not going either," she says. "He's part of the family now. There is no way I'm leaving him on his own."

"Of course not," I say, exasperated. "We wouldn't want the poor thing to melt in front of the fire. Or fall out the window. Because, you know, Sue, he'd fucking *bounce*."

But by that last salvo Sue has already walked out and I am talking to an empty bedroom. "Who gives a shit anyway? Bring it along. I don't care. I don't. My father was a fucking loser." Yelling now at the space above the door, where there is a spider and something else.

A tiny patch of mould.

*

I let Alfie take his scooter to the funeral. It may not be appropriate but at least it is Darth Vader black and not stormtrooper white. Father of the year: he wanted the stormtrooper and I bought him the wrong one. I ask him to leave it outside while they turn Dad into ashes, usher us out, and bring the next grieving family in. Life is not so much a circle as the conveyor belt in *The Generation Game*, in which we try to remember all the things that have passed us by.

As we stand outside, Alfie with his scooter, Sue with her reborn doll, and me with my recently acquired knowledge of my father, we shake hands, kiss cheeks, and say thank you and goodbye to those who came, a parade of mostly complete strangers. Which is the moment I realise that we are now outside the crematorium and I have missed my chance to say goodbye to *him*. My own father.

"I need to go back inside," I say to the man minding the exit door.

"Sorry, sir, the next family will be starting their service at any moment." And true enough, peering across his shoulder I can see through the glass doors on the other side of the building an array of sad, dejected faces (sadder than ours certainly; some of them tear-streaked, bawling before the eulogy even begins) as the end of my father's coffin disappears behind the red velvet curtain.

This is the moment when I realise the silence in *my* heart is gone. Want and expectation and disappointment slowly eating itself. The slowest of deaths, like a thousand cuts in which I'll forget the knife until it revisits my flesh, and so every slice feels like both the first *and* the thousandth. He died.

He died.

Watch it sink in.

*

We catch a bus into Salisbury city centre. At the crematorium, a few people asked if we wanted a lift (we were even offered a ride in the Wintercroft minibus) but we made our excuses and left. Sue wants to walk the rest of the way home. She thinks the air will do us all some good. Alfie doesn't complain because he likes riding his scooter; the doll *can't* complain, and I go along like I always do. On the way, Sue stops at a bench close to the busy Exeter Street Roundabout to change the doll's nappy; she seems surprised to discover it isn't soiled. I need to keep this freak show moving, I think. Passersby are slowing down for a peek at the blue bundle Sue is carrying, which is hardly surprising considering the rest of us are dressed in black (the contrast alone must draw the eye), but with my hand firmly on Sue's back we blow past them all like a cold breeze.

Then we reach the park.

Churchill Gardens.

"Mummy, can we go? *Pleeease*. I want to play on my scoo'er."

Sue looks at me. Alfie looks at me. Sue pulls the blanket down under the doll's face so that the doll can look at me too.

"Don't," I tell her.

The sun is out but it is cloudy and threatening to rain. How busy can it be? I think. Most children will be in school. Besides, part of me wants to know if the old man is there today, sitting on his bench, making the parents uneasy.

By the time the play park comes into view, it is too late to turn around and walk away. We are committed (we *should* be committed, I think), otherwise we run the risk of a meltdown from Alfie. The Fenwick boys are rigid thinkers, set in our ways—or so I used to believe.

The play park is full of mothers. It feels like a biker gathering, only with prams and buggies instead of Harleys. There are between eight and a dozen women, various ages, shapes, sizes, all talking and peering under each other's hoods to coo at what they find in there.

Of course: the older children are all in school but the young children and the *babies*, they're all right here, penned in by a wrought iron fence that looks like a heating coil.

And we are going in there.

O-O spells no.

Despite my efforts to the contrary, the first contact comes from me. Alfie wants to ride on a swing, so I volunteer to push, if only to keep Sue—not Sue, the time bomb she is carrying—away from the others. There is a woman in her mid-thirties, no makeup, hair in a bun for convenience, pushing a young girl, maybe two-years-old, on the swing next to ours. The mother looks tired and bloodless, while the girl looks pink and satisfied. A little vampiress with her own personal blood supply.

I push the swing. Alfie laughs. Life cannot get any easier.

But then curiosity gets the better of me.

"Excuse me... Have you seen the old man who sometimes hangs around here?" I do not need to say any more; the woman's face darkens visibly (not difficult as she looks virtually anaemic to begin with) and she snatches the conversation away from me before it really has a chance to begin.

"The man in the suit?" she says. "The one that didn't fit?" Then she proceeds to answer her own question. "They moved him on or took him away. A group of us got together and put a complaint in to the council. He was scaring the children."

Push.

"Is that so?"

She hears the doubt in my voice, decides to ignore it.

"He used to sit on that bench over there," she says. "Same one every day. Just sit there and constantly stare at them."

I see her point. After all, if looks could kill, hers would have had the old man castrated and hung by the neck from the nearest branch.

Then what would she make of Dad? I think.

"I spoke to him once," I tell her, pushing Alfie so high each swing ends in a moment of weightlessness then that inevitable bump as the chains rein him back in. "Sitting over there, right enough." I point to the bench where I had stumbled upon him that night and for a moment all the air is sucked out of my lungs. Draped across the back of the bench is an empty suit jacket; *his* empty suit jacket. A parting gift or a parting shot, I cannot tell. "I think his name was Dullcut. He seemed harmless enough. Pleasant, even."

The woman looks at me as though she wouldn't mind seeing another neck in the noose, and within three more swings her daughter is scooped out of her seat and led (more like dragged) by the hand back to the huddle of mothers.

"Looks like I got that one all wrong, buddy," I say to Alfie.

"Why?" he asks.

"Well, for starters, I had the little girl pegged as the bloodsucker."

"What's a *budsucker?*"

"A budsucker's an alcoholic. A bloodsucker is a—never mind. We could do this all day. The rain's coming and it's time to go. Where's Mummy?"

"There she is!" he cries, pointing out Sue over by the other mothers.

My heart beats faster as she approaches the women, holding the bundle up and away from her body; not quite as an offering but certainly presenting it to them. She is beaming, her coffee-brown eyes wide and glistening with happy tears.

I stop the swing and lift Alfie out of the rubber-cage seat to let him run around. Actually, all I want is for us all to leave, go home, *now*, but when it comes to Alfie it can be like trying to land a plane without it blowing up on the runway. There are specific stages and procedures to follow. But let's keep Alfie in a holding pattern for now. Sue is the one I am worried about.

The women's faces are warm and welcoming until Sue peels back the blanket to reveal what she is carrying. I envisage not a baby's face or even a doll's but a digital display, red digits counting down the final seconds: 00:03...00:02...00:01...

Silence.

Watching Sue's face is like watching a star go supernova: that sudden increase in brightness at the precise moment of total collapse.

And I am seeing all of this in terms of aeroplanes and timers and stars because similes and metaphor—*language*—creates a barrier from what is really happening around me. So, when the plane burns on the tarmac or the bomb explodes or the star collapses it is all...figurative.

Or at least it used to be.

Watch it sink in.

One of them laughs and elbows a couple of the women standing next to her. The nudged women, who were talking among themselves, turn to see the face of the thing that Sue is so proud of—and laugh into their hands like children. From them, my mind flashes to Alfie, who I find standing by the rope tower with four or five children surrounding him. A boy of Alfie's age is talking to him, pointing at Alfie's scooter, which appears to have become the rope in a game of tug-o'-war. Alfie's thick eyebrows are having a fit, scrunching and stretching by turns as he watches the boy's lips move but struggles to process the words he is saying. The boy gets more animated and forceful as Alfie's brow goes into retirement and fixes itself in the furrowed position. He looks like a kid with psychic powers trying to stop someone's heart, but I know there isn't any power there and there isn't any real aggression. He is simply confused by the *rifty* boy in front of him pulling at his scooter, taking it away, *riding* it away.

The children laugh.

The women laugh.

And Alfie looks around for his parents but fails to spot either one of us, and in a moment of desperate panic he looks so lost my heart breaks and everything inside it pours out.

I stride across the mulch and pull Sue away from the women and Alfie away from the children. I lead them both out of earshot, and for a moment I think about how odd this scene must look, with all of them in their bright everyday clothes and the three of us in our funeral. But then a light rain begins to fall and the children shriek and the women shriek even louder and everyone runs for the shelter of the nearby trees or the pirate ship hull. Except us.

We close our eyes and let the rain land on our faces.

People run from rain but sit in bathtubs of water.

Charles Bukowski's words to me in my dream.

Not me, I think. I can't run anymore.

"Dad...he liked to dress in women's clothes."

Sue doesn't laugh but only looks at me wide-eyed and waiting as drizzle clings to her hair like dew.

"He does, Mummy," Alfie says. "Grampa tole us when we went to see him. He tole us about the *whores* and the undead too."

"Okay," Sue says and laughs. "I *think* I know what you mean."

"One day Mum came home early and caught him red-handed," I tell her.

"Really?" she says. "Wow. What did she do?"

"She made tea and scones."

"You're joking?"

"Nope. He told me. I suppose it could have been the dementia talking, but I don't think so. It kind of fits—right?" The distance, the secret drinking (perhaps leading to the liver cancer), shit, even the aversion to facial hair.

I am welling up (thank you, rain, for the camouflage) so I let my father tell the rest of the story, not quite as he told it to me in his room in Wintercroft—without the forgetful pauses or the meandering side trips. He was, however, as lucid as I have ever seen or heard him since the onset of his dementia, so perhaps this memory was the one vessel that even the worst fog could not sink.

'*Your mother and me never talked much, but that day she found me— we sat down and had ourselves a good, long conversation. The best. And then later, when the tea and scones were finished your mother turned to me and said, 'I'll need my husband back now.' So I went upstairs, changed into my old clothes, and came back down the man she expected me to be. I owed her that much, and more besides. Those were intolerant times, and intolerance makes fools and monsters of us all. What your mother showed me was love. Real love. She believed in my madness. Because if anyone had found out it would have destroyed not only me but her, too. She kept it secret for thirty years. Not only that, but every once in a while she drew the curtains, put on the kettle, made some scones, and let 'Evie' come to visit. I swear your mother and her could talk all night, but at the end of the evening Evie left and I came home. I always came home. It was hard saying goodbye to her but giving her up completely would have been much, much worse. Your mother understood that and took pity on me. She was a truly wonderful woman.*

'*Skip forward thirty years and she ends up in this place. By this point she doesn't know who I am anymore. You can't imagine how that is, how* humiliating *that is, to be living in a place like this with the woman you've loved most of your life passing you in the corridor like you're a complete stranger. It was like it had all been for nothing. And when you're this close to the end there doesn't seem to be time for second chances. So, I stayed in here, inside my room. I didn't want to see her. In all honesty, I was waiting for one of us to die. But then Emily, she convinced me to try one last time. She talked me into a wheelchair—I had that bad hip, remember?—and she pushed me up to your mother's room on the second floor. I got out and held onto the door jamb with one hand while with my other I held out the flowers I'd brought with me. Calla lilies; her favourite. And because I had no free hand left, Emily knocked on the door. We waited. Finally, your mother answered, took the flowers from me, and said, 'Thank you, Evie.'*

'I lost it. I called her a word I'd never called anyone before and I refuse to repeat it now. She slammed the door in my face. I stood there and listened to her sob into a pillow. Then I turned to Emily, told her to take me back to my room. She did, but the whole way she kept trying to cheer me up and I...I just couldn't. I told her to leave me in the chair, I'd manage to get out on my own, and to close the door on her way out. When she was gone and the door was closed I could still hear your mother crying on the other side. I started crying myself then, but I didn't want Emily or anyone else hearing me, so I held both my hands over my mouth and nose until the sound couldn't get out and the air couldn't get in, and I slid off the wheelchair and lay like that on the floor until I nearly passed out.

'You see, I called her what I called her out of embarrassment, nothing else, but really that was the first time she'd recognised me in two years, and maybe—maybe the first time in forty.'

I take Sue's hand and squeeze it in mine. Tears and rain run down our cheeks.

"I know that sometimes I am a bad husband and a poor father but maybe things can still turn out all right." I wait. Nothing. "And now I am going to keep talking because when we don't that's when the problems start, when the rot" (*mould*) "sets in and the silence begins to gnaw away at everything we've built and—"

Sue kisses me. Long and inappropriately.

She pulls away. "Shut up." Kisses me again. "*Shut up.*"

If this was one of those old films I'd be the hysterical woman and Sue would be Humphrey Bogart slapping me across the face.

"Stop trying to control everything with words," she tells me.

"What about *them*?" I ask, meaning the women emerging from their shelters like zombies from the grave, the children climbing wild across the rope tower like giant scuttling spiders, and everyone else out there too. "They'll never accept this. They'll think we've both lost our minds. And they'd be right."

Sue shrugs. "They'd do well to lose a bit of theirs too," she says. "You said it yourself. We are the inside."

I lean over Alfie and kiss my wife on the corner of her smiling mouth. Seeing that smile through her tears is like catching the last gasp of sunlight on a day full of rain.

"What about him?" she asks, meaning the doll, meaning our baby, meaning our son.

I take him from her arms and cradle him in one of mine as I pull the blanket aside to reveal his face. Everything is screaming at me: this is not going to end well, and this—whatever this is—is not the ending I was hoping for. But sometimes we don't choose the ending, the ending chooses us. And we are powerless to resist the things we want.

"I think he has my father's eyes," I say.

Looking for Landau

1. The Silence Will Be Beautiful

Here we are again. On my knees in the dust. This time we are in the Sun Belt; this time it is Arizona dust. But the blood in my mouth always tastes the same.

I know he isn't here, but they've seen him, I can tell. They've *talked* to him. It's written all over their hate-filled faces. They have murder in their eyes. I have to hand it to Landau: he has a knack for getting people to do what he wants. For showing them the way.

"Whatever he told you, it's a lie." Hands behind my head, dust on my knees, it's what they expect me to say. I am probably a rapist or a paedophile, and they are Landau's appointed death squad, except they don't know it. I bet they would love the title, though. It would chime with their jack boots, the Reichsadler pins on their leather jackets, or the swastikas hand-painted on their motorcycle gas tanks.

I look around, one eye swollen shut. Seven, eight men in a bowling pin configuration. The prospects look wiry at the back, not a lot of meat on their young bones, but useful with it. They hit the hardest since they have the most to prove. It's manufactured hate to get them into favour with the club president, to earn their full patch. Isn't it always though? Manufactured? A means to an end? I fucking hate that. Hate *is* the end.

When I rode in, they were fresh back from the white power rally up in Phoenix, drinking hard, celebrating, trying to impress the drunk wives with their battle wounds (so called). I gathered that much before the beat down started. I should have known some roadside hole-in-the-wall called *The Tumbleweed* could never be as harmless as its name suggests, not with the motorcycles leaning outside the saloon doors and the metal playing so loud the whole dirt lot shook like they were panning for gold. And maybe I did know. The truth is they probably spent the entire rally yelling and cursing at some poor, defenceless Rosa Parks wannabe. And the battle wounds? Old scars from a time when they actually had a pair. Now this bunch of has-beens or never-weres *all* have something to prove, not just the prospects, and they will fuck or fight to prove it. Looking at the calibre of broad this outfit attracts, better they get to knocking teeth than catching clam.

Broad. Now there's a word I haven't used in seventy years. It's funny how they sink for a time then come bobbing back to the surface, like bodies carried down the long river.

"What's your name?" the president asks, jabbing the smouldering end of a thick cigar close to my face. This one is meat more than muscle but he hits like a slow train in that the hurt keeps coming. One day soon his heart will stop. I pick that up from people sometimes; a vibration—and in his case, a *good* vibration. Another jab of the cigar. "What's your goddamn name, asshole?"

"Is it necessary?" I ask. It's not like they intend to erect a marker beside my shallow grave in the desert, is it? He hits me by way of an answer, a hundred wagons dragging across my face. "Fine," I say, spitting blood from the side of my mouth. I'm surprised to see no teeth. "Call me Rust."

"Tell me, *Rust*—what is that fucking thing on your arm?"

I am wearing a leather cut-off, plain black T underneath. I like the freedom of movement it provides. With my hands clasped behind my head, he can see all the way to my biceps.

"This?" I say. "It's a scar. It's called a Lichtenburg figure. It's what happens when you get struck by lightning and live."

"*You've* been struck by lightning?"

Why do they say it like it was winning the state lottery? It ain't. It damn well hurt.

"Twice," I tell him. "This one on my left arm continues across my back. I've got another, on my leg, but only men I *like* get to see that one..." Provocative smile. I need to hurry this along. Landau is getting away.

"You a faggot?" the president asks.

Seems I am not the only one to revert to outdated nomenclature.

"Look at us," I say. "Out here. Drowning in a sea of dead words. What say we head inside and talk? I can show you my scars, you can tell me the direction he went. I'm buying."

"He's a faggot for sure, pres," says one of the prospects, blonde, barely eighteen years old. The vibration coming off this one is strong too. His heart ready to stop, like a broken clock. "Let me do him. I'm ready."

"Is it really relevant what or who I am?" I ask, fixing the kid with my eye less swollen. "In three minutes, unless one of you tells me where Landau is, you, your pres, every one of you, will be dead."

Cue laughter. But this is the saddest movie; sad because they don't seem to have read beyond the next line.

"At least let me buy you a drink to see you on your way," I tell them.

The president looks over his shoulder at his vice president and one of his lieutenants. Their faces don't matter. None of them do. "You getting all this, boys? We got ourselves a confident son of a bitch." He turns back to me slowly, spits something dark into the dust between my knees. "You're used to being confident and getting what you want, ain't that so? But we—we ain't no ten-year-old boys."

So, a pederast it is. I am a different monster in every state. Thank you, Landau. The blows land harder when they have that picture in their minds, like maybe they are punishing their own fathers.

Pres nods to his VP on his left, who turns and nods to the blonde prospect at the back. Prospect turns and signals the barkeep, who until now has been watching proceedings from the backlit doorway of the bar. The signal sends him inside, and all the lights go off. Now he has deniability if anything should go wrong here tonight; wrong being that the cops get wind of what happened. He closed early and went home to his wife, although something tells me he has no wife—a different kind of vibration, I guess. Regardless, the dirt lot is plunged into darkness for a few seconds before a single motorcycle headlight illuminates my face.

In front of me, the men become dark, wavering columns standing before a curtain of light. I can no longer see any of their faces or, better yet, the faces of those who surround *them*: the bleachers; the skrik.

"Can I ask a question first?"

Their president shrugs. "Shoot."

"Landau... If you won't tell me where he went, will you tell me when you saw him last? Are we talking days or hours?"

Pres does not answer for a moment, and a moment feels like too long in the short remainder of his life.

"Days or hours? Please..."

"Hours," he says finally. "Five. Maybe six."

"So we're down to that," I say. "Good. Thank you. Thank you so much."

"Why are you *smiling*?" he asks.

For the first time, the president sounds unsure. Mine is not a face for smiling. They say muscles have memory, and the muscles in my face have never forgotten.

"Holy shit," says someone else from behind the curtain. The blonde prospect, I think. "Doesn't this asshole know the real beat down's coming? What you got so far was nothing but a taste, motherfucker!"

"Last month it was eight," I say, ignoring him. Eight hours.

I'm closing.

Then pres sends his freight train of a right at my face again. I see it coming all the way but choose to let it pass on through. His knuckles seem to carve a tunnel through my smile, hollowing out my skull, leaving nothing behind but blood and echoes ringing down a long, long, empty space.

I'm scared, Rust... They're going to kill us, aren't they?

(Not me)

Give me your hand... Give me your hand... I won't let you go.

Then the pres hits me with his left. Inside the tunnel in my face, the walls crack, and water first leaks then sprays from each widening fissure. Like rain.

Like showers.

I won't let you go.

Mortal men have no patience. But some of us have time on our side; some of us have learned there is a long game and how to play it. When the klaxon sounds and the game finally ends, the silence will be beautiful. Until then...

I go to my hands and knees. I pick up a pair of rocks from the dirt lot that are a little too large for my fingers to grasp comfortably. I hold my hands out to my sides. I like the symbolism. The dead are the cross I bear, and later, there will be blood on these hands. So much blood.

Where the rocks come from I can only guess, but I like them too. They have a history longer even than my own, even than that book, and they fit with a comfortable awkwardness in the palms of my hands, my fingers curling around their sharp, roughened shells. When the fighting starts, they will inflict a world of pain, and they will transmit that pain—through my fingers—back to me. This will be a shared experience.

In some ways, we are all going to die tonight.

2. A Fish on the Hook

The barkeep pours me another drink. He doesn't try to hide the fear in his hands, and I don't mind the bourbon moat he spills on the bar just as long as the glass ends up full. Darkness has fallen hard outside. In more ways than one. A moonless sky choked with cloud no one can see. The barkeep—his name is Rick—finishes pouring my drink, shakes the uncapped bottle neck at my scraped knuckles, my red-slicked palms.

"Can I get you something for those?" he asks. "I got bandages somewhere, I'm sure of it."

I look up from my glass on the bartop to Rick. He is tall, middle forties, which is young enough—maybe—to know better, but old enough—maybe—to not care about having a future and try something stupid anyway.

"This is a biker bar, so it goes without saying you have weapons stashed around the place, right? I'm thinking a shotgun behind the bar at the very least. Listen to me, Rick. That would be a mistake. Your *last* mistake. And I don't want that. I want you to have a lot more mistakes in your future, do you understand what I am saying?"

Rick nods, sweat on his brow, fear pouring out of his eyes. It's the fear that gets to me most, little else does these days. Fear is like a cigarette. You take a pull, it gives you what you need—a jolt of something—but it is killing you slowly and you know it. So, what do you do? You stop smoking. I see that look on a man's face now and all I wanna do is stamp it out.

"Bandages would be appreciated, Rick. Thank you. Go get them while I drink this."

And please...don't look at me.

Rick emerges hesitantly from behind the bar and heads for the backroom. I wave him on, turn my back to look out the window, at the night. I have been shot before, many times; like being struck by lightning (*twice*) it is not an experience you look to repeat. But if I misjudge Rick the barkeep, I'll recover. He won't.

"Did you see him?" I ask, although by appearances I am talking to an empty bar. There is the sound of rummaging from back there but he doesn't come out with either twin-barrel or bandage.

"Who, the weird guy?"

The weird guy.

"Yes, him. Did you see him? Talk to him? What did he say?"

I get up from the barstool—

can't sit

—and walk to the window that offers the best view of the dirt lot outside, leaving a spattered trail of blood in my wake. Nothing a mop and bucket won't fix. I peer through the grime at the eight bodies lying peaceful as sleeping steer, and at the equal number of bleachers left behind, huddled like nervous children at their first ever party.

Landau's children.

They glow with a strange luminescence. Watercolours drowned down the canvas of this world, running like tyres once afire but now only melting in the yard, giving off a different kind of noxious smoke, odourless and yet capable of filling your lungs with an overwhelming sense of doom and dread. But I have learned to breathe the dead, and maybe even come to enjoy it, like some exotic tobacco for the soul. It's hard to quit when that's all you've got.

He never comes right back for his children. I have laid that trap for him before. Landau keeps moving forward, like a black tsunami, or a shark. For the children of Landau it is the longest party: bleachers must stick around until he comes their way again, which might be a week from now or a century, who knows but Landau himself? Otherwise, I would have found him by now.

He leaves behind a trail of ghosts, and I follow.

Rick returns from the backroom with some plasters, a roll of bandage, and a tube of antiseptic cream. We sit at one of the tables. His hands are still shaking but he manages to pour whisky over my palms to clean the shallow cuts and wash away the dust and dirt that may have got worked in there. As he applies the cream, sticks the plasters, winds the bandage, his eyes dart to the window and the lot outside.

"They're gone," I say. "They're not coming back."

But they aren't gone, they've only changed, and now the eight bleachers stand at the window, peering in at us, their faces stretched and twisted but emotionless. I *could* say they are going to be a fixture around this place for a while, until Landau returns, but Rick doesn't need to know that.

"What am I supposed to tell the cops?" he asks, his shock clearing just enough for him to start worrying about what is going to happen to *him*.

"Tell them they picked the wrong fight and lost. There are other outlaw gangs in this area, they'll start with them. Say there were at least twenty, it was dark, you couldn't see their patches, but your guys put up a good fight. That way, the club's reputation won't take a beating around here."

He nods like a fish on the hook. There is sincerity in it; I believe him. The fear has subsided from his eyes. All I see in them now is a darkened room and two shapes writhing.

He finishes patching me up, but doesn't let go of my hand. He takes a long pull from the whisky bottle. Another. He offers me the bottle without wiping it off. He looks at me. I look at him. The eight bleachers, pressed to the glass, they look in at the two us looking at each other.

"Ain't this a Disney moment," I say.

We laugh.

And Rick puts down the bottle.

3. The Scream of the Sonoran Desert

By three a.m. the heat of the Sonoran Desert relents only a little. I build a fire at the foot of a rocky outcrop but lie on a bedroll some ways back, at the edge of the flames' reach. It is enough to stare into the fire so that when I look away I cannot see for a while. Until my eyes adjust. And they always adjust. Beyond the firelight, in the surrounding darkness, I glimpse the silhouettes of cacti stretching up from the ground like giant daggers or middle fingers.

I cannot sleep. So, I climb the outcrop and stand at its summit instead, gazing down across the desert toward Interstate 10. Off to my left and still some miles away, a singular glow rises from the horizon to greet the darkness: the suggestion of Phoenix. Meanwhile, below me, the desert plain seems full of Christmas lights. Distance allows me to make such a quaint comparison, but should I venture down from this outcrop, I would see them for what they truly are: bleachers, skrik, their faces stretched with the anguish of their eternal waiting like that of the subject in Munch's work, The Scream. I call them skrik because they *are* the scream: the silent embodiment of death. Pale, wavering figures of sickly light that I must watch and follow in anticipation of their winking out, because in that—in the darkness they leave behind— there is a way to finding Landau.

But he is not the one who keeps me awake tonight. That blame belongs to another.

Machiel.

I see him sometimes, a familiar face among the bleacher crowds. To the untrained eye, he is no more than a point of light among these thousands of other points of light. But I am familiar with the constellations of the dead, with the terrible beasts their disparate lights join together to form: rage-filled faces, powerful limbs and jaws, rending teeth. And yet all of them ineffective as a child's drawing of a monster. His light is the aberration: the one that does not belong in their firmament. He is the loneliest star among these other lonely stars, one which I recognise from watching and wishing upon, from pouring my dreams and hopes into, from incalculable nights screaming back at his silent scream, my frustration, my loss.

Give me your hand... I won't let you go.

But, of course, I did: then, not now.

Then the cacti change, middle fingers joined by the others, flexing themselves into starfish, into hands reaching from the body of this world—*bodies* of this world: a tangled floor of torsos and limbs pressed together to become one green and yellowed mass, the hands reaching and rising from the narrow spaces in-between. And I sense below the hands: mouths, nostrils, *faces* open in a rictus of need but ultimately just holes choked by dust and sand and the shit of lizards.

And I feel guilty for the thing I want most, for I get to walk on their silence and breathe the very air they craved and *still* crave. But the silence always feels temporary, as if their screams will reach my ears at any moment, a tsunami of anguish and sound. Yet the moment never arrives, which makes it worse somehow, the anticipation of a thing that will never be, no release, no retribution, but miles of waiting gnawing at my peace.

I raise both hands to my face. Inflate my lungs with guilt and air.

Tonight, on top of this rocky outcrop in the Sonoran Desert one mile north of the I-10, I give them a voice.

4. Kites to Crawfish

The following day I sleep late, rising to the midday sun and soaring temperatures. The sun doesn't affect me much. I am numb to its charms. However, its light does provide some respite from the skrik. I know they still surround me but there are moments in the day when I can almost convince myself that I am alone.

I swallow some water, shake the desert's gifts from my bedroll and head for my ride. Many moons ago, in a place as far from the Sonoran Desert as anyone can imagine, Machiel used to tease me about how I would be late to my own funeral, not knowing of course the joke would be on him. Most days start with such bittersweetness, then it's usually downhill from there.

After a few bites of cornbread (while I'm in the city I should pick up some fresh supplies) I am back in the saddle, cruising at sixty, heading east on the I-10/Papago Freeway. The first motorcycle I ever owned back in the fifties, a Harley Sportster, had a rigid frame and rode me as much as I rode it. They were like wild, unbroken horses then. You felt every bump, crack, and hole in the road. These days, the ride is smoother, meaning you can go for longer. Maybe it's me, but what is the point? If by the end of the long ride you can still walk straight, you ain't done it right. That applies to most things in life, and maybe to life, too. I don't want no green broke horse.

I could sell the bike—hell, I could give it away—but I am a man of habit. Besides, Landau has *his* wheels. I need some of my own, otherwise I will never catch him up.

But it seems like every time I get within a certain distance, he finds some way of stalling me, setting me back, making sure the two of us never meet. I take the beatings, I hand them out on bad days, I heal, and I keep riding. And all I have to show for it is a collection of scars, like stamps on a passport, and a long bleacher trail at my back.

Scars are hope, I tell myself. If nothing else, mine prove lightning can strike not only once but twice. *I saw Landau before and I will see him again.*

Perhaps that is too strong a word: I caught a *glimpse* of Landau— or rather the red stare of his taillights—in the moments before the clouds rolled onto Fulton Street, Lower Manhattan after the collapse of the south Tower. People were running in panic and as the dust cloud chased and grew it swallowed the sun and everything with it, including Landau.

That was nearly twenty years ago.

On the Papago Freeway, the odometer kisses eighty as Phoenix rises in front of me and the wind rakes the dust from my hair.

Helmets are for pussies or anyone with a life expectancy.

Phoenix is my limit for today, though. An hour or two in the saddle with these hands is enough. I can barely hold onto the grips.

Dumb move going at those bikers with rocks.

Yeah, maybe. But I'm down to the moment. I think too far ahead or look too far behind, and it's over. I will see how far-off everything truly is, the past, the future, Machiel, Landau, and I'll come to a dead stop. I'm down to the moment, cruising in the cold space between two not-so-distant walls of fire when all I want to do is burn, baby. If I *could* just come off my ride and bust open my skull on the road—if it were only that simple—then maybe I could take my seat on the bleachers and watch the endgame with the rest of the skrik. But I don't need a helmet and if I really did come off this beast, it's the goddamn road I'd feel sorry for.

Why stop, then? Why not keep riding?

"Because I need to hit something." I say it out loud, the words a quarter-mile behind me already, incinerated by that wall of fire at my back like bugs tossed into a zapper. "I need to hit something bad."

*

I wait until nightfall before entering the city, pacing a shallow groove in a diner's lot meantime. Finding Landau depends on a continuing strategy and not as the result of a single impulsive play. Much better to wait at the city's borders until darkness illuminates a way, otherwise I might miss some vital clue. It has happened before and cost me years. Landau is the slenderest of needles in the haystack, but he is also a needle that does not wish to be found. With nightfall, the trail is not so much too cold as too *hot*. The lights of the city overlap with the bleachers and it becomes difficult to pinpoint a clear path—or even if Landau has passed through here at all. The falling dark invites me in for a closer look. I rev my engine and give myself over to the mercy of the city.

Sometime around midnight, after roaming the streets of Phoenix for hours and finding no trace of him, I find myself frustrated on East Van Buren. It is quieter than it was in the old days, the beast now tamed by the county Sherriff's Department, but on some side streets the prostitutes still outnumber the skrik. I have had to train my eyes over the years to focus on what I want to see, a kind of tunnel vision, otherwise it becomes a disorientating melange of skin and ghostlight. I don't know whose company I prefer these days.

A few minutes south of Van Buren, I pass bars, motels, and apartment complexes where half the streetlamps have been shot out by rocks to create the right *ambience* for the cars in the parking lots to rock to music and fucking. The beast it seems perhaps not so much tamed as caged and kept out of the way. Meanwhile, in the shadows clinging to these buildings, the drug dealers do a decent trade, shuffling their feet and blowing into their cupped hands, as clichéd and inconspicuous as the cops sitting in their blue-and-whites a short distance back from this arena of sex, at the edge of deniability in fact, drinking their coffee and eating their jelly donuts. Meanwhile, around the cars in the parking lots, people and bleachers crane to watch, peeping Toms and Janes beating off in time to the soundtrack, in time to the sex, bleachers gathered around them like so many limp dicks and dry pussies, their screams of silent anguish never quite so fitting. And the cops—*these* cops on *this* night anyway—seem content to contain the problem and maybe enjoy a little piece of the show themselves. After all, they work long hours and maybe the uniform doesn't do it for their wives anymore, stuck indoors with two, three, four children. What they don't know is that maybe grandma or grandpa agreed to look after the tribe so that mum can escape for a few hours to enjoy some good ole carnal barbecue—spit roasted by a couple of strangers on the back seat of her beige Prius in a parking lot south of Van Buren, folks gathered round, high on crystal or spice, or maybe just eating donuts, watching.

The head eats the tail. I've seen it all. I've seen too much.

Such bullshit. Some of it. Most of it. Some. I've pulled into the parking lot of a cheap apartment complex and there is one car rocking, a small crowd (people and bleachers alike), a pusher, but no cops and no *wives* of cops, none of that circular wishful-thinking bullshit. That is just what I want to believe—that everything has a circular nature, nothing is random, nothing just *happens*. There is a meaning to everything, even if the meaning is one I arbitrarily apply myself, like slapping a factory sticker onto the side of a plain cardboard box. At least it is a label; a purpose.

Because six million Jews don't die for nothing. Ten thousand homosexuals don't die for nothing.

Because Machiel did not die for—

I can feel myself slipping. Losing focus. The scent is cold again— not cold, more like the scent is lost among the stench of the city—and Landau is out there, at the forefront of my mind and yet as mythical as a unicorn.

Big cities make me melancholy; sex makes me melancholy. Barkeep Rick was only last night but it was over so fast. After the fight with the bikers and the rocks, I was about ready to pop anyways. My bad. The band Queen said it best when they sang: *Pain is so close to pleasure.* That feeling of dissatisfaction rises within me again, filling my sack. I feel dirty and I feel *dirty*.

Landau can wait. I need this interlude. I want this interlude. And nothing provides it like the city, it's thick, greasy heart beating in my ears with a kind of irresistible music.

At some point during the public sex show, somebody stands next to me. What never fails to disappoint is how ordinary this sometimes—too often—feels. That is, when it feels like anything at all. People read about this kind of thing in newspapers or online and screw their faces in judgement, but when you are there, when you are part of something depraved, it starts to feel normal, routine even. We were all kites once, beautiful, hand-built, diverse creations. And now we are crawfish. Break us in half, suck the head, eat the tail, throw us away.

This one is tall but a little emaciated. He is interested, though, which is enough. You can see it in their eyes, the dirty corona around the dilated pupils. We may be surrounded by a crowd of skrik but he is real, *alive*, which, again, is enough.

"You gotta be, you know," he says.

I look at him, unsure of what he's talking about. He has a good mouth.

He smirks, indicating there is a punchline coming.

"Mad," he says. "You gotta be—to live in this neighbourhood, right?" He points at the bottom rocker on the back of my jacket, where it reads: NOMAD.

"I get it," I say. "You're a funny guy."

If he drops some stupid line about fungi or fucking mushrooms, I *will* send him to the ground, fuckable mouth or not.

But he doesn't, and we're good.

"You live round here?" I ask.

He nods and points to one of the windows on one of the floors above us.

It sounds like the perfect place to me.

"Let's go."

5. Never Very Far to Fall

My name is Rust and I am an addict.

This one's apartment is a shithole, windows closed and curtained, pizza boxes and beer cans littering the floor. I don't know his name (can't remember, didn't try) but I know he leaves the crusts, drinks Pabst Blue Ribbon, and has an aversion to fresh air. This one lies sprawled on the floor, naked, skin still blushing in all the spots where we crashed against each other. Either he let me have the mattress—in which case, who says romance is dead?—or he rolled off and onto the floor, a drop of inches. In a neighbourhood like this, there is never very far to fall.

I sit up, feel the hard wooden floor against my buttocks through the mattress, and rub the tiredness from my eyes. The only light comes from a lamp in the corner, and at some point he threw something red over it to create a mood. Now it has slipped partway off the shade so that there is a divide in the room. He lies mostly in unfiltered pale light, while my lower half is doused in colour. Legs, crotch, hands. I stare at my hands. Itchy and red. The bandages that Rick the barkeep fixed me up with are a little spotted with blood but it's my thumb and fingers, the ones you use to make the shape of a gun to point at your head: they feel like they've been dipped in PVA glue or something.

Oh Christ...

Then I am up and hurrying for the bathroom and the sink. There is a flat sliver of soap that not even a small kid could use and a nail brush with brown stains on the base of its bristles. I stab the soap-sliver with the brush and under a raging faucet scrub and scrub the memory of this one off my hands. Who would have thought he'd have so much in him?

Look at you.

I can't. The only consolation is that the bathroom mirror is cracked down the middle and he—or someone—has used it and a marker pen to play a game of Tic-Tac-Toe. The Os look like screaming mouths, the Xs like the eyes of the dead. The thing with this game is that if you know how to play, you cannot lose. Likewise, if your opponent knows how to play, you cannot win either. Landau is out there somewhere, and if there is one of us who is not playing the game with a favourable strategy, it isn't him.

On the broken mirror over the sink, there is one space left and no way of winning for one of the players. But whose turn is it?

Am I screaming or am I dead?

6. The Folding Man

The elevator is working but I take the stairs. On every landing there is drug paraphernalia and the stairwell is crammed with bleachers. I do not know if the skrik know that I have the sight or if they are merely drawn to the living like some kind of ghostly parasite, but they stand and watch me with their silent screams as I pass, beggars looking for a currency I do not have. We are packed so tightly in the stairwell that I am forced to walk through them, my face passing through theirs, our mouths kissing across planes, their screams swallowing my face, and me tearing through the back of them like a ghost myself, carrying with me the touch of the coldest feather. It is strange and disorienting and by the time I open the door and emerge onto the now empty lot I am gasping for air, having held my breath for several floors.

Elevators are worse.

Outside, the show is over and the lot appears to be deserted, but that doesn't mean there is no one here. There are skrik, there are always skrik, but there are people too, lying in pockets of shadow around the lot. You glimpse a protruding sneaker here, a hand there, the kyphotic back of a topless middle-aged male sitting cross-legged and bent forward as though in prayer. As I cross the lot, heading for my ride, I step over the bruise-mottled legs of a long-haired young woman high on a few dollars of spice. Slumped against the fender of a twenty-year-old Nissan Sentra, she looks like she is trying to kiss the ground between her splayed feet but isn't nearly flexible enough to reach it, so instead she simply lolls forward then springs back, rambling incoherently at my passing. Even the skrik appear to give her a wide berth.

Back on my bike, I cruise through downtown Phoenix. Traffic is light, both on the roads and the sidewalks. At an intersection crosswalk, the stop lights come on in pairs, like red eyes trying to stare me down. I could run them all and be on my way, but I stop and observe the rules. Nobody steps onto the crosswalk and crosses the street. The lights remain red. It happens sometimes. Man built the traffic light to control his fellow man. Officially, they exist to keep him safe, but control comes in many guises; it wears a mask, like a clown or a president or a simple fucking stop light. We build the things that control us because we want to be controlled. Control is purpose, an end to the chaos and the meaninglessness. It is everything to the people, and everything to the skrik. The only difference is the skrik have learned the truth and that truth is written all over their faces. Control does not belong to us. It belongs to the next guy. Landau is control. Landau is purpose. He is the anchor that stops this ship from hitting the iceberg. And so I chase the next guy. I get on my motorcycle and I follow, like there is some invisible length of tow-rope tied to my fork. But maybe the next guy is just a myth, something to seek out, to fill the time between the drinking and the screwing and the screwing and the drinking, and maybe one day I'll come to the end of the rope and find nothing there but more empty road.

Maybe it is time people woke up and smelled the spice.
Maybe it is time I did, too.

*

Whenever I pass through Phoenix I end up in a familiar neighbourhood,
standing outside a familiar door. I park my ride three streets from the
house on E. Cambridge Avenue to avoid announcing my presence: the
sound of its engine enough to rouse the dead never mind the living in
this suburban neighbourhood, where the only sound at this time in the
morning is the quiet conversation between lawn sprinklers and perfect
green lawns.

There are fewer bleachers in this kind of neighbourhood. Few
remain here, but then what was their dream in life can be a punishment
beyond it. Peace and solitude are, it seems, enjoyable only in finite
measures; in endless supply they become torturous things. And so the
bleachers are drawn to the most populous areas, the places where life
still thrives. They pack out the slums, stations, bars, and sports venues
like moths drawn to the flame that burned them so the first time. So I
come out here as much to escape them as to see *him*.

Those bleachers that do remain here tend to keep off the streets.
They stand at empty windows and scream their silence at the world. I
wonder how many times one of the kids has spotted a curtain twitching
or just sensed he was being watched and called a timeout in their game
of street basketball to direct his friends toward Mr or Mrs So-and-So's
house? How many insults or mudballs have been thrown at windows
in error because of a curtain that never twitched? Bleachers aren't that
effectual, but the kids sense they are being watched by *something* and it
troubles them enough to react. What they don't know is that it isn't Mr
or Mrs So-and-So watching them shoot hoops out here but the thing
that sits in wait for them all. That's right, kids, it's *death* watching you,
always watching you. But if you're one of the lucky ones, that feeling of
flies crawling across the back of your neck will be the closest you ever
come to him until the end of the fourth quarter.

The house was built in the mid-seventies, the year Patty Hearst
went to prison, Gerald Ford was in office, and California's sodomy law
was repealed. Pueblo style, brown stucco walls, no garden out front
but a tiny square of the desert, two towering cacti framing the eastern
mountain views.

His name was Dallas. Still is. But he used to be *my* Dallas once upon a time. And Dallas used to live in New York with me. Now, Dallas lives in Phoenix and for a while that was all too confusing until it inevitably made a kind of sense. Most things do in the end.

Five a.m., one hour or so before sunrise, and Dallas as an old man sits out on his driveway in a folding chair, small wooden folding table beside him, uncapped bottle of beer by his foot. An open book lies on the table, facedown, like a body dumped on some dry lake bed.

He does not touch the book and only sips the beer, as though these things are just props for some scene in which he is forced to act. I think forced because even from the shade of a tree down the street I can see the pained look etched on his face as he waits for another Arizona sunrise.

Or maybe that's just more of my circular wishful-thinking bullshit, I don't know.

Dallas always liked the sunrise. He used to watch it from the rooftop of our apartment block in New York. Sometimes I joined him; too often I did not.

For one so rich with time, I have spent it badly.

Now in his eighties in this one storey house in Phoenix, we are fifty years and two thousand miles from New York and our high-rise apartment; closer to the worms than the angels, I guess. A folding chair, a folding table; a folding *man*. Able to put himself away into spaces where I could not reach.

Time is supposed to make us cynical and wary of taking risks. I had years, *centuries* to build up my resistance, to witness first-hand how these things must go. The flower of love inevitably perishes, each petal falling like a fist onto an unmoving chest. *Live, dammit. Love, dammit.*

But Dallas had an allergy to risk.

He was my first and only love after Machiel. Machiel would have liked Dallas, and he would have wanted me to be happy. But to fail at love, to stand idly by as the petals disconnected and fell, to watch the corpse of us just lying there, unmoving—that was my betrayal. And so I left Dallas and New York behind.

I folded.

But it seems the flower grew once again, here in the desert of all places.

An elderly man emerges from the house carrying another folding chair and shuffling barefoot across the driveway until he stands next to Dallas, whose face changes as though some internal light has come on and the director called for action. The man unfolds the chair, sits, settles his legs, his breathing, and takes Dallas' hand in his. But first, he moves the book, placing it face up on his lap, and I can almost hear the words breathe and gasp at the air, at the second chance they've been given to live. But we see what we want. Hear what we want. Books close, men die. I choose not to read and I choose not to...read.

The two of them hold hands forever. From down the street, I see their lips moving as they talk; words as elusive as the words within me.

Such bullshit.

It's control.

A mask of convenience.

Dallas is an old man now, and some part of him feels he needs to hold onto someone's hand when his time on this rock comes to an end. He could live alone but he cannot die alone. It is a convenient happiness, or *love*, and love is control. Every time I see it, my heart breaks, though it's only partly for what I have lost—because behind the smiles and the words and the hand-holding, I have seen the scream that awaits.

I turn away from the house Dallas will die in, his waiting room before the next, and head back to my bike and the open road. I walk past similar houses, skrik stood at nearly every window, beseeching me with their eyes, and when I am past, when it is clear I cannot help them leave this place, their eyes narrow into stares and rake me with their frustration and disappointment, that fire at my back, that scalding heat.

On my way, my mind wanders to my recent dalliances with Rick the barkeep and the other one. What little conversation there had been between us inevitably focussed on my twin scars. Sometimes, I comment, "Who else is lucky enough to be struck by lightning twice in one lifetime?" Other times, I say, "Who else is lucky enough to be struck by lightning twice in one lifetime?" The same words but said in a different tone. And that is all we are: the same words in a different tone.

I find there is comfort in repetition.

To drown in it, to chew and swallow the same tasteless food, to fill and empty the same hopeless lungs, to ride the same fruitless roads, to stick the same parts of ourselves into anonymous cookie-cutter men— to fuck the emptiness only to have the emptiness fuck you right back: what else is there for it?

There is comfort in repetition...somewhere.

But I am yet to find it.

I left my bike on a small hill overlooking the eastern edge of the city. As I take my seat and flex the pain and stiffness out of my finger joints (although maybe it is my lingering reluctance to leave Dallas behind), I find myself going from looking to staring at the distant ghostlights—or rather the pattern in the darkness between them.

I see something.

A thin trail of darkness through the outskirts of Phoenix, through the ghostlights, and a point, just beyond the city's borders, larger than the trail leading to it, where the skrik have perhaps been pushed back or...cleared out of the way.

I have seen it before, but never this close. Twenty miles, less.

A clearing, like the spot where a tear lands and melts the snow.

The head of the snake.

Landau.

7. Superstition Freeway

Over the centuries my eyes have grown accustomed to the ghostlights. From a distance, the skrik appear much like the stars in our skies, numbering in the billions, as though whatever god put them there went mad from their obsession. As it is with star-filled skies, it is the space *between* the stars that most fascinates and draws the eye. Where there are no ghostlights, no bleachers, no skrik, there is that depthless and mysterious dark, and somewhere in that, perhaps, lies the path to Landau. It is like a trail of black smoke, the contrail of a flaming jet across the sky, dissipating back to absence, but his is the thinnest vein of darkness winding its way between the lights, like a crack forming on a wall or a gossamer black thread dropped onto a sheet of white, as subtle and hard to see as a single finger-trail across a sandy beach. I have so many comparisons collected over the years. But stare at the sand for long enough, stare at the sky for centuries, and you can see, you can see them all.

And you can see *him.*

The Harley's engine roars against the rising morning, driving back the imminent sunrise, echoing down the suburban streets. I imagine Dallas on his driveway, jerking upright and wide-eyed on his little foldaway chair, letting go of his partner's hand for just a moment. Then his eyelids slipping back to their usual resting place, his back curling forward, Dallas settling into his chair again, hand finding the other in the lifting darkness with a reassuring squeeze. *I am still here.* I hope he will give me at least a moment for what I gave to him (not years: years I had to give; *me*). In that moment, our minds rise and meet somewhere over Phoenix, above all of *this* down here, and we circle like birds, happy to glide together for a time and then separate and slip back into the dark. Then, with a twist of my right wrist, I accelerate through the quiet streets, away from Dallas and toward Landau, trying to follow that thinnest crack in the wall at sixty, seventy, eighty kilometres per hour. Within minutes, I am southbound on North 48th Street, where I narrowly avoid a collision with a restaurant delivery truck. On East McDowell Road, it is a drunk driver in a Prius that almost takes me out. I forgive him: if I owned a Prius I'd drive it shit-faced too. By the time I hit the Hohokam Expressway, I am swerving left and right to avoid the skrik; this is the spill-off from Sky Harbour International Airport off to my right. Here, they outnumber the vehicles on the road by three to one. Minutes later, I open this baby up, doing one-twenty eastbound on US-60—Superstition Freeway. The skrik practically blockade this route (drawn towards Landau? That is my hope). Usually there is a way around, but at high speed, trying to follow this slightest of paths, I have no choice but to go through. Bleachers won't move out of my way as they have no need to do so. Even their instincts have died. They stand where they stand and allow themselves to be ripped apart like cloud, swirling in the exhaust of my bike, smoke and spirit, screaming faces curling and spiralling within the plumes. Steeling myself against the onslaught of their faces breaking across mine, wishing now for that helmet, I am covered in their memories, their final, dying thoughts clinging to my clothes, my skin, like water after plunging into some death-cold lake.

Now and then there is a gap in their numbers and I manage to steal a glance eastward, at the dark space that has piqued my interest. It seems larger now, but whether that is through the closing of distance or by some action of Landau's it is impossible to tell—and then I tear into another chorus of skrik and my vision beyond even a few feet is impeded by the stroboscopic flashes of ghostlight and those tortured thoughts behind it. That is when my heart stops—when the snake disappears and I am left careening along Superstition Freeway in a kind of blind, hopeless freefall, until another glimpse, another surge of hope, picks me up, tosses me back into the air.

8. A Whisper Through the Blood

The tail of the snake is disappearing. The bleachers moving to fill the dark space between them, grasping what little comfort they can from their impossible numbers, closing Landau's path behind me until all that is left is the head of the snake, the small clearing, like a drop of oil on a floor covered with fairy lights.

But it is not the clearing itself that excites me; it is the intensifying of the ghostlights around it. The contrast of that clearing, that dark space, with the brightness of the bleacher presence—that's what lures me.

It looks to me like a gathering.

Westbound traffic slows to a crawl on my approach, the drivers leaning out of their windows, rubbernecking the scene of the accident. Phones shame the faces of those who hold them up to record the events, probably to upload onto social media later, faces not as lifeless as the skrik but uglier for sure. At least the bleachers maintain a respectful distance.

A Mack truck has driven through a small car. Debris lies strewn across the road, mostly twisted metal pieces of the car and the soft insides of a suitcase that during the impact was ejected from the smaller vehicle onto the side of the freeway. One or two vehicles navigate the debris and drive on to their destinations, the rest form a queue while they wait close to their vehicles for someone to deal with this mess. The tailback isn't long—it is early morning and this is a quiet section of Superstition Freeway some way east of the Phoenix metropolitan area—so I am able to ride between the vehicles to the actual scene.

I climb up to check the cab of the Mack truck and find the driver alive but barely conscious inside, the phone still gripped in his hand, screen cracked where his thumb pressed into it at the moment of collision. Texting while driving. It isn't even the booze that kills them these days; it's the act of communication. They can't talk without someone getting hurt.

The driver hasn't seen me yet, which is not a huge surprise considering he failed to see an entire car in his path, but this time it looks like shock has numbed his senses rather than distraction. I give him a moment.

The Mack's hood is pretty beat up, but it is the equivalent of a bloodied nose; the bulldog hood ornament still intact and standing proudly, defiantly, as it looks upon the devastation scattered across the freeway in front of it. As for the car—from this angle I cannot tell what make or model it used to be. I can see there are people inside—*were* people inside. But I am not too hopeful they will still resemble people either.

When the driver of the truck finally sees me, he recoils in fear. Odd but not unexpected. The shock clears in an instant and he fumbles to unlatch his seat belt, with the broken phone still gripped in his hand.

This asshole cannot even remove his belt while holding onto that thing but earlier he thought he could steer forty tonnes and eighteen wheels with it. His reaction, the futile effort of trying to get away, tells me everything—almost everything—I need to know. Landau has been here and this asshole has seen him. Up close, too, by the looks of it.

"Where is he?" I ask. "Which way did he go? East—out of the city? Or west—back in?"

He looks dumbly between me and the phone in his hand, his thumb fused to its insides like he was going for second base right before his truck entered the other vehicle, partly hearing my speech, partly replaying the last words he sent his unwitting accomplice. For the sake of a few minutes... Assholes like him don't deserve time. They abuse it. But look who's talking.

The paramedics and the cops will be here at any moment, and this is one of those times, a crossroad, where every second counts, every decision could lead me one way or the other, closer to Landau or heading in the opposite direction. I leave the truck driver to his superficial cuts and walk toward the mangled wreckage that used to be a car.

Every so often the morning breeze picks up and a sock or shirt or someone's underwear leaves the open suitcase lying on the road to make a doomed bid at escape. It starts as an inspiring effort, like those passengers that leap into the ocean from sinking or burning ships, but the breeze quickly dies—and the passengers usually drown—and the item of clothing, be it sock, shirt, or panties falls to the ground, only to be dragged in fits and starts through the dust to the whim of the desert wind, snagging on everything in its path. A men's white shirt makes it only as far as the freeway barrier before it finds itself pinned hopelessly to the concrete, going nowhere.

Before the Mack drove into the back of it, the car had been a silver Kia Forte. Now, it is a concertina of crushed metal, rear wheels lifted off the ground, nose crushed into the freeway. A single taillight staring redly at the sky. Inside, one passenger in the rear and the driver, both adults, both male. Only something the size of a mouse could have survived in the back. A pair of women's panties sit on the crumpled roof like a delicate yellow flower. Duck my head inside and the driver's face is gone; a different kind of bloom. The air bags either disconnected or misfired. His teeth—some of them; too many to count—lie in the footwell like dropped change. I turn my head to one side, peer through the hole in the windshield. His other passenger—wife, girlfriend, sister, would-be wearer of the panties on the roof—lies perhaps forty feet in front of the car, although it looks as if she was airborne for twenty then slid the rest of the way. No belt. They'd have to scrape her off the road.

Sirens approach from the west. With the growing traffic queue still to navigate, I figure I have a minute or two before the EMTs or the cops arrive and clear the scene. I leave the car and hurry toward the woman on the road. Besides, I cannot bear to look at the driver for a moment longer. Mr Inside-Out. I expect the woman won't be much better though, abandoned as she is like roadkill. I walk alongside the trail of blood, which feels like walking a red mile, and drop to one knee at her side—

—Ms Roadkill lifts her head from the road—*peels* her head from the road—and swivels it one eighty to face me. I let out a startled cry and scramble backwards. One side of her face is completely denuded, the right eye gone, probably part of that long smear on the road. She stares at me with the other eye, bloodied but intact, red as the Kia's one remaining taillight. There are patterns in this world, rhythms, beats I don't always want to see, but sometimes I have little choice; my mind goes there and makes those connections without me. I look around and see no reaction to her sudden and unexpected movement. The one other human being on the scene who isn't skrik or filming on a mobile device is talking to the driver of the truck.

The westbound traffic is at a standstill now, and all I see are hideous faces bathed in the glow of iPhones and tablets, holding those things up in the air with both hands, like placards that read: *hey, I'm a real sack of shit*. Sometimes I think the only difference between them and the skrik is that they have the comfort of sitting. Besides that, we are all the same: dead inside.

It looks like Ms Roadkill and I are going to have a moment. She tries to push herself up from the road, a strange sucking sound, until her left arm snaps and folds under itself, sending her to kiss the hardtop. It is another cruel twist of fate, and she does not attempt it again, resigning herself to her resting place.

"Rust," she says, her head turned again to face me, ear pressed to the road as though listening to what it has to say. She knows my name, or at least the name I have chosen to carry. "Rust," she says again, a rasping voice despite the blood filling her throat and frothing from her mouth. "Turn, back... Please... Left, me...to...message... Said... *promised*...he, would...come, back." A deep breath, although I wonder if it is through instinct rather than necessity. "Soon, said."

Soon? Was that the message? Or was it what Landau said to her? That he would come back for *her* soon?

I look around. More people have left their cars, edging toward the scene for a closer look. Can they see this? *Why* can't they see this? Why aren't they running, yelling, screaming? Why do they move like they are underwater? The people of this world, drowning. And me—I cannot save one of them never mind them all.

I turn back to Ms Roadkill.

"Can he hear me?" I ask.

A whisper through the blood. "Yes, I can hear you."

So, more games. Hiding behind the dead.

"Landau."

Saying his name, knowing that he can hear the name I have chosen for him, knowing there will be a moment of confusion while he ponders it, feels like a small victory. Like a beach landing only to find no army, no resistance waiting, just one lone figure stood on the empty sands. In my mind, at least. In reality, right in front of me, the puppet master has somehow animated Ms Roadkill's dying form.

"Not this way," I tell him, shaking my head. Not through a can of flesh and arterial string. "Face to face, or not at all."

It is a brave or dumb move, and Landau leaves me to contemplate which one it is for several long moments as the wails of the distant sirens make themselves *less* distant.

"Show me the door," I say, shooting for the moon.

Ms Roadkill—Landau—laughs. A mirthless sound tinged with sadness.

"I want through," I say.

"I cannot do that, Rust."

"Why?"

"It is not for you," he says. "This world is yours. You cannot leave it. Not by *my* door." His hollow laughter again.

It feels like my heart stops.

If only it could.

But it is only playing cruel tricks, as it always does.

"You get to live, Rust," Landau continues, "in the knowledge that you will always breathe, but you will do so with one hand—*his*—squeezed tightly around your throat."

"Wait," I say, replaying not only his words but the pauses and subtle inflections. "Are there others? Other doors? Tell me."

He pauses, and near to the ground Ms Roadkill's one good eye shuts, squeezing bloody tears into the cracks on the freeway.

Whatever power Landau possesses over her appears to subside then, and I am left kneeling on Superstition Freeway waiting on a vacant corpse to answer all of my questions.

The sirens grow louder, sucking all other sound from my immediate area to rise and loom over me like a wave to end all waves. The stars in the sky and the skrik on the ground begin to fade as sunlight pours over the Superstition Mountains to the east like warm butter over praying hands, morning finally arriving to push back this darksome night. The circle of bleachers closing now around the crash scene, filling the open space even as they continue to fade from sight, like a milling crowd after the street parade ends and the sawhorse barriers come down. Even the rubberneckers leave their cars, still holding onto their mobile devices but lowered, their blinking, human faces visible for the first time. The night can make us do some crazy, thoughtless things.

True story.

Or maybe that's just more circular wishful-thinking bullshit.

He opens Ms Roadkill's eye.

As she pins me with her baleful stare, I wonder if Landau can see through her as well as use her as his mouthpiece.

"Death opens the door," he tells me. "Your fight is not with me. When a ship crosses the sea, leaving its wake, would you say the ship created the sea? No, you would not. Would you blame the ship for the sea's current? No, you would not. The ship is merely a vessel, just as I am. I pick up these migrants and show them the way to death's country. I do not cut the cord that keeps them here. They do a far better job of that than I—or he—ever could. I am merely the one who shows them the door and ushers them through."

I detect the impatience in his words, and I realise that this is a concession. I am the mosquito that has buzzed at his ear for decades: he wants me gone. He has tried to slow me with tricks and violence, but here I am.

"Let me through or answer my question: are there other doors?"

And then he sighs through Ms Roadkill. There is no sound, no breath left inside her lungs to expel, but the tightening and relaxing of the muscles in her chest mimic his own movements somewhere far from here. And so she sighs, but not air, *blood*, casting a fine spray towards my face.

"If there are," he relents. "They are yours to find."

"Tell me where."

"Not where, Rust, *who*. But I will say no more."

"I won't stop, you know," leaning in close to Ms Roadkill's remaining eye. "I'll keep coming for you until you give me what I want."

He laughs.

"Oh, I think you will be much too busy for that. Lightning strikes a third time...if you wait long enough."

I step back as he raises Ms Roadkill's head and torso from the road, pulling on unseen strings to bend her spine into an impossible curve. The bones of her neck crack and click with a sound like broken insects until she fixes me once again with her tearful, red stare.

"My baby," he says, but with her voice. Or perhaps it is Ms Roadkill herself channelled through Landau and her own body from the other side of the door; whatever—it is enough to send me off balance for a moment.

"Your husband, he... He didn't make it."

"No," she says, glaring at me with that one taillight. "My *baby*..."

The word runs down my throat like a spider.

I turn to face the Kia. From the crushed tangle that is the rear half of the vehicle, near the bottom sill where the door has bent to reveal a cruel smile between it and the chassis, the pink star of a tiny hand. Backlit by the Mack truck's full beams, in defiance of the morning pouring across the mountains, a faint but monstrous shadow reaches for me along Superstition Freeway, stopping inches from where I kneel beside the body of its mother.

No.

NO.

I can't.

And my mind is in flight again, not over Phoenix with Dallas but soaring past eighty years of history, dive-bombing into a camp of mud and barbed wire and German monsters.

Dachau.

I am lying in a pile of the dead, pretending to be one of them, and beneath all of the cold flesh, the jutting bone, the sightless eyes, my hand searches for and holds the hand of someone I can only pray is Machiel. We held each other in the darkness even as they introduced the gas, but in the violent panic that followed we were separated. The last I saw of him, Machiel was clawing at the walls, naked, thin, testicles gone, boiled off in one of their many tortures. I used to tell him that when they were done with us, the pink triangle badges on our shirts could finally be placed together, one on top of the other, to form a six-pointed star. Then no one could hurt us again; they could only gaze upon our happiness as a distant, unreachable light. Now I squeeze the hand I hope is his and plan how I might escape the furnace as broken Jews tasked with removing our bodies throw more of us on top of the cart. My greatest love stolen from me like the precious fillings from our mouths. And in those moments, as they wrench out my teeth, I learn what it is to be the skrik and scream in silence.

Back on Superstition Freeway, my boots walk me through the long, reaching shadow to the soft hand of flesh and bone at its source. Behind every shadow, there is always something real and the light from which it is born.

In the Kia's footwell, crushed between the rear seats and the driver's seatback but still intact is a child's car seat, torn free, flipped over, wedged in-between front and rear. It reminds me of a turtle shell.

There is a moment when I don't think it will budge, and part of me is relieved, but then the door opens a little—enough for the Kia to give birth to a boy of around ten months.

I unfasten his restraints and pull him out of the car. A miracle amongst all of the carnage. Or maybe not a miracle at all; maybe someone built to survive, like me. Only time will tell.

In the morning air, with the sound of the sirens so close, so loud, he squeezes his eyes shut against the intruding world and starts to cry. One tiny voice screaming against the world.

Such a beautiful sound.

Around us, the bleachers have moved in to all but fill the space left behind by Landau's passing through here. I glance up from the child and toward Ms Roadkill to see a narrowing path through their vanishing crowds, a funnelling down the centre of Superstition Freeway toward another clearing about a quarter-mile from the scene of the accident.

The snake has many heads.

My feet carry me toward the next. They need no instruction. When I arrive at Ms Roadkill, I stand beside her unmoving body and shield my eyes with one hand to gain a better view. What I see is a clearing in the skrik multitudes and, at the centre of that clearing, a vehicle with familiar taillights parked a couple of feet off the side of the road. It is the final act of the bleachers on this long night before vanishing into the morning sun: to turn as one toward the car and its occupant, indefatigable in their mission to try and leave this world for any other.

The vehicle is a 1966 Cadillac Landau hearse.

Vertical taillights. Feline aspect. I feel like I am staring into the eyes of a panther, crouched and staring back.

I glance at Ms Roadkill lying on the freeway and instinctively turn the child's head so that he cannot see his mother.

"Why the hearse?" I ask, watching the other vehicle and memorising every last detail, knowing that I will see it again in life and dreams and perhaps somewhere betwixt the two.

Ms Roadkill jerks and tenses beside me as though a small electric current passes through her body.

"I give the people what they want," Landau says through her. "They fear the hearse, what it represents, but they also appreciate the comfort of its familiarity. I tried other means—a Volkswagen van, even an ice cream truck—but they did not take to them with the same... enthusiasm. The hearse simply works. The dead want no surprises."

Ms Roadkill's body relaxes onto the freeway again, and Landau is gone.

As the first emergency responders begin to arrive on the scene, I stare at the back of the hearse and fix upon the rear window with its white curtains drawn not quite all the way but enough to leave a tantalising gap through which I could see what lies inside—if I could just get close enough.

I run for my ride, still cradling the baby in my arms. He has a cut on his left cheek, but it is no worse than what he will inflict upon himself when he shaves for the first time in twelve or so years from now. And what of those twelve or so years? Will they be a drop in his ocean? How much time does he have? Is he my third lightning strike or my third strike?

Am I out?

The front wheel of my Harley Sportster points east along Superstition Freeway and a place called Landau. I realise now that Landau is not a man but a destination.

My engine idles, indecisive as the one holding its throttle.

The dead want no surprises.

And a child, still crying in my arms, with one thing on its brain.

Like some tiny, helpless addict.

This House is Not Haunted

1. The Fields Only He Could See Beyond All of These

Describe your perfect morning. What would it be like?

My perfect morning would be a Saturday. The start of the weekend. I would get out of bed without a groan and not feel the first twinges of middle age. I would kiss my wife, Sue, and she would kiss me back and the old electricity would still be there (now our love is more like Bluetooth; the connection is there but there is no feeling it). We'd kiss. We'd have the best sex of our lives. Twice. Later, for breakfast, we would drink coffee and eat eggs and bacon. Alfie would join us, rubbing sleep crusts from his eyes, a tuft of hair jutting from his head like a tick mark. He would laugh when I tell him to pull up a pew because he'd think I said something else. The summer sunshine would be slanting through the window, falling on his smiling face, and maybe a bird would be singing in the garden. There would be conversation and laughter. We would finish breakfast and I'd go upstairs to write for an hour, maybe two, the best prose of my life.

But this isn't that morning. *This* morning finds me standing in a field off Odstock Road in the middle of December, about to bury our son in a shallow grave.

He's not your son. Your son is dead. Your son was never born.

All of which is true, but tell it to Sue when she finds out what I've done. Tell it to Alfie when he says I've murdered his brother.

The field is covered in a hard layer of frost. The grass crunches underfoot. It's like the world is breaking apart underneath me. This is the spot near the copse where Sue and I shared our first awkward kiss over fifteen years ago, where Sue, Alfie, and I had a picnic last year, in which we got back on the same page when it came to our pregnancy, right before Sue told me on those stairs in The House of Mould that she was bleeding. It seems right that it should come to an end here.

Across the road, looking down on this spot is Wintercroft, the care home where my father spent his final days. He'd sit and stare out of his window at this field and the fields beyond this one and the fields only he could see beyond all of these.

I wish I knew what he saw.

I find his old window. The curtains are drawn. It is a detail that has eluded me until now but the curtains in the windows of the other rooms are all neutral, all beige, while the curtains in my father's room are red. Were they red at the time he was in there? I don't remember. And I am irritated that I don't, because for all this time I did not know that about him, along with everything else I don't know about him— and worse, never will.

Was it me?

Was I not paying enough attention to know him? To know my own father?

But I was the child. He was the adult.

And now? What's my excuse? Why don't I know my own son?

This isn't why I am here, I remind myself. But standing in sight of the red curtain of my father's window, I can feel his judgement.

No.

I *want* his judgement. I *want* to feel his eyes watching me dig this grave.

"See me, Dad. Just fucking see me. Does this make you proud?"

But he is lost now behind the curtain, forever. Trapped in the Black Lodge. In the footwell. In the eyes of the doll I am holding at the end of my arm. In every atom there is. Ghost particles haunting my universe.

The lights outside Wintercroft flicker into life, probably via a timer or some light-sensitive trigger, and there, there is my shadow back again, cast across the field and into the trees; the sense of a man, long, stretched, with the shape of a spade extending from one arm and the shape of a child extending from the other.

This is something from a horror story. It is exactly how I will write it someday, how it is playing out right now. Art should imitate life. The stark image of me standing in this field, begging my father to see me, holding onto the symbol of our dead child is one I won't soon forget. The cruel irony, the nasty twist is that, while this is me wanting to bury the past, it actually means I am burying my future along with it. There is no doing one without the other. They are a black centipede eating itself. And putting it into these terms, into fiction, is what makes me see the reality of what I am about to do.

Can I go through with this?

That is the question.

But you can stop reading here if you want, because no matter what I do next, this is The End.

1. Eating Blue Banana on the Way to the Lonely Mountain

I park our yellow Fiat at the mouth of the *cul-de-sac*. Turn on the radio to *Spire FM* to keep Alfie amused. Look at the house where I grew up. But the house where I grew up belongs to someone else now. Alfie doesn't listen to *anyone*, never mind Salisbury local radio, and cul-de-sac is a French term from the mid-eighteenth century, meaning 'bottom of the sack'. It's from the Latin 'culus', meaning bottom. Welcome to the culus.

"Cold, Alfie?" I ask him via the rear-view mirror. "I think the heater might still work."

"No, fine," he says. He is playing in his car seat with my Funko Pop vinyls of Jack Torrance from *The Shining* and Dale Cooper from *Twin Peaks*. He holds them as high as both the seat belt and the car's roof will allow then lets them fall to their deaths in his lap, landing on their oversized heads to his loud, wet sputterings. There is saliva on his chin. If it isn't this, he is usually smashing two figures, any two figures, against each other, both of them taking it in turns to die over and over and over.

"Why don't you sit up front with me, buddy?"

"No fanks."

"Alfie, sit up front. Please."

The truth is I don't want to be alone.

It's awkward but I manage to reach back and unclasp his seat belt and help him climb through the narrow gap between the front seats. He reaches up and stands Torrance and Cooper on the dashboard, where they face each other with those lifeless black-drop eyes. Why did I ever collect those things? It took me until I had twenty-one of them before I finally snapped out of it. Funkoholism. Sue said I was trying to buy back my childhood. Now I realise that it is as dead as their fucking eyes. And yet here we are.

"This is where your grandma and grandpa used to live," I tell him. "The house at the end."

"Mm-hmh."

"I lived here when I was your age."

"Mm-hmh."

"With Grandma and Grandpa."

"You already tole me that."

"I know, Alf. I just wanted to see if you were listening..."

"I'm *lisling*," he says. "You live here with Gramma and Grampa but now they're dead."

"No, I live with you and Mummy."

"I know," he says testily. "But you live here too. When you was a boy. With Gramma and Grampa. You just said!"

Alfie mixes tenses in the same way he still confuses gender. Past, future, male, female, with none of the barriers in between. We should all live on the spectrum (if that's where he lives; no one has been able to tell us yet). For me, though, the spectrum was an inferior home computer to the Commodore 64, not what it is now and all it entails. It took me a long time to adjust. It's *taking* me a long time. And to be fair to Alfie, I also find tenses difficult. Too often I confuse the past with the present.

The house was sold when Mum and Dad moved into Wintercroft. The proceeds paid for their care at the home. Meanwhile, a new family moved into ours. Husband, wife, son. Mum went downhill fast; her memories seemed to evaporate into thin air without a place of her own in which to keep them. Dad buried his memories deep, stored them away like boxes in a garage. So, I started coming here. Sometimes, it was just a glance at the windows as I walked past. Sometimes, I stopped for a while to drink in the memories, to stare at our old front door. Our old home seemed as reluctant to forget as I was.

At first.

Everything is gone now. Mum. Dad. And with them, large parts of me too.

Looking at the red-brick bungalow with its new locks, unfamiliar curtains, its repainted door (when did we go from green to blue?), I feel like I am standing at the bottom of a well, looking up at the bright circle of the past as night is falling.

It is getting too dark, too quickly.

Dad left us only a few months ago but, with the house sold and packed up long before that, I was deprived of that traditional final act as his son. Instead, he went up in smoke and that was it. Done. Dusted. No sifting through old belongings. No deciding what to keep, donate, or bin. It was the end of that chapter of the Fenwick story. And the people who replaced us have had years now to erase every trace we left, to walk the spaces we once walked, to fill each room with their own laughter, their own tears. To write their own story.

"And Sam too," Alfie says, seemingly out of nowhere.

"What?" I ask, my attention now back—confined—inside the car. "What about him?"

"He lives with us too. You said you live with me and Mummy but you forgot Sam. Sam lives in our house too."

"I didn't forget, Alfie."

"You did."

"No, I didn't."

"You did. You never said his name."

"That isn't the same as forgetting."

"Oh." Whenever Alfie relents and accepts that he is wrong about something, even if he does not fully understand the reason why, he will cap the conversation with an oh and shut down for a while.

But I can't let it go for some reason. Maybe because we are sitting too close to the dead past, a place where the face of a ghost staring back at me from the lawn looks like a football no matter how much I will it to be a face.

"Where did you get those?" I ask, meaning the Funkos, Torrance and Cooper.

"Um..."

"From the bookshelves in my study, right?"

"Mm-hmh."

"We talked about this, didn't we, Alfie? We don't help ourselves to other people's things."

"But they're toys," he says. "You're too old for toys."

I am also too old to be hanging around outside a house that belongs to strangers, and yet...

"Maybe so," I say. "But they are my toys." And this is *my* home... *my* precious. "Do you understand?" Before he can reply, I add, "Oh, what the hell—keep them." He doesn't know Jack Torrance from Jack-in-the-Box (although Jack-Torrance-in-the-Box would make a fantastic toy) and he's always been drawn to the Dale Cooper figure because Daddy likes his damn fine coffee too. "Just... in future—*ask*. Okay, buddy? We don't go into someone's space and help ourselves."

"No, we don't," he says with such disarming clarity it gives me pause.

It is one of the writer's curses, and there are so many, that nothing can just be what it is; everything has to mean more than it does.

"When did life get so complicated, Alfie?"

"I don't know," he says.

I reach over and muss his hair.

"What do you say we get you back into your seat and then go to Sprinkles for some ice cream?"

"Okay," he says, but not without smashing Torrance and Cooper into each other first, sending them both tumbling from the dashboard to yet another wet and explosive end on the sharp rocks of his knees.

Sprinkles is empty. It's December. Christmas is looming but only a small number of people are out shopping. Salisbury is dying a slow death. Poisoned by the Russians. Besides, who wants to eat ice cream on a cold day? Only us, it seems.

Alfie orders a cup of Blue Banana. I am vanilla.

"Daddy," he says, halfway done, his lips and chin painted radioactive blue. "Sam doesn't do anyfing. She's boring."

"He," I say. "Sam is a he, Alfie. And no, I don't suppose he does do much. Sam is meant to be a baby, and babies only do four things: eat, sleep, cry, and poo."

Alfie giggles and touches his chin. "But Sam only does one of those fings. He sleeps all the time. He never cries or poos. And Mum only pretends to give him food."

"That's right. And you know why, don't you?"

"Mm-hmh. Sam's not real."

"Close. He's real in the sense that we can hold him or give him cuddles or kiss his cheek—"

"Or hold his hand."

"Yes, that too."

"Or tickle his feet."

"Yes. We can do *all* of those things, but—"

"Mummy thinks he's real, doesn't he?"

"*She* does, yes. Like I said, it's very complicated these days, isn't it?"

Nodding, he says, "Mummy lost the special and now she wants Sam to be him. But Sam's not my *real* brother. My real brother is dead, like Grampa's dead, and they're both in Heaven togever. Right, Daddy?"

Stunned by his insight, I say, "Yes. Yes, they are. Eat your ice cream."

"I miss the special," he says. "And Grampa. Sam doesn't talk. She doesn't do anyfing. She just sits like statues all the time."

"*He*," I say tiredly. My mind carries me back to my father's room in Wintercroft. "*He* sits like statues." Although Alfie is talking about Sam, the idea of my father as a statue seems a good fit. A perfect fit. Tears fill my eyes with no warning. Fat, unwanted guests at my door wanting to take me on a long journey to some lonely mountain. And if *The Hobbit* metaphor is too laboured or too long, it works just fine for me in that it keeps the tears from falling. This time.

"I miss him," Alfie says.

He means his brother, of course, but nothing can just be what it is. Not for me.

"I miss him too," I say. "Now let's be quiet and eat our ice cream before it melts."

1. Like We're the Waltons

In the living room, I sit on one settee, Sue and Sam on the other. Alfie's asleep in his room upstairs. In The House of Mould, I got so used to hearing his laboured, rasping breathing that here, in The House of Air, I find myself, whichever room I'm in, listening out for it and wondering why I cannot hear him breathing at all. Sue says I get used to living with tragedy and when it's no longer there I go looking for the next one. That while conflict carries fiction, it should not carry life. I think I'm just one of those people who, when the rain stops falling, wonders *why* it stopped instead of simply enjoying the sun breaking through the cloud.

On the settee beside her, Sue has unfolded the changing mat and laid out a packet of wipes, a nappy, and a fragranced disposable nappy bag, open and ready to swallow a nappy that is never soiled. I watch her lie Sam on the mat, pop the three buttons around the crotch of the bodysuit, carefully remove Sam's nappy, use two wipes to clean the area, roll the nappy up, deposit it and the wipes in the bag, put the bag out of Sam's reach, close the three poppers, then prop him on her knee again. Sam does not cry or resist at any stage of the process. In many ways, Sam is the perfect baby.

He is a reborn doll.

And Sue is, in some ways, a reborn mother.

"Daddy, guess what?" she says.

I pause the documentary we were watching on Netflix on a close-up of *Making a Murderer's* Steven Avery. Netflix is a godsend for the parents of children and dolls. I wonder what people did before the pause function was invented. How much good material went unseen, unheard, unappreciated because of an impromptu conversation or a senseless nappy change? Prison hasn't been kind to poor Stevie. Stuck in that one place, getting older, going nowhere. His whole life on pause.

I switch off the television. My reflection in the darkened screen tells me I could stand to lose a few myself.

"Simon..."

"Sorry, what?"

"Did you know Sam is five months old today?"

"No," I muster. "I did not know that. Well, happy five-month birthday, Sam." Then, to Sue, "Did I tell you what Alfie said today? About Sam..."

Sue shakes her head, so I relay the conversation Alfie and I had over ice cream in Sprinkles.

"I think it bothers him that Sam isn't—doesn't... do anything."

"He's a baby," Sue says. "A five-month-old baby. Five-month-old babies don't do much. Did you tell him that?"

"I did, it's just... difficult to explain this—any of it—to anyone, never mind a four-year-old with Alfie's issues. He comes across like he's closed off" (*on pause*) "but he's actually really sensitive to stuff. He needs watching, Sue."

"I know that."

"I know you do, but a gentle reminder never hurts—yes?"

"No. I'm perfectly aware of what is going on with my children. I don't need *reminding*."

Children. Plural. As much as I am on board with this—our situation—there are times when it sticks in my throat, like a tiny bone that gives me enough reason to consider my next bite.

"Sue, I don't want to fight."

"We're not fighting."

That's when I quit—when Sue won't allow me the reality of an argument. I have to walk away before I make it indisputable. Otherwise, I will say something I regret then apologise for it over breakfast tomorrow, and I refuse to be that kind of arsehole.

"I'm going to bed," I say. "Are you coming up?"

Sue shakes her head and holds Sam tighter to her body. "I think I might read him a bedtime story."

"Not one of mine, I hope."

"Hardly," she says.

Ah, the passive-aggressive is strong in this one.

"And then you'll both come up to bed, yes?"

Sue hesitates. "Of course."

"All right. Goodnight."

"Goodnight."

"Goodnight, Sam."

"Goodnight, Daddy," she says on Sam's behalf. Like we're the fucking Waltons or something.

Trudging upstairs, I hear Sue's voice behind me, carried up from the living room, soft and low and sweet and cadenced. Not reading a story but singing a nursery rhyme instead.

Three Blind Mice.

I feel like I've been here before.

1. Footbrints and Angels

After a dreamless sleep, I wake at 6 a.m. and shuffle bleary-eyed through the dark in search of coffee. I don't need to put on any lights; one of the ways in which you know a house has become a home is when you can navigate through it blind. It's not until I step on something unfamiliar on the kitchen linoleum floor and my toes flex that I have any reason to feel uncertain. Reaching back through the dark without stepping off whatever I have stepped on, I flick on the lights and squint at what surrounds my right foot.

Flour.

I step back.

Next to my footprint in the flour is a Sam-sized outline. Around Sam's outline, partly erased by my own size eight, are a number of Sam-sized footprints. They are not in a line but a chaotic little cluster. It seems that while we were asleep Sam has been down here dancing and making flour angels.

I sigh as I reach for a dishtowel to wipe the flour from my foot. I sigh again as I fill the kettle from the tap, watch the water come to a boil, and pour the water into a cup. Sitting at our small dining table, the morning's light creeping up my legs, I sigh between every sip of coffee.

Twenty minutes and two cups later, I watch a pyjamaed Sue and Alfie enter the kitchen. One face lights up; the other clouds with curiosity.

"What is that, Mummy?" Alfie asks, seeming to direct the question at the floor. "Did Sam do it?"

Sue, standing beside him with Sam cradled in her arms, smiles and shrugs. Sam has flour caked along the bottom of his tiny feet and between his toes. He even has a contrived spot of the stuff planted on his cherubic cheek. Alfie hasn't spotted any of it yet.

"She did, didn't she?" he says. "She did this when I was sleeping."

"He," Sue says. "And yes, he must have. What do you think it is?"

"*Footbrints* and angels," he cries. "Is Sam real now, Mummy?"

"I think you mean foot*prints*, and of course Sam is real. He's always been real. You can see him and touch him and he listens to every word you say."

"Why wasn't he sleeping like me?" Alfie asks.

"Maybe he woke up. Maybe he came down here during the night and had himself a little fun."

"Can Sam walk now, Mummy? He has footbrints. I see them."

"I don't know. Maybe a little."

"Wow! Did he get up and walk down here on his own?"

Sue leans against the kitchen counter, predicting more questions from Alfie as he tries to process what has taken place here in his absence. His brow is furrowed and yet he wears a shy smile. He rubs his chin, mirroring the cartoon characters he watches on television.

"I think maybe he slid backwards down the stairs on his tummy," Sue continues. "I've seen him do it once or twice before. You did that too when you were a baby."

"What's back-words, Mummy?"

"Backwards. It means feet first."

"Well, not really," I say, ever the pedant. But it's all I've got since time and caffeine have not helped me to process this either. Besides, this scene is being written without me and I am sitting right here; here being less than ten feet away at the dining table.

"Aw, but *I* want to see him do that," Alfie says. "*I* want to see him do backwards."

"I know," Sue says. "But Sam is a special baby, remember? That's what you used to call him before he was born. The special."

"But does he only be alive when I'm sleeping?"

"I think so," she says. "For now."

"Like Woody and Buzz?"

Or Chucky, I want to say but don't because I want the questions to stop. Please. Stop.

"A little bit like Woody and Buzz, yes," Sue answers.

"Sue?" I venture. "Don't you think..." But Sue can hear the growing disapproval in my voice, the sigh infused in every word. She tries to silence me with a look. Stupid me, I refuse to listen to her face. "... don't you think we should have talked about this *before*?"

"What does Daddy want to talk about, Mummy?"

"Nothing," she replies with a pointed look at me. "Daddy is hungry and wants breakfast. Don't you, Daddy?"

"Apparently so."

Breakfast is bacon and more questions. Too much of either gives me heartburn.

Sam is put in his highchair and pulled close to the dining table. A plastic bowl of Cheerios is sat on the tray in front of him, spoon alongside. The flour flower is still visible on his cheek.

"Why did you make a mess on the floor, Sam?" Alfie asks, both curious and amused.

"I think it was his way of saying good morning," Sue says.

Alfie's face screws up as though he's smelled a fart at the table. "*Good morning?*"

"Yes. Sam can't talk yet," Sue tries to explain. "I think it's his way of saying it *without* saying it."

"Well, I hope he's going to tidy up his good morning. It's all over the floor. Can I have more cereal, Mummy?"

Over the next four days—or rather, nights—Sam leaves his mark or message or whatever the hell it is he's supposed to be doing. Ask Sam: he's the one calling the shots.

The next morning, on our living room rug, he's arranged Alfie's wooden building blocks into a facsimile of Stonehenge. Alfie refuses to touch it, as though Sam's version somehow holds the spiritual properties of the real thing. The morning after that, some of Alfie's Hot Wheels cars are neatly arranged in rows alongside our blockhenge. "It seems Sam is building us a popular tourist attraction," I quip of his midnightly efforts. Day three and *Toy Story*'s Rex has left a swathe of overturned Hot Wheels (not to mention a pile of insurance claims) on his destructive path towards knocking over most of our 'henge with clumsy green sweeps of his tail. Alfie is positively thrilled. "Sam is playing with my toys," he enthuses.

"You're building a bridge to break your own back," I tell Sue in a stolen moment in the kitchen one evening. It was a popular saying of my mother's, and I thought I understood it when I was a boy and she used to say it to my father but, like her (and my father, it turned out), there seemed to be something hidden there in plain sight. "He'll never want this to stop. You know that, right?"

"Keep doing what, Simon? It's not me, it's Sam."

Sue can do this. She can stick to a story way beyond the point of confession. She did it to me with the affair. She is doing it to Alfie with Sam. It's like when she used to read *The Hobbit* to him; she would try to convince him that the spreading patch of mould was in fact the shadow of a troll burned onto his bedroom wall by the rising sun.

"Alfie is really buying into this thing, Sue. I'm worried."

"You're always worried," she says. "But how is this really any different from someone getting lost in one of your stories?" Before I can answer, she adds, "This is good for Alfie's imagination. He *wants* to get out of bed these days. The children teasing him at school, your father's death, it's taken its toll on him. Now he runs downstairs every morning and his face... it just lights up."

I cannot argue with that truth and I won't argue with the tears in Sue's eyes.

Sometimes, Alfie sits at the table to eat his dry cereal and his eyes are empty. I'll ask him how he is and it takes a dozen attempts to elicit as much as an "all right". Sue and I agree that there is so much more then speech and language difficulties there, but the teachers, the TAs, the specialist doctors, they cannot see it yet. It is a time bomb ticking to its inevitable, destructive end. And the irony is that Sam, a *doll*, born not from a womb but a box of cardboard and polystyrene popcorn, knows which wires to cut. He has my son engaging with the real world more than anything or anyone that *is* real.

I cannot argue with that truth either.

1. In a Forest on the Back of a Dead Dragon

When the world makes little sense, I retreat from it. My father did it by dressing up as a woman, although that explanation may be a little too simplistic. Alfie does it practically full-time because he's teetering on the autistic spectrum, or so we suspect. It is something in our DNA, that when the going gets tough, the Fenwick boys don't get going, we get gone. We retreat in order to make sense of the senseless, to find meaning in what seems meaningless, to remove that suffix less in an attempt to discover more.

The Post-It Note forest. When the words won't come, I draw trees on green squares of gummed paper and fix them to the walls of my study. Right now, the forest covers the upper half of one wall and the upper corner of the next. Sometimes, when the words won't come, I stare up into the forest and glimpse those I have written and left behind among the trees, buried there like bodies. Words like DOUBT and

DISTRACTION and EGO and AWARDS. And yet I know they are in there, somewhere, staring back at me sightlessly from their Post-It Note graves.

Looking for a way back.

After Dad died, this room lay empty for months. The words I would have written vanished into thin air just like him. Not burned like him; never even born. Now the Post-It Notes on the walls have begun to curl from the cold and neglect, like the scales of some dead dragon, lifting to reveal the sickly, beige flesh underneath.

I live in a forest on the back of a dead dragon.

Hm.

A good opening. A striking image. An intriguing idea. But that is all I can come up with these days. I struggle to make the story move forward, to go anywhere but round and round in slow, fading circles. Maybe it's time...

I write the word HOPE on a green Post-It, quickly drawing a half-dozen tall firs around the word, each one a long vertical line intersected by carets. Then I stare at the letters staring back at me from their makeshift grave. Should hope join the others in the Forest of Forget?

But then I imagine my father's hand shooting up from a half-filled grave, reaching for me as I stand next to the hole with one foot raised, poised, ready to be brought down, and I realise that it comes back to this, that it *always* comes back to this: if I cannot bury what has truly died, how can I bury what almost lives?

1. A Stillborn Idea

Something's happening.

I wake at 3 a.m. as though it is seven. If I'd been dreaming, I don't remember it. I simply snap from sleeping to wakefulness in an instant.

I sit up in bed. My body feels completely rested but it is an illusion that will crumble later at work when the hounds of tiredness catch up to me and try to pull me down. For now, though, my mind is racing, freefalling through the dark, turning to look back at where it is falling from, reaching hopelessly for it, whatever it is.

A story idea?

Maybe. Whatever it is—whatever it *wants*—eludes me. Ideas have come to me this way before, strange little gifts from my subconscious left out like barely-breathing birds on the doorstep of my mind. Sometimes they make it; sometimes they expel a few short, encouraging breaths and then expire.

Someone is whispering in the dark.

Maybe this is what woke me. A susurrus. My body reacting to the shift in the night-rhythms of the house.

Who's up at this time?

I sit in bed for a moment, listening. The whispering is so faint my mind doubts itself. Then it comes again, rising through the house from one of the rooms downstairs.

It doesn't sound like words.

I glance at Sue lying beside me. She is asleep under the covers, snoring softly. I get up and walk through the darkness to the top of the stairs, listening all the way. On the second tread, the floorboard creaks under my foot.

The whispering stops. Its soft sibilance retreats into the darkness like a snake's tongue that has had too much taste of this world. Silence rolls up the stairs and finds me as the skin on my arms, on the back of my neck, reacts to the fact that the whisperer has reacted to *me*. We are not afraid of a strange guest being in our home so much as the strange guest knowing we are there too. We both listen, waiting for the other to do something, while I tell myself these goose bumps are because the house is cold.

I take a deep breath and continue down the stairs. All of the lights are off, as they should be. From where I am standing in the hall, I can see the vertical blinds in the living room are open slightly, allowing bars of orange light from the streetlamp outside to enter our house. I stand in the doorway and look inside.

Sam is sitting on the rug, propped against a cushion. His eyes shine darkly in the light reaching him from outside. Shadows flit across his face, giving it a sense of movement, of animation, but it is just the moths hurling themselves at the street lamp outside, projected onto him. Sam appears to find the futility of their efforts entertaining. Sam appears to understand what futility *means*.

I turn and walk quickly back through the hall into the kitchen. I switch on the cabinet lighting, which doesn't flood the kitchen with light but illuminates the countertops. Just enough light to see by. I go to the fridge (more light) and drink water straight from the jug as I listen to footsteps crossing the living room floor. Somehow, I manage not to spill a drop. I find an opened packet of pepperoni slices on the top shelf and remember that Sue and Alfie made homemade pizzas earlier, although earlier is now yesterday. And this is a delay, this, this, my reaction to what I just glimpsed in Sam's face. No, to what I *thought* I glimpsed. I tease a couple of pepperoni slices from the packet and push them ungraciously into my mouth. Chewing slowly, I listen as the whispering starts up again in the living room. Standing in the fridge light, cool breath on my face, I wish I was the kind of man who finds comfort in meat.

Maybe he *is* walking now, I think. Walking, running, climbing stairs (didn't Sue mention something about him sliding down on his belly?). Shit, maybe it's time to install the stair gate she bought and keeps asking me to set up. Why not? We change his nappies. We've bought him a buggy, clothes, toys he'll never play with. I even put up a height chart. So, what am I afraid of? We invited him *in*. All of us. Maybe this is just a natural progression.

I close the fridge. Turn off all the lights. At the bottom of the stairs, where I once stood in The House of Mould as Sue looked down at me with mascara tears running down her cheeks, I pause and stare at the first step. That was reality back then—a miscarriage and some real fucking pain—but this, this is something else. A stillborn idea we found on our doormat, took inside, and tried to nurse back to life.

"Go back to bed, Alfie," I say without turning from the stairs, from the very real memory of Sue bleeding down her legs. "And put Sam back."

1. You Die Lots of Times Too

The road to hell may be paved with good intentions but what concerns me as Alfie and I walk to school the next morning are puddles. It is a typically drab December day. Grey clouds. Drizzle. Alfie walks slightly ahead of me, weaving between the puddles, making a game out of it. So far, his shoes have remained dry. So far, he's winning.

We've been playing I Spy. When Alfie slips into one of his quiet moods like today, I take this page out of my mother's handbook to try and bring him back. Ironically, I used to play it with her when the dementia started chewing up chunks of her memory. It worked as a great distraction technique: sometimes I hardly even noticed she'd forgotten who I was.

"It's your turn, Alfie. I spy with my little eye..."

"Um, okay... somefing beginning with..."

He pauses to look around. We've already covered sky, trees, car, and road, so we're going to have to go next level with this one.

"I don't know," he says.

"Keep looking."

He does. Finally, he looks up, settles on: "Somefing beginning with S."

"We've already had that," I say.

"But you don't know what it is."

"Is it sky?"

"How did you know that, Daddy?"

"Daddy knows things. Try again."

"Okay. I spy with my little eye, somefing beginning with..."

"Z?"

Alfie looks at me like I am from another planet. "There's no zeds, Daddy."

"How about X?"

"No. No X eiver. It's my turn. I spy with my little eye, somefing beginning with... *Eww.*"

"That isn't a letter, Alfie."

"*Yook.*"

Look.

Ahead of me, Alfie stops and points at something lying on the road close to the kerb.

A dead pigeon.

"*'gusting,*" he says. "It's like a pancake."

I almost miss it because of the dead bird. I just look at him for a moment, staring. While it isn't the joy of witnessing his first steps, it's still something pretty special. I've seen dead birds before, seen roadkill before, but I've never heard my son say the word *pancake*. It's been *woe-cake* for as long as he's been able to talk, which to me always sounded like the saddest thing on the menu. Alfie loves his *woe-cakes* and *maypole syrups*. But maybe it's time to say goodbye to *woe-cake*. Consign it to history. Bury it in the Post-It Note forest. And if I am honest, I am a little saddened by that. Is my boy growing up?

"Daddy?"

"A car must have hit it," I say. A car and maybe a dozen other vehicles after it, each taking their turn like some kind of vehicular gangbang. The poor creature somehow dragged its crushed and broken body to the side of the road. Half of it is like a pressed flower fallen out of a book, the other half is relatively intact. Except the eyes. The eyes are gone. Eaten by maggots.

"He's just lying there," Alfie says.

"Don't worry. Someone will come and take him away."

"Like Jesus?" he asks.

"I was thinking someone from the council, but yes, I suppose so. Someone like Jesus."

"Is he an angel now?"

"Yes, he is."

"Can he see Gramma and Grampa then?"

"I don't know. Maybe. Let's just keep walking, okay?"

I manage to get him moving again but he keeps glancing over his shoulder at the dead bird and seeing his grandparents. At least he doesn't notice that I'm barely keeping it together.

"Did it hurt him?" he asks, not ready to let this conversation go.

I consider my answer for two dozen steps through the rain as the morning traffic passes us by; oblivious drivers hunch over steering wheels inside their cocoons of heated bliss. I regret not taking the car now.

"I expect it did," I say, finally. "But only for a moment. And then he was free."

"How many lives did he have, Daddy?"

I think about my father and want to say *two*. The life he presented to the world and the other life he kept to himself for all those years, until my mother found him out. Different sides of the same man but neither one the absolute truth of him. In the end, I tell Alfie, "We only get one life."

"So it's not like Battlefield...?"

I laugh even as the first tear escapes and makes a run for it down my face. Children can do that, lighten the mood in an instant, like tiny magicians pulling paper flowers from the bowels of a hat.

"*You* get lots of lives in Battlefield," Alfie continues, encouraged, "and you *die* lots of times too."

"That's right, I do. That's because I'm not very good at games. They're just pretend though. They're not real."

"Do *I* get one life?"

"We all do, buddy."

"But that's not enough," he all but yells. "I won't last five minutes."

I muss the hair on his head. "It's just how things are, Alfie. That's why you have to be careful crossing roads." I cringe inwardly at the shameless road safety lesson but this conversation has slipped through my fingers like sand, leaving me clutching at thin air, thin similes, thin metaphors. Thin chance of escape.

"And if I lose a life and I'm dead I go to heaven but only if I'm good," he muses, no longer craning to look back at the diminishing carcass of the bird on the road. His expressive eyebrows pinch together as his gaze falls to the wet pavement sliding below his feet. "If I'm good," he whispers.

"That's basically how it works, yes."

I want this conversation to be over. But it isn't.

Not yet.

"It's not really fair," he says, without looking up.

"It isn't about fairness," I tell him, immediately regretting my poor choice of words. "Sorry... What I mean is—one life can be enough. One life is fine."

He doesn't reply to that, which is slightly worrying but also comes as a relief. I never envisaged this particular father-son conversation would involve dead pigeons and videogames but I think I did okay. I think I scraped a pass.

We walk the rest of the way to Alfie's school in silence, each ducked inside our own mental foxholes. At some point, Alfie stops dodging the puddles and chooses to walk and then stomp through them instead. By the time I watch him pass through the school gates, his shoes and the bottom of his trousers are wet-through, and I wonder if I passed this test at all.

1. Looking for a Place to Land But Never Coming Down

The supermarket is the size of an airplane hangar. Within moments of us passing through the automatic sliding doors, Alfie is running down the nearest aisle, arms stretched out to either side, looking for a place to land but never coming down.

I offer to push the shopping trolley but Sue wants to do it so she can smile at Sam while he sits in the child seat facing her. I push my hands deep in my pockets and count the loose change instead. People cast curious glances at the way Sue is cooing at the doll in her shopping trolley while Alfie the Airplane strafes the dairy aisle and I make it 67 pence and a button for a shirt I probably no longer own.

Sue can tell there is something wrong with me. She isn't particularly tuned in to my moods these days: that all stops after the arrival of your first child. The storyline changes: it's no longer boy meets girl, boy and girl fall in love, boy and girl live happily ever after. It's boy and girl have a child, child gets in the way of boy and girl so that boy and girl drift apart because boy is a man but essentially still a boy, his pathetic male pride wounded because girl would rather kiss the child with a clean mouth than one she's used on boy. The question is, in this timeless tale of love, whether boy can grow up fast enough and become a man before the whole fairytale falls apart. We do, most of us, but it takes some boys longer than others to get there.

"Why are you walking behind us?" Sue asks after a while.

"I didn't realise I was."

I did. It isn't embarrassment; it's the writer in me leading me over to the edge of the scene to allow me to see it from the outside, in its entirety. I have always had the ability to step outside, to detach myself and drift away. Another one of the dubious heirlooms my father passed to his son, it seems.

"Why is he so hyper tonight?" I ask.

We have stopped walking. Shoppers step around us as we stare along the bread aisle at Alfie at the far end, brandishing a baguette like it's an automatic weapon and spraying imaginary enemies in his own videogame. As we're watching, he takes a slug to the chest and down he goes, spluttering and writhing on the floor. There are gasps and even a collision or two between trolleys as people try to avoid this KillCam being played out right in the middle of their weekly shop.

I imagine the dolly zoom shot from *Jaws*, Brody on the beach, that look of horror, only it's happening to me.

"What is he *doing*, Sue?"

She seems composed. "Stimming," she says. "His version of it anyway. It's stereotypic behaviour. He does it a lot. It's just his way of dealing with all of his pent-up emotions. You've seen him do it before. "

"At home, yes. But he's never done it in public before, at least not like this."

"Uh... *yes*, he has. Maybe you've just never noticed it. You don't usually come shopping with us unless the well has run dry. Sorry to break it to you, dear, but welcome to the desert of the real."

"People are staring at him, Sue—wait, did you just quote *The Matrix* at me? In Tesco? Wow."

"You don't have to beat me, Michael—you just have to try and keep up."

"Oh, *Lost Boys* too? Really?"

"Why are you so worried about what other people think?" she says.

"I... I'm not. It's just... *look*—look at what he's doing. The whole Novichok thing wasn't that long ago. People are on the lookout for strange behaviour, and if that isn't strange I don't know what is."

"He's five years old, Simon. I doubt even the Russians recruit them that young."

"You know what I mean."

"I know and *I don't care*. He's your son. Be his father."

There it is. It feels like a gutshot from one of Alfie's imaginary bullets. My palms are sweating. I'm losing my breath.

"I try, Sue," I tell her, backing away. "But in case *you* weren't paying attention, my father... he didn't exactly leave me any notes on how to do that, did he?"

"Where are you going?" she asks. "You know I didn't mean anything by it. Come on."

Still backing away, removing myself from the scene, I shake my head. "I just need to get something."

"Simon..."

"I'll be back in a couple of minutes."

"Simon..."

"Couple minutes, okay?"

I turn and wander off to the report of gunfire drifting across the supermarket. Alfie has respawned it seems, baguette in hand, determined to prove his old man wrong. That he gets all the lives he needs. Meanwhile, the one life I have is sometimes more than I can stand.

My first stop is the book aisle. Words I *can* control. When I sit at the laptop, I can choose which ones, how they line up, and rearrange them to my heart's content. Not these words, though. Generic thrillers and Fifty Shades variants on special: two for seven quid. I think I saw the same deal on cheese.

Is this really what I'm working towards?

I spot Sue and Alfie heading in my direction. Alfie seems calmer now, his hand underneath hers on the trolley handle, so it looks as though they are pushing it together. But is his hand held there by restraint or affection? Is there any difference?

Sue picks me out of the crowd and waves me over. Am I so predictable that she knows exactly where to find me, standing amongst all of the shitty books like some sulking child?

Boy meets girl, girl knows boy.

But I'm not ready to go back inside the scene. I hold up a finger to let Sue know that I need another minute and then duck out the far end of the aisle. I wander across the checkout lines. Squeeze around trolleys. This is where the real drama is. The crush of people. Forgotten items

("Did you remember the toilet rolls, honey?"), missing bank cards, credit cards, club cards ("I thought *you* had them."), inflated totals ("Sorry, *how* much?"), money-off vouchers that won't scan ("It should be fine; it only went through the washing machine once."), emotions running high everywhere in a veritable Netflix of dramas.

Then I spot my father in the crowd.

And it's dolly zoom time again.

1. The House of You

Two hours later, we are back in The House of Air and I still haven't quite caught my breath. Sue is annoyed at me for walking off in the supermarket. We put the shopping away in silence (although there is one comment from Sue: "Are you actually going to help or do you want to go for a walk around the block first?" Which I suppose I deserve). Now she is lying on our bed, door closed, night light on, singing Sam a lullaby, leaving me to get Alfie ready for bed. Only, my laptop is switched on in the next room, its screen blank, and an idea I had after what happened in the supermarket is decomposing in my brain like a body in time lapse. Right now, we are at the maggots stage. My fingers and palms are literally itching, I am so desperate to sit at the keys. But the words are disappearing so fast I am heading towards having the bones of nothing.

I run a bath for Alfie but forget the bubbles. He needs bubbles. So I add them, running him a deeper bath. The waterline reaches his chest when he sits down. I spot a bruise sitting high on his right arm, dark, floating above the surface like a solar eclipse. I am not surprised he has a bruise the way he threw himself around the supermarket earlier, but it looks days old, hinting at previous wars. I decide I will mention it to Sue later. For now, I cannot stop thinking about the old man.

It was one of those familiar-face-in-the-crowd moments. Pushing across the checkout lines, I saw him twenty feet ahead of me, walking away. His shirt was stained, with two great sweat-wings yellowing the back, the seat of his trousers smeared with mud. I had this surreal thought: you're not climbing out of the grave without getting a little dirt on your clothes.

Except my father was cremated. Therefore, unless a man can be put back together from ash, it was not him. So, I followed my-father-who-was-not-my-father (and if there are seven words with more truth to them than those I do not know what they are) halfway around the supermarket, him leading, me following, until we arrived at the spirits aisle. Here, the old man finally turned and allowed me a proper look at his face—or his profile at least—while he stood, hands pocketed, stoop-shouldered, wetting his lips as he took in the whisky selection.

It wasn't him.

Of course it wasn't him. This house is not haunted.

It seemed like a strange and incongruous thought to have in a supermarket then and an equally incongruous one to have now, while bathing my son.

This house is not haunted.

No, it was not my father.

And yet I knew the man.

After donning his pyjamas and brushing his teeth, Alfie climbs into bed for what he used to call *stowzee* time. Story time. In the past six months, I have held small funerals in my head for the words and phrases Alfie no longer uses. Now, I can add *woe-cake* and *stowzees* to the list of the dearly departed. As for those Alfie-isms that stubbornly cling on, they will leave soon too, replaced no doubt by these physical displays of his, what Sue calls stimming. With the death of words comes curious behaviours.

We never finish a book. Alfie grows bored easily, meaning that a hundred stories float in that place where stories go to await their ending. We only ever add to their number, an ever-growing flock of lost birds, a pollution of unfinished tales. Despite our many attempts, Charlie has never found his golden ticket or made it past the gates of Wonka's factory, Harry has never found his way to Platform 9¾, never mind Hogwarts, and Bilbo has yet to wander far from his hobbit hole, where Rivendell and the Lonely Mountain remain but a distant and comfortable rumour. All of them are fated to stay in one place, to sleep in a bed with their grandparents or in a cupboard under the stairs or a hole in the side of a hill—as is Alfie, as am I.

Maybe there is something to that, maybe there is not. Maybe the best stories reach no ending but leave you to wonder about their fate. Maybe that's just crap. My father's story had an ending and yet all I want is a few more words.

I read to Alfie until Bifur, Bofur, and Bombur come tumbling through the hobbit's door, and then I kiss his forehead and say goodnight. He never asks if Bilbo and the dwarves make it back from the Lonely Mountain. I suppose he likes the promise, the comfort of beginnings. And I don't blame him.

I am back in the supermarket. There is nothing like seeing someone who reminds you of your father to drive home the fact that your father isn't around anymore, that he's smoke and ash, or that he will never again visit a supermarket or look at you with the same trapped look *this* old man offers you when he notices you are staring.

"Can ah help ye?"

"I think we know each other," you said. "I think maybe we've met before... somewhere."

"Dinna think so, pal. Best ye move along now."

It came back to you. Churchill Gardens. The children's play park. A shrinking man.

"Your name's Cutler, right? You used to sit in the park. That's where we met."

He turns to you with a bottle of Bell's Original in his hand. "Oh, aye. I remember ye now. Got ma name wrang then as well. It's Cutter."

"Sorry, Cutter." I wrote a story about you, you thought. I named you Cutler instead of Cutter because of the negative connotations of that name. And now you're here, standing right in front of me.

A few hours later, standing in the doorway of Alfie's bedroom, hand poised over the light switch, remembering the conversation in the supermarket, I consider writing about my father in my next story to see if I can bring him to life, too. It would be a pretty cool trick, if perhaps a blatant rip-off of the King short story, *Word Processor of the Gods*. Besides, my brain catches up and I remember that Cutter existed *before* he appeared in my story, *Perception*, and that I do not have the power to create life, only to interpret it, like a fool seeing patterns in the dust.

"Where did you go?" you asked. "I never saw you again."

"What do ye mean?" Cutter said. "Yer seeing me now. Am right here."

And he is—he's standing in Alfie's bedroom, at the foot of my son's bed. A man named Cutter. The fingers of one of his dirty hands drumming absently on the bedpost. He looks perilously thin, thinner than the last time we met, as though his bones are trying to push themselves out through his shirt, out through his skin. He looks at me with wet, sunken eyes. The eyes of a man resigned to his imminent drowning. And he reeks of urine; a well of urine.

"You left the park," you said.

"Aw that," he said. "Aye. I had nae choice. The kiddies' mothers organised themselves intae a posse and rode me right oot o' there. They wis protecting their bairns fae shadahs when it's no the shadahs they need tae fear—it's the wans that *make* the shadahs, you know?"

You thought you understood what he meant at the time but now, here, in your home, it makes no sense at all. Nothing does.

Cutter turns away from you to look at your son asleep under the covers.

Why is he here? Where is the supermarket?

"Ye've got yersel' a nice wee family there, son."

"Thank you."

"Don't lose 'em."

"Excuse me?"

"I said don't lose 'em." In your home, in the supermarket, he looks over your shoulder at something going on behind you. "They're leaving by the looks o' it."

"What do you mean?" you asked.

"Your missus is wheeling her trolley right oot the door. Doesnae look too pleased."

You closed your eyes for a moment.

When I open them, Cutter is gone and Alfie is sitting bolt-upright in bed, eyes wide, with a frightened look on his face that seems to make his eyes glow preternaturally in the semi-darkness.

"Daddy?"

Barely audible, like a whisper from another room.

"What's wrong?"

"*Daddy...*"

A smell wafts over to me from his bed as Alfie shyly peels back the covers to reveal what's underneath. Like a sad magician ashamed of his newest trick, he reveals the dark patch on the crotch of his pyjamas and a larger patch on his bed sheet, which has turned a darker shade of blue.

And the room—the room reeks like the bottom of a well.

This is where the scene should end, I think. When the connection is made and the drama reaches a climactic point. But here we remain, with me looking at Alfie sitting up in bed, waiting for him to say something, anything, instead of simply looking down at his wet crotch and then across the room at me.

"Let's get you cleaned up," I tell him.

He says nothing but climbs stiffly out of bed to stand on the carpet with his hands held out and up from his sides, like an airplane with a fluid leak, or a graffitied statue powerless to clean itself, or a fainting goat frozen in panic. And if the third simile seems a bit harsh on the boy it is because I am irritated at having to run him another bath.

Something about the act of repetition snaps my fuse shorter than it already is. And what did Cutter mean by *don't lose 'em*? Don't lose them *how*? How did he even *know* I had a family? Or what Sue and Alfie looked like?

Maybe he noticed Sue shooting me dirty looks in the supermarket and put two and two together to get four and married. It's possible. It's also possible he meant nothing by it and I am reading more into it, looking for meaning where there is none. Something with which to drive the narrative.

I run the bath hot, letting steam fill our small bathroom and coat the walls with moisture. When I add the cold water to bring the temperature down, the water on the walls starts to trickle down the tiles.

"Daddy?" Alfie says. I have become a question to my son, just like my father was to me. "The walls are crying."

For a while, I don't know how to respond to that. I am both touched and irritated by his words. There is a kind of poetry to what he said that I can appreciate, but at the same time I am aware that Alfie meant it, as always, in the literal sense. He has no grasp of the figurative and that is something I have known for a long time: known and wilfully ignored. One of the tools by which I make sense of the world does not appear to exist in my son's toolbox, and I don't know how to reconcile that.

"Alfie, are you even sorry you wet the bed?"

He nods.

"Then can you say it?"

"No..."

"Why not?"

"I don't want to."

"Alfie... when you do something wrong, you need to say sorry for doing it."

"I don't want to do something wrong."

"But you *did*, so you should say sorry."

"I don't want to."

"Just say it."

He shakes his head.

"Say it, Alfie. It's one fu—it's one word. Just say it."

"... Sorry."

If it was supposed to get him to show contrition or make things right or make him—or me—feel better, it doesn't. Instead, I feel like a bully.

Don't lose 'em.

"Alright. Hop in and let's get you washed."

After his second bath, he stands in a pair of clean, plain pyjamas (his refusal to wear his favourite *Marvel* ones seems to me a manifestation of his shame—or maybe I'm reaching) while I strip his bed and change the sheets. I kiss the top of his head and usher him under the covers. Room light off, I switch on the lunar night light on the wall and set it to full because it's been just that—a full moon kind of day.

In my study, the laptop is asleep. When I wake it, the screen gives me the same blank look Alfie too often gives me, and I just know there are going to be no words tonight. The idea I had is gone. Besides, I can't work around all the clutter (Cutter) in my brain.

Don't lose 'em.

Maybe Cutter meant the words.

Maybe it's too late. This isn't a study or a writing room anymore but a shrine to what I have already lost.

I live in a forest on the back of a dead dragon.

I close the laptop and brush my teeth instead. Something about the mechanical when all I want is the inspirational leaves me irritated, though. Creativity draws so much energy and yet demands so much more, like some needy, insatiable child. Or doll. A lifeless thing into which I must instil life. Here I go again: looking for meaning where there is probably none. I dump the toothbrush in the sink and go to bed.

Sue is lying awake in the dark, looking for her own answers on the ceiling, while Sam lies in his cot in the corner of our room. Under their respective blankets, the chests of both mother and son appear to move mechanically.

"What happened?" Sue asks.

I sit on the edge of our bed. "Alfie happened. He wet the bed again."

"He's picking up on the mood in this house," she says.

"And what mood is that, Sue?"

"Yours, for starters. You've been so stressed lately. More than usual. He can sense it."

"I doubt that very much. He's more interested in what Sam is doing than he is in me or my moods. I'm fine, by the way—thanks for asking."

"You're not fine. What happened in the supermarket?"

"What do you mean?"

"Why did you walk off like that? You just left us."

"I didn't leave you," I say, although we both know Sue is right and I bolted. "I went to look at the books and to clear my head."

"Because you're not stressed..."

"All right, I'm a *little* stressed."

"Why?"

"Let me see... You have Sam. Alfie has his own little world he inhabits *and* Sam. Me? I can't seem to write because I don't see the point anymore—in any of it. Whatever I do—or write—it's never going to be good enough."

"Who isn't it good enough for, Simon? Have you asked yourself that?"

"I don't get to decide. Other people do that. If I make it as a writer it's almost out of my hands. It's going to be based on whether my face fits or not, and you know how that goes—it *never* fits. The same goes for Alfie. It's going to be up to other people to decide his happiness, based on how much they are willing to accept of his... his oddness. *Our* oddness."

"You've never taken to Sam, have you?" Sue asks. Beyond the glow of her night light, I can sense a palpable weight hovering in the darkness over us with that question.

"That's not true."

"He was good enough when you were grieving for your father though, wasn't he?"

I want to say I am *still* grieving for my father but I am tired. Alfie wet the bed and I cannot write. Sam is... Sam. Would that we could all be reborn like him.

"We were both grieving, Sue," I say despite not wanting to say it, but fuck it maybe it's time. "We were looking for answers. You lost a baby and found yours in Sam. I thought maybe he was my answer too. But now? Speaking honestly? I don't know that he is. I don't know anything. I mean, is he good for *any* of us anymore? I'm worried about Alfie—his connection to him. Maybe it's unhealthy. I just don't know. I'm lost, Susan."

Sue responds by switching off the night light. In the darkness, the weight I cannot see seems to swing precariously above my head like a pendulum—until I realise that the displaced air I can feel on the back of my neck is in fact Sue's warm breath and she is sat up on the bed with her face inches from mine.

"Kiss me."

One ever-so-slightly lingering kiss and then Sue turns her back to me, lies on her side, and holds open the blanket like a door. When I join her inside, she lowers her underwear to her thighs and moves her apple bottom against the most appreciative part of me, breathing faster.

Here, now, *us*—all of it fades as you find yourselves—body and brain—trying to connect to the past, like two people visiting the same stretch of beach they once walked on their first date together. The summer they held hands and smiled and shared freely of themselves. This, this is a walk along the same beach, only ten feet apart. Both of them are pretending not to see it, the distance between them, the empty sand, but it's there. Even the pleasant intensity of the meeting of the waves can do nothing to bring them closer together. And if the air seems colder now as they rewalk this old, familiar path, it's because it *is* colder; it's because they are walking the beach in a difficult winter with just one thing in common: their longing for lost summer days, lost summer nights.

When it is over, Sue says nothing and drifts off to sleep. I roll onto my back and feel the weight I cannot see still hanging there in the darkness above me. I shrug. It might as well have ended in a handshake, I think.

This day has gone on too long. Some days do that. Like a scene that doesn't quite know when it is time to end, that outstays its welcome with the reader or audience, that says the same tired old thing the same tired old way, repeating itself, saying the same tired old thing—

I get up, adjust myself, make my way through the dark to the bathroom. Wash my hands. Splash my face.

It used to be that after sex we cuddled. Talked. These days, I sneak down to the kitchen, walking the whole thing off like what just happened was a muscle cramp. Which isn't fair or entirely accurate, but the guilt I feel thinking it *is*. I creep downstairs, seeking the comfort of food. Chocolate or ice cream will do, because I need to add a sweet ingredient to all of this, and because I want the punishment of nightmares if I am to commit infidelity with the fridge.

I thought about having an actual affair once, but it seemed like a lot of work. What would be the point of bringing a thing back to life only to watch it slowly die again? Masochists pursue affairs.

I turn from the open fridge. In the monstrous shadow I cast across the linoleum floor and the dining table in the adjoining room, something is waiting. Something sat on one of the high-back chairs.

The doll stares back at me.

I gasp as my hand reaches instinctively, uselessly for the heart it cannot reach.

"Sam," I breathe. "Holy shit, Sam."

It is a scene from a thousand bad horror films. A cheap jump scare.

"Alfie? Where are you?"

He doesn't answer, but I imagine he is nevertheless crouched in the shadows under the dining table or somewhere else on the ground floor of this house, watching or listening to my reaction, a smile on his face.

"Take Sam to bed, Alfie," I tell the quiet.

And, "Alfie, you shouldn't be up."

And, "Come out. The game is over, buddy."

"Alfie, come out."

"Come out, Alfie."

"... Alfie?"

I run up the stairs, bare feet thudding on every second tread, racing the boy in the shadows back to his room... where I find him asleep in bed, snoring. Even a nudge, a firm shake won't wake him or break the pretence.

I head back downstairs, heavy-footed, one tread at a time.

The doll—Sam—did not get down here on his own, I think.

Did he?

Shut up.

In the dining room off of the kitchen, Sam has fallen to one side on the high-back chair. He hangs precariously close to spilling onto the floor. I just know that if he was to fall off that chair, he would pick himself up and dust himself down and—

Shut up.

He doesn't fall, and I spot that one of his arms is detached and lying in front of him. Loosely L-shaped. Short fingers splayed.

I approach the chair a little more tentatively than I should. My bare feet stick to the cold linoleum, making each step sound as though I am peeling stickers from a sticker book or Post-Its from a wall. My dressing gown hangs open. I stop and take the time to tie it closed.

This is stupid.

I am teasing out the moment, I tell myself, but it is scaring no one, least of all me. Sue wants me to believe in Sam, so she sneaked down here and set up this little scene behind my back while my head was in the fridge, and then she sneaked back upstairs. Immature, Sue. *Really* immature.

I pick up the doll's arm in my left hand and the doll in my right—pick it up by its hair. The pretence gets exhausting sometimes. Then, at the foot of stairs not unlike those in The House of Mould, the house

246

in which I stood as Sue told me she had lost our baby, lost our *special*, I stand and look down at what I hold in my hands, and think, Now we've just lost the plot.

I drop the arm and the doll on the first tread and then step over it to climb the stairs alone. I am a fool shuffling his way through the dark, along the landing, around the bed, struggling not to knock into anything. It's always the knee, I think. Where you bend is where you get hurt. So, never bend. And I tell myself to stop finding meaning in *knees* for fuck's sake and just try to get some sleep.

In bed, I lie on my back, hands behind my head, and stare at the ceiling. I hate the dark, these days. It reminds me of mould; three-dimensional, permeable mould. I feel claustrophobic in it sometimes, as though I'm trapped inside a giant spore. I close my eyes and the darkness only deepens, and that roughness I feel on my eyelids isn't because my eyes are dry but because there's mould back there too. I am made of mould.

Eyes open again, I think of the doll lying face down at the foot of the stairs. I think of it twitching to one side then twitching to the other, like something inside it is alive and trying to get out. The doll rolls on its face like it is an egg readying to hatch. A host. And the head is rising slightly off the carpet as waxy fingers squeeze from its eye sockets then splay themselves, the folds between them clogged with vernix. Fingers as long as the doll's arm, eight of them, with two long, curving, front-projected thumbs, split at the nail like the claw of a hammer.

The Sam-thing walks on these new hands, pulling itself across the carpeted stairway, a cold whisper that reaches my ears even as I lie in the bedroom upstairs imagining this. *Please*, imagining this. It drags the rest of Sam behind it, body, remaining arm, legs, all undulating lifelessly as it climbs one stair and then another before taking to the wall, using those front-facing thumbs like picks to alternately grip and pull itself up, up, up, while the eight long fingers flop uselessly beneath. There is something of the octopus about it; something of the squid. Or the spider. Or the crab.

As the Sam-thing nears the top of the stairs, the boiler mysteriously fires up and the pipes within the walls start to click like unused limbs working out their kinks. The Sam-thing stops in its waxy tracks, its eight fingers retracting into its wall-pressed face, sensing perhaps other presences nearby. Suspended, it grips the walls with its hammer-claw thumbs as the rest of Sam dangles like a hanged child, and the house— the house just clucks its unseen tongue and cracks the stagnation from its bones.

"*They're coming, son. Hordes of the undead, riding on the backs of giant spiders.*"

The words of my father, uttered many, many times while he was deep in the fog of his dementia, right before the monster of cancer came and snatched him out of the mist.

Somehow he knew.

Knew what? That Sam would give birth to some grotesque version of himself through his fucking *eyes*? He knew nothing. All he left me were meaningless words, as insubstantial as the fog he wandered in until his last breath.

This night... I am haunted by so many ghosts: mould and fathers and sons that never were.

Sometimes, the doll helped with the pain, I think. Sometimes, it serves only as a constant reminder of what we've lost.

But isn't that what children are?

I feel ashamed for thinking it, and yet in the dark I find myself opening to its uncomfortable truth.

They're the ghosts that haunt the house of you.

I think, Is that what it felt like for you, Dad? Were you haunted by me? Unable to escape this *thing* you could not understand, did not want?

I push my head deeper into the pillow, inviting it to swallow me at the same time as the Sam-thing is climbing onto the foot of our bed, teetering on the mattress' edge and looking at me with eyes that are now hands, hands that are the start of something new, new and terrible, terrible smell filling the bedroom, bedroom walls pressing, pressing, the smell of vernix cloying, cloying, *clawing* at the back of my throat, my throat tightening, the tightening grip on my foot, my foot gripped in the Sam-thing's hands, hands that are the start of something new, new and terrible—

I yank my foot free. Even so, the sensation lingers. The black centipede of the Sam-thing's touch crawls across my skin as the black centipede of words crawl through my mind, eating itself.

Sue saves me then. She stirs and wakes and turns on the night light. She peers at me sitting on top of my pillow, pressed hard against the headboard, legs drawn up to my chest like some frightened little boy.

I glance at the foot of the bed and the Sam-thing is gone, scuttled back into some dark space, and yet its presence remains apparent inside this house.

Everywhere.

Confused, still half-asleep, Sue asks, "What's wrong?"

"A nightmare," I tell her. And it's the truth. She doesn't need to know the part about how I wasn't asleep when I had it.

An hour later, I finally endeavour down the path toward just that, counting the horror clichés of tonight like sheep.

Today feeling like a scene that has gone on too long.

That doesn't quite know when it is time to end.

That has overstayed its welcome.

1. The Ghost of Our Doubt

The morning is particularly cold. Frost clings to the ground outside. A chill is in the air.

"The heating came on last night," I say as Sue wakes in bed and stretches beside me. It's an opening to discuss what actually happened last night—or at least an ominous tunnel leading to a whole cavern of conversation I'm not sure I want to enter into just yet. "It kept me awake half the night. The timer must be set wrong."

"Can you reset it, then?" she says. "It's freezing."

This is what becomes of us. We used to have plans, hopes, dreams. Morning kisses. Morning fumbles. Now, we greet each other with commentary on the central heating. Sometimes, it's like we are starving and scraping the bottom of the cake tin for a flavour to lick.

Sue sits on the edge of the bed, her naked back toward me. Where I used to see smooth, soft skin, now I see the moles halfway down her spine, like three spots of mould that never seem to scrub off. She reaches for her towel robe and pulls it on with as little show of flesh as possible. The whiteness of the robe used to bring out her coffee-coloured eyes; today, it's the rosacea on her cheeks as she turns to face me.

Is this what they mean when they say familiarity breeds contempt?

No, not contempt. Love is the thing that burrows. At first, it's all about the surface, about it finding a way *in*, and then it digs into all of our secret places until there are no more secret places left to dig. It is at this crucial point that the thing either calls us home or looks for somewhere else to burrow. A new host.

"I'm sorry," I say, although I am not quite sure what I am apologising for—this tired male gaze, perhaps. Sue is home to me. But sometimes when I wake in the morning I am reminded that there was a time when I wasn't her one and only parasite. She loved someone else. Briefly, futilely, but still—sometimes I stumble upon one of *his* tunnels and feel momentarily lost.

"What are you sorry for?" Sue asks, echoing my thoughts, or at least one of them.

"I don't know," I say. "I look at you sometimes and just feel the need to say it. "It's like trying to fill a tunnel her lover left behind using a child's plastic spade to shift the dirt. "I wish I could have given you more. Or given you better. Or given you *something*."

Great. I woke up this morning both philosophical *and* pathetic.

"Shush, you. You gave me Alfie and Sam." But she looks away from me then. "I don't need anything else."

With the affair, Sue learned how to lie. No, everyone knows how to lie. The affair meant Sue learned how to lie to *me*. And that is like standing inside one of those tunnels of his and listening to the sound of Sue's voice echoing along his walls before finally reaching my ears. A conspiracy of sound. A distortion of the truth.

"Where *is* Sam?" Sue is looking at the empty cot in the corner of the room.

"You left him downstairs," I say.

"When?"

"Last night. After we..."

"No, I didn't. He was here."

"Well, he wasn't, because when I went down to the kitchen for something to eat, he was sitting in one of the dining chairs. I assumed you were pranking me."

"You assumed wrong. Where is he now? Still down there?"

"So you weren't doing that Elf on the Shelf thing then? The thing you've been doing for Alfie."

"Not last night, no," she says. "We were *busy* and I was tired. I fell asleep as soon as you left. Sam was right here, in his cot. I think I'd remember if I took him downstairs."

"Okay—"

"It must have been Alfie. I've told him before to leave Sam alone. He's not allowed to touch him unless one of us is around. *Alfie, get through here.*"

"He's downstairs playing," I say. I can hear his staccato footsteps, feel the shudder rising through the walls, through the floor. We live in a house of straw. One huff and puff and the Big Bad Wolf wins. "Sue? I don't think it was him."

"Sam didn't get down there himself. *Alfie, get* up *here.*"

"No, of course not, but I don't think it was him—Alfie, I mean." He was asleep in his bed last night. I checked.

Didn't I?

"What are you saying? That it was you?"

It seems we have reached an impasse. I don't answer.

"Will you please stop messing around? What is *wrong* with you today?"

Messing around. Poor word choice there, Sue. The real question is why is betrayal at the forefront of my mind this morning? The past is the past. We shook on it. We made love on it, many times. But sometimes a nightmare is so real that even when you wake from it, there is a time, sometimes a *long* time, in which you *believe*. In which what was unreal is not only real but right in front of you again, breathing its foul-smelling *realness* in your face.

Before I can answer, Alfie appears in the doorway of our bedroom, still dressed in his plain, non-Marvel pyjamas, rubbing sleep from his eyes. I did not hear him climb the stairs and he looks too tired, too newly awake to have been playing anywhere, never mind downstairs. And yet the staccato footsteps below us, shuddering through the walls, the floor—they have all stopped.

And the Wolf says to the three little pigs, "I'll huff and I'll puff and I'll blow your house in."

Sue doesn't notice the... the *discordance* here. She has already barged past Alfie standing in our doorway, heading toward the top of the stairs, to even consider placing him inside his room at the same time as the sounds of activity downstairs a few moments ago. To be fair on Sue, I find I am doubting my own hearing too. The walls are thin, sound travels, etcetera, etcetera. His alibi, if it is one, is thin. And why is he doing that new thing he does when he feels nervous? Making that C-shaped claw with the index finger and thumb of his left hand, always his left hand, and pushing it into his mouth, cramming it right in there like a boxer's mouthguard. Only, his arm is attached, and so it looks like his arm is growing out of his face—and after last night I have had *enough* of that sort of image for a lifetime. But this, this I get. It's an odd habit but one that is part of his sensory processing disorder. I get it. C is for comfort.

If this house *is* haunted, I think, it's by the ghosts of our doubt.

"Oh my *God*," Sue's voice echoes up to us from the hall at the bottom of the stairs. "What have you done? What the hell have you done?"

I grab a pair of jeans from the floor and pull them on along with a creased polo shirt. No buttons are fastened. I leave our bedroom and stand at the top of the stairs. Sue is already standing at the bottom. It occurs to me briefly that stairs have hosted some of the most important moments of our lives and that we are invariably at opposite ends, facing each other. It's where I pieced together the affair and confronted Sue, and where she broke the news that she had lost the special. It has a symbolism I am just starting to pull apart in my brain when Sue holds up Sam's torso in her left hand, his head in her right. His arms and legs are scattered all over the stairs.

"What the fuck, Simon?"

For a moment, I am speechless.

"Simon, what the fuck?"

Sue rarely swears. In that respect—and in many others—she is better than me. But it is not Sue dropping f-bombs that makes the impact: it is the sight of her slumped shoulders and the vacuum of silence that follows her words. It feels like some teetering moment before a long fall down a flight of stairs.

"Why would you do this?" she says, when she is able to say anything further.

"What do you mean? I didn't. His—his arm was already off last night and I left him there. I meant to fix it back on this morning before you got up. It wasn't me, Sue."

"Great, just fucking great. So it *was* Alfie then? Where is he?"

I turn to find him standing behind me, using my legs as a shield. And thank God he is standing there, because if I felt a hand on the back of my leg and turned to find no one there, I don't know what I would have done.

"Sue, I don't think it was Alfie either."

"He didn't do this to himself. One of you stripped him and pulled him apart. He's in pieces, Simon. *Pieces.*"

"All right, I know, I *see*, but let's turn it down a notch..."

"Fuck off, Simon. Just... fuck off."

Already holding Sam's head and torso, Sue gathers his scattered limbs into her arms, drops a leg, picks it up, and then rages into the kitchen. A moment later, we can hear her sobbing right before she turns on the cold water tap and rushes water into the sink to drown the sounds of her grief.

I turn to Alfie and take a knee.

"Did you do that to Sam?"

His fingers are clawed into a C and jammed inside his mouth. Saliva slicks his hand.

"Alfie, buddy, please. You need to tell me what happened. Was that you?"

He shakes his head.

"Okay. Downstairs," I tell him. It sounds like a threat even though that isn't my intention. But words can be fluid and slippery sometimes. They can take on new meaning when spoken at the bottom of a flight of stairs looking up or from the top looking down.

Everything changes depending on where you stand.

1. Circle of Rust

On the walk to Alfie's school, I try to talk to him, to coax out a few words other than *Is Sam going to be okay?* but he walks either four feet behind or ten feet in front, a small moon orbiting my angry red planet in an ellipsis of silence. He is angry about something too; his face tells me that much. So I try the usual things to get him to open up a little. A game of I-Spy or idle talk about the cows grazing in the small farmhold we pass on the way; even putting words into their bovine mouths. None of it works other than to raise the flicker of a smile, rapidly hidden by his returning scowl. Besides, the smell of manure in the air on these frosty winter mornings fills our mouths with the taste of shit. It's best to walk fast with our mouths closed, and then I can just blame the livestock on the other side of the road for me not finding a way to communicate with my son.

It is at moments like this, when I will my mind to distance itself from reality, that my subconscious throws me a lifeline.

I see a man. He is tough but different. He gets answers. Wouldn't that be nice, Alfie? I think. You know, answers?

A motorcycle roars past us then, the rider deliberately revving the engine, calling attention to himself. My main character might ride a motorcycle too, I think. It's something I've always wanted to try. A Harley, maybe. But what's the hook here? How is he different?

He's immortal.

Okay, but remember *Highlander?*

He's immortal but he's on a path of self-destruction. He wants to die. He's addicted to meaningless sex while he's chasing something or someone who has all the answers to his questions. His final solution. That's interesting wording... maybe there is a World War Two connection here. Maybe he lived through the war and lost someone very close to him. So, he's chasing his final solution: his own death. But how does he get out of that? If this thing is to have any kind of legs, he'll need to fail.

He finds a child.

A child he must choose to abandon to its death or take with him. It sounds trite but I'll stick with it for now. Besides, write about what you know or write about what you don't know and you might just learn something. This could work. What about a love interest? Maybe someone during the war... Yes, he lost the love of his life in the war. The Germans sent homosexuals to the camps too. So, maybe they were both sent to the same camp and he survived the gas chambers. And that is the reason he wants to die. He is haunted by his past, his lost love, a man who becomes more out of reach to him with each passing day. I know what that is like—right, Dad? Jesus Christ, Freud would have a field day with the sexual angle here. Failed or unresolved Oedipus Complex. Whatever. I need something to anchor this idea, this story, novel, *series* of novels, in reality because maybe a motorcycle-riding, sex-addicted, homosexual immortal is just a little too much? Maybe this whole idea is a loser. You cast your line into the word-lake and what you reel in sometimes, what eventually lies in the cradle of your hands, is not some exotic, silver fish but some old shaving mirror reflecting back your own disappointed face framed by a circle of rust.

Rust.

His name is Rust.

This idea won't let go or I won't let *it* go. That is when I know it needs to be taken seriously, when this kind of mitosis takes place and my mind fills with interconnected ideas and images and even excerpts. The story takes on a life of its own. And if Alfie is angry about something right now then let him stay angry, because this thing growing inside my mind is bigger than him and it may even be bigger than me. He has no idea how long I have waited for something like this to implant itself.

We arrive at the footbridge over the railway line. We are a few minutes' walk from Alfie's school but I am already thinking about when I drop him off at the gate and I have the rest of my walk to work to *think*. We stop in the middle of the footbridge and wait for a train to come, as we do most mornings. Alfie will wave at the driver while I think about what it would be like to let go of everything and jump. At this time, there's one every five or ten minutes. The tracks wait underneath us like a fallen ladder.

Standing here, I often think of the film *Stand By Me*, about four American boys who follow a track just like this one in order to see their first dead body. The track here is empty; a saddening reminder that stories aren't real. I've often wished I could write something like *Stand By Me* (or rather *The Body*, the novella on which it was based), something that people would remember and talk about for years, decades, to come. But those kinds of stories don't seem real either anymore. The publishing deal never materialised, the story collection took eight years to be released and sold poorly when it was. My stories sink like badly thrown rocks pitched across a deep lake, lost in the water of words. Besides, the world is apathetic to words (and to words like 'apathetic'), caring more about selfies, memes, pictures of cats. I like cats but I have followed this track for twenty years and I want to find my dead body.

Maybe Rust will be different, I think. Having lived for so long with ghosts, he can see the dead. He can speak to them. He has all the answers except one: how to be a father to this boy. Maybe he can find out the answer to that too.

Time runs out.

Alfie and I cross the footbridge in silence.

Behind us, the track remains empty of both boys and trains.

1. We're Never Moving Forward

For the next seven days, I am back at the keyboard. Every spare moment, I'm there. Early morning. Late into the evening. The weekend. Staring at the keys that will somehow help me make sense of everything. Snow falls outside my window. The wind howls against the walls like some tempestuous child trying to get in. Go away, I think. Sitting in my study, the coffee tastes good, and day by day the words begin to taste even better.

On the second day, Alfie wants me to help him build a snowman in the garden. There is enough snow cover but I am too busy to lend a hand; Rust is riding his Harley Sportster across North America, hot on the heels of someone called Landau, who will give him (and me) the answers, *all* of the answers, if only he can catch up to him and pin him down. So, Alfie builds the snowman on his own. He gives up after rolling the head and the body. He doesn't put them together. The best part is the details, creating the arms, the features of the face, maybe adding a hat, a scarf, a carrot for a nose. But Alfie abandons his project and the snowman is left not knowing who he is. By day four, I'm tired of seeing this unfinished thing sitting out on our lawn, and so I put on a pair of boots and a jacket and slip outside to kick it back into nothingness. A few minutes later, I am back at the keyboard, back on the Harley Sportster. Back.

Sue fixes Sam. One day he is an assortment of pieces lying on the kitchen countertop, the next he is whole again, Sam again. When Alfie steps closer to say hello to Sam, Sue sends him to his room, where he makes so much unhappy noise it sounds like there is someone else in there with him.

I tell him to keep it down so that I can concentrate.

Just like that, the glue begins to come unstuck. Sue spends time with Sam. I write. Whenever we pass each other (usually on the stairs; the scene for not just our biggest moments but, in that silent passing, our most indifferent), we exchange a look or even a perfunctory kiss on the cheek. I don't ask Sue about Sam and Sue doesn't ask me about Rust, and neither one of us asks the other about Alfie. The glue *unglues* and the whole thing doesn't quite fall apart (not yet; not right away) but we both know that it's gone and even a nudge in the wrong direction will see the working parts of us begin to fall off. Meantime, I ask Alfie how he is and he masks and says he's fine and, because my father was always too busy to ask me that same question when I was a child, I tell myself I am doing an okay job and go back to Rust. There's been a crash near the Superstition Mountains in Arizona and Rust is about to meet a child born from the twisted metal that will change everything for him. There is a car in the story, a hearse of course, and in that car is death and the answers Rust craves. But in another car, the one broken and ravaged by the crash, there is a boy who needs saving. And that is where I hit the wall or the wall hits me and I stare at the empty part of the screen and the Post-It Note forest on my study wall and the place where the snowman stood on the back lawn a couple of days ago and it finally gets through. It finally gets through.

A boy who needs saving.

Life does not imitate art: it *is* art.

Cruel art.

I lower the laptop screen. Check the time on my phone. Dinner time. Check the day. Saturday.

Trudging downstairs, I am disorientated, because I feel like both the character of Rust as he walks toward the wreckage *and* the little boy he's about to pull from it. I am the father *and* the son. And yet I have missed all the clues, missed all the *cues*, just like my father did with me so many, many times.

The dining table has been set by Alfie. Forks and knives in unique arrangements. Sam sits in his high chair, his empty plate in front of him. A plastic fork, a plastic knife. I can't see the places where Sue put him back together again as they are hidden by the Mickey Mouse bodysuit Sue has him wearing. Mickey Mouse in sunglasses. Mickey Mouse in Ray-Bans. I stare at that for a moment before I get everyone their drinks, then take a seat at the table.

My timing is perfect and terrible. I am on time for the chicken fajita wraps Sue has prepared and I am days, perhaps weeks, late for this conversation, in bringing myself to the table as it were. Sue distributes the wraps from a serving platter, two each for the living, a wrap cut in half for the non, with the other half as well as several extra wraps left on the platter for the still-hungry. She sits to my right, opposite Sam. Alfie and I sit facing each other across the round table.

We bite, we chew. Sue smiles across at Sam, who looks back at her with that inscrutable smile of his, the one that hints to her of worlds of mischief but of monsters to me. And I don't look at him anymore; I can't. I look at Alfie instead, the dark circles under his eyes, and the rheumy look that reminds me of my father on what became his death bed. Before that, what caused that look were the sleepless nights of cancer and dementia, the hidden pain and worrying over some undead army coming to claim him even as it secretly advanced through his organs, planting black flags along the way. We bite, we chew. We swallow. But I can't. Thinking about dad, I can't. The chewed food simply sits inert in my mouth, getting cold, losing its flavour.

"You look tired, buddy," I say to Alfie. "Are you sleeping okay?"

"Don't talk with your mouth full," Sue says matter-of-factly, because—you know—we've got to have standards, right? Meanwhile, Sam smiles at us all, and that metaphorical glue that supposedly holds us together? I can smell it. Literally. Coming off him in waves, like he's eaten it, like that fucking monster inside him has gotten high on the glue of us.

"Is something wrong, Alfie?" I ask.

He shakes his head and keeps eating.

"What is it? What's wrong?"

"Nuffin'," he says.

But the circles under his eyes seem to darken right in front of me, and those rheumy eyes become full-on wet as tears well but don't fall, like he's drowning behind glass.

"Alfie... Something is wrong. What is it?"

"I said nuffin'."

"It's okay to tell us. Whatever it is, we won't be mad."

It sounds like I mean Sue and I, but I am two people right now: father and son. Perpetrator and victim. The one who does not see and the one who is not seen. But Dad is not in the room with me and this house is not haunted. He *is* a part of this thing, but only in the way that the dream of last night can linger long into the next morning or a phantom limb can still inflict pain.

Three times. I have asked Alfie three times if there is something wrong. It is three more than my father would have asked me. But I still don't have the answers, and writing about Rust isn't going to provide them because *life* provides the answers, fiction only provides the prism through which we view them.

"Alfie... I promise, okay? It's okay to tell me what is going on."

"Nuffin's going *on*," he says, exasperated.

But the tears don't lie. The flicker of annoyance, anger even, shows that I am getting through to him. The door has opened a crack and a little light just shone through.

His left hand moves toward his mouth, index finger and thumb slipping inside, pressing his teeth.

"Have you had another accident?" It's what we say when we mean wetting the bed.

He thinks about it, then shakes his head.

"There's something though, isn't there, buddy?"

The smallest nod.

"Okay. That's okay. Why don't you just say it? See what happens. I bet you'll be pleasantly surprised. Mum and I, we won't be mad, and you, I bet, will feel a lot better than you do right now."

Sue, who has been watching me interrogate our son, reaches across the table and places her hand on my arm. "Simon, what are you doing?"

He's falling into a cave, I think. But I am not letting him fall in there on his own.

"Sue, please, let him answer."

She withdraws her hands, folds her arms on the table in front of her. Glances at Sam.

"I'shit myself," Alfie says when Sue is looking at Sam and I am looking at Sue and no one is looking at him.

With his hand pushed into his mouth the way it is, I think he said,

I shit myself. Part of me wants to laugh. The son part, not the father.

"I asked if you'd had any accidents, Alfie, and you said no."

"What? I didn't have accidents. I told you."

"Then what did you say? Can you take your fingers out of your mouth and say it again? Just one more time so we can hear. Okay?"

The fingers stay in his mouth but I can make out the words this time, wrapped as they are in saliva.

"I's hit myself."

It's not the confession I expected. Sue and I glance at each other and in that look there are four, five years of failure. I grab my fajita and bite into the wrap for something to do while I think about this. Cold chicken, tasteless peppers, nothing-sweetcorn, wrapped in a cardboard circle. I drop it back onto the plate.

"What do you do?" I ask. "When you—" I cannot say it "—do that?"

"Punch," he says.

"You *punch* yourself? Where?"

"In my room."

"No, I meant *where*—where on your body?"

"Oh," he says, like he just got a maths homework question wrong but now gets it and feels a little embarrassed by his mistake. "On my arm. Uh, sometimes my legs. And here." Alfie points at his tummy.

"Anywhere else?" Sue asks.

"Uh..." He nods. Reluctant.

"My *teef*," he says, and in case we don't get it, he slips his hand out of his mouth and shows them to us. "I try to take them out."

You want to stop this conversation right now. You want to run out of that dining room and maybe inflict a little violence of your own, on a wall, maybe, or a door. Pound pound pound on it with your fist until this house reveals all of its secrets. All of its ghosts.

But I don't do that. I'm still here, sitting at the dining table.

"Why would you do that to yourself, Alfie?" I ask.

"I don't want Sam to go," he says.

Sue takes his hand, the one not rammed into his mouth, and says, "Why would Sam be going anywhere? Don't you like him being here? Being your brother?"

"Ye-es," he says, stretching the word out like it's a piece of gum he's teasing from his mouth. "But Sam does nice fings. He builds Stoneshenge and does footbrints on the floor and uvver stuff."

"Isn't that a *good* thing?" Sue asks.

"Yes, but it makes we want to..."

Red-cheeked, he cannot seem to hold it in any longer. The glass breaks and the tears spill down his cheeks, collecting on the back of the hand he has pressed into his face (as opposed to the hands that push *out* from Sam's at every chance he gets), fingers buried deep deep in there like the world's most awkward attempt to whistle. But the only sounds actually coming out are plaintive sobs.

"It makes you want to what, Alfie?" I ask. "It's okay. You can tell us. No one's mad at you; we just want to know. Okay?"

"Hubbt im," he says.

"What? What did you say?" It comes out sounding less patient than I intended but it is as hard for me to keep what I am feeling inside as it is for Alfie to stem the flow of tears.

Sue's back straightens on her dining chair. Her eyes are locked on Alfie.

Sam smiles his eternal smile, as though he's enjoying the show.

"Take your hand out of your mouth, Alfie," Sue says. "Then we can hear what it is you're trying to say."

Nobody told me it would be like this. Talking to your own child like it's a hostage negotiation, the words like prisoners he is reluctant to release. All I want is to see them free and see the situation resolved.

"You're not in any kind of trouble," I tell him. *Let the hostages go.*

Somehow, this softly-softly approach is only making things worse: he is sobbing openly and still won't remove the hand pincering his tongue. Saliva is stringing down from his hand now and forming a pool on the plate in front of him.

"Hey hey hey, it's okay. Alfie, listen... You can tell Mummy and Daddy *anything*. You know that. Whatever it is, we still love you."

It crosses my mind that if this was a story I was writing I'd have to get out the red pen or start tapping that delete key because it feels like I keep saying the same thing over and over and we're never moving forward.

The clawed hand slides slowly and wetly out of Alfie's mouth like some kind of strange birth. I find myself thinking of Cutter, the old man from the park, the old man from the supermarket, the old man from Alfie's bedroom the other night, sitting on the park bench where I first met him in that awkward suit that didn't quite fit, feeding himself brown lettuce from an old McDonald's carton. Shoving those wilted leaves into his mouth like he hadn't eaten in days. He reminded me of my father but what if he is my son in fifty or sixty years? The ghost of a Christmas yet to come.

How do I stop it?

But Alfie is talking and Cutter, the ghost in my mind right now, edges back into the darkness.

"When he—when he does nice fings," Alfie says, pulling me back into our conversation.

"Yes?"

Don't interrupt, I tell myself. Let him release the hostages in his own good time. The alternative is a kind of Waco situation where, instead of a compound, this entire conversation burns to the ground.

"When he does nice fings... I... I..." More tears. He glances up at the ceiling as though he can hear someone moving around upstairs. His slick, clawed hand inches toward his mouth to choke down the words. We're losing him, I think. He's going back inside to start the fire.

"It's okay," I say, my voice cracking now, because this shit is getting real. I can't hide behind the Waco metaphor anymore. "Tell us, Alfie. Please. What happens when he does nice things?"

"I... hurt him?"

He poses it as a question almost, because maybe that is easier than presenting it as a statement. Maybe he thinks it gives him some wriggle room to deny it later. Maybe he's simply confused by what he is saying.

"Hurt who?" Sue asks, but she knows. She just took away his wriggle room by telling him to step inside a dark cupboard with the bad thing he has done. To spend time alone with it as it breathes heavily on the back of his neck.

Alfie's face pales as he glances at his brother propped in the highchair.

"Sam."

"You hurt Sam?" Sue says. And the temperature inside this room, inside this house just dropped fifteen degrees.

Alfie looks at Sue now, nods.

"Why would you do that?"

"I-cause..." *because* "I-cause, um, he does nice fings."

"You mean Stonehenge and the flour angel on the kitchen floor, right?" I ask.

He nods.

"What did you do to him?"

Alfie's hand creeps toward his mouth again.

"I... I squeezed her." He means *him*, he means Sam, but he is distancing himself.

"Where?" I ask.

"Her tummy. And..."

"Yes?"

"Her froat."

Throat.

Sue stands up and walks unsteadily over to the kitchen sink. She fills a glass with water but her hand is shaking so much she cannot hold it steady enough to drink.

"But those were nice things Sam did," I say to Alfie. "Why would you hurt your brother like that?"

"I-cause, uh, the nice fings."

"You hurt him *because* he did those nice things?"

He nods. "I wanted him to talk. He just stares and stares and says nuffin'."

"Like a statue," I say.

Nod.

"The voice... tells me to hurt him."

"Wait—what voice? You said Sam just stares. Alfie, what voice?"

"Bad Alfie."

"So there is a bad Alfie?" I ask, making it a question because I don't want it to be a statement." And is bad Alfie the one who tells you to hurt your brother?"

"No, bad Alfie is me. I'm Alfie. I'm bad."

"So then who is hurting Sam?"

"Me."

"Alfie, I'm confused."

"Are you going to send him away?"

"Who?" I ask. "Bad Alfie?"

"No, *Sam.* My brother."

"No," Sue says from the sink, where she is leaning back against the countertop. "Sam isn't going anywhere. He's part of this family now."

I open my mouth to say something but realise there is nothing I can say to Sue at this moment that will not escalate this. Later is a different story. When the children are tucked into bed and darkness can hide our faces and my shame, Sue and I will talk. It's long overdue.

I turn back to Alfie at the dining table.

"Do you want him to go away?"

He looks at me and just when I think there can be no more tears, there are.

"Do you want Sam to leave?" I ask again.

He looks down, toward his lap, toward whatever thing may be

hunched under the table and looking back up at him through the gap in his bony knees. The troll under the bridge. My father on his death bed. Cutter in his suit. The spider-like hands that pushed out of Sam's eyes. The special lying in a toilet bowl full of blood. And I realise some of these monsters, some of these ghosts belong to Sue and I, because we've brought them into this house, given them our time, our energy, *all* our energy, and allowed them room to breathe.

Alfie nods, ashamed of his feelings. Feelings we *inflicted* upon him by taking Sam into our home.

Sue starts to say something.

"Let him speak," I interrupt. "Why, Alfie? Why do you want Sam to leave?"

He raises his terrified eyes from the monstrous things under the table and looks straight at me.

He looks more frightened of the words he is about to say.

"I-cause I don't want to hurt him anymore," he says. "I don't want to hurt Sam. Daddy, *please*. I don't *want* to."

"It's okay, buddy," I tell him. "It's okay. I won't let it happen again. And you don't need to hurt yourself either, okay? That stops now, too."

He nods, and I believe he has good intentions, because it's clear from the pain etched in his face that he'd rather hurt himself, rather try to pull his own *teeth*, than hurt his little brother ever again.

And I want to say to him, *you can't hurt Sam anyway*, but it's like we've all been conditioned to step around the idea that he isn't real. Like astronauts on some treacherous space walk, knowing one misstep will plummet us all into a vacuum. Or some kind of collective self-hypnosis. The Cult of Sam. We are the inside. We are the inside. Our mantra and the soundtrack to our fucking lives. But we're really victims who don't want to talk about the crime, because part of us believes maybe we brought it on ourselves. Got pregnant. Lost a baby. Invited the monster in while never letting our ghosts leave. And we are reading every chapter of this horror story except the last because we don't want the story to end, because The End leaves us in an even more vulnerable position—with a choice to make: what now? The End is a monster. All endings are. It is the silence that drops after the final full stop on the final sentence, when we think the nightmare is over, the story's been told. But it hasn't. The monster won't be done with us until there is nothing of us left. And I am doing that thing again, burying the problem under an avalanche of the figurative; simile and metaphor held firmly over my face like some sweet, chloroform-soaked rag. And there's another. Any more? No? Good. Because enough is enough.

Enough is enough.

Alfie is crying like I've never seen him cry before.

Tears and snot. It's not like in stories. It's messy. It's real.

And I am crying too now as he cries along with me and Sue takes Sam out of his highchair and walks out of the kitchen, cradling him in her arms, cradling the pain of the child she lost and had to put back together again.

And I get it. I do.

But the hurt has to end.

Sam has to go.

1. The Eternal House of Sam

Some days are like this. They're about how they begin and how they end, and the middle, the filling—it fades from memory. Like the words in a long sentence: you will remember how the sentence began, you will remember how it ends, but those middle words… you might as well save your energy and not them read at all.

The House of Air has become The House of Sam. The air we gave him, along with our time, affection, and collective belief has made this his house. Alfie is asleep in his bedroom, door open, lunar night light on. After he brushed his teeth and before he climbed into bed, I inspected him for new bruises. Finding none, I waved him through my security checkpoint toward the country of uncertain dreams. This is what we've come to; this is the kind of father I am now.

Sue is in bed, lying on her left side and clutching Sam to her body as though she fears some dollnappers will come for him in the night. I tried rubbing her upper arm for comfort earlier but gave up when I saw Sam smirking up at me from between her breasts.

The House of Sam.

I lie on my back in the dark, staring not at the ceiling but the high corner of the room, searching for mould in the shadows, disappointed I can't seem to find any. Easier times, you might say. Today, I kept picturing my son trying to pull out his own teeth because he hates himself, hates that he's hurting his baby brother. I can't shake it. And now it swings over my head like a pendulum, inching towards cutting me in half. Alfie's bloody, toothless mouth; a circle of teeth left under his pillow; one pissed-off Tooth Fairy saying that isn't how this shit works. It's almost funny, but there's the rub: almost isn't enough. We're *almost* happy; Alfie's *almost* normal, sorry, *neurotypical*; I'm *almost* successful. What we are is *almost* fucked.

His teeth...

His *teeth*...

What next?

How far?

This all began with a miscarriage and I don't want it to end with another death. I don't want those bookends for my collection.

"Baby?"

Sue doesn't respond. Maybe she's forgotten that's what I used to call her. But Sam is *baby* in this house now. And Sam is going to remain baby forever.

The Eternal House of Sam.

"Sue, we need to talk about Alfie..."

"Sam isn't leaving."

Cupping the back of Sam's head, Sue presses him harder to her chest. In the darkness, she could be breastfeeding him. She could be, but she isn't. She usually pumps and puts it in a bottle first. It's a comfort thing for her. Just like Alfie putting his hand in his mouth is a comfort thing for him... right before he tries to wiggle free a molar. Comfort is a lie; it's a soft, plush cushion for your head but with a spike underneath. There's no such thing as comfort in The Eternal House of Sam.

"It's time. Sue, we need to move on."

"We don't. We need to talk to Alfie. Help him understand."

"Sometimes I think *I* don't understand, Sue, so I'm not sure how I'm supposed to explain it to him."

"We try. Both of us, together."

"Yes, we could probably do that... but I don't think I can."

"What do you mean?"

"I can't do it, Sue. I'm sorry."

"So that's it," she says. "It's over?"

"For Alfie's sake—his mental health—and ours, I think it needs to be. Don't you?"

She lies there in the darkness next to me and I can no longer hear her breathing. I can hear *Sam*, the mechanics of breathing, the pretence of it, but not Sue. She is holding her breath and, I guess, shutting her eyes too. Against me. Against the whole world. We all did. Three Blind Mice.

"No."

There it is. Sue's breath. A long exhale after the word. Like she'd been holding it in for minutes, days, weeks.

"No," she says again.

"No," she says, a trilogy of denial. One for each of us blind mice, as though she is speaking for us all.

"I'm not ready," she says.

"To let go," she says. "I'm not ready."

"I can't lose another one," she says.

"You will, don't you see that? If we don't fix this thing, and soon, you'll lose that boy through there. He needs us."

"I want my dream, Simon."

"I know."

"It was a good dream."

"It was. It was good. The best. But..."

Sometimes a dream has to end before it becomes a psychosis. A dream like having two perfect children. Or even having *one* perfect child. A dream like leaving the day job to live and work in a garden of words. Or like getting to know your father before he no longer knows himself. Or or or.

"... dreams have a price sometimes."

"So what happened to 'we are the inside'? Was it a lie?"

My hand on Sue's shoulder. Cold skin.

"No, it wasn't, baby," I say, trying to take it back, the lie, the word *baby*, to take it all back in this Eternal House of Sam and somehow make things good again. "But when things go rotten on the inside, you have to get out. There's no other choice."

"There is."

"What is it?"

"*You* leave."

"*What?*"

"Leave. Go. You're what's rotten here. You've been pretending the whole time."

"I wasn't pretending, Sue. I was... asleep."

"Fuck you, *asleep*. You never wanted Sam. You never wanted the one we *lost*, never mind Sam."

"That's not true."

But maybe it is, I think. Maybe one child was enough.

"He would have just got in the way of *your* dream, isn't that right?" Sue says. And she rolls over in our bed, onto her back, the cover pushed down below her naked breasts. One is exposed in the dark, my eyes have adjusted enough to see its familiar shape; the other is occluded by

Sam's head. I can't see it but at the same time I *can*: the smirk on his face as her nipple accidentally brushes his lips.

"I wanted our other baby, Sue. I just wasn't used to the idea yet, and then you lost him and it was all over."

"*I* lost him?"

"*We*. I meant we. Don't read into that—please. It wasn't your fault. It wasn't anyone's fault except maybe the—the mould in that house. Or fate."

"Yes, well, fate is a cunt."

"Maybe so."

"Sam isn't leaving this house, Simon."

"What about me?"

"That's up to you."

"How is it up to me? Are you saying you don't have an opinion on whether I stay or go?"

"Do you want Sam gone or not?"

"You know my answer to that. He isn't real, Sue. And for something that isn't real, he's causing a *lot* of fucking problems for us right now."

"Okay, so there is your answer."

And just like that I am sleeping in the car.

1. What Makes This Thing Hard To Do

I wake with the winter sunrise and the singing of the birds in the trees behind our house. Sam's house. The Eternal House of Sam. Each breath I take hangs in the air of the car like I'm in the film *Titanic*. There's frost on the windows. White mould. It's one of the most uncomfortable sleeps I've ever had, curled up like a foetus in the back seat of our little Fiat, the pillows from my side of the bed and a throw from the settee for warmth. I'm born into the morning with what feels like a hangover but I haven't touched a drop. The punishment when I haven't committed the crime. Not yet.

Not yet.

In the footwell, I find the Funko Pop figure of Dale Cooper that Alfie must has left in the car. Cooper's head is now aslant, the spring holding it in place pulled this way and that until it has lost its tension. He gives me a kind of sideways look as though he's trying to figure me out. The hand that once held a damn fine cup of coffee is missing. Snapped clean off. My son, the would-be killer of dolls, must have practised on Dale before graduating to bigger dolls, it seems. Jesus

Christ, what next? Burying mannequins under the patio? Didn't I write a story about that a long time ago? It doesn't matter. It would be funny if it wasn't my life at this moment.

I drop the vinyl figure back into the shadows of the footwell. Send his ass back to the Black Lodge.

"Sorry, Cooper. Not today."

I let myself into the house. I haven't relinquished my key yet. Besides, this isn't a separation; it's a fight that simply went too far. Sue and I have had other fights and come back from the brink. Come back *stronger*. But this one... this one feels different somehow. The house feels different, like it's forgotten me after just one night apart.

In the kitchen, I make a cup of black coffee and raise my mug to my compadre out there in the footwell. There's no cherry pie in the fridge but there are slices of Tesco ham. I fold a couple of slices and call them breakfast.

The house is freezing. The boiler hasn't fired up yet and the bones in the walls aren't creaking-clicking into life. Back in the hallway, I stand at the bottom of the stairs and take a moment to see if my breath fogs the air in front of me. Nothing. That boat has sunk. Everyone is asleep and I am a ghost in my own house.

Maybe this house is haunted after all.

The stairs.

I try not to think about what stairs have done to us. These stairs in The Eternal House of Sam; the stairs we thought we'd left behind in The House of Mould. Even as I climb them to reach somewhere I know I need to go, I am aware of the fall *growing* at my back. This might be the last time I ever do this. At the top, I turn and look down, unsure of how I came to be here or why. Everything changes depending on where you stand.

That isn't true, I think. I know why. I know why I'm a ghost right now. Why I'm creeping into Alfie's bedroom to check he's not awake. Why I'm tiptoeing out again, then across the landing toward the bedroom where Sue is asleep with Sam cradled in her arms.

Except he isn't.

Sam is sitting in the space between Sue's pillows and one of mine, propped against the headboard, facing the door like he's been waiting for me this whole night, just like that. His tireless face, his tireless smile under a facsimile of my father's eyes.

Our eyes meet.

Sue knew she would get to me with those. She even had them made to order. She did not know that my father would die before Sam could join our family but she knew what they would do. I spent over thirty years struggling to win the affection of my father, to understand the distance in his eyes; Sue bet on me being willing to spend a few more on Sam.

I get it. I do.

And I love her for trying to repair the irreparable in me.

It's what makes this thing so hard to do.

My shadow falls across the bed, across the sleeping form of Sue, across Sam propped between the pillows and looking at me.

A moment later, my shadow is gone, like I was never there, never existed. None of this ever happened.

And Sue is still asleep with nothing but the space between our pillows.

1. This is not The End

Go back.

Go back and start reading this story again.

This is not The End.

dragonland

I live in a forest on the back of a dead dragon.

I stop writing...place the quill on the warm shelf cut into the dragon's heart to keep the tip from freezing...and read the first line again. It is proving to be the most difficult. Why does it read like a confession, or at the very least like the path to some shameful secret? The decisions we make lead us to where we are; mine have led me to where I am—an orphan alone in this frozen valley, trying to understand the brother who left him for a fool's errand. He left me. Abandoned his king. Why am I even writing this? No one will ever read it, least of all him. He has joined our father and mother by now. But these were Cai's pages; this was his quill and ink. Perhaps this is just my way of finding him again—on the page, in the snow. Tomorrow, I will write a new first line. Start over. Today, it is too cold to do anything more.

I fear it has become my bones.

1.

Sometimes I stand at the edge of the forest of shoulder and look out upon the tiny kingdom Father bequeathed to me. From the towns of skull and tail's end to the dragonspine road connecting them, to the plains of wing—it belongs to me now. But what does that mean? To belong... With our father gone, each nightfall seems colder. My breath-clouds linger longer than they once did. The sun falls behind the distant mountains earlier each evening, splashing the valley floor in long bloody red. It is like watching death seeping through a sheet from some unknowable wound. I witness each day end like this, as a boy watching a man die, knowing guiltily that his time to rise has finally come.

I retreat to the fire. I am grateful for its warmth and for the young trees encircling us that do what they can to divert the bitterly cold wind from our camp. I remember the day Father planted them: it was our second day and I was fifteen years old. I remember watching, helpless, as he walked out into the falling snow in search of something, anything that might prolong our survival. It almost killed him, and maybe it did play its part just six days later, but to see him return on *that* day, walking up the dragonspine road with a clutch of saplings in each hand, was like watching a giant return with a forest. And lo—it became one. The forest of shoulder. Named apropos of its location and ability to hold back the bite of the wind. Sometimes a boy's idolisation of his father is not fanciful but a true measure of the man.

If only my little brother, Cai, saw it so.

He sits next to the fire inside the ring of trees. Cross-legged and hunched in his patchwork coat of furs, he glances up as I approach. I sit beside him and look into his grey eyes ringed with wood ash to reduce the snow glare, like mine. We both must look like we have been in a fight and lost. Indeed, we are almost the same in appearance, differentiated only by fourteen months and two hand-breadths of height. It is only our minds that have chosen different paths.

"Is it still there?" he asks.

I grunt in answer. He means the light on the mountain, of course. It has become a regular aspect of our days here—as regular as the conversation that inevitably follows any sighting of it. It is a pale and uncertain light high on the mountaintop to the west. So high, in fact, that on some nights, when the dark is at its fullest, it looks like any other star in the sky. My brother sees romance in that. Hope. I just see something insufferably distant and out-of-reach.

"I like to know she is still there," he says. "Still watching over us. Especially on nights like this."

I know what he means. On nights like this...when the cold is so brutal the heat of Tyrandir almost fails to reach us. They say dragons can live for centuries and that death is less an inevitability than a choice for them; a resignation from life. It takes many months, sometimes years, for their hearts to cool (some scholars claim the world is heated by a similar kind of heart). It is why small creatures and large predators alike, even now, tend to give Tyrandir a wide berth, or at least approach with ample caution. Several months after he crashed down in this far-flung valley with my father, brother and I on his back, he protects us still. On nights like this...when the frost grips our furs and it hurts our bones to move... when the blizzards sweep through the valley and across dragonland like an assault of icy knives, I wish he would just open an eye to show us that he lives, that this is naught but a deep slumber. Of course, I wish my father would do the same, but his grave beyond the green moat outside of skull is disturbed not by his own hand but only the pawing of creatures willing to risk even a dragon's ire for a taste of his corpse.

The snares we set see to them, though.

"It means she is alive," Cai says.

It takes me a moment to realise what—or who—my brother is talking about. My thoughts are still on Tyrandir and my father. Then there is this damnable cold dulling my mind to a near-useless blade, incapable of swinging easily from one subject to the next, never mind cutting to the heart of anything.

"It may just be a trick," I say. "Or some conspiracy between the mountains and the moon to lure us into a hopeless situation."

I leave him to go drag my bed closer to the fire. Each of the dragon's fur-lined saddlebags are large enough for one of us to fit comfortably inside. They play their part in keeping us alive.

"Or it could be our mother," he insists.

"You do not know that."

"And what do *you* know, Brother? With any real certainty, I mean. No more than I."

He stares at me across our small fire. His face remains partly unlit, as though this madness has yet to reach the rest of him.

"She is lost," I say. "Like our father, the king. You would do well to focus your attentions on what needs to be done here. Otherwise, the light on the mountain may outlast yours..."

"Her dragon fell like ours, Stephen. I saw Sauro come down west of here—the same direction as the light on the mountain. It is her, I am convinced of it."

"I believe you *are* convinced, but it is far and it is high. And it is a journey neither one of us could ever hope to make and live. We have grown weak and slow as old men here, in case you haven't noticed..."

"Not *that* weak," he says. "Or that slow."

I sigh and shake my head. "We were three in number. She was alone. Father, a strong man and a king no less, perished within two weeks. What hope had she alone against all of *this*?"

He reaches over and squeezes my shoulder with his gloved hand. "Have you seen a corpse, Brother?... No. Have you buried it like you buried your father's?"

Worse, I think but do not say to him. I have buried her so many times I have lost count. When dark is full and the howls of the wolves are silenced by the screaming of horrors far worse than them, yes, I have buried her, far and deep in the recesses of my mind, where she might be safe from their violent attentions.

"Enough, Cai. Please. I do not wish to discuss it any further."

"But what of the light," he insists. "What is it, then, if not her?"

I shrug his hand off my shoulder. Climb into my saddlebag for the night. He does not see me reluctantly curl into a cradle for the catching of dreams.

"It is nothing," I tell him, knowing I will surely bury her again tonight.

2.

Thunder entered my bed chamber within the palace of Kuhl Amar. The door shook in its frame like something afraid. All the doors in the palace had known such fear at one time or another; my father spared none of them. I was never afraid of him though. I worshipped him too much to be afraid. Besides, I had the uncanny ability to hear the manner of his approach, to know when his mood had soured. There was a saying used by the old dragonmasters: to tame a dragon, you must know a dragon first. I had little hope of ever taming my father, but I knew him well enough to avoid his fire. Most of the time.

That night, I had heard him yelling at the guards and servants alike—those that remained—long before he arrived at my chamber door. He entered, although he invariably gave the impression that any room moved to accommodate *him* while he stood ever in the same place. He wore his riding furs, heavy boots, and thick gloves. His beard had mostly gone to grey by then, the colour leeched from it over the past few months, betraying what he refused to reveal in his mannerisms and words: that he had grown tired.

His eyes found me sitting on my bed doing nothing—waiting for him, in fact. Blue eyes, flecked with green if you got close enough, if he let you, but strangely unfocussed of late, as though he were trying to look at several things at once, all of them outside of the room in which he stood.

His face was the thinnest I had ever seen it, and flushed as someone who has newly-finished unloading a wagon down to its boards. My father did no such thing in life, of course. Anger was his main exertion, if you discounted chasing handmaidens through the secret corridors and hidden rooms of the palace. I gestured toward the flagon of water on the table by my bed. He shook his head and then threw a drawstring sack at my lap.

"Fill it. Take what you need and one or two—*only* one or two—things precious to you. We leave soon."

I stood from the bed and went over to the tall wardrobe that loomed in the corner of my room. I opened it and retrieved a modest-sized bag from inside. Held it up for him to see.

"Where are we going?" I asked.

My father smiled and my heart skipped like a pauper who discovers the only gemstone in a long seam of rock.

He would never smile at me again.

"North," he said. "Dress for warmth, not comfort."

I cringed inwardly. So keen had I been to impress him with my foresight in packing, I had forgotten to change out of my nightclothes.

"We go where the land cares nothing for the sun," he said. "Where those ungrateful bastards will never think to follow."

I reached in with my free hand and pulled a long-coat and cloak from the wardrobe's innards. My father would recognise them from our hunting trips. He nodded his approval.

"Good, Son," he said, though I chose not to hear the pause.

While I dressed, he picked up the empty sack. "Your little brother will need this, I expect."

"Doubtless he will. Though he'd fill it with books if he could."

"Indeed. I am fortunate to have you to rely on, Son. *You* understand..."

"Thank you, Father."

"Let us leave this nest of snakes and ingrates. May we return one night to avenge this savage injustice upon our house and name. And may you hold down every man, woman, and child while I draw my sword across their neck."

"Yes, Father."

"A traitor's knighthood for them all!"

"Yes, Father."

I was dressed.

"Come, Stephen. Do not tarry. Your mother is preparing the dragons as we speak."

3.

It is the kind of morning that makes me regret not putting on a dozen shirts that day instead of three. Too cold even for the sun, which now hides behind the clouds to the east. The vast mountains surrounding us are partly hidden too, the massive peaks plunged inside the corpse-grey bellies of the clouds, inviting them to spill their frigid guts upon the valley floor in a snowstorm unlike any we have seen thus far. Frost crusts our brows and eyelashes. The thin air blasts across dragonland in icy gusts. We tilt our faces to breathe inside our cloaks—stale air, yes, but warm enough not to burn our throats—and we crouch as we move around our camp.

Earlier, I made the journey from shoulder to skull. Forty to fifty steps to a child who is upright, but a near-endless, energy-sapping drag when forced to undertake it on my stomach, using spines and scales as handholds to pull myself along while drawing what little warmth I can from the close contact. And for what? Two snow voles—one caught in our snare, one lying dead in the snow—the latter useful only for patching our coats, judging from its mottled liver.

"You will need to gut the other," I inform Cai, who sits watching what I am doing from the other side of the fire. He merely looks at me aghast.

I remove my gloves and set them aside to be boiled free of any infection later. So far this morning, the gusting wind has blown out our fire twice. Father may have dug up and carried armfuls of earth from the green moat around dragonland, sought and fetched the saplings from the woods scattered throughout the valley, planted them around the hollow between the dragon's shoulder blades, themselves a wind break to some extent, but he could do nothing to speed along their maturity. He had wanted to prove something to us: that dragonland was not the road's end but a place on which things could not only take root but grow and thrive.

"What are you waiting for, Cai?" I yell, perhaps a little louder than he deserves, but my frustration with the storm needs its voice.

"Can it not be done later?" he replies.

"No. The meat will spoil. It must be done now."

"The meat will freeze. It would keep for weeks."

"I already cut its throat. That is one less thing for you to do." I left a spattering of the vole's blood around the snare to lure other animals, but most of it had already frozen in its veins. "Here..." I hold the carcass out to my brother.

"My hands are cold."

"When are they not, Cai? Take it."

"I do not want to."

"You want to eat though."

"Yes, but—"

"Then do it. Use the knife. It is on my bed. Make a small incision in the stomach, push your thumbs inside then peel the skin outwards. The legs can be tricky to get free, but then you get to the best part: twisting off its head."

"Stop! You know I can't."

Laughing, I leave the carcass near the fire in the hope that it might thaw. I crawl over to my saddlebag bed to retrieve the knife myself. It once belonged to our father but, like everything else, it is mine now. When I return, Cai is leaning close to the flames, head bowed, inviting the rising heat inside his hood. I take a moment to let the fire warm my frozen fingers.

"Let me borrow your gloves, Cai. I should not be doing this with bare hands. The last time I checked, there was no apothecary here."

Without looking up, Cai tugs off his gloves and hands them to me. I go to work skinning the vole.

"Our father taught me this," I say. "Mother taught you how to sew…"

"You would have frozen to death long ago if not for her and that."

"And you would have starved to death if not for him. And me."

"You thrash in your sleep," he says. "How many times have I had to repair your bed?"

"Yes. But *you* eat like a horse, little brother. How many times have I had to do *this*?" I reach over and shake some of the vole's innards underneath his hidden nose. He leans back, out of reach. When I imagine the grimace on his face I can feel the frost crack on mine as I smile.

Cai returns to the fire cautiously, leaning close to the flames once more.

I drop the offal into a shallow bowl Father carved from a piece of wood he found. I will add the head and bones to it so that later we may enjoy a few precious mouthfuls of soup. I wish he was here to share it with us: Father. Huddled in this hollow between a dragon's shoulder blades, surrounded by snow fields in a valley of vast, white emptiness, ringed by towering mountains that rend the sky, time and distance seem to both shrink and stretch somehow. He is gone but he is here still. Beyond all reach and yet with us now, and now, and now. In every moment; in everything. He is the knife. The bowl. The towering mountains and the barren valley. He is dragonland. And yet he is no part of it at all. Everything and nothing. Nothing and everything.

"Do you think she will be on the mountain tonight?" Cai interrupts.

"I do not know. The meat on this one looks good. We will have some breakfast this morning, at least. What I'd give for some eggs."

"What do you think she does up there?" Cai asks.

"Nothing. Much like her second born. Now fetch me one of the sharp sticks. We need to eat something. Cai? Cai!"

Instead of looking for the skewer, he crawls over to one of the trees our father planted and tears off a thin branch dense with green needles. He hands it to me. I say nothing of his thoughtlessness but set the branch aside; I may find a use for it later. I find the stick we use to skewer the meat myself. It was lying close to him the whole time.

"*This*," I tell him, holding it up in front of his face. "We use *this*."

"Do you think she has enough to eat?"

I ignore him, but he takes it as an invitation to carry on; to fill the silence with talk of her.

"What grows on mountains anyway? What lives so high up?"

"Not much," I say. "Maybe some birds. Mountain hares. Nimble-footed goats. Creatures that talk to the clouds like you. I would not know. But it would be deathly cold up there, exposed as it is..." I feel guilty for saying the last part, for planting that seed.

"She'd have her dragon though," he says, unmoved. "Or maybe she's found herself a nice little cave... Yes, I expect she has by now. Mountains are full of caves... so she would have food and somewhere safe and warm at night. Why, she's probably better off than us."

"I doubt it, Brother. I doubt it very much."

I throw a few sticks on the fire, frowning at our dwindling supply, and then punch the skewer's sharpened tip through two small chunks of frozen pink meat followed by several even smaller pieces. I hold the skewer over the flames as the blizzard continues to howl all around us. Between our fire and the storm that would puff it out like a birthday candle are the shoulders of our dragon, the forest that encircles our camp, and two coated and cloaked boys, all of us working in unison to keep the wind from the fire just long enough to cook these few simple scraps to eat. It is exhausting work even before Cai speaks.

"I think we need to go look for her," he says. "Or at the very least find out what that light on the mountain is." Rubbing his cold, bare hands together over the flames while rocking on his rump, he looks at me with those wide, ash-circled eyes of his: a foolish young boy trapped down a well who sees a silhouette interrupt the circle of light, the *hole* of light, and confuses it with hope.

"And what if it is not her?" I ask. "You will have risked our lives, our father's line, only to discover you were wrong. Let me save you some time, Cai—you are wrong. Mother is dead. Father is dead. And it disturbs me greatly that you appear so keen to join them."

The silence that follows is sweet but short-lived.

"Why must you say such insufferably cruel things? I am your brother..."

"The *light* is the hole here—can't you see that? And hope is nothing but the long fall into it."

"What are you talking about?"

"I am simply saying that we must protect the kingdom. As the only surviving sons of King Stannard of Kuhl Amar, it is all that matters now."

"But ...protect *this*? This terrible, awful, hideous place? *Why?*"

"It keeps us alive. For good or ill, we call it our home now."

Cai stops rubbing his hands and looks at me across the fire. "This is not our home. It is a dead dragon. Its heart cools every moment of every day we are stuck here. See the moat where its heat has melted the snow and ice? It is shrinking daily. I've seen it."

"This dead dragon has given you life since it brought you here."

"And it seems to have taken so much of yours. Where is the older brother I looked up to?"

"He is here."

"Back at the palace, you rode horses...you leapt rivers...you flew above the trees instead of cowering amongst them."

"Your mind is playing tricks again, Cai. Those were ponies not horses. Puddles not rivers. And the trees I flew above? You must be thinking of when I leapfrogged Mrs Rowe's shrubs in the palace gardens. I got my hide tanned for that, too. Do not change the past to make some silly point."

He stands and walks to the edge of our camp. "Fine. But do not change the future to make yours."

I glance up from cooking the skewered meat. Cai is looking over the forest of shoulder at the mountains to the west. "Meaning?" I ask.

"Meaning no one is coming to save us."

The blizzard wind howls across dragonland like a chorus of wraiths agreeing with him. I push the sound out of my mind and focus on the fire and not burning the vole meat.

"You are wrong," I say. "Many were loyal to our father."

"When he was alive, yes. When he put coin in their pockets, even more so."

"They weren't bought, Cai. They were rewarded, and amply so. Our father was loved."

"By you and I, yes. And by our mother? Most deeply. But does a servant ever truly love their master? Do we love the snow these days? I mean love it like we once did, when we could build knights and monsters out of it and it did not threaten our lives. Now that it is the master of our fate, I must say I am beginning to loathe the very whiteness of it."

"Things have changed, I grant you that. But the duty of a king remains the duty of a king: to protect his kingdom."

Cai turns then from his beloved mountain and says, "You are not a king and this is not a kingdom. It is a place of last resort. A refuge. And a pitiful one at that. Mark my words, dear Brother, it will kill us both if we do not leave."

"Then maybe it is a kingdom, after all," I say. "For didn't our father's kill *him* in the end?"

Suddenly my brother is stood before me, arms spread in disbelief. "You have spent so long together you have become him—only writ small. Where he had a kingdom and lands, you have this dead thing and a place that does not want you. Can you not see it? Or is this stubbornness of yours supposed to convince someone—yourself, no doubt—of some kind of entitlement?"

"Get to the point," I tell him. "The meat is almost ready and you give away words like trinkets." I want to hurt him and the only way to do so is to shame his talent with words just as he has shamed mine. But is mine a talent, I think. To be the mirror of someone else? Who am I, really? What am I?

I am the ghost of my father. And I know nothing else because there is nothing else to know.

Cai sits beside me and places his hand on mine. His fingers look red and painful from the cold.

"We must leave this place soon," he says, and I can hear a tremor rising in his voice like a high, errant note through a symphony score. "Before the heart of the dragon turns cold and we're both lying face down in the snow beside it with maggots living on our backs."

"And why would I do that?" I ask.

He throws back his hood as if it is full of bloodflies. "Why? To find your own way. Father isn't watching you now. There is no longer any judgement save your own. His eyes are closed and you are free."

I shake his hand from mine. "To do what? Find Queen Gessalla?

She is dead, Cai. Dead and picked clean."

"Do not say that. And call her what she is: our mother."

He moves away from me to nurse his melancholy at the edge of the forest of shoulder. The trees, barely reaching his chest, shake their leaves as though they object to his presence. I have to remind myself it is merely the work of the wind and the blizzard and not some lingering eldritch influence of my father's.

The vole meat cooked, I eat my share straight off the skewer. It is delicious but a tease to my empty stomach, which grumbles in protest even more than Cai. I pass him the skewer with his share still on it then place our pan—the tin keepsake box he brought with him when we fled the palace; empty now—onto the makeshift rack over the fire in order to melt the ice for our bone soup later. There is something reassuring and calming about watching ice melt in the box while we are surrounded by so much of it that will not.

"Cai?"

"Mm."

"What is it you see? I don't just mean the light or Mother. I mean what is it to you, truly?"

Biting the meat on the skewer while looking thoughtfully at the blue-grey vastness of the mountain, he says, "I see a stair. It rises out of this snowy hell to a doorway. In the doorway someone stands, holding aloft a flaming torch. I want to see who it is. I want to see the golden light reflected in their kind eyes. I want to climb the stair."

"You sound as touched as one of Hegis Ky's flock," I say, shaking my head. "It is an impossible journey. And winter is pressing—"

"All the more reason to remove its foot from our throats now and run while we can. Come with me."

"I cannot."

"Leave him behind, Stephen. His eyes are closed."

I stand and walk over to Cai, placing my hand firmly on his back and between his shoulders.

"I am not ready."

"Maybe so," he says. "But in the great reckoning there is only the before and after. Your foot is trapped in the before. Pull it free and walk with me. That is all I ask."

"This is why you could never be a king," I tell him. "You speak in near-riddles half the time. Talk of reckonings...befores and afters... trapped feet. You go around a thing rather than attack it head-on."

"And yet I am the one prepared to climb that mountain..."

"You are not the king. I am. And I forbid it."

"I am deeply sorry," he says, stepping away from me and the hand on his back. "I would not wish such a fate upon my darkest enemy."

"I do not ask for your apology," I say. "This was my father's last gift to me. You are simply jealous."

"Really? How so?"

"You wanted what we had. You always have."

"A father?" he says. "Yes. I cannot lie—I wanted one desperately. But *this*—me and you arguing in a blizzard in some lost and forsaken place? You can have it—"

I turn to him, rage heating my face and burning his next words right out of his mouth. "This is all I have left of him," I say.

Cai nods, looking out from the forest of shoulder at the distant mountain with wet, imploring eyes.

"Yes," he says. "And the light on the mountain is all I have left of her."

4.

On our third day in the valley, Father took me aside and predicted his fate. When I say he took me aside, we left Cai sitting in the camp in shoulder and took a walk together down the dragonspine road to tail's end. We stood in our cloaks in the green moat that surrounds dragonland, where both the impact of Tyrandir's landing and the heat still radiating from his heart had cleared the snow up to five paces from his body. A short distance away, a pack of seven wolves studied our every movement from a copse of silver birch. My father turned to me, clutching his left side, and for the first time I noticed the sag of his broad shoulders.

"I'm dying."

There was no preamble or forewarning, he merely announced it like he might the arrival of sunset.

A blast of frigid air came between us then and sent both of us staggering back a few steps, away from each other, even as his announcement stole my power to speak. My head swam and I faltered as I fought to catch a breath. We moved toward each other again, and pushed our heads together as snow began to fall heavily around us. He saw the tears in my eyes and brushed them away roughly with his gloved hand.

"Don't," he said. "Your eyes will freeze shut."

"H-how do you know you're..." I could not bring myself to say the word.

"When the dragon came down, something must have...broken inside me. It hurts to breathe. And there is this—" He hawked and spat a bright clot of blood onto the snow nearby, where it lay in stark contrast to the white. "There is much to do," he said. "But there are one or two things we must speak of first. Catch a breath, Son."

He saw that I was faltering and waited for me to collect myself, but the longer I made him wait the harder it was for me to find a fulcrum. Somewhere off to my left, one of the wolves howled, and while my hood prevented me from seeing them without turning my whole body around, my mind helpfully presented images of the pack breaking into a run across the snow field between us. My father cupped my chin and tilted my face up toward his. I saw the flecks of green in his eyes.

"Calm," he said.

I nodded—and kept nodding—until slowly my breath settled and the sneering pack fell from my mind's eye as though swallowed by some hidden crevasse.

"Listen and listen well," he said. "Soon it will be just you and Cai left. He is not built for this, but you *are*—you must be, as the eldest. Look after him and stay close to Tyrandir. Someone will come for you."

"Who? Who will come?"

"A friend. When we fail to arrive in the northern city of Pelardruin, they will search for us and they will find you here. Do not stray from the dragon's side, except to hunt or forage, and then—bring my sword with you *always*. Do you understand?"

"Yes, Father."

"You will be safe here for a while—long enough, I trust. Tyrandir will confuse the wolves and stay warm for some time yet. Though he appears asleep to them, it is a fragile curtain you must hide behind. They say the only thing to die slower than dragons are worlds. Pray that is true, but make no error in judgement here: death is the end of this and every road. All things are temporary: dragons, kingdoms, men. Let him be a stopping post but respect him as you would your own kingdom and he will keep you both safe until the Northmen come."

Father coughed and spat another clot in the snow. Double the size of the first, it sank from its own warmth and weight.

"What about Mother?" I asked, knowing Cai was already struggling with the separation. "Should we try to find her? What if she lives?"

He lowered his gaze for a long moment. I watched his shoulders sink. Finally, he looked up at me, and his eyes spoke of an anguish festering within him that could not be simply spat into the snow.

"I am afraid they are gone," he said.

"They?" I asked. I assumed he meant Mother and Sauro (pronounced like the very thing that had befallen us).

"Your mother was with child," he said. "Not long, not enough to be seen, but she was no longer bleeding. You know how such things work, yes?"

I knew enough.

I nodded but said nothing. A brother or a sister... What cruelty was this to be informed of their life *and* death in the space of a few breaths?

"Time is limited," Father said, interrupting my thoughts. "We push it from our minds as though it is plentiful. We deny it has any power over us, when what it has is absolute. But it is better to know it is the end and gorge on life than pick at its bones and never feel truly satisfied. I still have time to teach you some things, and you still have time to learn. But we should return to your brother or he will grow suspicious of our absence."

"He will want to search for her," I said. "They are the closest of us all. He will need answers."

But Father began to climb back up the dragonspine road, a different man from the one who had walked down it some moments before. He seemed wizened and slow, as though telling me of these things had eased no amount of the burden he carried but merely allowed his mask to slip for a while.

I stopped him with a cry into the wind that was all but stole away into the mountains.

"What will I tell him?"

"Tell him nothing. Tell him everything. Tell him Sauro fell with Tyrandir but that altitude separated them and she was carried many miles to the west. Tell him the mountains would not have welcomed her but dashed her against their rocks and outcroppings. Tell him she is lost."

He turned away once more but I called out a second time to stay him.

"Why did they fall together?" I meant the dragons and not Mother and my unborn sibling. "As Tyrandir fell, I glanced toward Mother and Sauro and saw them hurtling toward those western mountains. But isn't it strange for two dragons to fall from the same sky?"

Father looked down to his left hip and then to his right, at where he would have kept his sword sheathed. It was an old trick of his from when he held court in the throne room of the palace of Kuhl Amar; a feint meant to earn himself time to make a decision and to put others ill at ease. I had seen him use it before both executions and pardons, so feint or not, it left me feeling deeply uneasy.

"A good question," he said finally, in an impressed voice that sent me reeling as much as the feint itself. "And very wise. But one best saved for another day. We must be getting back. I have something I wish to show you boys besides how to set snares and prepare an animal for the plate. It is a game involving, of all things, *dragons*. And where better to play such a game than on the back of one?"

I spread my arms wide to remind him of where we had found ourselves and of the dangers we presently faced, seven of which watched us with cold eyes and snarling stomachs. He paid no heed.

"You will need a clear, strong mind as much as anything in the trying times ahead. First, let me show you this thing. Then, if you wish, pass your judgement on me."

He seemed oblivious to everything in that moment. Perhaps between what he had already lost and the falling sands of his own mortality his senses had been numbed beyond all restoration. Perhaps he had merely hoodwinked me into dropping my question. I shrugged, though he would not have seen such a tiny gesture hidden within the folds of my cloak, and began, thoughtfully, to follow his footsteps up the dragonspine road.

My mind circled that most unlikely image of two dragons falling in tandem from the sky like spiralling maple seeds—until a nervous glance to my right at the copse where the wolves had gathered revealed they were gone: their pack scattered by some new animal presence.

I stopped and stared as my insides plummeted as from a towering cliff top.

In their place, gathered on its two hind legs to gain a better view, stood a menacing beast of bulk and horns.

5.

A violet sky of twilight... The sun slipping behind the blue mountains to the west.... The snowfields around us fading from blinding brilliance to the colour of old bruises.

Every night, Fortûn Eld, the world of second chance, falls asleep, and this place shows a little more of its true self. A cold confession. But

I have learned that when too much is revealed there is often some regret, and regret is followed by a rebalancing, some terrible price to pay.

And so, though there is little wind this evening, the cold is especially brutal, the vast emptiness stretching farther than before, gripped by utter stillness, like a predatory breath held and held, willing us to perish.

Father died at twilight. On a night such as this. When every night is the same, memories lie in shallow graves. When every night is the same, he refuses to remain buried.

In shoulder, we hang our cloaks on the trees to create a makeshift shelter. Cai insists we leave it open facing the west so that the light of our fire may speak to the light on the mountain. I do not protest as it is not worth another argument. Besides, our shrunken stomachs are full for the first time in as long as I can remember.

Earlier today, while melting ice over the fire to give us water to drink, I spotted something lying in the snowfield north of dragonland, a dark shape perhaps three or four hundred paces beyond the edge of the plains of wing. I grabbed my father's sword, leapt onto my feet, and ventured out to investigate.

Wading through deep snow is akin to swimming upstream. It demands a complete bodily effort just to keep moving slowly forward. The cold gnawed at my fingers through my gloves. The falling snow clung to my face and clothes. Each flake was an icy whisper trying to persuade me to lie down and surrender myself to the eternal white. But by then I could see the shape ahead of me was a carcass and a carcass meant food, so I pushed onward. Eventually, I arrived at the body of a wolf: an adult male, easily as heavy as me. I had found one other wolf lying dead in the snow some weeks before but it had been diseased, inedible. It was from it that I had taken a shoulder blade bone, boiled it, and fashioned a saw by cracking it in half and cutting teeth with my father's knife. Today, I used that saw to cut meat from its kindred, though there was no need to open its carcass as some other creature had already torn it asunder, spreading its ribs like the petals of some grisly flower, leaving them jutting at strange and unnatural angles. Most of the good meat was gone, wrenched from the bone, but for two boys used to snaring snow voles and drinking bone soup seasoned with nothing but flakes of lichen, there was a veritable feast to be had. I went to work cutting the largest pieces I could, filling my pockets and then a pouch I fashioned by folding my cloak. All I could carry.

Returning to dragonland seemed much easier when spurred on by the thought of the mouth-watering smell of roasting meat and the sounds of fat popping and sizzling in the fire. I did not spare a thought to what could have killed an adult wolf so brutally. A mouse does not think of the cat when it steals from its hole in search of a few crumbs to eat. It takes its chance and prays the swat never comes. But good fortune comes with its price just as twilight's violet confession must lead to a dusk of deepest regret.

Huddled inside our shelter of cloaks and by the light of our small fire we both roll our dice.

They strike each other and rebound...for mine to reveal a shield and Cai's a sword.

"Shield blocks sword," I say. "Roll again."

We roll but the dice miss each other and therefore do not count. Lucky for Cai: my two swords to his shield would have won me the point. We roll again. The dice make contact. It is valid.

"Ah, the mounted knight," I say before I look at what my brother has rolled.

"Phalanx," he announces brightly. "Your knight charges blindly into a forest of my spears. His body is left looking like a cushion for pins. One point to me!"

"Again," I say.

We roll. The dice clash. A shield once more for me. For Cai, it is the mounted knight.

"My horse kicks the shield from your loose grasp and then my knight runs you through. *Blegh.*"

"Save the commentary, little brother, and just keep score."

"Two—naught."

"Roll."

Two swords versus one. Cai wins.

"Roll."

His mounted knight encounters mine. A draw.

"Again," I say. Then, "The phalanx..."

"Meets...*the dragon*," he squeals. "My fiery breath melts your spears and burns all your soldiers to piles of ash. Four to naught. Why, your luck seems to have left you, Brother."

"It is merely slow to warm," I say, but Cai has a point: the dragon dice have little regard for me on this night—or *any* night, for that matter. It would seem Father taught me a game in which I was destined only to lose. He had good intentions, I am sure. When interpreting the crude pictograms, he said, it fires even the dullest imagination into action. The game of dragon dice diffuses tensions. Creates hope.

All things being equal, of course.

But when a player such as Cai has both the luck of a street gambler and the imagination of a born storyteller, all things do not seem equal to the hand that rolls the dice on will alone.

"There she is," Cai says later, when the score lies at a dismal eight points to two.

I glance up and peer through the gap between our cloaks and see the light on the mountain. I turn back to our game. "Roll again."

We both roll and, tracking mine, I see that I have found the dragon at last. This point is won. My little brother's only hope is to roll—

"The shield," he says. "I crouch behind it as you spend your breath and no harm befalls me. I get to roll again."

"You need the dragon," I remind him. "Only a dragon cancels out another, and getting it we must both roll again for triple the stakes." Three points would seal him the victory but it will never come to that.

Cai's face is tight with concern, as though he has forgotten this is a game. He rolls his lonely die. It bounces off the ring of stones around the fire and—

"The dragon," he announces in a flat voice. His fervour seems to have deserted him suddenly as he places the two dice, the two dragons, alongside each other, and stares at them for a moment. Finally, he shuffles closer to the gap in our cloaks and gazes out at the darkening night. "You can have this game," he says. "I don't want to play anymore."

"But Cai..."

"I just want to sit here awhile."

"You are but one roll away from winning the game."

Or, I think, I am one roll from the start of the greatest comeback in the history of dragon dice.

He turns to me again, a sad smile on his lips. "Two dragons together... I would say that would be a win for both of us."

"Don't," I say, shaking my head. "Don't turn this into *that*. Roll the dice and claim your victory or let me claim mine."

"I already said you can have it."

"I mean let me earn it. I do not want it given to me like a trifling thing."

"Why must there even be a winner and a loser?" he asks.

"Because that is the nature of the game. Of all games. Someone loses, someone wins. Father told you that."

"Maybe Father was wrong," he says.

"Roll, Cai."

"I won't."

"You are such a child."

"And you are such a man."

"What do you mean by that?"

"Nothing," Cai says, shaking his head forlornly while watching the light. "Only that we are different. One of us grows while the other..." He shrugs and wipes something from his eye. "I am just a little sad, Brother. Never mind."

"But the game..." I say. In truth, I do not care for it—trust my father to find some way to demean me from his grave—but I do not know what else to do except go on as we were. "We should finish it. The bragging rights alone might keep you warm."

Cai turns and frowns at the two dragons. "Why must you turn them into a competition? Mother and Father were never at odds. One never tried to best the other. They were two hands; opposites, yes, but interlocked."

"Spare me."

"Why," he says. "Why must you be spared what I suffer?"

"And I do not? Look around, you fool. I am the king of the smallest kingdom in the world."

"No, Brother. I meant why must you be spared from *hope*? Our mother is alive. On that mountain. She is alive. Knowing it is a kind of suffering—one I endure every day I remain here eating dog meat and rolling dice with you."

"Then bury her as I have."

"My imagination will not stretch that far."

"Then let me help you," I tell him, the words falling from my lips like the followers of Hegis Ky, who it is told flung themselves headlong from the cliffs of Ord in search of spiritual redemption at the bottom of the sea. I know of their cautionary tale from my father and yet— and yet I cannot stop myself. Father told me that even as they fell to instantaneous death their arms were flailing, not in an attempt to prevent their dying but in readiness of the swim to the sea floor.

"This was her fault," I say to Cai.

When I think of the tale of Hegis' followers, I see some of them turning to look at the ground they left behind; ground that would never know their feet again. That is me now. The deed is done. "She was the one who made my father have the dragons' fire glands removed when they were younglings. She convinced him to give away his greatest weapon and turn them impotent as old men. How different it might have been, Cai, had she not done that to them—to *him*. We would not be here, foraging like animals. The uprising would have been squashed with its clothes and hair afire and its face melting like cheese on the hearth. This was Mother's fault."

Cai's face pales. He looks stricken. "She did not know the people would rise against him. He, he mistreated the poor, he—"

"She poisoned the dragons."

"What?"

"How else could they have fallen within moments of each other? Think on it."

"Our mother? I don't believe it. I won't!"

Cai scoops up the dice and arranges them on his palm so that the dragons remain facing upward, side by side. He stares at them as though they might reveal some truth hidden from him all this time. But he has missed the true lesson of dragon dice—that luck and a prayer are never the answer. We make our own luck. We become our own gods.

We believe our own truths.

Cai would see it were he to look up from the dice long enough to find the tears in my eyes before I brush them away.

I stand and leave our makeshift shelter built for the rolling of dice to return to the real world of dragonland. The violet sky is darkening; the confession made. Solitary trees reach from white drifts like long, bony fingers caught in their final attempts at escape. Not firs but trees of the south that lost their way, found themselves trapped and rooted in this valley where all things come to die, it seems. Birds, stretched and thin, rarely fly here but wade the snow fields on long legs, leaving a path of tiny footprints that soon forget them, plunging long, scooped bills into the snow in search of ever-dwindling morsels, often finding none, so that their footprints lead only to the spot at which they succumb and perish. And there they are swallowed by the white wickedness, preserved for the next wretched creature to happen along, foraging not with a beak but a hardened snout and raking claws or perhaps great horns with which to drag and dig through the snow, panning for meat like men pan for gold, and all to reach the bird that sought the worms that maybe never were. And these larger beasts either find the bird and live (a while) or fail and fall themselves, to lie alongside the thing they sought so desperately, that had the power, in death, to sustain them.

Cai joins me and we don our cloaks and stand shivering as we look over the forest of shoulder at a night that approaches like a dark army on the march.

"Truth is cruel, Cai," I tell him. "Sometimes it is better eaten; sometimes it is best left buried in the snow."

"She would not have poisoned our dragons," he says. "And you can bury it, eat it, or choke on it, Brother. I do not care."

"Only the four of us knew of our father's plan to flee the palace," I say. "He would never have taken the coward's way, and I know it was not I who poisoned them, so that leaves just you and her. Was it you?"

"No!" He tries to push me but I barely move.

"Then you have your answer, Cai. She tried to kill us all. Lucky for us she was a poor murderer."

"But *why*? She loved us, loved Father. It makes no sense. If she convinced him to take away their fire, why years later would she turn them into a different kind of weapon? For what purpose, Stephen? Tell me that."

I see the light on its distant, blue mountain. Burning, burning, burning. It *could* be a flaming torch, I suppose. Or a fallen star. Or even some large glowing insect sputtering and twitching towards its final darkness. Regardless, I turn away.

"I am afraid the truth has died with her on the mountain," I say.

6.

The following day, the sun rises spectacularly over the mountaintops but fails to melt as much as a handful of ice and snow. Cai has not thawed either after the night of the dragon dice. He keeps his distance throughout the day by moping on dragonland's extremities with his book. He does not notice the rabbit in the snare outside skull or the large footprints in the snow approaching tail's end, a confusion of tracks just fifty paces from our green moat, as though the beast of bulk and horns had paced to and fro, still too unsure of the larger, unmoving bulk of Tyrandir. I am certain it was him: I have seen no other creature capable of leaving such an impression in the snow that could fit my own two feet, heel to toe, inside it. Perhaps he was drawn by Tyrandir's heat as much as he was wary of it. When I try to tell Cai of my findings over supper that night, he only nods and writes in his book of his present misery. And some unkind things about me too, I expect. The harbinger. I am tempted to scoop the ink bottle from where it snuggles against the rocks around the fire and use it as fuel (to roast this rabbit). What use are words anyway? In the time it takes him to compose a sulking sentence I have readied our next meal for the skewer.

Eat your words, Cai, I think. I will be dining on coney tonight.

I reach behind me for another piece of wood for the fire but my hand finds just one scrawny branch. No, not even a branch. A *twig*.

"We have a problem," I say to Cai. "The fire is low."

"Then throw some more wood on it," he says absently, not looking up from the page he is spoiling. What does he write about that matters more than dragonland? Or unusual tracks in the snow? Or the next piece of wood for the fire?

"How do words burn?" I ask him.

He glances up at me. "What?"

"There is no firewood," I say. "That is our problem."

"Where is it?"

"Gone. I thought we had enough but we've been burning more of it lately. With the dragon cooling, I am not sure its heat alone will be enough to see us through the night. We need a fire, Cai. I will have to go and find some wood."

"Burn some of the saplings then," he says.

"Out of the question."

"You cannot go out there now."

"Father planted those. I'd rather burn *you*."

Cai looks at me for a moment, trying to read the story of my face, but it is a tale only I can tell.

"It will be dark soon," he says. "You cannot see where you are going. You will get lost out there."

I stop listening to his protests as I stand and pace the camp. To run out of firewood near nightfall…how could we be so fatally careless? I will hear no end of it. There is but one thing to do. I draw my father's sword from its scabbard to punctuate my instructions with each stab of its blade.

"Stay here. The fire will burn itself out when I am gone, so stay low to the dragon's hide. It still provides warmth—snow barely lies here; Tyrandir will not allow it—but if the wind picks up it will make little difference. Take the stones from around the fire. *Carefully*. They will be hot. Place them in the foot of the saddlebag you sleep in. Climb in beside them and curl up tight like a fist. The stones will provide some heat, but still—try not to fall asleep until I return."

"Maybe we should both go," Cai says.

I shake my head firmly. "I will move faster alone. Besides, one of us needs to stay and guard dragonland." I give him our father's knife. "Keep this close while I am gone. He lives on in the things he made and the things he carried. He protects us still."

Cai takes the knife and looks at it and looks at it, and I can see his back straighten and his shoulders rise from the mere act of holding it. His small hands and thin wrists make it seem as large as a short sword. In his mind, I believe, he is fending off his nightmares. But to the monsters of this valley, he holds naught but a needle, a thing with which to scratch. Cai does not need to know this, however, just as he does not need to know his mother was with child when Sauro fell or what my father's lips confessed to me as he lay in my arms. I know now why parents lie to their children. Life to a child is a story, a fiction in which they play the hero.

The truth is the death of their story.

Let them enjoy the lie while they can.

7.

Dusk arrives. Snow begins to fall, lightly at first then heavy and hard, as though thrown down from the baleful sky. Stars appear between the clouds, between the flakes of falling snow, and you wonder if they might begin to fall too. Out here, away from the comforting warmth of dragonland, the worst seems possible. As though in reply, the howls of wolves celebrate the rising of the moon. Distant but not distant enough.

Although the dragon's heat fades every day, it has become the foundation of life here in the lost valley. In dragonland, you can place your palm to its scales and, yes, feel the buried heat radiating outwards, but also something else, something more important.

Reassurance.

False assurance, you think.

The dragon is dead and hope is dying with it. You reach for it, live on it, but it seems only to slow your walk to the door that stands ever open and welcomes all...

Hush, Stephen. You are cold and alone and you are not yourself.

A man dying of thirst cannot survive long on a few drops of water, but take away those few drops and you leave him nothing. Something is hope. Something is time. You must hold on to *something*.

Cai to his light on the mountain.

You to the kingdom of dragonland.

The invisible crown.

But...what good is the crown that no one can see?

The sound of footsteps a short distance behind you. Where there was nothing a moment ago, there is now someone—something—following you, close, brazen, unafraid to be heard.

"You let the firewood run out, you fool."

You are not surprised to hear your father's commanding voice. You have spoken many times since his death. The body dies, rots, turns to nothing, but part of it lives on inside those it made. It must, you think.

"You left your brother in grave danger."

You pull your cloak tighter and try to walk faster, away from the judgement in your father's voice. But the snow resists, seeming to grow deeper with each step.

"I had no choice," you say. "He would not survive out here. Or worse—he would."

"Why would it be worse?"

"He might come to the false belief that he can walk anywhere in this snow."

"And?"

"He might start to believe he can climb a mountain..."

"Maybe he can."

"So you would separate us?"

"No son of mine should fail."

"So a father may fail but his sons may not?"

"Careful with that tongue, boy. You brought this on yourself."

"You left us. You—"

"I said, be careful. I may not be able to reach for your throat but do not forget I live in your mind. Show me some respect or I will leave you raving in the snow."

A chill overwhelms you and your body begins to tremble uncontrollably. Seeing weakness, the cold bites deep, sending ice through your veins. Within moments, you are shaking bodily.

"F-forgive me, Father. I just meant he is still a young boy, and—and a boy of books at that. I have seen him nights curled up in his bed, writing in the journal he brought with him. Poems or stories. Pathetic odes to nothing of import."

You stop in your tracks and try to rub and slap some heat back into your body. You sense your father circling as he waits. Somewhere beyond him, the wolves have stopped howling, which seems worse somehow: their silence like a hole in the darkness from which they might leap at any moment.

"You let the firewood run out," he says again. Father always believed that a point should be made not once but many times.

"I did not mean to, Father. We were playing the game of dragon dice you taught us and—"

"Once again, you would try to blame me for your failings."

"I only meant..."

"It is easy to blame the dead for anything. But you forget that we give you life. Me. Tyrandir. Would you be here at all if not for us?"

"No. I would not."

"But we do not forget you," he says. "We give you comfort. We give you direction when it is needed. And yet you only call upon us when your need is dire. My fair-weather son, you disappoint me. In fact, you fail me. There, it has been said."

Hugging yourself, teeth chattering, you turn again and again in the falling snow in search of him.

"No, Father. Please. I *will* try harder. I swear to you."

"I fear it is too late for trying. You cannot even defeat your brother in a game of dice. You get lost in a flurry of snowflakes. And you leave him to guard what should be yours to guard. No. It would seem I was mistaken about you. You are an unworthy king."

You tell yourself to remain silent. That the nail cannot argue with the falling hammer. That he will grow bored and leave you alone. But when did he ever leave you alone? In the palace. Here. Days. Nights. Besides, the dead have patience unbound.

"We needed firewood," you say. "Cai is too young and too weak to fetch it alone. It had to fall to me, Father."

"So you chose to gather wood rather than defend your kingdom from those who would take it and cast you out into the snow? Do you not see my point? Must I spell it out?"

"What should I have done? Risked sending Cai out here? What?"

"A king does not let the firewood burn to nothing. A king thinks ahead, always ahead. He *anticipates*."

"Okay, Father. I will do that. I will anticipate—"

"He controls."

"I will—I will control."

"He leads."

"Yes." Nodding now.

"And he sacrifices."

"Okay, I will give myself—"

"*Others*, mooncalf. He sacrifices *others* for the good of the crown, even one invisible as yours."

294

"I understand, Father. Forgive me. Give me one more chance. I beg of you."

"*Here* is your chance." A gust of wind whips across your face and you can feel the crown you do not wear slip from your head—or was it struck?—and fall into the snow. The next moment, you are on your hands and knees searching for it, a thing that does not exist and yet you feel desperate to find, digging through drifts in a fit of hysteria. It would seem that not only can you know you are losing your mind but you can readily invite madness inside to replace it.

Soon your arms grow tired, burning from your fruitless efforts. Your father's footsteps stop circling you and you glance over your right shoulder to see if he is standing there, but where you thought he stood there is nothing but a curtain of swirling snow and an invitation to the plunging darkness that lies behind. Then, over your left shoulder, his voice whispers in your ear, close as an insect landing there and rubbing its wings. "It would seem you want to replace me, boy." You flinch and fall away from the sound, rolling through the snow until you find yourself buried up to your knees, with arms swallowed elbow deep. "Maybe you will get your wish," he says. "Keep digging. I wait for you in the snow."

Looking around, you cannot see him. You never see him. "What is it I have done wrong, Father? Truly. Tell me and I will learn and do better. What is it? I am all that is left. Cai lives in a fiction. Poems in a book. Lights on a mountain. I am left with what is real." You look and you look but you fail to see the ghost of your father anywhere. You fall forward into the drift, burying your face as you might in a pillow, and shout at the coldness. "I am left with what is real!"

"Stephen?"

A voice, soft and concerned, reaches for you through the blizzard, and then a small hand touches your shoulder, giving it a reassuring pat. You lift your face and brush it clear of snow so that you may see. Cai stands behind you, peering out from his voluminous hood with worry etched on his boyish face.

"What are you doing here?" you ask.

"I came to find you," he says.

You leap to your feet and throw your arms around your little brother. After a century, you let him go.

"I followed your voice," he says. "Who were you talking to?"

I cannot tell him. If he knew our father visited me and not him, even in death, after what I revealed to him about his mother's betrayal, it would be too much for him to bear. The truth would be the death of *their* story, such as it is. Father's visits should remain my secret for now.

"I was talking to this place," I say. "I think it wants me to die."

He draws me close. "Then tell it, 'no, not yet'."

Our hoods meet and complement each other, joining to keep the wind and falling snow outside for a moment. In the commingling darkness, I tell him I will try.

"But wait—what are you doing here? You are supposed to be waiting for me in dragonland."

"Oh, but I am," he says.

A startled scream hurtles through the wall of snow around me, seeming at once to come from far-off *and* nearby. Cai steps away from me, his face receding inside the hood as though drifting into the distance, smaller and smaller, until finally it vanishes and the cloak falls and folds upon itself in the snow. A second scream reaches me then, more terrified than the first. I look in the direction of the sound...in the direction of dragonland.

And I start to run.

8.

During the days leading up to his death, Father seemed like two different men. It was true: dragonland changed you. In the span of a few hours the snow valley could go from being a place of grandeur and beauty to a cruel prison of empty snowfields and mountainous walls. Father, like it, moved between two ways of being: there was the man who crouched behind a barricade of snow and kissed the back of his hand to make a sound like a wounded mouse in order to attract something larger that might feed us all; the man who showed us how to dress for the cold—collar up, hood over your head, tie your cuffs and tuck your trews inside your boots; how to build a fire, skin an animal, cook its meat; how to make lashings from the inner bark of the wood he collected, and to use those lashings to tie the tools and utensils he'd made to the dragonspines so that they could not be stolen by the next blizzard. So many things, small and large; things he had been taught himself as a boy but had all but forgotten as a man and a king. He found a renewed zeal for a brief time, albeit in gulps, or maybe it was that for those few days he was able to forget at times who—and what—he was.

The rest of the time he would seem bent and old and defeated, like a once-great tree finally beaten by the relentless pushing of the wind, all but fallen over. He spoke of avalanches and of freezing to death; he warned us of black toe or black finger—*it chooses where it starts and what it calls itself,* he said; he spoke of wolves and how they run and run and run their prey to utter exhaustion and eventual collapse. He described a thousand ways in which to die in the stark beauty of this place—of the crevasses hidden under the snow like waiting mouths, the loose rocks on ridges that might send you tumbling to a crushed skull, and of the constant murmur in your ear, how it tried to persuade you to give yourself to the snow right there at your feet, to just let yourself fall, like Ky's followers, into a cold and final embrace. Indeed, he spoke so much on the subject of falling that it began to inhabit my dreams and became a part of my night's tapestry here in dragonland.

Our last conversation on the evening of the eighth day. He had returned with firewood in his arms and two eggs he had somehow managed to spill from an owl's nest. He had placed the eggs carefully inside the hood of his cloak and then walked back through the snow unprotected from its savagery. I met him at tail's end, his face all but hidden under a grimacing mask of ice and snow as he stepped onto the dragonspine road and began his unsteady climb to our camp on shoulder. He instructed me to remove the eggs and raise his hood as he had no free hand with which to do it. Afterward, I held onto those eggs, one in each gloved hand, as though they were crown jewels I had sworn to protect. There was blood on his lips as he spoke but he seemed oblivious to it—the cold numbed all sensation—and I did not mention it to him. I wanted it to remain part of him and not spat and left on the ground.

He stopped and turned to me.

"Son? A word with you if I may?"

A request—and spoken with such tenderness too. I had only heard such a quality in his voice when he addressed Queen Gessalla, our mother, and then it was a thing of exquisite and puzzling rarity. It pricked the ears. It stopped the heart.

"Of course, Father."

"I will die tonight," he said.

The silence that followed his words seemed to come from inside my chest as my heart refused to start beating again. The world seemed hollow. The mountains became the unscalable walls of some deep, deep hole. I looked up and the sky—the sky was the blank, answerless face of a mooncalf. I could not breathe.

"It is time I became the past," he said. "I am tired. So very tired. And my story is tired too. The time has come to write 'The End' on this final chapter."

I had no words. They were locked inside my heart that refused to beat.

"I am sorry," he said. "Sorry I could not leave you more. Sorry I could not take back what I have done."

I nodded to indicate that I was listening. In truth, what he said to me next may be the only words I ever truly heard in my life.

"A dead dragon as your kingdom... It pains me so, but it is all I have to give. Yours now. Sorry it isn't everything. Sorry it isn't the world. But maybe—maybe the smallest thing can become the greatest in time. Shoots become flowers, don't they? Saplings become trees—trees become a forest. And my sons—my sons *will* be men someday. My last hope—such as it is—is that this dragon can become a home, a comfort, a surrogate, a—"

"Land," I said. "A dragon*land.*"Nodding, nodding, the tears shaken loose from the grip of his eyes, he said, "Yes, Son. A dragonland."

And then I saw it as it would be seen from that moment: dragonland, with its towns of skull and tail's end, its forest of shoulder, its plains of wing, each connected by a single road: the mighty dragonspine.

"Here," he said. "Take this crown." He lifted nothing from his head and placed it upon mine. Seeing the light return to my eyes, he nodded and turned from me then. "Come. We still have those eggs to boil."

I rushed to his side and, with the eggs in one hand and the other hand free, I held onto his arm as we walked up the dragonspine road together for the very last time.

9.

As I run through the dark and the snow toward the screams of dragonland, I am followed. I sense them at my heels and sometimes catch a glimpse of them: wolves, running alongside me; long-bodied, lupine shadows racing through the blizzard as they seek to surround me with their unnaturally patient hunger. Their steady, rhythmic breaths are a torture to my ears.

If not for my father's sword, which I use to prick their flanks when they veer too close, I would be overwhelmed within moments, brought to my knees with a series of draining bites until the strength to defend my throat left me and my arms fell uselessly to my sides. Instead, spurred on by that image and still haunted by my brother's screams, I swing the sword at any shape that darts within range. But I am tiring fast. My arms feel heavy and slow, and I struggle to reconcile the burning desire to live with the physical weakening of my body. It is a terrifying betrayal, and though the prospect of my bloody end urges me to keep moving my legs, keep swinging the sword, it also invites me to give myself over to it. Maybe the followers of Hegis Ky saw that; maybe it was not madness that drove them from the clifftops but a simple desire for the pain of waiting to end when they chose it. I could stop running now and my death would be mine to give, not theirs to take... But then a cry rises from the soles of my feet, through my entire body, to gather in my throat, to spill from me as I spill from them— slashing the foreleg of an audacious wolf whose muzzle and throat are painted crimson with someone else's surrender. Blood sprays and the animal tumbles into the snow, yowling in pain.

I feel the teeth of another pinch my left thigh in retaliation, the skin pulled taut beneath my trews, and a tearing as it relents. Warm freshets of blood flow down my leg, past my knee. A blind stab backwards with my father's sword finds something satisfyingly soft, and the teeth and the wolf fall away from me. I stumble but do not fall. I will not fall. Another cry escapes my chest, pained, defiant, full of empty fury. I want to cleave their leader's head with this sword, to warm my face with his blood, smear it over my skin so that I might wear him from head to foot. *I am wolf. I am wolf.* The words repeating over and over in my mind, spurring me onward through the deep, clutching drifts of snow, under the lidded eye of the moon until, at last, dragonland appears in front of me, doused in moonlight as something born from a dream.

Home... I am home.

10.

On our eighth night in dragonland, I found my father lying dead in the snow, a short walk beyond the town of skull but still hidden from the view from our camp in shoulder. The light of the moon fell upon him like something from a nightmare. Upon his lips, a stain that told the story of his death—a story I did not wish to hear. My father had fought wars against men, monsters, machines. He'd flown on the back of giant dragons, moved forests with his bare hands: he did not...he did not do *this*.

I pocketed the vial. Later, I hid it inside the cave under skull, in Tyrandir's mouth, wedged between two teeth, inconsequential as a scrap of flesh to be pecked loose by a dragon-friend. But those birds do not venture this far north and so the vial lies there still, violet as the twilight sky he died beneath. And just as empty.

Sometimes I sneak away from Cai to gaze at the bottle, wondering why I did not bury it in the snow that night along with my father. Why I held on to this last vestige of him—something so shameful and... poisonous.

I have no answer.

Kneeling in the snow on the night I found him, I asked the same question.

"Why? Why, Father?"

I beseeched. I begged. But he would not say, not then, not later, when his ghost returned to taunt me and threaten me with madness.

I suspect he meant to die quickly and secretly and selfishly as Cai and I slept unaware in our saddlebag beds in shoulder. I suspect he meant to kill us all at first, perhaps to spare us the shame of opening our hands in supplication to the men of the north. With the taking of the palace of Kuhl Amar and the collapse of Father's kingdom, we had been reduced to a family of homeless beggars. And so he had killed the dragons, Tyrandir and Sauro, killed his wife, Gessalla, killed himself, Stannard, King of the Southern Kingdom of Fortûn Eld, and though he had original intentions of killing his sons too, at some juncture he'd had a change of mind—if not heart—and chosen instead to leave us to the dictates of fate and fortuity. I suspect we were the smallest parts of him that wanted to live on, to not drink from the vial or jump from the cliff; the best and worst of him, his pride, greed, regret, and sorrow, for all of these are nigh on impossible to douse as dragonfire itself. But in finding him, in letting himself be found, he had doomed me to follow a similar path as his. Tied me to it, in fact, like a rock, then rolled that rock down the long mountainside and left me to fall.

But all of that—my suspicions—were arrived at much later on, long after I dragged his body through the snow to bury it as best I could in the softer ground near dragonland's green moat. What came before all of it were tears, a lot of tears, both bitter and funereal, and a boy, lost at fifteen, tied at fifteen, holding onto his father's cold hand for dear life.

11.

My legs are no longer mine as I run from and with the wolves. I reach the plains of wing and start the climb to shoulder. We have no fortress there but we have the rumour of a living dragon and the advantage of elevation.

The wolves stop outside the plains, uncertain muzzles sniffing the green moat and the melting snow. The moat is not green at all but brown and grey where the snow has thawed to reveal the rocks and earth underneath. The green is just flecks, grass shoots between the rocks that hint of fields and meadows but never truly deliver. The wolves appear unsure, milling around, their wedge-shaped heads low to the ground. If only the whole of dragonland could rise up against them now and burn them to ashes where they stand. But Mother took its fire with Father's consent and the dragon is dead and the wolves are close—close enough to realise that now. Their leader takes a first, tentative step onto the plain, then jumps back. When there is no movement from the dragon, no fiery retaliation, he steps forward once more, confidently this time, smiling cruelly and growling like one who has been fooled for a time but will be fooled no more. The other wolves, five now, fall in behind him, an advancing cohort of bared teeth.

I turn and run to shoulder, yelling Cai's name, but find him gone. The camp appears untouched, no sign of any struggle. Then I turn to look down the dragonspine road and see him crawling on his hands and knees toward me, followed by a beast on four legs that rises onto two when it sees me standing beyond my brother. The creature rises taller in hands than I can begin to count or estimate, unfolding like a terrible reverie. Its body is a land in itself, vast and defined by the hills and valleys of muscle hidden only partly by a forest of coarse, pale fur. Upon its head, a crown of horns, twisted like those of a mountain ram, with several pairs of smaller horns jutting from the underside of its jaw like daggers. It opens its mouth with a deafening roar that snaps to a piteous and angry squall as the horns underjaw sink into its upper chest, now matted with the blood of its own cries, and the sound that pours forth is like fire, ravenous and yet somehow aching to be quenched. The beast throws its head back and rages at the dusk sky, from right to left, breath plumes rising in clouds. For a moment, the stars are lost among them; for a moment, the moon appears to tremble.

"Crawl, Cai! Crawl to me!"

I am unconvinced he hears me above the howlings of both blizzard and beasts, for the snowstorm grows worse and the wolves form an unholy chorus with the beast of bulk and horns. Icy winds whip us as I am forced to plant my feet, to brace against the dragonspines of the road, to prevent myself from toppling from my land. Cai looks up and sees me at last, and that alone emboldens him to crawl apace in my direction.

"Faster!" I yell. "It follows!"

I have no plan here other than to be reunited with him. If this is to be our end, we should meet it together, as brothers.

His coat is torn and his arm is bleeding heavily. A cuff from the beast, I presume. What happened here? All that is evident is that he had a fortunate escape or that the beast had not wanted to kill him outright, for he surely would have been nothing but scattered pieces by now.

You let the firewood run out. My father's voice... accusing me with the words he leaves unsaid.

Cai stops crawling and rises onto his knees long enough to point behind me, even as I feel the presence of the wolves gathering at my back. I stagger toward him, mindful of the blasting wind, the creeping wolves, the advancing beast, and at the centre of this maelstrom, at its peaceful heart: my wounded brother. I reach my hand out for his. He crawls toward me, reaching for me with his blood-soaked arm. Our fingers almost meet.

The wolves bundle past me then, knocking me off balance. The arm I reached for my brother with is flailing along with the other as I fight to keep my balance on the dragon's back. My brother closes his eyes and curls himself into a tight ball. He covers his ears to drown out the sounds around him, or perhaps it is in the hope of not hearing his own screams when they come. But the wolves have lost interest in us for now, nary a snap as they pass. They seem more taken suddenly by the settling of some long-standing feud with their rival for this valley. I see them queuing up behind their leader to attempt to scale its mountainous bulk, seeking to climb and claw to the summit of that thing and conquer its throat. One, two, three, they hurl themselves at it, holding on with their mouths, their teeth, paws scrabbling for purchase both on the dragonspine road and the beast's dense fur, ripping clumps of it free but naught else. However, this is a mountain that not only moves but fights, and the last thing I see before I lose my balance and fall from the dragonspine road to the snowfield below is the beast of bulk and horns tossing the first two wolves to either side like useless rags before crushing the skull of a third between its two hands, the wolf's head collapsing like a melon under a mallet.

And then I fall.

Into a long, long dark.

12.

I wake up at dawn, inside the dragon's mouth. Cai, already awake, sits peering out between two of its huge, serrated teeth as sunlight charges down the mountains to chase the darkness from the valley floor. The light even reaches us here in our cave beneath the town of skull, splitting as it might through the bars of a prison window. I sit up, rubbing my head.

"Are you hurt?" Cai asks.

"My skull aches," I say. "And my right side—ribs, leg. Bruised for the most part. It is my pride that is wounded. How is your arm?"

"It hurts still but the bleeding has stopped," he says, without turning from the breaking morning. He does not show me the arm but even in profile his pale, sweating face speaks gravely of a fever. "We were lucky," he says. "Had it been just one of them—the wolves or the beast—we would both be dead by now. As it turned out, their hatred of each other outweighed even their hatred of us. This place makes bitter enemies of us all."

"How have I come to be inside the dragon's mouth?" I ask.

"I dragged you here. Through the snow." Now he looks over his shoulder, but only to nod his head at some place behind me. "There is a gap in its teeth just over there. Large enough for us to slip through. I managed to drag you inside before any of them noticed we were gone."

"Are we safe in here?" I ask, glancing at the spaces between the dragon's teeth for other possible points of entry.

"From the beast, yes," he says. "For now. Perhaps a wolf could squeeze through the same gap as we did, but I doubt there are many of them left. Or any with a want to return. The beast was merciless. Rarely have I witnessed such anger and cruelty. The fight, such as it was, lasted no time at all, and those wolves who could ran away like beaten pups. I can still hear their yowling."

"And the thing? The beast. Where is it now?"

Cai shakes his head slowly, sadly. He is lost... not in the morning but his sad daily ritual: he must say goodbye to the light on the mountain and start another long day of waiting for its return. "It is still out there, somewhere. I watched it drag a wolf's body—the leader's, I think—toward the wood, leaving a trail of blood through the snow. I expect it will follow that red path back to dragonland as soon as it feels hungry again. It knows the dragon was a false threat all along. A rumour with no truth."

"It may not return," I say, though I am unsure for whose benefit I am saying it. I might as well proclaim the moon blue or my father a saint.

"It is a matter of when, Brother, not if," Cai says. This time his sadness is fleeting as he shifts his whole body around so that he can face me. Such a strange meeting place this is: the two of us sat upon a dragon's tongue lapidified in death, our roof its palate, our walls its teeth. As an eerie breeze drifts from the tunnel at my back like the ghost of a breath, my brother lowers his hood and looks long at me, waiting. For what, I do not know.

They were called living fossils by some. Dragons, that is. Others say they simply refused to die out, and that it is evidenced in the way in which their bodies refuse to perish and rot as all other living things do—by giving themselves back to the land—instead, turning into a kind of organic stone. A monument to themselves, they say. Worshipped by some, loathed by others, who see their stubborn refusal as an offence against the gods.

And Cai is *still* looking at me, deep in thought—no, not thought. I recognise his countenance. The furrowed brow. The rapid breathing. The way his eyes do not focus on any one part of me but dart from my face to my hand to my shoulder, and so on. He is restless and frightened. Short of wringing his hands, a confession is coming.

"Speak, Brother," I say. "What is it that preys on your mind?"

Closed eyes. Deep breath.

"My mind is made," he says. "Do not try to alter its course, I beg of you."

There is something of the dragon about him too, I realise. A reluctance to let go of life. And in the same moment I feel both proud and deeply disappointed. I decide that I will save him the effort of his confession.

"You are leaving."

13.

The walkways inside The Gardens of Kuhl Amar were concentric. Ovals within ovals within ovals. Seven in all and all connected: from The Road of The Undecided, the outermost, widest and longest of the seven, to The Path of The Ready, a short and narrow course that encircled their common centre, The Tree of Great Decision, which stood at the very heart of the gardens. Each path was intended to provide its walker with a different view of both the gardens and their own mind. They led past countless plants and small trees as well as fountains and pools, all of it home to turtles, geese, hens, and peacocks. On most mornings, my mother could be found walking with The Undecided. Not that other people were permitted inside the gardens during her scheduled visits, but the breadth of that walkway and its unpaved, well-worn surface spoke of the many who had walked it before her, wrestling with some inner torment while readying themselves to make a choice of great import.

On the day that I recall, the king, my father, had publicly chastised and humiliated me for looking away as both a young man was hanged to the end of his life for stealing food and his parents flogged to within a breath of theirs for giving life to a criminal. I had made some weak excuse and fled to the gardens.

My mother did not know that sometimes I would watch her, hidden behind a cabled column, as she paced the great quadrangle in her flowing green morning dress, brushing her fingers across the heads of the flowers as though they were an adoring crowd bending not toward the light of the sun but the lightness of her touch. I wished—from behind my column—that I were one of those flowers: a tulip, a peony, or even a blue rose. I wished it, and then shrank into a shameful ball within the empty, echoing cloisters.

On the day that I recall, I peeked over the low wall dressed with purple bougainvillea and saw her looking around for the source of a sound she seemed sure she had just heard: a boy crying. I ducked out of sight, but not before I saw her spinning on the spot like a dancer uncertain of her steps. Pressing a hand to her belly. On the day that I recall—a recollection dreamlike in its distance from this dank mouth-cave we find ourselves in now—she found me, perhaps by tracing the pathetic sobs to their source or perhaps by glimpsing some treacherous tuft of hair jutting above the gallery wall.

"Who is it?" she asked in a voice startled but still mellifluous as birdsong.

"Me, Mother," I replied, erasing my tears with hurried swipes of my sleeve. "I have found you, it seems."

"Not seems," she replied. "Have. Or have I found *you*? Why are you crouched back there, hiding? Stephen... what has he done?" As she said those last words, a shadow entered her voice and fell across my heart. "Come. Join me. Please."

Satisfied the tears were swept from my eyes, I stood from my hiding place and climbed the gallery wall, careful not to tread on the bougainvillea. The combined scent of the flowers was heavenly. I lowered myself into the bright gardens and walked to my mother's side. The sun's light stung my eyes at first, as though berating me for crying, but Mother placed her hand on my left shoulder and guided me on the path she walked most mornings alone. She gave me time to settle into it, to take in the flowers and get accustomed to the chaos of colour that was the orange roses and rainbow hyacinths of The Road of The Undecided.

"So what is troubling you?" she asked.

I took some time to answer. "Why do people have children, Mother?"

She seemed surprised by my question. Of course, in false hindsight, I realise she was in fact startled by its pertinence. She was, unbeknownst to me at the time, with child.

"A child," she replied, "is an expression of the parents' love for each other. And in some ways it represents a continuation of that love. Love dies though, as everything must."

Again, I heard the shadow enter her voice. Like a stranger in a doorway. It blocked a room I was afraid to enter.

"Why do parents have a second child, then?" I asked, returning to my point. "Is it to recapture the feeling of the first? Or is the first not enough, they feel the need to repeat—and repeat and repeat—until they find themselves with a mob of children?"

"Are you jealous of Cai, Stephen?"

"Why would I be? I am your firstborn. Cai is a... a *dilution*."

"That is not a very fair thing to say of him. He is your brother."

"I am not jealous. But by the same measure, why do you prefer him to me?"

She stopped walking. Her hand did not leave my shoulder but turned me gently so that we faced each other.

"That has no truth, Stephen. You are both equal in my eyes."

"But you spend all of your time with him."

The hand that had sat on her belly rose to cover her throat. "Because you are so busy with your father. As you said, you are the firstborn. With that comes certain responsibilities."

The tears threatened to return. "What if I don't want them?" I asked. "What if I don't want to learn how to fight or hunt or tell people what to do? What if I just want to *be*, like you, now, in these gardens? Or like Cai writing in those books of his. What if I don't want to hurt people or—or decide who lives and who dies?"

The shadow did not just enter her voice then but flitted across her entire face. "Your father... your father... he... he loves you, Stephen. As only a king can love."

"Then love is unfair," I proclaimed, looking down at my feet, at a beetle struggling across the sand on which so many others had walked. I felt like that beetle, and at once I wanted only to crush it underfoot. "You love my brother and leave me to *him*. He is cruel, Mother. And the farther I stray from him, the crueller he becomes."

"It is a bondage, I admit. But do not think I have no understanding of it or that I somehow love you less."

"*Time* is love," I said, unable to hide the anger in my voice. "You give all of it to Cai and very little to me. You share your love of poetry and books with him while I learn which ribs to push my swordblade between in a fight. Or where in a deer's throat to shoot an arrow. Or how to smile and lie to a man's face as I have his home burned to the ground behind him. It is unfair. Do you hear these words, Mother? It is unfair. And now my brother wishes to try and find you when you are lost forever on a mountain and neither time nor love can change that. And yet he *will* try because—because he is braver than me, not a dilution at all but a second attempt at getting something right—"

"Wait," she said, looking at me, searching my face for answers to her questions even as I searched hers for mine. "Of what mountain do you speak?"

And then the scent of all of the flowers of The Gardens of Kuhl Amar conspired in an instant to lift, carry, and drop me back into the dank mouth of this dead dragon.

From bright day to bitter night.

And now I lie awake, rushed forth from a most unsound and feverish sleep.

Of course it never happened that way. My mind was forging new memories from the pieces of old ones like a smithy making swords for a coming war. The gardens were real, my mother real too, once, but no longer. Our conversation, however, was fanciful, only what I wish had been said. In truth, on the day that I recall, I had simply wept in the cloister as Queen Gessalla walked her path alone. And by the time she stood in front of The Tree of Great Decision, I was either back inside my room, punching my demons from my legs, or I had already done so and returned to my father's side, eyes raw from crying and thighs warm with the bruises about to flower.

"It came to me as I lay in bed the other night," Cai says. He is peering out between the dragon's teeth. The light on the mountain is visible to me over his right shoulder, seeming to sit upon it in fact, like my mother's hand in my idle dream. His now. "Actually," he says, "the idea came from you."

"Me? What idea?"

"The stones from the fire," he replies. "Last night, before you went looking for more firewood, you told me to put them in my saddlebag for heat. After you left, I did what you said and crawled in there with them. How we laughed at the cold around us. I even burned the sole of my foot but that is not the point. It gave me an idea of how I can search the mountain for her. For Mother."

I sit up then. Stretch. Rub the ache from my legs. No broken bones but plenty of bruises from the fall. Despite knowing how I came to have them, each feels like a strange little gift carried over from my dream.

It is dark inside the dragon's mouth. We can see only by what little moonlight slips between its teeth. It reaches like pale arms across the floor of our cave, seeking to drag us from our safety.

"What do you think?" Cai asks. "Of my idea..."

Ironically, I use the light on the mountain to find him in the dark. The same mountain that is intent on luring him away from me. "You mean the stones? They won't remain hot long enough for you to reach the foothills." Let that be an end to it, I think.

"You're right, they *won't*," Cai says brightly. "But a dragon's heart *will*."

Shaking my head even though he cannot see me do so. "No. No, no, no. You are *not* taking it. We are not going up that mountain. I am going back to the trees. I am getting the wood I set out to find and more of it besides. We can take dragonland back and defend it from this beast. We can collect branches and make archer's stakes. We'll place them around the moat, a single row at first, then a second if there's time..."

"There won't be time for that before it returns for us," Cai says with a pitying tone, as though he is my elder by two winters or a king with the power of decision. "And the next time we may not be so lucky as to have the distraction of wolves."

"The next time we will be *ready*," I tell him. "We can make spears. Traps. Start work on a shelter. Build a structure we can defend. We have options here, Brother, and a chance at survival. Surely it is better than taking the heart and running off into the snow on some mission fated to end only with our deaths? But enough of this. What is there to eat? I am famished."

"Not much," he says forlornly. "A coney that wandered into the only snare that isn't broken beyond repair. But a paltry meal he will be: he's all bones and skin. And there is a small bird I caught with my hands when it flew too close. Can we talk of this? Please?"

"Wait—you caught it with your *hands*? How did you manage such a feat with reflexes like yours?"

Cai ignores my gentle teasing. "The dragon's gums are like rocks covered with a kind of moss or lichen. It smells foul and draws an even fouler-smelling worm. They look like maggots wearing winter coats. Birds feed on those worms. One of them flew in here and I managed to catch it. The bird, the coney... they're lying around here somewhere. Stephen, I really need to tell you something—"

"What do the worms taste like?" I have no mind to find out but I do have a mind to keep playing this game of dodge-the-rock until my brother gives up throwing it.

"I don't know," he says. "The smell puts me off trying one. But go ahead, your *highness*. Eat a worm."

Surprised by Cai's tone, I choke on a surge of laughter. It seems near-impossible to stop it, though. Soon, it is filling the darkness and echoing down the dragon's stony throat. It is like listening to a lunatic falling down a well.

"*I have already begun,*" Cai all but yells, killing my amusement in an instant by providing not only the bottom of the well but the archer's stakes of which I spoke moments ago.

"Already begun what?" I know, but I want to give Cai the opportunity to not say it.

"The excavation of the dragon's heart," he says. "I will reach it in a day or two. And then I mean to take only what I need for the journey—a small portion, no more. I will lash it to my back, underneath my cloak, and then I will set out to find our lost mother."

"And what will you do for food?"

"I have been keeping a little back," he says. "Enough for two, maybe three days' march. It is buried in the snow, close to where we put the snares. I can forage along the way too, but I expect there will not be much to find out there."

"Unless you enjoy eating rocks," I growl.

We do not talk for a time. Sitting at opposite sides of the dragon's mouth, we observe the darkness between us and wait for the other to speak. Still hurting from my fall from Tyrandir's back, and with the dream still fresh in my mind—a dream in which I foretold this, foretold Cai leaving in search of her, choosing Mother over me—I yearn for this conversation to be something else I have dreamed. That, or a false memory in which none of this was said and we spoke only of catching birds and the kinds of worms that come to live on the teeth of dead dragons. But the smell drifting up from deep within Tyrandir's long throat, the reek of Cai's work down there to remove the dragon's heart with his unbidden surgery, offends me so deeply I cannot remain quiet for long. I am only grateful that darkness shields my brother from the look on my face and the hand stroking the dagger-handle at my belt, for he would see then that I am truly haunted by the ghost of our murderous father.

"What of our plans?" I ask him.

"What plans?"

"Our plans for dragonland! What of all the nights we lay underneath the stars and moon and spoke of what we would achieve here, in this place, together? Was it all a lie? A ruse?"

"No," he answers in that small, reedy voice of his. "It was neither. But if you remember those nights well, then you will know that you were the one who spoke of such things while I mostly listened. I wanted it for *you*, Brother, and I still do, but I made no secret of the light on the mountain nor my desire to see whose face it fell upon. I spoke of it many times."

"I did not hear you," I say.

"Then you were not listening."

I rise to my feet too quickly and stumble. Straightening, regaining my balance on the uneven surface of the dragon's hardened tongue, I am suddenly overwhelmed by the smallness of this place, its low, ridged roof, its wall of teeth, the tightness of egress. The heat is oppressive too—still—months after the dragon's death.

"Why can't a thing die?" I say. "A dragon. A parent. The subject of this conversation. Just die and grow cold and disappear from the world. Closed eyes. Light out. Gone. Why must they appear to keep pace with the living when they have no life to speak of? Why do we nurture their pretence? I am so tired of ghosts and kingdoms and of conversations that lead to the foot of the same accursed mountain. So very, very tired."

Cai says nothing. It seems that I have lost him again in the dark, although I can still hear his loud breathing. I know that if, through some gap in the dragon's teeth, I can locate the distant light on the mountain again, I will find him posited between me and it, but no—no, no, no. I have said what I have to say. Let the words find him themselves or not at all.

"I need to get out of this crawlspace. The stench has become unbearable."

"Where will you go?" he asks, his voice floating to me from somewhere off to my right.

"I will take a walk," I tell him. "And if I can I will sleep in our old camp in shoulder tonight. Where I belong."

"But it is not safe outside."

It is not safe in *here*, I think. Not for you, Brother.

"Don't go," he says.

"Don't go... And yet, when the time comes, you will *skip* out of here in search of her corpse. Listen to yourself. Do you not hear the folly in your own words?"

If he does not, I can hear it in mine; the folly of arguing with a rock in flight. And yet I must try, because maybe that is all that separates the living from the dead: the ability to fight the pretence of this, of everything, whilst knowing that day by day, piece by piece, we've already succumbed to it. What a sad hypocrisy we are.

"I mean to leave this place," he replies calmly, slowly. "I will not stay here with our dead father while you wait to join him."

"Instead you go off to be reunited with your mother in *her* grave—if she has one."

"If she does not, I will dig two. Side by side."

"See? You fool. You *know* the outcome of this thing."

"I know that I would fare better if my brother were with me. Two halves make a stronger whole. But I also know that he will not join me because he too has a notion of duty to one who is no longer here. That he will do what he must to protect their legacy, such as it is, because to do anything else would be considered a betrayal. But I assure you, Father cannot rise from his grave to punish you... and yet—I can tell he already has."

"I... I should cut your throat now and save you the time and the heartache."

"Do what you must, Brother. But know this: he lives on in you. There is no greater compliment I can give or deeper wound I can inflict than that. So, do what you must."

I pray the moon stays back. Do not let Cai see this face or I his, for he will glimpse truths that should never be told and the true distance between us will finally be unveiled. Not opposite corners of a dragon's mouth but opposite ends of a dragonland. Between us there lies only death, and worse: those things that refuse to die.

I turn and crawl out of the dragon's mouth but thrust my head back through the narrow gap in order to say these last words.

"Remain in here with the smell and the worms if you wish, Brother. But do not touch his heart. It does not belong to you."

14.

Forgoing a long walk in the snow, I return to our camp in shoulder, stepping over and around the broken carcasses of the wolves that lie scattered along the dragonspine road. The camp itself is relatively untouched, but the smell of death remains pungent in the air, likely to draw scavengers willing to risk a dragon's ire in order to eat. It will take just one to encourage the others to follow. Or perhaps the beast of bulk and horns, unsated, will return to drag away another meal. It encourages neither travel nor sleep but a kind of despondent paralysis to grip my bones.

There is no blizzard on this night; no snowfall at all. The cold is a thing I am not accustomed to but instead a constant harassment I have learned to accept. Meanwhile, the mountains surround me like a noose, and near one particular summit to the west an innocent light flickers while speaking softly too of our destruction. I lie down to wait for the end that seems to never come.

Inside my saddlebag, the warmth of the dragon against my back, I listen to the growl of my empty stomach and consult the stars for a while, whispering new, more favourable versions of my conversation with Cai earlier. In all but one, he agrees to remain in dragonland with me. And in the other, he promises to return. If only they would mediate—the stars, the moon, the mountains—but they seem only to listen as a wish-well does to those who drop a hopeful coin into its gullet.

When I tire of talking only to myself, I think about my plans to build a shelter, a hut, a village, an entire *city* in this place. Walls of wooden stakes would keep our enemies out and our citizens safe. Visitors from far and wide would enter through an impressive and yet daunting tunnel of tall, leaning ribs before passing through a pelvic-bone archway into dragonland's majestic main square...

Why can Cai not see it? That the best way to honour our dead is to build anew, not chase some light across a mountain like some foolish kitten pouncing after a mirror's reflection. Maybe he will realise his mistake in time. Maybe I can convince him in the morning that my plans for dragonland are not conversations with the stars but something real. Something within our grasp if we want it. I need to show him the possibilities, just like Father showed me. But how?

You let the firewood run out.

Father's words to me in the snow return in my thoughts, threatening to blow out the tiny flame of hope kindling within me. It falters but does not fail. If anything, it begins to burn with a stronger flame as I realise that he is showing me something—a path: a way for me to right not just one but two wrongs.

Maybe I will go for a walk, after all.

15.

I return to dragonland before sunrise and stack all of the wood I have gathered throughout the long night in front of Tyrandir's mouth like an offering to a god or a pyre on which to burn all of my brother's doubts. As the sun peeks over the blue mountains, wishing to see for herself what I have planned for this day, I cup my hands to my mouth. "Cai! Come outside. See what I have done. And this is only the beginning..."

I remember the day when my father, the king before me, returned with armfuls of saplings. I want to make the same impression upon Cai today as my father made upon me then. To prove that if a man can carry a forest then a boy can move an entire wood, if he is willing.

"Wake up, Cai. We have work to do."

My hands are blistered and bleeding from swinging a hatchet through the long night—a dragon scale makes for a most resilient axe blade—but if the fruits of my labour provide us with a shelter, and the shelter with just one reason for Cai to remain with me in dragonland for a little while longer, then my efforts will not have been ill spent.

"Cai! Hear me!"

Time.

It is the thing that can heal all rifts and douse all lights.

All lights.

He will stay.

He will stay.

He will.

"Cai?"

But now his name is a question. Nothing stirs within the dragon's maw; no sign of movement at all.

"Stop playing games, Brother. Join me outside. It is a fine morning. Even the cold has retreated some way. Come out."

No reply. Nothing stirs. Something catches my eye though, far above my head. A lone bird with a broad wingspan circling the blue skies over dragonland. Sensing the death of my excitement, perhaps. Readying to touch down and pull the flesh from this moment's bones. A light snow begins to fall. To inter my woodpile.

"Curse you, Cai. Show yourself. If you have hurt feelings after what I said last night, then know they were just idle words. I would never harm you, Brother. That was someone else speaking, not me. Someone else." The ghost who inhabits this place, I think. "Please, I am sorry. Come out."

I walk around the dragon's mouth as the snowfall grows heavy and thick. The clarity of a few moments ago is utterly erased, and I struggle to see what lies right in front of me. Finally, I find the gap in the dragon's teeth and crawl through it into the dark, private chamber of his mouth.

A moment later, I emerge back into daylight, pale of face and trembling.

Have I died? Has the beast of bulk and horns returned in the night to finally claim its kingdom? Is this another dream? Like meeting Father in a blizzard or Mother in The Gardens of Kuhl Amar. Both conversations I never had; both confusingly, agonisingly real.

My mind is raving. I do not trust my thoughts anymore.

"Let my flesh be a lie. Let my bones be resting in the earth. Let me be the ravings of someone else. Anything but *this*."

I search for what seems like an age, looking in every district of dragonland—from skull to tail's end—for a grave mound or a marker should I be buried deep. But in the end, my search is in vain. I cannot find myself.

And back in the chamber of the dragon's mouth, I gaze into the dark secrets of its throat and urge myself to step forward. It is hotter than I remember it being last night, and then I realise that a heart has been exposed. The heat reminds me of the steam rooms in the palace, where Father would retire—sometimes with one or more of the queen's young handmaidens—sometimes with me. Bright roses appear on my cheeks, brought forth by shame as well as the heat greeting me with its sullied tongue.

I will not look.

I will not look at his divided heart.

And then, turning to leave, I spot something in a corner of the dragon's mouth, propped between two of its teeth like a piece of undigested food.

My brother's book, its leather cover softening in the heat. A note tied to its cover with a cordage of bark curls around its bondage like a fallen leaf.

I remove the note and hold it up in the scant light that reaches us here. The note reads:

My dearest brother,

Forgive me. I am ill-equipped for goodbyes. I have been forced to say it to one parent and deprived of saying it to the other, so forgive me if I refuse to say it to you now, my only sibling. I have left you a parting gift. A gift of two halves. During these long, frozen nights, while you slept, I kept my sombre vigil on the mountain and wrote in this book that I now leave to you. It is not a crown but it is my hope it will have some value to you in time. Within its pages you will find stories and a few scattered poems— some true, some make-believe, some a glorious blending of the two. They are all, every last one, dedicated to our beautiful mother and queen, and titled collectively, Our Light on the Mountain. *For it was our* light, *and she is our* mother. Mine *and* yours. *Yes, yours too, Brother. Now it is my hope that these stories will allow you to find her again in your heart, even as I seek to find her on this frozen mountainside, searching in every cave and nook. We both owe a debt to our parents, though yours is a different and a dark debt I cannot begin to fathom. To this purpose, I pray these stories bring you the light you need to turn your back on the darkness of the past.*

Always,
Your brother
Cai

P.S. The second half of your gift is the empty pages at the back of this book. Empty except, that is, for another title:

dragonland

Although it has given us this time together, sadly, for what it has also taken from us, I feel it is not quite deserving of its capital. So, dragonland it shall be.

These pages are for you, dear brother. Do with them what you will. Fill them with stories of your own making or close the book forever and come find us on the mountain.

Until then...

The silence of their absence overwhelms me. Father, Mother, Cai, gone, with me left on my own at the end of this world. My grief feels insurmountable. Never before has the cold bitten so deep. Clutching Cai's gift to my belly, I collapse to my knees on the dragon's hardened tongue, unable to move, paralysed by wave after wave of fear, loneliness, and memories. It seems as though hours pass if not days if not months if not years... and still I am yet to move.

I wonder if I ever will.

Acknowledgments

My deepest thanks to my wife, Summer, who understood my madness and gave me the time and space I needed to create. A special thank you to Andy Cox, who originally published all but two of these stories in the pages of *Black Static*, *Interzone*, and *Crimewave* magazines. And to all of the kind hearts who not only gave up their time to read my writing and offer their honest opinion but who picked me up and dusted me off on more than one occasion – to Ray Cluley, Amanda Campbell, Ralph Robert Moore, Johnny Mains, Paul Townsend, Rich Dodgin, Priya Sharma, Michael Abel, and others (you know who you are): you have my undying love and gratitude.

BONUS MATERIAL

A Peek Behind the Curtain: Story Notes
(contains spoilers)

Men Playing Ghosts, Playing God

In February 2004, I started work on a short story called *Of Bee and Undertow*. It was about an elderly gentleman named Henry Eddowes who lived in a care home. Back then, I was writing literary fiction more than horror, searching for my voice, my niche. I got about 5,000 words into *Of Bee and Undertow* before it completely ran out of steam. Henry was breaking out of the home for one last night of freedom but didn't make it much farther than a few steps outside of his window before I set the story aside to work on something else. I never forgot poor old Henry though. Nine years later, when my family and I were living in The House of Mould, I would pass a care home every day on my walk to work. I often wondered what it was like for the residents. Henry was soon at the forefront of my mind again. Now, he stayed up late and played poker with his friends; now, he was deeply in love with one of the other residents, Constance; now, he wanted to ease her grief by pretending to be the ghost of her husband leaving little gifts on her pillow; now, death was a regular visitor to the home. Needless to say, it took a very different direction from the original idea. Wintercroft care home makes its first appearance in this story. It is where Simon's father lives in *So Many Heartbeats, So Many Words* (in fact, you might have noticed Simon's father complaining about Henry and his friends in that story). I'm glad Henry found me again. I'm glad he got the chance to tell me the rest of his story.

So Many Heartbeats, So Many Words

In March 2014, my wife suffered a miscarriage while pregnant with our second child. Of all days, it happened on our son's birthday. Even though it was early in the pregnancy, she was devastated. I do not think men can truly understand the pain of that loss; we're simply not connected physically to the creation of a life in the way women are. It's fair to say I could have handled the situation better. In May/June 2015, I decided I would write a story that would attempt to capture the emotional impact and turmoil of that time. I also wanted the kind of closure that comes from writing The End.

Simon is a failing writer. Sue is his wife and soulmate. Alfie is their son with speech and language difficulties. While Simon is the narrator, it soon became apparent during the first draft that Alfie was the perfect symbol for this family's communication difficulties and the real star of this piece. The words he uses, the unique phrases, they all came from my son. The countdown of the chapters (from 10 to 0) was inspired, I think, by Richard Bachman's *The Running Man*. I write 'I think' because although that novel clearly wasn't at the forefront of my mind when I wrote this story, the counting down of the chapters was something that had stayed with me since I read the novel in my teens.

This was a strange and difficult story to write because a lot of the core emotions and events are true or at least truth subtly reshaped to fit the narrative. The most interesting parts for me were where the lines blur (we never grew up in Salisbury, for instance, but my wife was leaving for Australia around the time we got together; our first kiss *was* pretty awful; my father isn't in a care home; we *did* live in a house with a mould problem – and still wonder if it contributed to what happened; and the way in which the tragic news broke on the stairs is exactly how it happened). If you can hit that sweet spot between truth and fiction it gives the work verisimilitude, an authenticity that is very difficult to create in something wholly fictional.

The Space That Runs Away With You

Since relocating to Salisbury, my family and I have moved house several times for various reasons. I wrote about The House of Mould in *So Many Heartbeats, So Many Words* and wrote another story, *The Suffering* (which is not included in this collection) based on the creepy woods at the back of another property we lived in. It got to the point that whenever we moved I'd write a story about our new house. *The Space That Runs Away With You* was based on a property we rented in which the tenancy agreement stated that we were not permitted to enter or use the loft space. I had the idea that the family that moved into my fictional house had suffered a huge loss (this was before the miscarriage) and that through their collective grief the loft would come to symbolise hope and 'infinite possibility'.

The Broken and the Unmade

I wanted to write a story of two distinct halves, told from different perspectives, and this is the story that grew from that idea. I also wanted to give this story some historical context and the concentration camps of World War II have always interested me in that they evoke very powerful emotions (*Auschwitz* by Laurence Rees is a fascinating read). On top of all that, I wanted to write about survivor guilt and explore how the past is an heirloom we pass down through generations, not necessarily through the retelling of stories but through our emotional recollection of events, or, in this case, the emotional damage those events inflict. I wrote the material set in the present day first and then went back and filled in the scenes set in the past. That way, I could focus on one time period at a time. The two boys in the story, Joshua and Thomas, are named after my eldest son and the son of a friend. At the time, I wasn't sure why I would do that, put my son in this unenviable role where his grandfather would try to murder him. It only occurred to me some years later that I was channelling something, anger or bitterness perhaps, towards my own father, because he has never shown any interest in my son, his grandson (for all intents and purposes, he is dead to him). Coincidence? I don't think so. Art imitates life.

The Things That Get You Through

Break-ups can be devastating. I don't think you ever forget the worst ones; in some ways, they change you forever. I had the idea of writing about the five stages of grief in my mind for a while. I knew I wanted to present them in distinct chapters, dissecting the grieving process. Often, the starting point for a story will come either as an image or a part of a scene or, if I'm extremely lucky, through a dream (sometimes delivered in its entirety). Here, it was the image of the main character painting a wall just hours after hearing the news of his wife's death. I had the line 'Lilac is the colour of denial'. It wasn't enough, however, to simply describe someone going through the stages of grief, and so I added some urgency to the mix. The protagonist decides to force himself through the five stages over a short period of time. The question this story asks is: could that work?

Writing this was a lot of fun. Each 'chapter' has its own flavour, its own style and emotion. I wanted the chapter headings to be more than just breaks and somehow contribute to the theme, which is that the stages of grief should be given their due respect. They are as important as, say, our five senses. Therefore, *Lilac is the color of denial / Anger is the smell of turpentine / Bargaining is the sound of one man talking to his mannequin / Depression is the touch of a dust angel at your back / Acceptance is the taste of a mocha latte with a beautiful blond.* Some readers may not pick up on small stuff like that but it is something I enjoy immensely: leaving little details (like buried treasure) for the reader to discover should they ever care to read the story again someday.

Pendulum

For years I had wanted to write a short story with a structure that closely reflected the content, but I never could land on the right idea. Then, in March 2019, *Pendulum* landed on my lap or rather in my dreams. This one arrived one morning fully formed, and I remember jumping out of bed and writing the idea down in a hurry. At the time, my son was being bullied regularly at school. Every member of staff we talked to was reluctant to believe him because he is on the autistic spectrum and so *of course* he must be lying or at least exaggerating, right? Or maybe it was the thought of the extra paperwork, I don't know. But I was *living* with this idea – of a boy who is being ignored by the world around him: not just ignored but beaten down by it.

The first draft was written over the course of a week, the second draft the same, which is fairly fast for me. Like many of the stories in this collection, it taps into the fears of being a parent, parental guilt (can we ever be there enough for our children?), and so on. This is another story that has a number of facts and real life detail buried under the fictional stuff, such as how the child in the story was born (our first son was also born by ventouse) and the mother's waters breaking during an episode of *Boardwalk Empire* (yes, that happened too!). Other details simply serve the story, of course. I now believe that dream was a flare sent into the sky by my subconscious. We fought long and hard with the school to keep our son safe and it turned out he *was* being bullied (we had no doubt, but it took an admission from the boys involved for the staff to take the appropriate action. Too little, too late; he attends a different school now). Some of my anger, some of my guilt ended up in this story; the rest spilled over into *This House is Not Haunted.*

The Sound of Constant Thunder

I love end-of-the-world stories. King's *The Stand* and McCammon's *Swan Song* are two favourites. Let's make it a Top 3 and add *Long Voyage Back* by Luke Rhinehart to that list. The idea for this story came when my wife and I were pushing our son in his buggy across a bridge in Salisbury the day after watching one particular episode of *The Walking Dead* in which some of the characters smeared themselves in zombie guts in order to pass unmolested through a crowd of the undead. I thought that was a pretty cool idea at the time and I was still thinking about it the next day as we walked across the bridge and a woman walking in the opposite direction stared into our pram with what I can only describe as a look of horror. Whatever the reason for that look was, my mind flashed to the possibility that he was choking in there, unseen by us, or, god forbid, he had already choked and died. Parents worry about *everything*, but a parent who writes dark fiction can take it to a whole new level sometimes. So, the image of the smearing of the guts and that stranger's reaction to my child in his pram nudged me towards the character of Charlotte, a woman who moves relatively untouched through a post-apocalyptic world (I mean, who is going to mess with a 'crazy woman' pushing around a months-old corpse in a pram, right?). I also wanted a main character who wasn't your typical hero. A quiet loner who didn't get very far in the world as it used to be but has found a fragile peace since the bombs fell. I wanted to see what would happen if I brought them together. Theirs is a love story of sorts, a beginning at the end of all things. Sometimes, I wonder if Alan managed to survive, escaping the soldiers. Sometimes, I wonder if he ever found Charlotte and if he had it in him in the end to tell her the truth she did not want to hear. Maybe I'll find out the answer someday.

The Harder It Gets the Softer We Sing

While this story starts where *So Many Heartbeats, So Many Words* left off, more than three years passed between the writing of the two. Following its publication in *Black Static* magazine, *So Many Heartbeats, So Many Words* easily became my most popular and well-received story. I got emails and messages about it, particularly about how authentic it seemed. Readers picked up that it was based on actual events and experiences. I also enjoyed writing about Simon, Sue, and Alfie Fenwick. I knew these people. After all, they were a fictional version of my own family. I felt that their story wasn't quite finished yet. But after the success of *So Many Heartbeats, So Many Words* I was adamant that any follow-up had to move the story forward and not just simply repeat what had come before. I started the process with character notes, briefly summarising the impact of the miscarriage. I wrote scene ideas on scraps of paper and, yes, Post-Its, in no particular order, and collected these over a period. Eventually, I sat at the computer and created a plot outline, slotting in these scenes where I thought they should go and setting aside those that didn't yet have any place, for possible use later. This all sounds more organised than it was. For me, the early stages of creating a story are usually pretty chaotic. I have the story germ and I think about it constantly over a number of days, weeks, or even months, adding ideas as they occur (usually randomly and often with no clear reason why it should be part of the story). I have a sense of what I want to write about but with something like *The Harder It Gets the Softer We Sing* it can be a long process of accumulating ideas and scenes and snippets of dialogue and even, sometimes, trawling through years-old unused notes, looking for something that feels right for the project.

I started writing the first draft of *The Harder It Gets the Softer We Sing* in June 2017. I finished two months later, in August 2017. In this instalment, I wanted to take the foundation of verisimilitude from *So Many Heartbeats, So Many Words* and move it in a more fictional direction. In reality, my wife and I had tried again to have a baby, suffered another miscarriage, which turned out to be an even worse experience than the first, but eventually got lucky and had our second child. However, I thought it would be interesting to take a walk down the road of what might have been had life taken a very different course.

My father is not the man I have presented in this story. I don't know my father, his likes, his dislikes (wait, I remember he was a fan of Bounty chocolate bars, the blue ones rather than the red, and I know that I inherited the same preference, but that pretty much covers my knowledge of the man). That said, much of this story is based on real emotions, moments, and fears, so while the actual events may be fictional, the underlying emotion, more often than not, comes from a real place.

Following on from the chapter countdown in *So Many Heartbeats, So Many Words*, I wanted to do something similar here with the chapter titles. This is a story about outsiders and accepting difference in other people, so to reflect that in the chapter titles and the story itself, I started with so-called writing rules and set out to break them (*never open a story with a dream*, for example; okay, fuck it, let's open with a dream). In amongst these are other negative statements that I try to disprove in the chapter or scene. The message, I suppose, is to not accept what the world tells you is right or wrong but to find your own way. *Be the inside.*

Those who have a keen eye will notice a number of references to other stories I have written (or were they written by Simon? Sometimes, I wonder). While this kind of thing can seem pretentious, I assure you it wasn't ego at play but a conscious effort to maintain the authenticity of these stories and to keep blurred that line between reality and fiction.

Looking for Landau

In 2017, I was invited to contribute a story to the first volume of *Tales From the Shadow Booth*, a horror anthology edited by Dan Coxon. I came up with an idea for a simple chase story. Or so I thought. *Looking for Landau* grew beyond the maximum word count of eight thousand words and kept growing until it became the novelette you read here. It didn't stop there either. I've written a second part to Rust's tale, an unpublished novella called *Like A Man Drowning*, and there is at least two or three more parts to his journey that I hope to write someday.

The scene in which the car crash victim lifts their bloody, ruined face from the road and talks to Rust is inspired by an unpublished story I wrote back in 1995 called *The Adam and Eve Syndrome*. It has the dubious honour of being the first story I wrote after I dropped out of university to become, you guessed it, a writer. Over twenty-five years later, I still laugh at how much of an idiot I was. Still, it's particularly gratifying that parts of a scene I wrote so long ago have found their way into Rust's epic journey. Things happen for a reason. We make stupid decisions sometimes for a reason. But if there is one point to take away from this it is to never throw away your old writing. Perhaps refrain from showing it to anyone else but *never* throw it away.

This House is Not Haunted

A writer controls only so much of what he/she creates.

There was never supposed to be a third part to the Fenwick story. My original plan was for them to get the reborn doll early in *The Harder It Gets the Softer We Sing* and for things to take a similar path as they do in this instalment. However, it didn't work out that way and I was left still wondering how the Fenwicks respond to the doll and what impact it ultimately has on their lives. So, it became clear pretty quickly that I would have to write a third part to find out. I just had to wait for the right idea to come along.

In December 2018, we joined the whole Elf-on-the-shelf craze. We called him Buddy. Buddy was very active in our house. My eldest son (who has autistic spectrum disorder) responded positively at first but his growing frustration was noticeable. He could not understand why the Elf did these things overnight or why he would not talk to him. Unfortunately, he became a little fixated and it did culminate in a scene very similar to the confession at the dining table that occurs in the story. There were other pressures on him at the time (the bullying at school, which I have already mentioned) and my feeling is that it contributed to his vulnerable emotional state. I realised that what had taken place between my son and the Elf in real life (which seems really strange to write now) was what should take place between Alfie and the reborn doll in the story. I had my idea.

I built a detailed plot outline (because of the complexity of the story) and wrote a significant amount of the first draft between December 2018 and March 2019, at which point it completely stalled. Somewhere around *that* confession scene, in fact. In retrospect, I think I was not prepared to write it at the time. And so, the story sat and sat until Luna Press showed some interest in this collection and asked for one or two unpublished stories to be included in the line-up. Because it had been over a year since I had worked on *This House is Not Haunted*, I picked it up and rewrote the whole thing. In a way, the delay was part of my extended run-up to tackling that painful confession. Now that scene has become a strange and inscrutable mix of truth and fiction, much like the rest of this trilogy of stories.

The chapter numbering and story structure is important in this story, just as it is in *So Many Heartbeats, So Many Words* and *The Harder It Gets the Softer We Sing*. Like the Fenwicks, the reader never moves past chapter one. They are trapped within the grief, the struggle to find some way out. The references to *The Hobbit* (subtitle: *There and Back Again*) underline the idea that their journey ultimately leads them back to the beginning. For the reader, I wanted this to happen literally – Simon asks the reader to turn back the pages and start reading the story again. This wasn't the ending I had in mind originally, but having (I hope) made an emotional connection with the reader, I liked the thought of having them now *physically* go back through the pages to read them again. It felt right.

With these three closely connected stories, it's sometimes hard to see where I end and Simon begins. Have we become so inseparable that we're indistinguishable from each other? Take Alfie playing innocently with the Funko Pops near the beginning of this story, for instance. I had no idea when I wrote that scene what they meant, if anything. But by the end of *This House is Not Haunted*, they came to symbolise Sam and Alfie's whole relationship. Who knows, maybe Simon wrote that part...

There are, again, many references to my other stories, both those in the book you are holding and those published elsewhere (some are obvious, some not so much). I wanted it to be the fictional equivalent of a greatest hits album, pulling together elements of my other work over the last eight years or so and somehow making them into something bigger, something better than a bunch of singles that never really troubled the charts. I leave it up to you, reader, to decide how successful that has been.

dragonland

In February 2019, while writing the first draft of *This House is Not Haunted*, I wrote the line, 'I live in a forest on the back of a dead dragon.' I loved that line. It refused to leave my thoughts in the days that followed. It seemed to open into something big, and I knew it was a story I had to write. It was also part of the reason I set aside *This House is Not Haunted*. At the time, I thought *dragonland* might have some influence on how that story developed, everything being connected as it is. With nothing to go on other than that first line, I wrote a couple of pages of general notes on dragons and who I thought my protagonist might be. Two weeks later, I did the same, two pages on the locale of dragonland, the towns of skull and tail's end, a little of the backstory, etcetera. I set it aside. When I returned to *dragonland* almost one year later in January 2020, I wrote an eleven thousand word first draft/ outline in a little over two weeks. In February, I started work on the first full draft of the story, and it took three-and-a-half months to write eighteen-and-a-half-thousand words. Then, another month and a full rewrite later, I added even more flesh to its bones.

dragonland was finished. Twenty thousand words and sixteen months on from writing 'I live in a forest on the back of a dead dragon' in a different story, this story lived and breathed in my hands.

I don't think it is coincidence that I named one of the brothers in *dragonland* Stephen. I don't think it is coincidence that he is torn between his loyalty to his family and his deep desire to write the story of dragonland to somehow get closer to the father he never truly knew. I don't think it is coincidence that he turned his back long enough for Cai to go on without him, or that he left Cai to tackle that mountain alone. I believe there are no coincidences when it comes to writing.

The path is long and lonely. Nobody knows where it leads. But it can also be breath-taking in its beauty. It can instil or even repair our sense of wonder. It can heal. The choice to walk it is a difficult one, assuming, of course, there is a choice at all.

Thank you for joining me on the path for a while.

I hope we meet again someday.

CPSIA information can be obtained
at www.ICGtesting.com
Printed in the USA
LVHW110803010921
696586LV00003B/112